AXIOM

WANDERER OF WORLDS

BOOK ONE

ACKNOWLEDGEMENTS

First and foremost, we wish to thank the wonderful folk who read our manuscript and asked pertinent questions. You helped us to polish a work that we hold dear; Sue, Kylie, David W., David S., Lorraine, Tam and Fiona. Also we must thank everyone who believed we had something great to offer and invested in us. Especially Steve Nguyen, Steve Strathdee, Sue Strathdee, Diane Meiklejohn, Robert Meiklejohn and Nigel Atkinson. We have to give credit where it's due and praise Sue for her editing work. We apologise for those commas.

DEDICATION

For David, Leonie, Kevin & Barrie

For David

TABLE OF CONTENTS

PROLOGUE

The Fold

BEYOND the crowded forest, the world felt huge beneath a watercolour sky. The air changed as shadowed coolness yielded to the heat of sun-soaked grassland. Father and son headed up a gentle slope and the wiry nine year old boy marvelled as warmth enveloped him, prickling the hairs on his arms. The separation between forest and field was only a few steps, spongy black earth quickly surrendering to the firmer sod.

As the grasses thickened and swarmed around their legs, he took one last look back at the trees. They stood like a council of men huddled together to glower their good riddance at the interlopers. A day's walk through the dark and densely-populated forest left an aroma of dirt and decomposing foliage on his clothes. The way had been gruelling and the footing erratic, but the boy hadn't noticed. He'd wielded sword-like sticks and leapt off fallen logs, crawled up steep embankments to escape untold savagery and hunkered in plant-choked gullies to wait for imagined enemies to pass. The dappled light and cries of retreating animals held many possibilities of adventure.

Dusk coiled above them, uncaring that they hadn't yet found a suitable place to camp for the night. His father's words became clipped, urging him to move faster, and a spark of nervous anticipation flared in the boy's belly. It was now that the long day spent walking took its toll. His muscles ached and he couldn't keep his hands still. He relied on his father's legs to mow a path for him through the long, tangled grass. Balmy breezes swept across the plains like the intermittent attentions of a toddler, tugging this way and that, and he was similarly distracted.

His father was a giant leading the way and the boy's worshipful gaze was always drawn back to him. He walked fearlessly, his pack laden with trinkets and souvenirs from the many worlds they'd travelled through, bouncing beguilingly with every step. His own pack weighed a quarter of what his father's did and he carried only his belongings. The responsibility of the necessary things, the mementos and the memories, were his father's alone to bear.

In that early evening twilight, the magic of a world undergoing palpable change thrilled him. His gaze moved from the grass he couldn't see over to the reds, pinks and golds streaking the sky above. He inhaled deeply the scent of warm spring air, of grass and life carried on the wind.

The boy reached up and watched his hand skim along the tall grass. The field was many different colours ranging from green to dark brown, though it gave an overall impression of wheat. This was no farmer's field gone fallow for they were in the middle of nowhere. There was not another person for hundreds of miles—he knew this for he saw it in his mind as surely as he saw the mottled colours in the meadow around him.

He looked up in time to avoid running into a saucepan strapped onto his father's pack. He squinted up past his mentor's broad, strong shoulders to the back of his head, trying to figure out why his father had come to so sudden a stop. The boy questioned him, a quizzical frown upon his brow, and when he got no response he knew something was very wrong. His father never ignored him, never failed him. Walled in by grass and his father ahead, the child couldn't see and panic took root. It shot adrenaline through his veins and left bitterness in his mouth.

It was the first time he'd tasted fear.

Confusion swamped him, holding him momentarily

inert and then he pushed past, ploughing his way through the grass until he saw his father's profile; he was rigid, his expression tight and his skin pale. His gaze fixed on whatever lay ahead of them.

The child turned to look, swiping ruthlessly at the few blades of grass still blocking his view. When the way was clear, he beheld a scene he wasn't prepared for. He whimpered a disquieted noise deep in his throat and it was then his father finally looked down and noticed him. With a gruff cry, he wrapped a large hand around his son's bony shoulder but it was too late to shield him. His hand stilled, not jerking the child away but gripping him reassuringly as they stared at the carnage together.

Twelve corpses were splayed out in a circular pattern before them. The eerily flattened part of the sward they'd fallen upon was also a circle, the grasses laying down in one direction. It was like a giant board had been thumped down and swept around in a smooth motion so these people could be sacrificed upon the natural altar.

The wind changed direction and blew the stink of putrefaction at father and son. They gagged their distaste, turning their heads and covering their noses and mouths. These corpses weren't newly-dead, they were days old. Turning back when the wind shifted once more (though still with his hand over his mouth), the boy scrutinised the scene, unable to speak past the horror clogged in his throat.

A moving black cloud pulsed around each cadaver—swarms of flies, buzzing excitedly with the promise of maggots soon to be hatching in softening, rotting flesh.

Two of the corpses held hands. Some were young, others old. There were dark-skinned people and fair, men and women, short, tall, fat and thin. There was nothing overt linking them, nothing obvious that was the same except they were all dead...with their eyes open. They looked mutely at the darkening sky as if beseeching their fate.

The boy knew nothing of cults, of religious zealotry, of fanaticism so intense it might drive a singularly-minded group of disparate people to commit mass suicide. He was too young for such concepts. He knew about Wanderers, though, that there were twelve powers and that when all twelve were combined, something magical and mystical happened. A Wanderer would be transported to Endworld, to the World of Worlds. There were twelve people before him—he knew, because he'd counted them a great many times to avoid looking too closely at their features—and his faith was stirred by it.

The closer he looked, the more signs that these were Wanderers took shape. Similar equipment to his father's pack were tied to their bags and backpacks. Most had placed their gear on the ground by their feet before their demise, though a couple still wore theirs and were arched over them like bridges of death. Colourless, odorous death curved over their worldly possessions.

This was a dead Wanderer Fold.

He saw no wounds, no bloodstains on clothes, no severed limbs or damage done. If it weren't for the grey tint to their flesh, their blank looks and stillness, they would look like whole—and possibly even healthy—people. What could have caused them to die? There seemed to be no foul play whatsoever... yet *something* had killed them.

His father removed his hand and placed his backpack on the ground. With a few neat flicks of leather ties and some clasps he removed a bandanna and held it over his nose and mouth. He then straightened and strode resolutely forth into the circle. Without speaking, he bent down and rifled through the pack of the nearest body, one hand holding the cloth to his face, the other searching for anything useful.

A cocoon of cold encased the boy and he looked away. The scudding clouds drew his attention and he became ice, too numb to be tainted by this moment. Later, he would understand his father's practicality and when he was older, he would scavenge for himself, wherever he happened upon the opportunity to do so. For now, he simply watched the sky change colours, frozen inside his glassy skin, his heart cold. He wondered, as he looked up, if the spirits of the dead Fold looked down upon them and whether they applauded or were appalled by these two Wanderers. If they really *had* reached the World of Worlds, surely they wouldn't care? He didn't wish them to be cursed for his father's insensitivity, so that was how he preferred to think of things.

The wind gusted towards him again and brought with it fresh odours of damnation. Suddenly, the boy was not sure of anything beyond feeling scared, alone and fragile, though he didn't have the words to express such complex vulnerability. All he could do was pluck fretfully at the grass seeds and steal glances at his father, needing to reassure himself that his family was still the constant he could rely on when everything else unravelled.

By the time the last streaks of light faded from the sky, the pair had moved on to make camp as far away as possible. They'd left behind a sight that wouldn't fade from their memories and carried with them a malodour that had invaded their pores. There was also an awful, undeniable knowledge that burdened their newly-disillusioned souls; innocence could die as surely and swiftly as the living.

And a Wanderer Fold meant death.

CHAPTER ONE

Hard Truths

HE'D been stuck in the roof for hours.

Armpit deep in thatching, Daeson's hands ached from holding on. Sweat plastered his brown hair to his face, tickling and itching but he couldn't let go to swipe it aside. His legs dangled limp in the cottage; he imagined them as some peculiar farming accessory, like something to swap out when the original set broke. Perhaps this strange fantasy was an indication of his suffering from heat stroke. He doubted it—it was only morning, though late. The temple bells had rung twice as he'd watched the sun move higher into the sky. It hadn't reached its peak yet but it would soon, and he was thirsty.

Daeson was between escape attempts, conserving strength and feeling sorry for himself. He would not yell for help. The townsfolk already looked at him with pity, he didn't want them hiding smiles as well. Some of them wouldn't bother, just as they hadn't bothered to avert their eyes.

Failure, their stares accused.

Daeson grunted, determined not to let his mind trek a well-worn path. He had to focus on getting out. He'd been an avid tree climber as a young boy but he'd also been a skinny lad. Now he was much heavier. His bulk was mostly muscle though, so he should be strong enough to free himself except he had no leverage. Stuck as he was, it would be much easier to allow himself to fall the rest of the way rather than climb up. Letting go wasn't feasible. He'd wrenched his shoulder when he'd caught himself and didn't want to risk hurting himself further.

His shoulder wasn't hurting anymore so he might've been lucky enough to escape worse injury. No sense testing his luck further. Daeson felt like a pawn in a battle between Malice, the God of ill fortune and Tamsin, the Goddess of good fortune. He could be the primary character in a Lesson, who'd blundered his way into a situation so dire that deities would argue over the outcome.

Stop imagining and start acting, Daeson. Get your future out of the hands of the Gods and into your own.

His father's voice in his head. A practical man, he'd never had time for the fancies of a son that wanted to name the farm animals, to grow the crops he liked to eat rather than what brought the most coin and who climbed trees when tasked to collect firewood. An old memory sparked, bearing the answer to his escape.

How'd you come down from that tree when you climbed up this one?

There'd been a mixture of confusion and pride in his father's voice. Daeson remembered the question because of its different tone. His father was often gruff, more so when he had to deal with their neighbour Kurgan. Neither Daeson nor his father had respect for a man who saw his land as just business.

He thought about that day. Daeson had leapt from one tree to another because the one he'd climbed had branches too far apart to reach. Swinging out, he'd hooked his knees over a bough in the next tree and let go of the first so he could hang upside down.

Daeson renewed his hold on the roof and swung his legs back and forth. It put more of a burden on his arms but he held on grimly. The momentum of swinging forward threatened to pull him the rest of the way through the roof, but swinging back made him feel like he could escape the hole. He could hear the reeds creaking under his weight.

At the topmost arc, when he felt the lightest, he heaved himself up to his belly and flopped onto the roof. A face full of straw was almost welcome, though the stuff that flew up his nose wasn't. He was exhausted and wanted to rest but also didn't want to spend any more time on the roof. He made himself crawl to the ladder.

The small collection of thatching bundles and twine waiting for him on the ground were no longer enough for patching. He grunted his discontent at them and headed for the water pump. The bucket was looped over the spout and inside was a battered cup. He didn't bother pulling it out, he just pumped until the bucket was halfway filled and drank deeply. The rough edge didn't bother him today. He hitched the bucket back onto the spout and wiped an arm across his mouth.

With a sigh, he moved around the cottage and went inside. In the middle of the dirt floor was a scattering of straw and the thick branch that had stuck in the roof last night during the storm. He stepped around it and looked up at the damage he'd caused. The hole didn't look as big as it had felt while he was in it but it was big enough—if he didn't cover it with something, the next rainfall would ruin everything in the cottage. Not that there was anything left to ruin.

Other than the pipe stove to keep himself warm, his bed and a solitary chair, he'd already sold or traded the rest of his furniture to keep the farm going. He realised now that he'd been throwing good coin after bad...there was nothing he could do to save the fields, they were already grown over. From his raised vantage point Daeson had stared at them all morning and been forced to accept the hard truth.

His last hope was his vegetable patch. It was meagre because he'd only planted enough vegetables for himself, but it was fertile and maintainable. He'd swapped half of it over to winter produce and yesterday had noticed the rest were ready for harvest. He could divide them into rations; sell or trade half of them for more thatching or an animal skin. He also had chickens to sell but knew better than to part with them, they still produced a good quantity of eggs.

It was too quiet. He hadn't heard his chickens all morning. He hadn't even thought about them. He'd missed their feeding time because he'd been trapped inside the roof. They should've been making a fuss by now. They were always clucking at one another even when they were fat and happy. His stomach churned. Had they broken free of their cage? Worse...stolen by foxes?

Daeson hurried out of the cottage. The door springs pulled it shut behind him with a squeal as he headed for the coop. The path rounded the vegetable patch and that was where he stopped. The churn in his belly became a tight knot and his legs turned watery, threatening to spill him onto the ground.

What happened? He didn't understand. What happened? Repetitive thoughts on top of vivid comprehension on top of broiling anger. He shook with the force of his emotions as he surveyed what lay before him.

Clumps of dirt and tufts of roots were scattered on the ground. No more neat leafy rows of spinach and kale, no more stalks of carrot and radish, no more growing heads of broccoli. Just smashed remains, broken stalks and piles of garbage. Everything had been purposefully ruined. Nothing was taken, all was destroyed. With his heartbeat drumming in his ears, Daeson walked stiffly to the edge of the patch. Every step closer felt heavier.

Huge holes were scooped out of the dirt; every bulb had been removed, every stalk pulled out and snapped. There was nothing left.

Who—? His mind gave him the answer before it finished forming the question.

Kurgan. Who else had motive for making his farm life difficult? Who else wanted him to sell his land?

There was nobody he knew to be capable of such a deed except for the hard-faced farmer that his father had warned Daeson to be wary of.

Despair soured in his mouth and sank into his belly. *The chickens!*

"No, no, no," he begged, turning and breaking into a run. He reached the coop at speed but dropped to his knees at the devastation that greeted him there.

Three limp, brown feathered bodies lay prostrate on the ground among smashed eggs. The yolk and albumen had long since seeped into the dirt, but the ruined shells were enough for Daeson to interpret what happened. He'd heard them squawking in his dream. In reality, he'd probably half woken, but it was well before even a farmer's early rising. The chickens had sounded an alarm and he'd only stirred enough for their screeches to register in his sleeping fantasy. The vegetable patch was planted snug against the cottage wall and he'd heard nobody stomping about outside.

Last night it had been storming, providing cover for the culprit and Daeson's farm was remote. The only person that might've seen what happened was his neighbour.

Doubt gnawed. If Kurgan was the only potential witness to the crime, why bother to hide beneath the cover of a storm?

Daeson knelt at the coop staring at three dead chickens until the temple bells brought him to the present. The final service was held at noon and he'd missed his usual mid-morning one. His daily routine had been severely altered.

His grief was choking him. He had an intense desire to escape the farm. Daeson hadn't been raised to run from his problems but he felt overwhelmed by them. Perhaps a few hours away would put things in perspective.

While walking down the sloped trail that led to the

village, Daeson saw Kurgan at the bottom. He broke into a jog, righteousness burning hotly at his core. Would his neighbour say nothing? Perhaps he would feign innocence.

Daeson caught up where the dirt road ended and the cobbled street began. The clomp of his boots alerted Kurgan because the brawny farmer turned to see his approach. There wasn't a smile of greeting on his face for Kurgan wasn't the kind of man to smile unnecessarily. Recently Daeson had become the same.

"Why did you do it?" Daeson accused, bypassing any polite chatter or explanation. Kurgan would know exactly what he was talking about. "Did you think I would give in and sell the farm to you?"

Kurgan's thick brows lowered. He placed his hands on his hips while he looked Daeson over, making an imposing figure. Though he was taller by a hand—an accomplishment, since Daeson himself stood a little over six foot—Daeson wasn't intimidated. He believed he was looking at a coward who would sabotage his farm in the middle of the night.

Doubt persisted. Why would Kurgan make a move last night, of all nights? It made no sense, except nobody else wanted him to sell up and leave.

"What are you talking about, boy?"

When Kurgan spoke, it wasn't thundering anger covering up shame like Daeson expected, but a question.

"You know well what I'm talking about. You're the one who tore it up!" At Kurgan's silent stare, Daeson continued. "I never figured you for a coward, but what you did—"

"Hold your tongue!"

Now Daeson could see the anger that he'd expected at the start. Didn't most bullies hide their fear through aggression? That's what his father had told him.

"You'd best not be calling me a coward," Kurgan

warned, one of his hands moving off his hip to point a finger not far from Daeson's face. Daeson slapped it aside, earning a look of disbelief.

"I'll call you by whatever name you earn. You came while I was asleep to tear up my garden. What else should I call a man who sneaks around at night?" he said.

"Why would you think I would?" Kurgan asked gruffly.

"Who else stands to gain, except you? I might not have seen you with my eyes but I can use my brain."

"Then use your brain to think of someone else."

Kurgan turned to leave. Daeson reached for his arm except he didn't make contact. There were some village folk staring at him curiously, likely watching them because of all the shouting. Daeson wasn't comfortable airing his grievances in public but he wanted Kurgan to admit his guilt. Even if Kurgan denied it, it would be as good as admitting it because Daeson knew when people were lying.

He would catch up with Kurgan after the service and question him again.

Farmers and villagers filed into the temple for its final service, accepting the bread rolls handed them by the acolyte at the door. One by one they dropped the rolls into the fire pit as a sacrifice to Ravina, Goddess of the Harvest. Daeson smuggled his bread into his tunic, where it pressed like guilt against his skin.

He isolated himself by sitting in the backmost pew. Soft sounds of greetings and whispered conversations became a hiss as words bounced off stone floor and walls. He imagined his name was among the sounds because of his stolen roll. He met their stares, brave only because he wanted to search their expressions for knowledge. The person who'd ruined his vegetable patch and killed his chickens would be unable to meet his gaze. He didn't know why he was bothering, he already had his answer in Kurgan...except the farmer hadn't addressed the accusation, and hadn't *looked* guilty. Would a man with no conscience show regret? Daeson needed either a confession or denial before he could know the truth and act on it.

His father had said only those who were weak would take the path of revenge. Daeson struggled with that advice; he saw no justice in allowing someone who'd done wrong go unpunished. He was old enough not to argue but young enough to think he knew better. Soon after, his father had succumbed to an illness, leaving Daeson to wish he'd paid more attention and respect.

When the time for service neared, Cleric Faelin appeared from a side door and looked over his congregation. Daeson averted his gaze, feeling the cleric's eyes boring into his soul. Did he know Daeson hadn't sacrificed his bread? Was the cleric condemning him for his hunger? His appetite had been a gnawing thing, begging Daeson not to waste food on a ritual. He'd been waiting for the right time to shove the bread into his mouth, but his appetite wilted under that iron gaze. Daeson sneaked a look upward, relieved to see the cleric standing behind the podium and looking at someone else.

Cleric Faelin was an imposing man, more so when he stood behind the podium shouting about paying dues. He was striking in his dark blue and yellow robes. His expression changed according to his thoughts. He looked kind when he smiled, cruel when he frowned, and thoughtful when he listened.

Speaking in a clear, booming voice, the cleric began with his thoughts on Ravina. She brought no festivals or feasts but demanded respect for the soil that provided the bounty of life.

Daeson sought out where Kurgan sat. He thought it blasphemous, that the man should come here this morning after what he'd done last night. When Daeson looked back to the front again, he was startled to meet the cleric's gaze.

Next temple service heralded the beginning of winter. Supfest was mentioned and his stomach growled. Daeson waited until the cleric looked away and worked his roll to the open collar of his tunic, where he could sneak a few bites. The crust was hard and scratched his gums but the inside was soft and delicious. He chewed as discreetly as possible. Eating the roll made him feel impossibly hungry, awakening the beast in his stomach.

He barely listened to the service. Towards the end, the collection plate was passed around to pay for Supfest. Daeson was concerned that he had nothing to put in it but the plate didn't reach him. Sitting so far behind everyone had caused the townsfolk to either forget or overlook his presence.

When everyone stood to sing a farewell to Gli, the departing Autumnal God, Daeson snuck away. He thought he'd managed to escape without notice except the acolyte was out the front. Daeson bid him farewell but the acolyte stopped him.

"Cleric Faelin would like to see you."

Daeson felt his eyes widen, his thoughts leaping to the half-eaten bread still shoved down his tunic. He considered pulling it out and apologising, but the acolyte had turned and was looking and pointing toward the path that went around the side of the temple, to the back.

"You can wait in the kitchen and help yourself. Cleric Faelin will be some time before he joins you. He has to farewell everyone first."

Daeson stared at the acolyte who continued looking

and pointing down the path instead of at him. It made the request more urgent. The promise of food beckoned. Daeson considered throwing his half-eaten roll into the fire pit as he passed, but believed it would be a greater insult to the Harvest Goddess. He also had nothing for her to bless. She hadn't failed him; he'd failed to keep up with her.

He passed the door that led to Cleric Faelin's den. Daeson had been in that room only a few times in his life. The first time he'd been so young he was barely walking; he remembered a cluttered room and the smell of wood varnish. His father and the cleric had explained to him about his mother, that she'd gone to the Endworld and would not return. Their words had little impact though he did recall sitting in a mud puddle many moons later and crying because his mother had gone away without him.

The second time was not long after his fourteenth season; winter had come and gone, taking his father with it. The den still smelled of wood polish and the room remained cluttered. The only markings he could make were the ones that formed his name, and the cleric had him signing it over and over to documents that had been explained to him and quickly forgotten in his grief. He'd watched the cleric press his seal to wax at the bottom, officiating them. Then they'd both walked to the cemetery where his father went into the ground beside his mother.

Willem and Marget, together at last.

Stop.

It was hard not to mourn everything at once. His dead parents. His ruined farmland. His few possessions. His murdered chickens. His destroyed vegetable patch.

When he entered the kitchen and beheld a bountiful fruit bowl on the countertop, his mood changed dramatically. Daeson rushed past the long wooden table and its benches to get to it. Greedily he plucked out figs, peaches, nectarines and plums. He ate two of each before finishing his bread roll to counter the sweetness of the fruit.

The cold storage box in the corner caught his eye. Fruit was fine but meat was better.

When Cleric Faelin came to collect him, Daeson was finishing his third ham and cheese sandwich. He shoved the last piece into his mouth, much too big for a single bite, and had trouble chewing. His face grew hot at his dilemma and when the cleric held out his hand, Daeson wiped his fingers on his tunic before taking it.

"No need to rush your meal," the cleric said kindly, pumping Daeson's arm in a firm handshake. Dressed in his finery, it was hard not to feel intimidated by the cleric's presence. "You look as though the weight of the world were upon your shoulders."

Daeson swallowed in large chunks, his throat protesting what was being forced down it.

"Maybe not the world, but the farm is," he replied. He could hear the waver in his voice and attributed it to the difficult digestion. He had no such excuse for the tightness in his chest.

Cleric Faelin nodded, an unreadable expression on his face. It was something for Daeson to marvel at; that he didn't know what this man was thinking. He didn't feel judged but he also didn't perceive sympathy.

"Follow me."

Daeson had intended to clean up after himself but didn't want to make the cleric wait. Aware of dirty plates and cutlery at his back, he fell into step and they went into his den.

Other than the room feeling cosier, it looked and smelled exactly as Daeson remembered. Every surface was littered with papers or items that Daeson associated with the temple. He closed the door and sat in the closest chair while Cleric Faelin moved around his desk, pausing to hang his robe on a hook.

Underneath he wore a simple tunic over pants and Daeson was struck by how ordinary he looked. It was strange to see him dressed in such a way; like catching a person on the privy.

He would keep that association to himself.

Cleric Faelin sat and moved a few bundles of papers aside so he and Daeson could chat without things in the way. He leaned forward, linking his fingers before asking a baffling question.

"You're a winter babe, aren't you?"

It was so unexpected that Daeson's response took longer than it should've.

"Yes," he confirmed.

"How many winters have you seen, Daeson?"

"Uh, this coming winter will be my sixteenth."

"Old enough to understand that failure can be inevitable, no matter how much we fight it."

Outrage swelled in Daeson's chest and worked its way up his neck like bile, hot and acrid.

"I haven't failed," he spat through clenched teeth. His fingers curled around the chair arms.

"Willem should not have made you promise to keep the farm. It was too great a burden on a boy."

He felt ambushed by the conversation. In a few simple words he'd been told he was a failure and his father blamed.

"He was dying! The farm should not have died with him!"

"Calm yourself," Cleric Faelin ordered quietly, holding up his palm. Daeson seethed. His hands ached from holding onto the chair so hard and they'd already been punished today, keeping him from falling through the roof.

"Willem would not have wanted you to throw your life away chasing the impossible. It was the sickness talking."

"It wasn't sickness, it was *truth*," Daeson argued,

unable to hold his tongue. He expected another reprimand for his outburst but the cleric quietly assessed him instead.

"You still have your gift," he said. "Then you know that I am speaking truth as well. I knew Willem deeply. He would not have wanted this bleak future for you." After his declaration, the cleric sat back in his chair.

Daeson made his fingers unclench and forced the tension from his shoulders. Relaxing made it easier for the wad of sticky emotions to ball in his throat, forcing his face to scrunch before he covered it with his hands. He fought for control with shuddering breaths. He hated crying. It made him feel like the child he was rather than the man he had become. With a few deft comments, the cleric had disarmed him and made him vulnerable. Had that been his intention all along? Was that why he'd insulted him? The cleric had told Daeson his biggest fears and then forgave them.

Daeson would never blame his father for the promise made, nor would he resent him. If Daeson had been more ruthless early on, made better decisions about the farm, or asked for help instead of running it into the ground because he was too proud...

"I never understood why you didn't sell the farm to Kurgan. I know he made an offer worthy of the property."

The sentence distracted him from his emotional battle. He removed his hands to stare at the cleric doubtfully. Was this another trick? Being a cleric meant he oversaw everyone's documents, mediated deals and understood how people did business. Surely he knew what kind of man Kurgan was?

"Kurgan is a cheat," Daeson said. He anticipated that he would be interrupted but Faelin remained impassive. "His first offer was well below the value of the farm."

"Any wry businessman would be ready to take

advantage of a fool. You proved your mettle and he returned with a fairer price."

"But it's not fair. It's repulsive to take advantage of someone. I was barely fourteen, how could I know what the farm was worth? It's only because he lied about it being a fair price that saved me."

The cleric nodded his understanding but had no response or explanation. Daeson wanted to ask if he would've allowed such an unfair transaction to go ahead but knew there was no point. The cleric wasn't supposed to mediate. He role was to oversee.

Daeson couldn't stopper his anger. "Kurgan is a criminal and should be marked."

"That is a harsh penalty for someone offering a low price," Faelin pointed out.

"Not for the offer. He came onto my property last night, in the middle of the storm, and tore up my vegetable patch and killed my chickens!"

The outburst felt ridiculous in the silence that followed but the cleric looked shocked. Daeson was bitterly satisfied with that.

"You say it was Kurgan as though you know," the cleric said carefully. "Did you see him?"

"Well, no, but—"

Cleric Faelin raised his hand again and closed his eyes in the same moment. It was a silencing gesture and Daeson complied even though he was feeling wronged. The cleric should be horrified at Kurgan's behaviour, not defending him.

"You should not make accusations of others without knowing for sure," he was told.

"Who else would—"

"Huphuphuphup!"

Daeson blinked in the face of the ridiculous noise the cleric had uttered.

"A heinous crime indeed," the cleric agreed. He linked fingers again. This seemed to be Faelin's favourite position.

Being silenced and then facing the cleric's superior expression was aggravating. His thoughts turned contemptuous.

"Perhaps you should take this as a sign from Ravina, that you are not meant for farming like your father, but should forge your own path."

"This isn't a sign from the *Goddess*," Daeson argued, bordering on blasphemy. Once again he relished the shock on Faelin's face, but this time he continued. "This is about a man being vengeful because I didn't sell him the farm and he wants my land cheap!"

He hadn't seen it with his eyes but he knew it in his heart. Nobody else had motive and Kurgan had made many offers. First Willem had told Kurgan no and then Daeson. Perhaps the frustration had become too great for their neighbour to take and he decided to remove all choice.

He would starve and he had no coin for food. Even though he was saying and thinking as much, the force of his loss still hadn't sunk in. He was sure it would tonight, when he went to bed hungry.

"Kurgan didn't vandalise your farm, Daeson." The words were gentle and matter-of-fact. Daeson's gaze lifted to the cleric who finally looked sympathetic to his plight. "He has long since given up on your land. He is negotiating a deal with the Briggs family now."

Daeson could feel surprise on his face. The Briggs farm was an inferior plot of land with a sharp angle to it that made planting arduous. They grew olive trees, also. What would Kurgan do with olives?

"So you see, he hasn't forced your hand. You forced his."

I don't care, Daeson wanted to say, but couldn't. His tongue was fixed to the roof of his mouth and he huffed. Apparently he *did* care.

"Have you any coin to buy more seed with?"

"I have nothing."

Shame suffocated him. Running the farm had changed his personality, he could feel his insides twisting with stress. Maybe he wasn't a farmer after all.

"What are your plans?" Faelin asked.

"I have none," Daeson replied, his voice breaking. What word had the cleric used to describe his future?

Bleak.

He felt it now, that bleakness. It stole through him, numbing his mind and body. His heartbeat echoed in his ears, making it hard to concentrate on what the cleric was saying.

"Perhaps you could sell the farm and purchase a house in the village? There will always be a need for a pair of strong hands in Cloverlea. You would easily find seasonal work."

"There is nobody who can afford the farm, save Kurgan," Daeson said, giving Cleric Faelin a wary look.

"Yes, it is unfortunate that the one man you're not comfortable selling your land to is the only one with the means. Have you considered travelling elsewhere such as Stonehearth, to entice a buyer for your farm?"

"Uh, no."

He hadn't thought of leaving Cloverlea to look for a buyer. He doubted he could find one now, the farm was a mess that would take a lot of work to salvage. But there was hope, and Daeson clung to it.

"Perhaps someone there dreams of moving to a small community. You could sell your farm and also your services as a farmhand. Then you would have some coin at your disposal and see your farmland restored to its former glory."

The solution wasn't perfect but it was as close as he could come. There was only one obstacle in his way.

"I don't have enough supplies to travel with."

He didn't need a horse or mule to carry his things—all he needed were his feet—but it would be foolish to leave without camping supplies. He had no equipment beyond a water flask. He would still need food rations, a bedroll and tent, and coin to pay the tolls when he neared Stonehearth. It was a typical method for a city's guard to keep out vagrants and thieves; if a traveller couldn't afford the toll, it stood to reason that they wouldn't amount to much within the city's walls.

"You should take the land ownership document with you. I will also give you the contents of this morning's first collection."

Daeson was aghast. He'd never accepted anyone's charity and he wasn't about to start now.

"Cleric, no, it's too much."

"The collections are to help those in need or who have a wrong done unto them. Are you not both these things?"

He wanted to deny it but couldn't. He watched the cleric produce a small golden key that was stitched to the cuff of his shirt, and unlock a deep drawer nestled among the bookshelves. He reached in and pulled out an overflowing pouch.

"It's too much."

"Huphup!" Cleric Faelin made the noise again to silence Daeson's protests. "Such an argumentative young man. I hope this is not the usual way you show respect?"

Daeson felt his cheeks grow hot with embarrassment and accepted the pouch filled with coins. He wanted to open it up and peer inside but knew the action would be inappropriate. He looped the leather thong through his belt holes and was impressed with the sensation of weight on his side.

Cleric Faelin took a moment to produce a document with a waxed seal on the bottom. The insignia of four arrows belonged to the Goddess Laliko, for she represented expansion and her seal was used on official property deeds stamped by the temples.

"Whether you are able to read or not, you shouldn't negotiate without a cleric or justice present."

"Thank you, Cleric Faelin," Daeson said dutifully, taking the paper. It already had a crease in the middle. Daeson re-folded it along the crease and slipped it under his tunic, keeping it flat against his chest.

"I was hoping it wouldn't come to this," the cleric stated with a shake of his head.

"That what wouldn't?" Daeson asked, thinking Cleric Faelin might have been speaking to himself.

The cleric's dark eyes found Daeson and regarded him in a way that Daeson didn't care for. Uncertainty trickled along his spine.

"Stonehearth is not a place for gentle hearts like yours. I pray that you find your buyer and are brave enough to follow your dream. May Portos be your guide."

Portos, one of the old Gods, the ancient beings that had multiple roles and therefore blessings could mean multiple things. Portos ruled not just destiny, but also adventure, wise decisions and free will as an illusion.

The blessing indicated to Daeson that his time with the cleric was over. He stood up, said thank you and farewell, and left the den, softly shutting the door behind him.

He moved up the path, heading for the front of the temple. After a few steps he came upon a sight that slowed his feet and offered a welcome distraction.

The acolyte was crouching at the temple's pump—a clever contraption that worked on two cogs and spun on a belt to keep the water flowing—scrubbing his hands raw. Daeson stood near him but the acolyte didn't notice, he was engrossed in his task.

"Have you been doing dirty work?" Daeson joked.

The acolyte sneered at the pun but when he lifted his gaze to see who'd spoken to him, he did a double take and shot to his feet like a man haunted. "I don't know what you're talking about!" he blustered, his voice lifting an octave.

He was lying. Daeson knew it but didn't know what it meant. He'd only asked about dirty work but the reaction he witnessed was excessive enough to heighten his instinct.

"Did you kill my chickens?"

He hadn't considered the acolyte might be a part of the crime, but it made sense that someone would pay him off to do the deed. Why go running around at night in a storm when you have a low-paid acolyte handy to do it for you? Any bribe would seem generous.

He half-expected an expression of confusion but what he got were rounder, fearful eyes that darted to and fro, unable to meet Daeson's gaze. Coldness seeped through Daeson's gut. The pouch of coins felt heavier on his belt loop.

"Who told you to?" Daeson demanded, wanting to frighten this weedy little creature into giving up the real culprit.

Was it Kurgan? his mind asked.

"Was it Cleric Faelin?" his mouth said.

The pump stopped gushing water. The acolyte's red hands trembled and he folded them into his armpits. Perhaps he was warming them up but the gesture looked defensive. Daeson waited for denial, for a question, for anything. He received silence. The acolyte obviously knew he'd said too much already.

Did he know that Daeson had a gift for truth? The only way the acolyte *could* know was if Cleric Faelin told him. Revealing such knowledge would be a betrayal. Even if he didn't know, only guilty people kept quiet.

He had to stop himself jumping to conclusions. He needed the truth.

Daeson stormed back down the path and threw open the door to the cleric's den. Faelin had been writing and looked up to meet his glare.

"It was you! All this time you sat across from me, pretending to help me, and it was you! You sent him!"

Daeson's heart pounded violently in his chest because of the confrontation and the fear he might be wrong. The cleric placed the quill back in its ink pot and slowly stood.

"What good would it do, to wither away on a farm because of a hasty promise to the man who raised you?"

The confession was very strange but Daeson couldn't focus on anything except the fact the cleric had turned on him.

"Did Kurgan talk you into it?" he said, stepping forward. The cold was at his back, causing the papers inside the room to ripple or steal away from their piles.

"Foolish boy. You fixate on Kurgan because of Willem's rivalry with the man. He has nothing to do with this. He is better than you realise, for honouring your secret."

"He doesn't know about my gift, unless you told him."

"I don't mean your gift for truth. Your *other* secret." The cleric stared at Daeson who didn't know what to say. "Where do you think your gift came from? Have you not thought on it at all?"

"I'm not here to talk about my gift. You took my farm away from me!"

"Your farm was already gone. You were drowning, holding onto a thin reed that would not last. All I did was take it from you so you could swim."

The metaphors felt ugly in his gut, swirling in that strange space between truth and lies. Silence ruled the space between them as Daeson boggled at the cleric. How could he stand there so impassively after taking away what little Daeson had? How was he not on his knees begging for forgiveness?

"I have no other secrets," he said finally, wanting

the silence to break.

"Kurgan knows you were not Willem and Marget's babe. He promised to lie about them being your parents, so the Flag Guards wouldn't take you to a workhome."

The shock ran deep, as though someone had scooped his insides out, leaving behind a hollow shell. His chest tightened, making it difficult to breathe. His hearing muted, noises sounding as though they were coming through a barrel. The cleric was still talking but Daeson was too busy trying to make himself feel normal. Darkness entered his vision before seeping away. When the sensation passed, it took everything with it except the feeling of being gutted.

Willem wasn't his father. Marget wasn't his mother. Kurgan and the cleric both knew it. Had Cleric Faelin thought Daeson knew or was he telling him the truth to disarm him? Did it even matter what the Cleric was trying to do? His intentions were impure, either way.

Daeson's mouth filled with spittle that he balled with his tongue and spat onto the den's floor, the act cursing the temple and all those within it.

"Daeson!" His name was uttered in a mixture of disgust and horror. He was satisfied with the reaction he got but it didn't make him feel better.

"You deserve it," Daeson said, his voice shaking. He left the den and moved up the path.

This time the acolyte was nowhere nearby.

CHAPTER TWO

Bunker Visit

S soon as the telephone rang, Synjan knew who it would be. Resignation filled her as she lifted the sleek white handset.

"Hello?"

"Is that Miss Walker?"

"Yes."

"This is Endam Hartley at the south branch of Gredann City Bank. Your deposit wasn't made this morning."

The man on the other end of the line sounded uncertain. He'd been warned to use caution when calling this number and to be succinct. Risk was implied. He was also bribed generously for performing this task.

"Thank you," Synjan replied and hung up. Her lips twisted as she contemplated the news. A glance at her wristwatch told her it was eleven in the morning; more than an hour after the day's money should have been banked. It was the third time in as many weeks that she'd received this call and she'd promised herself this would be the last. The pad of her index finger tapped on the cool plastic of the phone. A voice nearby pulled her from her thoughts.

"Who was it?" Ellis asked. He stood at the head of the hallway that led to the rear of their home. He'd come from his bedroom and his green eyes were alert as he looked her over, no doubt identifying her pensive mood by her body language.

"The bank," Synjan told him, unsurprised when his lips thinned.

Ellis headed into the living area, stepping off polished wood and onto the cream carpet of the sunken lounge. He moved around the low square coffee table where the pieces of an unfinished jigsaw hinted at snowy mountains and log cabins. The wraparound sofa's suede cushions were plush and he sank into them, crossing his legs and assessing her.

Synjan went to him. Though the sun was climbing to its zenith and filling the large, open plan space with a golden glow through the skylight, Synjan didn't feel warmed.

"So," he said mildly, his voice pleasant as he stretched his right arm along the low back of the couch. His expression was expectant.

She could only stare at him, not wanting to admit defeat yet unable to think of another way to salvage this disaster.

Ellis was a distinguished-looking man, though not classically handsome. The sixty years he'd lived hadn't been kind to his fair complexion, yet the lines on his face lent him character. His close-cropped salt and pepper hair gave him a vital air. He had a square jaw that balanced out the roundness of his balding head and narrow features in between.

His emerald eyes were his most notable attribute. Bright and intelligent, they peered out from behind rimless glasses. When Ellis spoke, people listened and it was mostly because of what they could see shining in those eyes. His voice was rich and deep but it was his *tone* that got people moving.

He always presented himself impeccably, his face cleanly shaven and his clothes immaculate. Today was no exception. Ellis was a man of demanding taste, impossible standards and harsh judgement. Synjan knew what his single word meant, as he'd trained her to know in the eighteen years she'd been with him.

"I'll have to take care of it," she announced, sounding calmer than she felt.

Ellis nodded, running the forefinger and thumb of his left hand along the fold in his pants. "Regrettably," he added, as if that would reassure her.

Synjan's task was confirmed. She pivoted and skirted around the dining table and headed for her bedroom. It was at the front corner of the three storey house, where she could get the modicum of privacy a single, twenty-four year old woman deserved.

She wasn't in her room long. The denim long pants and brown long-sleeved shirt she had on were suitable but she pulled off her joggers and changed into platform boots. She stood at one hundred and sixty-two centimetres and felt more confident walking into unpredictable situations with extra height.

Next, Synjan attached her bra holster before checking that her small automatic pistol's magazine was fully loaded and the safety was on. She holstered the gun and checked its concealment in a mirror. Her large breasts were the reason a shoulder holster was impractical but they effectively hid the gun. She doubted that she would need to draw the weapon but she wasn't going to risk being without it.

"Good luck," Ellis bade as she passed back through to collect her keys before leaving. Synjan didn't look at him or acknowledge his words. There wasn't anything she could think of to say.

The floor below was dedicated to the running of their business, with a single apartment for their housekeeper. Most visitors to this floor were employees coming to see Synjan. She acted as Ellis' proxy while he remained upstairs.

The second floor's spiral staircase led to the middle of the mechanic's workshop that occupied the ground floor. The stairs were concealed in a large support with a locked door. Select people had a key for this internal entry, most came up the back stairs and knocked. The workshop was a legitimate, family-owned business operating under the name of Minke's Garage. She and Ellis had nothing to do with the company apart from collecting rent each month and occasionally having them service the vehicle Ellis owned and kept garaged there.

Synjan left via the rear of the building. She was pleased to escape the cacophony of a workshop filled with mechanics banging on engines and yelling to be heard over the whine and zip of the machines they operated.

A wooden bicycle rack was built against the wall, a selection of four rides stowed within. She chose a rusty bicycle that had a basket-style trailer attached to the back. She would need it to get the money to the bank once she picked it up.

Their network of staff and business partners referred to this building most often as 'the Office', rather than their home, and it was a habit Ellis and Synjan had also adopted. The Office wasn't the only residence Ellis owned in Gredann. Six cobbled, hilly streets away was the Bunker and this was where Synjan headed once she pedalled out of the weed-ridden alley that ran between the Office and the row of houses behind it.

The ride to the Bunker required concentration as the streets weren't easy to negotiate on a bike that had seen better days. Nothing made of metal lasted very long in Dockside. The salt in the air ate at everything that wasn't fabricated from wood, plastic or cloth.

There were a few other vehicles moving around on the narrow streets. Most were patrolling Authority open-top vehicles and the rest were small trucks moving goods into or out of the many warehouses within the fishing district.

Chiefly, she needed to dodge pedestrians and she almost came undone at one point when she rounded a corner and an elderly man stepped out in front of her.

"Ho, there!" she cried as she struggled to steer around him. The Dockside roadways were angled towards a drain down their centre and though there were always promises from the Authorities to upgrade the surfaces, the cobbles were missing in some places or the whole thoroughfare was skewed at a steeper angle due to a lack of maintenance. Walkways on the sides of the road were extremely narrow or non-existent, despite the outcry of citizens who were run over more frequently than was warranted.

The old man stopped and wheezed a laugh at her efforts as she stood on the pedals in order to get the bike around him and up the hill.

Such things didn't happen in Portside or Hill End. The roads in the better parts of the city were smooth and grey with footpaths bordering both sides of every road. This was just one reason the Authorities weren't welcome in Dockside and old timers like the one she'd almost hit spat after saying their name. They were understandably bitter after more than fifty years of broken promises and neglect.

Synjan pulled into Breezy Turn at the top of the hill and coasted to a house about halfway down. There were two sets of stairs that led to different doors in the wide residence; the one on the right had more steps to accommodate the gradient of the land and this was the one she headed for. She angled her bike against the stair railing so it wouldn't roll away, confident that it wouldn't be touched by any of the guttersnipes in the area. Everyone in Dockside knew the Bunker was Ellis'. People didn't steal from him if they valued their health.

Synjan withdrew her keys and walked steadily up the stairs. She let herself in and shut the door behind her as quickly and quietly as she was able. Dust motes floated around her in the darkened entryway. This place had been her second home in Gredann and even now the smell roused a sensation of comfort and familiarity. There was unease too, because there'd also been many traumas here.

To her left were the common living area and kitchen. She knew—because she was experienced and this was a routine she'd performed too often lately—that her target was in there, but she wasn't ready for a confrontation just yet. Instead, she turned right and moved along the turns of the hallway that wound through the dormitory half of the house.

As soon as she was away from the foyer, the large house felt derelict and filthy. There were six shared and single bedrooms of various sizes as well as a few bathrooms in this half of the house. Synjan wrinkled her nose as she passed pungent toilets and untidy rooms. She was surprised that she didn't meet anyone as there were currently five permanent residents and they should've been returning for lunch. It was obvious that more than just the banking routine wasn't being followed in this dysfunctional household.

There was a tiny office at the very back of the house near the bedroom that used to be hers. When she'd lived here, the office had been the exclusive domain of Ellis and Charli, the woman he'd paid to be the live-in housemother to all the residents.

Charli had also been a savvy businesswoman and she'd been in charge of protecting all the funds Ellis had filtered through the Bunker. Synjan had been fourteen before she'd even had the privilege of looking into this hallowed room, which was little more than a glorified closet. She'd always wanted to see the computer, a very rare item most Docksiders would never sight in their lifetime, but Charli had been fanatical about keeping the office locked and Synjan's inquisitive gaze out.

Now, Synjan searched through her keys with one hand as she approached but tried the knob with the other anyway. The last vestige of hope died within her as it turned and swung inward. She was able to walk straight in.

Seven leather satchels were spread haphazardly

across the desk. The computer they were beside was not turned on, indicating their contents hadn't been counted or recorded as they were supposed to have been, before they were banked. She swore as she closed the door and moved to the chair in front of the desk. It squeaked as she sat, giving away her intrusion, but she knew no-one would notice. The days of people taking pride in doing their job well in this house were gone.

It took her half an hour to get everything in order. It was only because she'd used to collect these satchels as a child that she knew who belonged to what. Back then, she'd been a Runner. She would travel the reaches of Gredann in the early hours of each day and collect the illegitimate funds Ellis' network of employees had accrued in their various pursuits the night before.

From Hill End came the profits of selling drugs and alcohol to rich people—that was two satchels of money. Another was the spoils from contraband and under-the-table gambling at a pair of fancy hotels. Two more satchels held the takings from a gambling ship Ellis owned called *Lady Tamsin*. The last two were filled with cash from various Portside bookies. They were the earnings from illegal dog, cock or bare-knuckle fights held while the city-wide curfew was in effect. The return on such ventures varied widely—especially with the Authorities' bribes factored into the mix—but all turned a nice profit. The night-time events also gave Docksiders the empowering belief that they were rebelling in a small way against the Authority stranglehold on their city. It worked in Ellis' favour from many angles.

Once she was finished, Synjan shut down the computer, gathered the three satchels she'd condensed the money into and headed for the other part of the house. She was aware that her pulse rate had lifted. She didn't want to be here, do this, be the person she was about to be. She never did. But this...this was going to be particularly difficult. She took a few deep breaths to negate the adrenaline seeping into her system. She was anticipating a fight and even though she was confident she would win, she was too highly trained to ignore the many factors that could go against her.

She passed the front door with a regretful glance and stepped into the common room.

Her target was a past friend. Something in her was ashamed to think of her as a 'target', but it was also easier. Kate was sitting at one of the dining tables, her face resting on her arms and her eyes closed. There was a recently used kit not far from her elbow. As Synjan dropped her satchels onto the chair opposite with a deliberate thump, Kate sat up with a gasp and looked around blearily, taking a few moments to focus on the blonde woman who stood across from her.

"Synjan?" she queried, her voice thick and bewildered.

"Good dawning," Synjan greeted steadily.

A squeal that didn't sound heartfelt came as Kate staggered to her feet. She lurched around the table to embrace Synjan, hugging her brutally. She wore a food-stained singlet, hole-riddled pants and smelled like she hadn't showered for days. Synjan held her breath and kept her face away, allowing the hold to continue for a few seconds before she gently pushed the twig-thin brunette back.

"Whatchoo' doin' here?" Kate asked, her lips drawing back in a travesty of a smile. Once, she'd had beautiful teeth but only two of them remained and the rest were blackened stumps. Her skin was spotted with weeping sores and some muscles in her face had palsied, causing the lovely symmetry of her features to fail. Synjan didn't return the smile and pulled out a chair.

"Sit down," she invited.

Kate did so, making a show of swiping at her

knotted, unkempt hair and straightening her grubby clothes. "Wish you'd told me you was comin', I'd've made you some... lunch," she admonished, turning to look at the clock that was on the wall to confirm she had the timing right.

Synjan couldn't bear to look at her too hard so she grabbed the closest chair and set herself up opposite Kate.

"Never mind. I'm not here for lunch."

The money chair was beside them and Synjan nodded at it to draw attention to it as she spoke. Kate's gaze fell to the satchels and she frowned, scratching absently at the skin of her inner elbow. The tiny black holes in it wove an insidious and eloquent trail of tragedy. "I... was just getting to that," she said defensively.

"I already did it. The bank called me an hour ago to say it wasn't in. The office door wasn't even *locked*, Kate," Synjan criticised, her voice hardening.

"Well, the house is," the brunette argued hotly.

"You know how many people have a key."

Kate snorted. "It doesn't matter, no-one'd ever steal from *you*."

Synjan blinked. "It's not my money," she reminded the older woman.

"Well, from Ellis then," Kate dismissed, pulling a face and flicking a hand.

"They might, though. Like he says, 'It only takes one step to start a trail'."

"Oh, Synjan," Kate admonished, drawling her name in a manner that suggested they both knew that Synjan was just being some sort of fear-monger. "If anyone took his stuff, he'd just send you to get it back. And you would. O'course." Her grin was partly pride, partly contempt.

"That's not the point. The fact remains you're too relaxed and you're not doing your job. It's not enough.

I've warned you twice before. This is the third time."

Kate's expression shifted from cocky to frowning. Her eyelashes fluttered as she processed the meaning behind those quietly spoken words, mouth opening and closing twice. When she finally spoke, her reply was unexpected.

"Remember when you first came here?" she asked brightly, dragging her chair closer to Synjan's.

The sudden movement had Synjan tensing. She remained coiled as Kate's hand came towards her, resisting the urge to brush it aside in order to maintain the civility of the situation. Her shoulder was patted before Kate picked up the tail of Synjan's blonde braid, rubbing it worshipfully between her fingers.

"You were such a tiny little scrap!" she laughed, her bloodshot eyes taking on the shine of memory.

Synjan nodded, not trusting herself to speak because she *did* remember. She remembered how twelve year old Kate had looked; all long legs, taut skin and beautiful, shiny hair. The world was hers and she'd welcomed Synjan openly, becoming her closest girlfriend, advisor about boys and protector of the six year old orphan. It was difficult to believe the crone before her was that same girl, at just thirty years of age.

"Oh, everybody loved you," Kate enthused, letting go of Synjan's hair and pulling her hands back so she could rub them agitatedly between her knees. Her smile was genuine but there was a desperation in her haunted eyes that wasn't making her easy to watch. "Tiny thing you were."

Synjan breathed a laugh, wanting to end the awkward bout of reminiscing but feeling like she owed Kate this much.

"Little One, that's what he called you."

"He still does, when he's in a good mood." Synjan smiled slightly, trying to remember the last time Ellis had used the endearment instead of her name.

"An' you were so *fast*! Fastest, smartest Runner we ever 'ad. No-one could finish a run as quick and safe as you."

Synjan merely watched, distracted by Kate's scrabbling hands and not having anything especially uplifting to add. Yes, she'd been Ellis' best Runner and he'd shaped her into his most steadfast employee, his irreplaceable second in command. But it wasn't like she'd ever had a choice in the matter.

"You were so sweet, following Nick around like a lovesick pup and play-fighting with Ren," she giggled, hugging herself and curling her bony shoulders inward, as if enamoured by the cuteness of the memory.

Synjan couldn't let *that* remark slide. "I wasn't playing. I fought Ren because he tried to rape me and because he beat the smile out of you," she argued.

Kate flinched as if she'd been slapped, anger and hurt warring in her expression. "N-no, that's not true. Ren *loved* me!"

"Ren was no-good scum that never deserved you," Synjan countered quietly.

"He died for me!" Kate screeched, tears welling and her face contorted.

Synjan was at a loss, unable to argue such a tangled lie. Ren had been a mediocre assassin, trained as a sniper to do Ellis' bidding. He was an arrogant psychopath that had accosted every woman that came near him and he'd met his inevitable demise when he didn't scout his kill-spot well enough about eight years before. The Authorities finished him and Kate had spiralled.

"Forget about the past. We need to talk about your work here," Synjan said calmly, steering the conversation back to where it needed to go.

The sniffling continued before the brunette looked at her. Horror dawned. "Synjan... no! I can do better! I was just... havin' a bad day is all!" she gabbled, her fingers fretting against one another as she slid forward onto the edge of her seat to plead her case.

"I told you—"

"You said you'd gimme a chance!"

"This is the third time—"

"No! You can't fire me! I have nowhere else to go! I'll *die* if you kick me out!"

"We'll move you somewhere else, the farm outside the city has—"

"You can't send me away! Ren is buried here!" she pleaded, falling off her seat and onto her knees. The sharp report of bone hitting wood caused Synjan to wince. Kate grabbed for Synjan's hands, trying to press them together between her own in a gesture much like a prayer.

"Ren is dead, Kate. And you're going to be if you don't stop using."

"I can stop! I will stop – I *have* stopped! Today was my last day, I swear, just please don't send me away, Synjan, I'm begging you. This is all I have. I'll get clean, I'll do better. Please? For an old friend? Remember all those times I helped you when you were little? Huh? Remember how you could always come to Kate when you were crying and I'd look after you? Good old Kate, always there for you," she crooned, her words running together as she pawed at Synjan's face now, trying to stroke her hair, hands shaking so hard she inadvertently pulled strands more than patted them.

Synjan couldn't bear it any more. The proximity was stifling and it hurt too much to watch someone she'd once cared for discard her remaining shreds of dignity in a useless attempt to protect herself. She had to put a stop to it.

"Enough!" Synjan yelled, restraining Kate's wrists without any difficulty. Looking Kate in the eye made her feel out of control and she squeezed her eyelids shut momentarily. This situation, this place, did it rob everyone of their power? The worst part of it all was how this travesty of a woman could have been her, had Ellis not intervened. She opened her eyes, equilibrium regained.

"I'm sorry, but you're no use to us as a housemother. You can't take care of yourself, let alone the runners or the money. You'll need to get your things and I'll have you taken somewhere nice where you can get the shit out of your system," she said succinctly.

Watery eyes blinked up at her and there was blessed silence while her words sank in. "You fucking *bitch*!" Kate screeched, now attempting to gouge Synjan's face. "You think you're so much better than me because you're Ellis' personal little favour giver, but you're just a whore like the rest of us!"

Synjan clenched her teeth, lips drawing back in a silent snarl, amazed at the venom behind the words. More vile accusations followed, more descriptions of the many ways Synjan was no better and owed her privileged position all to Kate – except she was too much of a two-faced bitch to look after the people who'd helped her. She was cold and dead inside and her heart was a stone. Synjan held Kate's hands throughout the tirade, sickened by every insult but unable to think of a way to stop it until Kate took it a step too far.

"You little bitch," she sneered, "you stuck-up Wanderer bitch with your special powers and—"

Synjan backhanded her hard enough that she smacked her head against the wooden floorboards with a dull thud. Kate lay there groaning while Synjan's mind raced. How could she have forgotten that Kate knew her secret? How had she not thought about the danger that posed before now? Sure, friends made promises to friends as children but all bets were off when one of those friends was turning the other out onto the street.

Realising she was standing over Kate with her fists clenched, Synjan understood how this needed to be resolved and a cold wave ran from her head to her toes. She couldn't return to Ellis with Kate's knowledge hanging over her and she was loathe to use her gun... but there was another weapon she hadn't considered until now. She was looking at it.

"Kate. You have to go."

She tried to convince herself that the pitiable creature huddled on the floor was just a shadow of the friend she'd once had and that her plan might even be a mercy. *Was* a mercy.

"But... tell you what I'll do," Synjan hinted. She was pleased when the crying stopped. Kate unfortunately had plenty of practice recovering after being hit and she likely sensed that a change in her favour was coming. "Ellis wanted me to take you out of the city," she lied, "but I gather you don't want to go, so I'll give you some money and you can find a place in Gredann that you're happy with, okay?"

"Where'd that be?" Kate scoffed.

Synjan frowned, realising the brunette had a point. The only place someone like Kate belonged was Dockside, and it wasn't known for its rental properties like the more esteemed parts of the city.

"The Ship Inn?" Synjan suggested, naming a hotel not far from the docks. It was mostly frequented by sailors who'd decided to put in to shore overnight. It wasn't a pristine establishment but there were always rooms available.

Kate wrinkled her nose. "It's not real big. Or clean," she said, like she wanted to be convinced otherwise.

"C'mere," Synjan encouraged, helping the brunette to her feet. She grasped her by the upper arms once she was standing and held eye contact. "It'd be for the best if you went there. I know it's not great, but it will give me a chance to organise a bigger severance pay for you. You can look for a proper house later. Ellis wants you out of here today and it'll keep him happy if I can tell him you're gone and you're safe, even if you only have a little room at first. You don't have that much stuff, do you?"

"Mm-well, no," Kate admitted, swiping at her running nose while she considered Synjan's proposal.

"Go pack your stuff. I'll ride it to the inn for you and see you settled before I go to the bank."

The reference to money had the desired effect as a greedy light entered Kate's eyes. "How much c'n you give me?" she queried.

"Plenty," Synjan assured her, tilting her head conspiratorially to continue speaking, even though it was just the two of them in the house. "I'll look after you, Kate. Like you always did for me. Ellis won't even have to know how much I give you, it'll be between you and me, okay?"

A muffled squeak of agreement preceded another unruly hug, which Synjan endured. After Kate finally let go, she went to the dining table to grab her junk before she hurried away to pack. Synjan returned the satchels to the office, pocketing a wad of cash from one of them before locking the door.

She was angry at Kate. *Kate* had failed and allowed this situation to degenerate. Synjan knew she should feel remorse about what she was orchestrating but it was difficult, thanks to Kate's groundwork. Should she lament a necessary solution? Weep? There didn't seem a point. She *did* feel sad, but she was also relieved. She didn't have the luxury of choice.

Kate was ready in half an hour – she even showered and dressed in some decent clothing – and Synjan arranged her suitcase and box of belongings in the bike's trailer. Kate walked beside her as she pedalled the awkward load through the hilly streets of Dockside, rambling about what a positive change this was going to be in her life. For a short while, she was like the Kate that lived in Synjan's memory and it was harder to ignore the tight sensation in her chest.

When they reached the Ship Inn, Synjan laid down the deposit for Kate's room, opting to pay for a week. Kate's grin was triumphant, leaving Synjan regretful as she turned away to collect Kate's belongings. Together, they carried everything up the rickety stairs. Inside her little room, Kate eagerly accepted the bundle of cash she was given, thanking Synjan profusely and promising she'd use the money for sensible purposes as she turned to squirrel it away beneath her clothes.

"I know you will," Synjan told her sadly, summoning a smile as she gazed at her old friend's gaunt back. "Good luck," she bade and was barely acknowledged as she left the inn room.

Synjan rode back to the Bunker and took the satchels to the bank, checking on Kate with her Wanderer power. The distinctive strobing purple pattern that Synjan knew to be Kate's left the Ship Inn. Kate visited her dealer and scored. She probably bought more than she'd been able to afford in the last five years. Kate then headed back to her inn room. Synjan returned the bike to the Office and walked slowly through the streets of Dockside. Waiting. Mourning.

The shadows were lengthening across the rooftops of Gredann when Synjan arrived back at the Ship Inn. The door to Kate's room was unlocked and her body sat on her single bed, chin on her chest with her hands on her knees, palms up in a supplicating gesture. The spent needle was still in her arm.

"Oh, Kate," Synjan sighed her eulogy as she crouched beside the bed. Synjan's fight-roughened hands curled around Kate's and she thought again of when this woman had been young and vibrant and her friend. Tears rolled over her cheeks. She was sorry that Ellis had these drugs made, sorry that Kate had ever been sold to and infuriated by the way hard lives met even harder ends in Gredann.

Futility overwhelmed her and she hated herself for going through Kate's belongings, taking the leftover money and anything that could connect her to Ellis – including the drugs – before she turned and walked downstairs. She told the person behind the desk that they should call the Authorities to report the dead body upstairs. She nodded her assent when told she wouldn't get a refund on the money she'd paid for the room. It was expected.

As she headed for the Office, she wanted to run. Her instincts demanded action be taken to dampen the anger and despair swelling within. She didn't. Somehow, the tears continued to fall even though she wasn't actively crying. She swiped them away.

When she got home, Ellis was waiting for her, still sitting on the couch and reading a book. She went into the lounge this time and sat opposite him, knowing he wouldn't be satisfied if she didn't report in. He'd lit a fire and she stared into it as she waited for his opening remarks.

"You were gone a long time," he began, tenting his book upon his thigh. He made a show of looking at his watch. "It's almost six of the clock."

"Kate's dead," Synjan replied woodenly, sniffling.

Ellis tutted, adopting a sympathetic expression. "That's a shame."

Synjan glared at him. "Like you care."

"I know these things are hard on you," he responded mildly.

"Yeah. But *I* didn't do it. *You* did," she spat.

Ellis raised his eyebrows.

"You and your fucking drugs," she sneered, feeling the anger swirling again, too big to push down this time.

"Ah," he said, his eyes also beginning to glitter. He stroked the book's spine as he offered an observation. "I didn't force them into her system."

"It was *your* money I gave her to buy them."

"Well, that was short sighted of you," he frowned.

"They were *your* drugs anyway. The money will come straight back to you!" she yelled, laughing bitterly as she got to her feet and emptied her pockets onto the coffee table between them. Cash and little packets of drugs bounced haphazardly onto the jigsaw puzzle, looking even more ghastly for the refined environment they'd appeared in. "It's just one big, twisted circle, going nowhere but down."

"You need to *calm* down," Ellis warned, his eyes narrowed. He looked furious about what she'd dumped on the table but he hadn't moved.

Synjan bit her tongue in a gesture of self-preservation, taking a breath before she spoke again. "I didn't want to kill her," she admitted, her voice cracking as the reality of Kate's death hit her anew. "But she remembered I was a Wanderer. And she was angry over being fired." Even to her own ears, she sounded infantile and helpless.

Surprisingly, Ellis responded to her vulnerability, his expression shifting to something soft and compassionate. "Then you did what needed to be done."

Synjan watched the fire, releasing her pent-up breath when Ellis eventually came to her, positioning himself around her. His hold was comforting, despite the rage she felt towards him, and she leaned into it instinctively.

"I didn't *want* her to die," she whispered plaintively.

"I know, Little One," he murmured, kissing her forehead tenderly.

"She used to be my friend."

"That was a long time ago."

"I let her down."

"*She* faltered. She failed," he crooned, his fingers lightly tracing her face and neck, leaving goosebumps in their wake.

"She just... got lost. It wasn't her fault."

He remained quiet, holding her. Their breathing was synchronised and she could feel the soft bump of his heartbeat against her cheek as she rested her head upon his chest. One of his hands slid down her back, kneading the curve of her lower spine.

"Maybe—"

"Don't dwell. You did what needed to be done. You're strong. Invincible. Be proud of yourself. I am."

"I'm *not*," she snarled, pushing violently away from him. "What is there to be proud of? I knew she'd do it, I did it on purpose, but that doesn't make it *right*. I killed her!"

"As much as I did," he supplied slowly, his eyes unreadable as the firelight reflected off his glasses.

Synjan was distraught, aware that she'd made him angry by severing their embrace but unable to bring herself to fix it. "That's right! It was both of us," she retorted, her voice hitching on an errant sob.

"In the end, everyone answers to somebody."

Synjan flinched, hating that saying of his. She covered her face with her hands as she turned away from him and made her way to her room. He let her go.

Fighting with Ellis wasn't the answer and if she stayed near him, she'd only get herself into some serious trouble. She needed to deal with her feelings another way.

CHAPTER THREE

Lords And Horse Thieves

THICK winter clouds hid the afternoon sun, shielding the blonde boy from what little warmth its rays could offer. The estate was too far south for snow but not far enough to escape the sharp bite of frost upon fingers, ears and nose. Hawke looked back at the manor and imagined he could see his brother Denis waving from one of the fourth floor windows, but it was likely just a glint of light. Denis wouldn't betray Hawke's location to their tutor, a harsh woman constantly infuriated by Hawke's behaviour. At least when he wasn't around, he could only disappoint her once. He didn't often escape his lessons but dancing was boring and he was itching to ride his new horse, Silverprint.

The light grey steed was a gift for his eighth birthday, a reward he'd known was coming and impatiently waited for. Each child of Donovan Court received their own horse on their eighth birthday. His sister Giselle had been the last before him and she'd been charged with a highly spirited mare. She'd named it Wilder, and such a name couldn't be more apt. Hawke wouldn't go near Wilder but would never admit he was scared. He'd seen the large bruise his eldest brother Umber earned for getting too close to the mare; chomped on the shoulder for his insolence. If Wilder hadn't treated his sister gently, the mare would've been sold.

He opened the stable door a crack, not wishing to alert the stablehands inside. They were often chatting to one another or puffing harshly as they worked but all he could hear was the soft movements of horses in their stalls. Hawke had spied Togar, the stable master, taking the wagon towards the township after lunchtime.

Leaving so late meant he would be back just before nightfall. This left Hawke a couple of hours of daylight to ride Silverprint through the fields, and have him back before the announcement for dinner. He knew his absence during today's lesson would be noted but he wouldn't suffer the consequences for it until the end of the week, when a report was given to his father.

He heard a murmur coming from the far stall that didn't sound like a horse. He wondered if one of the stable hands was getting drunk on burnwater. He was conflicted; should he go and have a look or continue his mission to saddle and ride Silverprint? If the drunken stable hand was Mako, it would be an easy way to get rid of him. The way the brutish fellow looked at his sister unnerved him. Hawke had warned Giselle about it and she'd scoffed at his concerns but she'd stopped visiting the stables alone.

Wilder whinnied at him from the stall beside Silverprint. He stared at his horse while trying to decide. Even though he knew what he wanted, he also felt obliged to protect his family and the horses. A drunk could do a lot of damage in a stable and Hawke was positive that the voice belonged to someone who'd found themselves a hiding spot.

He approached without caution. When he pushed open the far stall door and found six people crouched within it, he wasn't sure what he was seeing. A dark-skinned man sprang up and grabbed him, covering Hawke's mouth and pressing something pointy under his chin. It was then that Hawke realised that one of the people 'hiding' wasn't doing so at all.

Mako was propped against the back wall, the tines of a pitchfork deep in his belly. Fingertrails of blood stained his coveralls. He was most certainly dead. Seeing his body didn't bother Hawke as much as realising he had a blade against his throat. Fear held him rigid. The dark man holding him was very strong.

The tip of the blade pierced his throat and he screeched in pain.

"What are you doing? He's just a little boy! Let him go," one of the crouching women hissed. Hawke looked at her with wide-eyes, grateful for her intervention and hoping his captor was under her influence.

"So he can run back to that big house and let them know we're here?" he replied. "No way."

Hawke made muffled promises, all of them lies.

"So tie him up, he's no threat," the woman suggested. Hawke didn't want her help anymore. He stamped the heel of his boot against the boot-clad foot of his aggressor but all he won for his efforts was a shifted hold. Hawke didn't try it again—there was something hard in the man's boot that protected his toes. He realised he should've gone for an ankle or shin. Biting was also out of the question because the hand was pressed so hard against his mouth that he couldn't move his jaw. He felt pinned and helpless and was reminded of the traps he and Denis set to capture wild animals foolish enough to investigate them—just like he'd been foolish enough to investigate the soft shuffling sound.

A hot stone lodged deep in his bladder, making him feel like peeing. He didn't dare disgrace himself in such a way, despite the fear nestled in his chest. He was dropped and landed badly, his shoulder taking a lot of the force. He cried out in pain and was roughly flipped onto his back and then knelt upon by the dark man. His tormentor's knee pressed firmly and painfully on Hawke's middle, forcing the breath out of him. Hawke gripped the leg that was on him but even though he tried to dig his fingers in, all he could feel was tense muscle. The man might as well have been made out of rock.

"Don't yell out, little boy," he warned, "or I'll fill you full of holes just like your boss there."

Hawke was incensed that he would be considered a stableboy and also under Mako's supervision. He looked towards the body and at Mako's slumped form. From this direction the stablehand's feet and legs looked like they belonged to a giant. Without their numbers, they wouldn't have been able to overpower him. The other stablehand was nowhere around either. Was his body lying in another stall?

The dark man moved off him and Hawke drew in deep, shuddering breaths. His chest ached and he rubbed where the knee had been planted on him. He didn't have long before his arms were grabbed and he was forced onto his stomach. When a rope was tied around his throat, Hawke cried a protest, tears of anger and humiliation streaking down his cheeks.

"Don't choke him, Eddie, by Junstill's sword."

Eddie grunted but continued to truss Hawke up so that his ankles were tied to his wrists and the rope around his neck connected to them both. If he wriggled, he would strangle himself. The rope Eddie used was for the horses so it wasn't coarse but it had been pulled tight. Hawke was left in the end stall with Mako's body while the group of five moved through the stables and took the horses. Now that he'd been left alone, a gamut of emotions coursed through him. Anger, indignation, frustration and hatred. His initial fear was well coated.

He heard a horse kicking and stamping, a great deal of whinnying and cursing and then an exasperated order: "Leave it." Hawke felt vindicated by Wilder's ill-tempered mannerisms and hoped the mare would give them a well-placed chomp on his behalf. His heart sank when he heard where Wilder's rebellion led. "Take the grey one next to it."

"No!" he shouted, dismayed. "No! No!"

His objections earned him a threat.

"Shut up, kid, or I'll kick your teeth out."

Hawke felt like crying. The choking, cloying

sensation filled up his neck and sat there like a hot, sticky wad of glue. Swallowing didn't get rid of it and it was a useless emotion. Crying did nothing but mess up his thought process; he'd discovered that early on when some of his tutors pulled out their switches to keep his sharp tongue in check. He'd learned to pick his battles but he'd not allowed them to beat him down. Instead he opened his mouth to take in a deep breath but not to call out. He kept taking long, deep breaths until the air melted away the emotional lump in his throat and he could think clearly.

He listened as they saddled the horses and could imagine his calm, trusting horse allowing them to do it. Beautiful Silverprint, whom Hawke had barely ridden himself, with his unusual light grey markings. They looked like someone had trailed silvered fingers down his neck and rump. He was the finest possession Hawke owned, including the weapons that were 'his' to train with—not really his because they'd belonged to his older brothers at one time. He had to wait until he was twelve before he could get his own sword. He'd had his eye on a *tayeta*, a lightweight, narrow, flat bladed sword, because he was the most proficient with it.

The rope wasn't slippery but it did feel slick because it was braided with waxed cord. Hawke worked his wrists around and around with determination, relying on the fact he wouldn't be checked on because the bastard was confident he'd done a good job tying Hawke up. The rope around his throat loosened and tightened with his movements. After a short while he could feel sweat dripping down his wrist from the exertion. He reconsidered; it was probably blood not sweat since his wrists were throbbing painfully. He had to hurry up, they sounded like they were getting up on the horses and once they were gone, any head-start meant the horses might be lost forever. Hawke had to release himself, escape out the back door and run to get help. The work-horses were in the back paddock but they were still rideable, and since Wilder was being left behind, there was a fast horse that would be able to trail them easily.

His plan clear in his mind, Hawke twisted and sawed until he could pull his hands free from the binding. He hadn't expected his legs to fail him as soon as they were freed and both feet smacked hard against the dirt floor. He froze, listening for the sound of footsteps but he could only hear the jingling of stirrups and conversation near the main door.

His plan went awry as soon as he got to his feet and peeked around the stall opening. One of the thieves was opening the doors for Wilder and Speck, the two horses that weren't being ridden. Wilder was the kind of horse to bolt for freedom and so she did, galloping past the group and causing one of the other horses to rear up. Silverprint was unsettled but didn't do much more than snort his discontent. Hawke was furious to see Eddie— the dark-skinned leader of the group—saddled up on his stallion.

Hawke glanced down at his wrists – in the muted light of the barn he could see that they had angry bracelets of red, but had only rubbed raw to bleeding in one spot on his left wrist. He'd expected much worse. They were hurting a great deal but he squashed their importance down.

The man that had released Wilder and Speck pulled Speck out of the stall but the sullen steed was obstinate about remaining in the stable. Eddie grabbed a crop and whipped it hard upon Speck's flank. The ageing horse wasn't prepared for this kind of abuse so it had the desired effect of forcing him to gallop away.

"You bastard!" Hawke screamed, disgusted that this monster, this murdering, abusive monster, was riding his horse and mistreating the other animals. Five faces turned his way, including the one who hadn't saddled up yet. Hawke was torn between running towards them or running away, until Eddie began to ride Silverprint towards him at a trot. Hawke realised his mistake and turned to the other end of the stable, lifting up the wooden beam that kept the smaller door closed. It was still big enough for a horse and man to fit through (if the man ducked) and he realised with a sinking heart that he wasn't going to be fast enough anyway. The hairs on his nape prickled as he listened to nearing hooves. Panic made his hands slippery as he grabbed the bolt lock release. Before Hawke could open the door, he was picked up by the back of his collar. His clothes were finely made; they supported his weight and didn't rip, and so he was indelicately thrown over Eddie's lap and ridden out of the barn along with the rest of the group of horse thieves.

They rode through the night. Hawke was eventually allowed to sit up in the saddle in front of Eddie, like he'd used to ride with his father as a small child. He asked questions that were ignored before finally holding his tongue. He paid attention to the towns they passed, looked at the stars and deduced they were bearing north to colder climates. He was hungry and his stomach and chest were aching, first from being knelt on and then from his abducted position on the saddle. One consolation was the lack of pain in his wrists, they'd gone numb. By the time the horses were allowed to slow to a walk, Hawke did what he hadn't wanted or expected he would do; he dozed.

They made camp. Someone carried him to a sleeping spot. He got the impression it was Eddie and something in him balked until a different sounding voice hushed him and he quietened. Through narrowed eyes he saw a pale man with brown hair. He hadn't been sleeping well while riding and his dreams muddled with reality; the smell of straw made him think it was Mako carrying him...then he got a whiff of leather and it was his father carrying him, his hold was tight but comforting...then it was Denis, who had somehow aged up. Hawke tucked himself into Denis' arms and welcomed real sleep.

He awoke with a strong urge to urinate, the pressure in his groin uncomfortable and aching. He was constricted in a strange kind of bedding that seemed to have no exit. There was no ceiling or sky because he was underneath a low-hanging beige fabric roof. He cried out as he fought the bedding, waking the blonde woman beside him. She knelt up and pressed her finger against her lips and then his. Hawke's heart began to beat frantically as he recognised her from the horse thief group.

It hadn't been a dream.

"Don't make a noise, little boy," she told him. Hawke didn't much care for the title.

"I am Hawke Aron of Donovan Court," he declared importantly. He was hoping to inspire fear in her for capturing a nobleman's son, but she didn't react.

"Alright, Hawke Aron, my name's Carmen. I promise I won't hurt you."

"Just like you didn't hurt Mako?" he asked acidly.

She was surprised. He liked that he'd surprised her because he felt like it gave him an advantage somehow. He didn't want to betray his fear to her, she would perceive him as weak and think him worthless enough to slit his throat. As he watched, her surprise melted until she was looking at him sadly. Was it pity in her eyes?

"I'm sorry about your friend," she began.

"He wasn't my friend."

He'd surprised her again, he saw.

"Do you need the toilet?" she asked eventually. The

reminder that he had to go made the desire more urgent.

"Yes, please." He understood that he needed her help to escape the strange bedding. She reached over and unstitched it with a single whirring noise. Hawke noticed small metal teeth and as soon as he was out he realised how cold it was. Inside the strange cocoon he'd been comfortably warm.

He heard the sound of trickling water and songbirds. Their twitters told him it was daytime. Carmen got to her feet, awkwardly bent over because the roof was very low. When Hawke stood, the top of his head brushed the roof of the small material room. He saw another sleeping woman nearby, using a book as a pillow. She looked younger than the rest of the group.

"That's my sister, Lyssa."

"I have a sister, too," Hawke said. Carmen smiled and nodded before reaching past him. She unstitched the fabric room the same way as the cocoon bedding, by pulling on a metal fastening that whirred, opening a flap for Hawke to step through.

There were no thoughts of escape as he stepped outside, just a pressing need for relief. He moved some distance away from the other fabric houses the horse thieves had and found some privacy behind a few scrubby bushes. After urinating he found he felt better and could think more clearly. He looked around to assess the area.

It was unrecognisable. He'd never come so far north before but had always wanted to. His father had taken Umber into the far north on an ice-serpent hunt but all they'd brought back with them were bear skins. Denis insisted serpents were extinct because nobody had slain any in their lifetime or even their father's. Hawke wasn't convinced. Their grandfather had disappeared on a serpent hunt along with his group of six men, and what else could overwhelm a team of seven skilled hunters if not an ice-serpent itself?

There was a high dirt bank on his left that he didn't think he could scramble up. It looked smooth and glossy like it was frosted over. If he tried he imagined he might slip and then would be caught before getting far. The running water was a creek bed not too far away and there were small areas at the edges where it had iced over. Hawke could see the horses nearby but they'd all been hobbled so they couldn't wander too far. He didn't have the time to approach, undo the hobble, hop on and then ride away. The three male horse thieves were gathered around a pit where they were making fire. Hawke watched as they manipulated a piece of flint that held the flame for them instead of casting sparks.

They must've come from a faraway place, to have such unusual equipment, but they sounded the same as he did when they spoke. His family held large banquets in the great hall several times a year, and nobility travelled from all over to attend. He'd been paraded before them and had to dance with all the girls that he might one day court, tying in families and political interests. He'd listened to many of them speaking, with strange pronunciations of their vowels and sometimes even using words he wasn't familiar with when they discussed their homes. The horse thieves didn't have accents like theirs, they sounded local.

None of them were looking at him. Carmen had returned to the fabric house where her sister continued to sleep and the men were all fire-building. Hawke's focus was on Eddie, the dark-skinned man, who was speaking to the other two.

Hawke crouched, shielding himself from their vision and considering his escape. He knew his directions with the sun and the stars so he could head south by day and night. Travelling would be hard though, for his breath steamed the air and his fingers and nose felt pinched by cold. He'd worn his riding boots so his feet were warm, but he hadn't dressed for a long trek north. His pants were unsuitable for hard travel, his under tunic with half-sleeves was of a thin weave and his winter tunic over it had no sleeve at all.

"What? Where is he?"

Hawke peered through the scrubby bush and watched as Eddie stood and whirled around, stumbling on the uneven ground. Hawke hoped he'd fall but he didn't. Eddie hurried to the fabric house. He looked upset.

"Did you let him go?" Eddie yelled into the door flap of the fabric house. There was a protest inside and then Carmen's voice. Hawke couldn't make out what she was saying because she wasn't yelling back.

Hawke wondered why Eddie thought he was gone when he hadn't even looked around for him; he'd just leapt to his feet and started yelling. He was joined by one of the other men.

"I don't see him. I don't see him," the man near Eddie said. Eddie moved away from the fabric house and started to turn in a slow circle. Hawke held his breath and remained still. If he moved, they would see him...but they saw him anyway. Eddie looked right at him and pointed.

Every instinct was screaming in Hawke to run but he didn't. He stood up and fidgeted with the hooks and loops on his pants, as though he'd recently pulled them up. Then he approached as Eddie marched towards him.

"What?" Hawke announced sullenly, playing dumb. His eyes widened and he flinched away but Eddie's hand was faster and he was struck across the face. He was unable to keep his footing and unbalanced. On the ground he caught himself with his hands and saved himself from being winded. "Bastard!" Hawke yelled. Eddie's boot pressed against his nape, forcing his face into the pebbled earth. It was unyielding and gritty.

"Stop it!" Carmen screamed. The boot disappeared and Hawke scrambled to his feet. Carmen must've shoved Eddie because of the way they stood. "He's just a little boy. What's *wrong* with you?"

Hawke raised a hand to his cheek. It felt both hot and cold, he couldn't identify which. Either way it was stinging and he shuffled closer to Carmen.

"He was trying to run away," Eddie said and looked to the man nearby, who was staring at Hawke with confusion.

"He wanted some privacy for toileting, you fool. Would you rather he do it inside the tent?"

Tent. The word sounded unusual and harsh amongst the rest of the words. It wasn't something that was a part of their language, he was sure. Which strange thing was the *tent*? Was it the fabric house or the peculiar bedding he'd woken up inside of?

"I still can't see him," the first horse thief said. Hawke stared at him and wondered who was the greater fool, because the man was looking directly at him. The lanky man who'd stayed by the fire finally joined them.

"You're right," Carmen said. "I'm getting nothing."

Hawke wished he truly was invisible.

"He has the blood," Eddie said, grabbing Hawke's wrist in a tight hold. Hawke immediately jerked back to try and pull out of his hold.

"Don't *enhance* it! What if he's an Elementalist?" Carmen cried out. Eddie let go and she had to catch Hawke who'd been arching away.

"He's not an Elementalist," one of the other men said. "Not if both of you can't see him."

"What power is that?" Eddie demanded, speaking to Carmen who stood behind Hawke. He was interested in the conversation in spite of himself. He didn't understand what was going on, but by context he understood they thought he had some kind of special ability. If the fact he was a nobleman's son wouldn't have them fearing the consequences of taking him, then perhaps this ability they were discussing would.

"It's pretty obvious," the other man pointed out.

"Yes, it is." Carmen squeezed Hawke's shoulder in a way that was possibly meant to be comforting to him, but he found it restrictive. The three men were all looking at him with renewed interest, like they'd found themselves a new prize.

"What's going on?" yawned a second female voice from behind Hawke. Carmen's sister Lyssa hadn't been so interested in the goings-on during camp, but she wanted a catch-up regardless.

"We've got ourselves a Shielder."

CHAPTER FOUR

The Tent Dwellers

IT was dark when Daeson shouldered his newly purchased pack and left the cottage. He'd surfaced many times from dreams that turned to mist on waking. Forgetting was a blessing, for vague memories left him with a lingering unease. He'd lain awake for hours, staring through the hole in the roof at a sky dusted with stars, thinking about the future that had been thrust upon him. When his thoughts began to circle, he'd risen and dressed.

The night was brittle with the promise of winter. Puffs of his warm breath on cold air were caught by moonlight. Crickets chirped their song and the fluttering of wings betrayed the presence of bats. Daeson could hear their squeaks and chatters when he passed—they could be warning him to not come closer, or they could be excited about having cricket for supper.

The path out of town took him past the temple and his thoughts soured. The cleric's hypocrisy tainted his good memories. His trust had been betrayed by someone who was supposed to protect him.

His thoughts dwindled at the sight of the cemetery. Daeson turned off the main street and moved up the hill to the location of the grave markers bearing Willem's and Marget's names. The few lanterns set upon posts lining the path had already burned out so he couldn't see the writing. He would only be able to read it by memory anyway, he'd long since forgotten how to identify letters and words beyond his own name. He knelt between the graves, wishing he'd thought of bringing gifts. He rummaged in his pack and pulled out some twine that he fashioned into a bow for his mother's grave. With another length, he made four different knots that his father had taught him, all used for farming.

Placing the knotted twine on his father's marker made him more emotional than he expected. His father, not a man who believed in displaying affection, had never ordered Daeson to halt his tears.

Get it out, son, and be done with it.

"You called me son," Daeson whispered, his words loud in the pre-dawn stillness. "You called me son and it was truth. I wasn't of your seed and it didn't matter to you, so it doesn't matter to me. You'll always be my father."

He wished he could say the same to Marget but she'd died too soon. He had always felt she was more his father's wife than the mother he hadn't the chance to know. He'd never admitted such a thing, knowing this opinion would cause his father pain. Daeson could only speak truth, but he didn't have to reveal all that he thought.

"Ten days' walk and I will have a new future," he said. He didn't know why he was explaining this, it shouldn't be important. He wanted to vow that he would return, that he would see the farm restored to honour his family. The words refused to come out. "I'll remember my Lessons."

He thought his father would be well satisfied with that.

He cleared his throat and startled a small animal nearby that leapt from the bushes and raced up a tree. Daeson barely noticed as he stood and brushed grass and soil from his knees. His pants felt heavy and wet where he'd knelt down and they stuck to him there.

Picking up his pack, he checked that his pouch was still looped through his belt and safely closed. His travelling supplies had cost him little, so it remained heavy with coin—though not bulging as it had when he'd first taken it. He looked at the headstones one last

time and because he didn't want to say goodbye, he
ended up saying nothing at all.

Sunrise beat him to the crossroads. He looked at the
signpost that pointed the traveller in three different
directions; Cloverlea, Everwood or Stonehearth. He
couldn't read it but every sign had the number of days'
walk tallied upon it. Cloverlea had a crossed out circle
indicating less than a day. One of the other directions
had four lines and a bar drawn across them; five days to
Everwood. The last pointer had ten tally marks.

Stonehearth.

He followed the sign, feeling good about defeating
his inability to read. He'd always wanted to learn, but
his father had been unable to teach him and getting a
tutor was a luxury.

He promised himself that one day he would learn
how to read. The promise lifted his spirits and lightened
his feet as his journey—and the new phase of his life—
began.

He was passed by two wagons filled with wares
heading to Cloverlea. The chance to catch an empty
transport to Stonehearth would be a gift but unlikely
due to the approaching Supfest. Merchants were keen
to be involved in the celebrations and ply their trade,
none would be ready to leave yet.

Daeson walked until the sun was above the trees,
casting a long shadow before him. The day was already
bright and warm, though it wouldn't match the
unforgiving furnace of summer. The breeze carried the
sound of flapping fabric. In a long narrow clearing that
ran parallel to the road were clothes pegged to
makeshift lines and thrown over tree branches. Beyond,
large tents dotted the meadow. Daeson watched four
young boys chase each other in a spirited game and

waved at them. Two of them waved back but the tallest beckoned his friends (brothers?) to join him before they disappeared into the dense brush.

Farther along, Daeson discovered that the few tents he'd passed were on the fringes of a much larger settlement. Tents were pitched closely together and the noise of community resonated across the field, punctuated by the squeals of playful children.

Be wary of the tent-folk, they're all thieves and bullies.

He remembered his father's warning, spoken to him gruffly after a quarrel with a tent-dweller who'd been squatting on their land. His father had rounded up some of the locals and demanded the man leave. The tent-dweller had packed up his things and gone without argument and Daeson had felt as though justice was done.

Looking at the people as he walked by, he saw men and women performing chores or sitting together and talking. They didn't look like thieves or bullies. Some of them watched him go by without acknowledgment but others raised a hand to wave. Daeson made sure to wave back, their friendliness contradicting his father's opinion.

When his shadow was a puddle at his feet, Daeson looked for a place to stop and rest. His stomach gurgled, reminding him that he hadn't eaten yet. There was a large rock on the side of the road, big enough and flat enough to serve as a seat.

He pulled out an apple and had bitten into it a few times before he realised he was being watched. A small boy with bare feet and curly ginger hair stood on the opposite edge of the road. Daeson assumed he was a tent dweller child. He waved but the boy didn't wave back. Thinking him shy, Daeson took another bite out of his apple. The boy moved forward to the middle of the road, surprising him.

"Hello," he said, belatedly covering his mouth to stop the boy from seeing spit and chunks of apple dribbling out. His father, who'd often pestered him not to talk while eating, would've been horrified.

Unless you've caught fire, there's nothing so important that needs mention.

The child was forced to finish crossing the road when a wagon trundled its approach (like all the others, the wagon was heading in the wrong direction). Smiling, Daeson reached into his pack and offered another apple. Still, the boy deliberated. Now that he was close, Daeson saw how young he was, possibly no more than his sixth season. Daeson gestured with the fruit. This time the boy took it.

"Tankey," he said before taking a huge bite. Daeson grinned but wondered at the strange thanks. Did the tent-dwellers speak their own dialect?

"Rory, by the Gods!"

Daeson looked towards the woman crossing the road, her ginger hair piled high on her head and her expression one of embarrassment.

"Sorry to be bothering you, he behaves like he's starving but he's fed well enough," she said, reaching for the apple in Rory's hands. The child held it behind himself, out of his mother's reach. Daeson boggled at this behaviour. He would've received a pinched ear for such insolence but Rory's mother shook her head and made no further attempt for the fruit. "What'll it cost to replace?" she asked, digging around in her apron pouch. Daeson guessed she was looking for a coin to pay him with.

"No cost, I don't mind. I like him."

The boy responded to the compliment with a scowl and a stuck out tongue.

"Rory!" his mother exclaimed, her face flushing. "I'm so sorry. I try to teach him good manners, I honestly do."

Daeson laughed and nodded.

"He'd eat every apple you had before demanding his lunch," she said, looking at Rory who took another bite of the fruit in his hands, perceiving that he was safe from his mother's grasp. "Would you care to join us?"

Daeson was surprised by the invitation. When he didn't give an immediate answer, the woman took the chance to persuade him.

"It's venison pie and potatoes," she crooned, like he might be one of her small children. In spite of the melodic declaration, or perhaps because of it, he found himself wanting to stay for lunch.

"That sounds good."

He picked up his belongings and followed Rory and the woman—she introduced herself as Anna—back to their tent. The tents Daeson passed were plain on the outside but distinctive and colourfully-decorated within. There were many ropes and stakes in the ground that they had to step over. The air was filled with delicious aromas as people prepared their midday meals. Many times Daeson had to wait as Anna was drawn into conversations that grew to include three or four people. The community here was closer and more vivacious than the villagers of Cloverlea. Daeson ached for that kind of solidarity.

They eventually reached Anna's tent. It had a large roof annex over the opening that was held up by thin poles. Unlit lanterns hung from a hook at the top of each. The overhang shaded a table, light reed chairs and a kiln. Daeson wondered what the tent-dwellers were going to do when winter came. It wouldn't just be rain that they needed to keep out, but cold. He wondered if they would pack up and continue north, fleeing the colder weather. Many in Cloverlea had predicted that the tent-dwellers would leave during autumn. They were still here and everyone looked well settled.

Anna directed him to leave his pack at the doorway

of the tent, declaring it safe there. He made stilted and trivial conversation with her as she busied herself preparing lunch, interspersed with unsuccessful attempts to engage Rory.

A short, stocky man arrived, flanked by two older boys carrying bows and arrows. They barely gave Daeson a look before dumping their gear into a wooden chest near the entrance. There was no padlock to stop anyone from taking the weapons.

"Feeding strays?" the man asked, pooching his lips out to kiss Anna on the cheek. He missed because she'd chosen that moment to reach for a spatula.

"Only when they feed ours. Hutch, this young man's name is Daeson." She gestured to Daeson and then folded her arms. "I don't see you holding any loaves of bread."

"Colton ran out," he said with a shrug.

"This is why you don't get the butter first," Anna sighed, then directed everyone to the table. Rory clambered onto his chair first.

"Nice to meetcha," Hutch greeted, capturing Daeson's hand so they could shake. Daeson was tugged a little closer to listen as Hutch leaned in. "I'd tuck that coin pouch into your pants. People here are good but some have it harder than others."

Daeson was surprised by a warning that mirrored the sentiments from Cloverlea. He took the man's advice and flipped the pouch on its belt loop so that he could shove it into his pants. It bulged uncomfortably at his hip.

"Did you get any rabbits?" Anna asked while cutting a steaming pie into large portions.

"We caught three," Hutch bragged. He joined his sons and slapped their backs heartily. Daeson waited awkwardly to one side and wondered what had happened to the rabbits, because they weren't in hand.

Lunch was served and Daeson was relieved he

didn't have to make conversation. Everyone was too busy eating. He'd been given a huge portion and he ate it all, burning his fingers as he held it and forgetting to eat like a gentleman after taking the first bite.

Afterwards, the three boys disappeared to play and Daeson helped clear the table.

"There's a small party tonight, with our closer neighbours. Music and dancing and a bonfire," Anna said in the same sing-song voice she'd used to talk him into staying for lunch.

"You in a rush to get where you're going or can you stay the night?" Hutch asked more practically.

"I can stay," Daeson said, feeling welcome enough to accept their invitation. He wanted to know more about the community—it was different to what he'd expected. Mostly the idea of going to a party appealed to him.

Hutch left to 'see someone about some rabbit skins' and Anna asked Daeson if he would help her with a few errands. He readily agreed.

It wasn't just Anna he helped. There were vegetable carts that trundled a daily path between the tents. One of the carts had broken its spokes after the wheel ground against an old hitching post. Daeson did the strong work; shifting crates of vegetables, helping to lift the wagon up so someone else could slide a sawhorse in place. The wheel was pulled off and someone ran it to the wainwright. A short wait later the wainwright arrived with a spare wheel and a small crowd. A few pitched in to help while the rest stood by and watched.

After the cart was mended and ready to go, Anna took what vegetables she needed off it without an exchange of coin. Daeson initially thought it was payment for helping out, but the ones who'd just been watching were doing the same thing. If nobody used coin, why had Hutch warned him about keeping his pouch out of sight?

"Anna, why didn't you use any coin?"

"The wagons are for everyone. Nobody goes hungry here." He could hear her pride.

"Where do the vegetables come from?"

"They're bought from the farming towns, like yours. They trade with us because our coin is good enough, even if we're not."

Daeson could feel his face flush. He wished he hadn't told Anna that he was from Cloverlea. She hadn't been any less welcoming, though it sounded like she was making a point of it. By the time they arrived back at the family tent, Daeson was over his embarrassment.

"Where does the coin come from to pay for the vegetables?"

"We all make things to sell."

"Does everyone do their fair share?" he asked.

"Some people do more," Anna said proudly.

"And some don't do anything at all?" he persisted.

He didn't know why it was important to him to make her admit that the community was imperfect. He supposed it was pettiness about Cloverlea's shortcomings. From the look Anna was throwing him, he wished he could take his question back.

"Someone who doesn't help won't feel as though they are one of us. Now stop looking for the bad and hold out your arms. No, not out to your sides...in front of you."

Stop looking for the bad, she'd said. Anna was right. Was that the kind of person he was now? Feeling better about his position by finding bad in others? He didn't remember ever being like that. He used to be happy.

Anna loaded Daeson up with baskets, woven bags and cushion covers. He felt like a two-legged packhorse. Then she led him to a different part of the community. Daeson's arms were aching when they arrived at their destination; a covered two-horse wagon waiting on the roadside. It was being loaded by several people at once as a heavily pregnant woman looked on, marking a tally sheet.

"Anna! Cloverlea or Everwood?" The woman scribbled on the sheet.

"Both. I have enough to halve."

"You keep busy. Your hands hurt?"

Anna set down her baskets and inspected them. "A little sore, but I'll still have that mattress cover for you tomorrow."

The woman patted her belly. "Still a few more days," she guessed.

After Daeson's arms were freed, he peeked into the wagon and recognised many things that were sold at Supfest. He'd always believed such items came from faraway places brought by travelling merchants, but now he saw they'd all been made down the road. He felt cheated.

On the way back, Daeson broached a subject that he couldn't work out for himself and hoped Anna wouldn't think ill of him.

"The tent—your community normally leaves before winter." He inwardly chastised himself for the verbal stumble. They didn't call themselves 'tent-dwellers' and he didn't want to use a phrase that could be insulting.

"We're oft further north by now but last winter we lost two of our trading wagons. The roads are full of rocks in the north and the going is slow. The wagons were rushing to get to Supfest and lost their wheels. Less coin meant we couldn't go all the way north to our families."

"Your families?" Daeson repeated, surprised. Looking at Anna distracted him from walking his path and he stumbled over a tent stake. He managed to keep his feet.

"Oop, careful."

Daeson nodded and scanned the ground as they continued on.

"Those too old, too young or too sick to travel stay

in the north. The climate is better there and the land is free."

"Do you have family in the north?"

"Hutch has his mother and sister. My folk and brothers are gone."

Gone? He didn't ask her to clarify. They could have travelled to a place so far they were out of touch, or they could have died. He didn't want to talk of death.

Hutch returned in the afternoon with three skinned rabbits in one hand and their pelts in the other. Anna immediately set to work, preparing a rabbit stew for the party.

As soon as the sky blazed orange, all three children returned.

Everyone had something to carry to the party. They walked single file to a dirt clearing where a bonfire blazed. Daeson took extra care not to trip while holding the large pot of rabbit stew. Colourful mats and low chairs encircled the blaze and long tables nearby held a stack of empty bowls and spoons. A trio of musicians played jovial tunes. Daeson placed the pot onto the middle table and promptly helped himself to a bowl. The stew had been steaming its wonderful aroma into his face, whetting his appetite. People lined up at his back.

Daeson thought the party quiet until night took hold, then the noise of music, dancing, laughing and singing became so loud that conversation was difficult. He was happy to sit and watch until two young women beckoned him to dance with them. He obliged and was taught some easy steps. After a few songs, they led him to a quieter spot, away from the bonfire.

As they spoke about their hopes for the future, Daeson got the impression that they were daring each other with pointed looks and playful shoves. He enjoyed the attention though his heart wasn't in it to flirt back. Talk of what might lay ahead for them in life led to questions about his past. They both quietened when they picked up on his sombre mood and after the silence extended, Daeson asked to return to the party. They complied, though their disappointment was clear.

He returned to the food tables, which were now filled with an array of platters. He tried a selection of meals throughout the night. The girls, as lovely as they were, had caused him to retreat into his thoughts.

He didn't want to return to Cloverlea. He'd known it at the cemetery, though he'd struggled to admit it. The instant he'd discovered Cleric Faelin's twisted assistance, he'd been embittered by the town. It had started to feel small and constraining. His livelihood was in ruins and there was no other opportunity for him. He hadn't realised how insular Cloverlea was until he'd left and experienced other parts of the world...even though he was barely down the road.

He was amused enough to smile. It faded when he realised how wrong his father had been about the tent-dwellers. They weren't all bullies and thieves. They'd welcomed him into their home, fed him, entertained him. They asked for little in return...nothing difficult, just helping out. He was awed by how generous they were to a stranger. They knew he was from Cloverlea—where the townsfolk shunned them—and still they took him in and treated him well. They were good people who deserved more than what they had.

What else was his father wrong about?

The thought sat so uneasily that he lost his appetite...except he'd already eaten too much. He was full to the point of discomfort. He poured himself a cup of water to sip and sat in one of the bonfire watching chairs—the seat a little too low for his liking—and let the party fill his other senses. He fell asleep and was awoken by Hutch shaking him.

"Time to go."

Daeson opened his eyes to see men shovelling dirt

onto the bonfire to stifle the glowing coals. The dark silhouettes of the musicians huddled nearby, chatting with one another. His cup of water had disappeared; perhaps someone had already saved him from spilling it upon himself as he'd slept. The chairs and mats were gone and as soon as he stood up from the one he'd slept in, a young man approached them, picked it up and hurried away with it. Daeson watched him go and Hutch chuckled.

He was led back to the family tent, the community looking different at night with hanging lanterns all about and people chatting quietly in groups. On the shallow breeze, Daeson could hear a light tune being plucked on the strings of a mandolin. When they arrived at the family tent, Daeson noticed all three boys were dressed in long tunics that reached their knees. They were immune to the mellow atmosphere and were bashing each other about the head with cushions. Hutch growled at them to get to bed and they complied with laughter.

The boys were asleep by the time Anna returned. She carried an empty wooden bowl and a small sack that she set in the middle of the table before grabbing herself a shawl and sitting with the two of them. Hutch worked the twine around the sack as soon as it landed and took out a handful of peanuts. He tossed the bag towards Daeson who shook his head, still full.

Daeson spoke. "I want to offer you both something. It might seem a lot but it comes with a request." He didn't know if Hutch and Anna would hear him out once he started explaining, so he thought warning them might be best.

"I'm intrigued," Hutch replied, freeing a peanut from its shell. Anna remained as she was, sat back with her arms folded over her stomach, keeping her shawl in place.

Daeson pulled out the piece of paper that was his

property deed and unfolded it, laying it upon the table and smoothing it out. Hutch stopped cracking peanuts and shifted the bowl so that he could better see. A lantern's glow above them gave enough light to read by. A group of people burst into laughter a few tents over, catching Anna's attention momentarily but then she was leaning forward in her chair to look at the document also. She scanned it quickly and her confused gaze settled on Daeson.

"What's the request?" she asked.

"This paper is a deed of ownership for my farm in Cloverlea." Daeson nodded towards it. "I've tried and failed to work it on my own because the farm needs more than one person working it. It's a family farm with a solid cottage...the roof needs some mending. It has two fields for planting and space to pitch tents nearby. You have three sons that can help you work it and friends to help you get started."

Hutch's gaze lifted. "We don't have the coin for this," he said slowly.

"I would rather give it to a family than sell it to a businessman. Any coin you have you'll need to last the winter, while things start growing again. There'll be some cleaning up before you can get started properly. My request is that you don't sell it, that you use it. It's an honest life."

"An honest life?" Anna asked, her tone harsh. Daeson realised belatedly the implication of his words.

"You aren't dishonest people, but you've told me you're judged unfairly. Owning the deed to this farm means you wouldn't be forced to move on."

He watched as Hutch looked at Anna, who shook her head. Daeson opened his mouth to protest but closed it when Hutch spoke first.

"Thank you for your very kind offer, you have a generous heart. But we're not farmers."

"And there are other ways to move people on,"

Anna said under her breath, but not so quietly that Daeson wouldn't be able to hear. He thought of the way his father had forced out the tent-dweller from their land and then of Cleric Faelin.

He watched as Hutch re-folded the deed along its crease, feeling foolish and confused by the rejection.

"We are doing well as we are."

"But..." Daeson looked towards the tent, where all he could see was a gaping space of black. Inside were three children sleeping on floor mats. Anna followed his gaze.

"D'you think they suffer?" Her question was hissed at him.

"No. They're loved...I'm sorry. I mean no insult, I just thought you'd want something more stable."

Hutch nodded, but his words contradicted his agreement. "You rely on the kindness of your Gods for the weather, for the bounty of the earth. You work a long, hard day with little time for pleasure. Yet here you are with us. Farm life is not stable."

"I was on my own. My father and I worked the land well together," he said, hearing the tremble in his voice and the tightness in his chest. He wasn't sure if it was because of anger, sadness or humiliation. Whatever emotion it was, it was enough to soften Anna's tone.

"You're a good young man, Daeson, with a kind heart behind your clumsy words. I won't take insult because I know you meant well, but you see us as poor when we are rich."

Hutch punctuated Anna's comment with more cracking of peanut shells and eventually Anna reached for a handful as well. Daeson was so filled with the epiphany of their attitude that he couldn't speak. They lived life as they wanted to and were happy with that.

Daeson slid the folded paper off the table and back beneath his tunic.

"Thank you for welcoming me and showing me how

you live. I've learned a lot. Almost as much about myself as I have about you." He reflected on his own words for a moment before telling them of his plans. "I'll be heading to Stonehearth in the morning."

"You better not leave without breakfasting with us. We'll have it before sun-up, so you can take advantage of walking the full day," Anna promised. Daeson agreed and they all retired to the tent. Hutch laid out a floor mat for him so that he could sleep very near the family and Daeson was touched.

CHAPTER FIVE

Distractions

SYNJAN never felt right approaching the front door. To enter the Queen of Hearts, she generally used the back door, but her purpose was different tonight. The sun was long gone and the curfew siren had sounded. She should be in her own home but this was where she needed to be.

Synjan's stilettos echoed on the wooden porch. The front door was painted white with a lead-lighting insert in the shape of a semi-circle at the top, broken into four segments. The inlay's colourful depiction of flowers and the four suits of a deck of cards prevented anyone from seeing inside, but the light shone through it warmly.

Synjan turned the glass handle and entered, musing that the front door was never locked. Beyond it was a cosy foyer and small counter behind which a red-haired woman sat.

"Welcome," the woman greeted, her tone friendly. Her gravelly voice was typical of a heavy smoker.

"Thanks, Dyna" Synjan replied, mirroring the smile. All business in the Queen was negotiated here with Dyna as gatekeeper. Though she looked isolated and vulnerable inside her little office, a peek around the edge of the open frame would reveal she wasn't alone. A large blonde man named Chad sat with her, holding his own counsel until he was required to act. Synjan knew that they passed the time playing cards and helping each other with crosswords.

"You lookin' for Nick?"

Synjan chuckled. It was a good bet that when she walked in she was here to see its manager, Nick Logan. "Do I look like I'm here for business?" she teased, flicking her long hair deliberately.

After her outburst with Ellis this evening, she had to

get out of the house. The best place to find a distraction was at the Queen of Hearts. She'd showered, poured herself into a tight black dress, curled her thick blonde hair and applied her makeup to dark and smoky perfection. Her knee-length coat was belted closed at her slim waist and hid her outfit but everything else advertised that her intentions in the club were far from mercantile.

Dyna gave a throaty laugh in return. "Ah honey, it's all business to me. S'just a matter of what yer' lookin' to trade."

"Isn't that the truth?" Synjan said wryly.

"So what can I do for you?"

Visitors to the club were usually not addressed in such a casual manner. Had she not been well known, Dyna would have asked her if she'd like to pick a card. "Ace of clubs," would get her to the nightclub level and, "King of diamonds," would buy in to Nick's elite gambling den.

Synjan had no understanding of how these pass-phrases travelled into all social levels of Gredann, but she'd heard farmers, sailors and even high-ranking Authorities quoted them. The fact the phrases didn't change probably helped, though Synjan disapproved of such a farcical attempt at security. Still, it was not her place to question the great Omerri Backhouse and her civilian methods. Considering their icy relationship, Synjan should be grateful she was allowed through the fucking door.

"I'd like to go downstairs, please."

"Sure thing." Dyna's hand slid below the counter to flick an unseen switch. Synjan thanked her and headed onward.

Across the foyer were two entryways. The right was an open doorway, beyond it a cosy waiting room filled with overstuffed armchairs. They were arranged so that they could take in the view of the street through the curtained bay window that dominated the front of the house. Brothel visitors waiting for their appointment sat there.

The second entry along the corridor was different. The polished wooden door was closed and there was no handle. When Dyna touched the switch in the booth, a distinctive snick permeated the quiet entry area. Had she moved faster, Synjan would also have noticed the door flinch as it opened slightly.

She walked up to it and pushed it open farther. The antechamber within had dark red pile carpet, cream wallpaper with red pinstripes and two chairs facing each other on the opposite side of a games table. Another anonymous polished wooden door without a handle was set in the far wall. In the centre of the room stood two large, muscular men in black suits and turquoise dress shirts. No ties. Their expressions were serious until they got a good look at her.

"Evening, gentlemen," Synjan greeted, closing the door behind her. When the locking mechanism reasserted itself, the older guard looked pleased. He opened his mouth to say something but was cut off.

"Hello, beautiful. Mind opening that coat for me?" the younger drawled.

Synjan raised an eyebrow. The older guard gave his companion a sideways glance.

"You're new," she announced, assessing the younger guard as he approached. Her shoes raised her to the height of his chest and he was more than twice her width.

"So?" he answered, looking back at his workmate.

"I'm Synjan," she said, holding out her hand to be shaken.

"Clay," he responded, engulfing her hand with his in a perfunctory shake.

"How long have you worked here?"

"Uh, not long."

"Right," Synjan murmured, disliking his inability to answer a straight question. She looked him over, thinking him young, despite his size and girth. Perhaps it was the blank quality in his hazel eyes that gave her that impression. "Well, I don't always come here at night but you'll see me around. I do a lot of business with Nick. I'm sure Jaxon here can tell you the rest once you've let me downstairs." She looked meaningfully at Clay, sliding her hands into her coat pockets.

"I don't... need to check you for weapons?"

Jaxon answered the question. "Not her, dung for brains."

Synjan grinned. "You'd find them." Clay's startled expression lifted her spirits.

Jaxon opened the other door by pushing up a lever set into the wall. The door slid into a recess, revealing a dimly-lit stairwell beyond.

"Should I go down with her?" Clay asked Jaxon.

The experienced guard's expression had Synjan giggling.

"No," he answered gruffly.

"I'll see you boys later," she bade, slipping between the two men and towards her destination. The switchback stairs were completely enclosed and as soon as she was beyond it, the door cut off the exit behind her, trapping Synjan in a confined environment. The walls were very narrow with lights set into them at regular intervals. They were only bright enough to illuminate a few steps ahead. Everything in the stairwell was covered in pale-coloured carpet, even the handrails, which gave them a ghostly quality. Noise was stifled and though she could hear a distant beat, it was softer than the muted sound of her shoes on the carpeted stairs.

When Synjan got to the bottom she was a storey and a half below ground level, facing a steel door. The wall that it was set in was covered with foam that looked like the inside of an egg-carton. She knew its material and shape had something to do with muffling sound but it had never been properly explained to her.

In the middle of the steel door was a fish-eye lens. Synjan picked up the metal knocker hanging on a chain nearby and used it against the door before squaring up. The guard on the other side would look through the lens and assess the threat level of whoever was trapped within the stairwell. Unknown visitors without a guard companion from upstairs would get no farther.

Within moments, the door opened. A cacophony of noise, flashing lights and movement assaulted her previously hushed senses. Sully gave her a nod as she passed him. He closed and barred the door before returning to his stool.

Every time she entered this space, Synjan was forced to acknowledge Omerri's genius.

Originally a brothel called 'Trinkets' owned by Ellis, the four storey terrace house faced Red Crescent, a curved street that swept into the more exclusive bordering suburb of Portside. Less auspiciously, the building extended so far back that it crossed into Dockside territory and backed onto a laneway that barely separated it from an enormous furniture warehouse.

Omerri had been offered a property by Ellis and selected this building from his portfolio of real estate, renaming it the Queen of Hearts. For a while it looked like a property straddling the boundary between Dockside and Portside might work favourably. The locals remained unconvinced and Red Crescent lost its status and title, often referred to as 'the Dockside end of Portside'. Still, the Queen did as much to promote a positive and up-market image as it could. The paintwork, building condition and entryway were immaculate and inviting.

Omerri's business savvy shone when she'd

purchased the two houses either side of the Queen. Below ground the walls were taken down, tonnes of dirt were excavated and the three basements were merged into one cavernous space well below the buildings' foundations. The first basement level boasted an expansive bar, nightclub and private entertainment area, as well as a few staff quarters. Below was another even more exclusive floor where approved punters could play cards or dice. It had been Nick's idea, created against Omerri's wishes—until she saw the amount of revenue it garnered. It took a great deal of loyalty and money to reach this room and Nick managed the running of it exclusively. It was *his* playground.

Eleven years on, Omerri had a legitimate reputation as a businesswoman but it was the illegal clubs below ground that made her rich and infamous. The Queen of Hearts was the only establishment in the city of Gredann that played off-world dance music in a nightclub environment. All of that under a brothel served to make the Queen an irresistible destination.

Synjan surveyed the large space carefully, undaunted by the pulsing lights. She couldn't see Nick anywhere and she had news for him; news that knotted her gut.

She approached the bar and took a stool. Misu greeted her immediately.

"Hello sunshine, what can I get for you?" he asked sassily.

"A Fisherman's Wail please," she replied. She could drink first, *then* find Nick.

He moved away to fulfil her request and someone sat in the stool beside her.

"Having a good night?" the stranger asked cheerfully.

Synjan looked him over. His clothing told her that he was from outside the city, likely a farmer. They frequently drove their produce in from the remote regions outside Gredann to sell at the city markets and stayed a night for some extra fun. She didn't have anything against such hardworking men, but they were a danger she wouldn't court. Locals came with potential strings. She had enough complications in her life without developing attachments.

"Just got here."

"I'm Martin."

"I'm meeting somebody," she rebuffed, then spun on her stool to scan the room.

At the end of the bar was a guarded door labelled STAFF ONLY. It led to the gambling den and the staff quarters. Beyond that were the public restrooms. Leaning back on the bar, she faced the dance floor with the D.J.'s box in the far corner. D.J. Hash—Synjan knew her as Kat—stood within, holding onto one side of her bulky headphones and swinging to the pounding beat. It was not the traditional music Synjan had grown up with but she'd learned to appreciate what played here.

A surprising amount of Authorities could be found here on any given night – surprising because it was their job to enforce the illegality of alcohol and restrict access to other-world technology and music. They came without their weapons but most arrived in uniforms.

"Somebody in particular?" the farmer persisted, drawing her attention back.

"Yeah."

"I could be particular," he hinted.

"No thanks."

The guy opened his mouth and she looked away. Thankfully, he didn't talk. Misu walked up with her drink and she took it with a question.

"You know where Nick is?"

Misu jabbed a finger upwards. "Dinner break."

"Thanks," she muttered and looked at her drink. There were three different sorts of alcohol in it and the rim was coated with a ring of salt. There was only one way to take a Wail; she drank it in one go, wincing as it screamed down her throat.

"That looked painful," the farmer said beside her.

She ignored his comment to ride the wave of fruity after-effects that left her head spinning. She decided she would go after Nick instead of waiting for him to come back downstairs.

"What was it?" the farmer continued, not yet dissuaded.

"A Fisherman's Wail," she told him as she got off her stool.

"Lemme buy you another!"

"No thanks."

Synjan headed for the STAFF ONLY door and went through it without looking back. She moved through the maze of corridors that had ten bedrooms branching off them. The rooms were quite sparse but permanent residents dressed them with personal touches. Nick had an elegant apartment in Portside that he called home but he was at the Queen more often than he was there, so he also had a room amongst the staff quarters—for when he wasn't sharing Omerri's bed. Synjan went to his room and swung the wardrobe forward. It was on castors and moved easily. Behind it was a chute housing a spiral staircase that continued both up and down. The wardrobe was weighted so that it would roll back into place if not held open.

Synjan felt her way onto the stairs in the darkness, climbing carefully upward. The chamber was just bricks and metal plates and rails, so her high heels echoed sharply. Relying heavily on touch, she was aware of every noise, the whoosh of her breathing and the warmth of the air coming out of her nose as it struck the curve of her top lip. The space was narrow and because she found it mildly restrictive to navigate, she thought that anyone with a larger frame than hers would feel claustrophobic in here.

The exit out of the spiral tube was similar to the entry, except it was a refrigerator instead of a wardrobe that she pushed aside. Two of the kitchen staff looked at her before going back to their chopping.

Nick leant against a metal bench beside the stoves, holding a plate in one hand and shovelling food into his mouth with the other. His legs were casually crossed at the ankle. A kitchen-hand stood beside him, stirring something in a large pot. His body language spoke volumes to Synjan; the tightness in his broad shoulders and his lowered head suggested that she'd likely interrupted a conversation between these two men that at least one of them hadn't enjoyed.

The kitchen-hand didn't look around at the click of her heels on the tiles so she didn't see his face, but his striking cobalt blue pattern was one she recognised. It was usually very close to Omerri's or Nick's whenever she spied on the inhabitants of the Queen. He'd been living there for some time but Synjan had never managed a conversation with him, despite her curiosity. He looked almost big enough to be a security guard, except he wasn't a fighter. Just the way he was subtly giving Nick the cold shoulder told her that. No doubt her old friend was enjoying whatever game he was playing with the kitchen-hand because he gave her a winning smile as she approached.

"Lil," Nick breathed, setting his fork down and looking her over appreciatively. "You look stunning."

He stepped forward and wrapped his arm around her shoulders, turning her from the man at the stove and walking her a few steps away. The nickname Nick used for her was an abbreviation of Ellis' pet name. He was the only one she allowed to use it.

Synjan smiled back, doing her best to ignore the way the compliment and his touch increased her pulse rate. He was eight years older than her and she was in love with him. It was almost a habit; she'd been in love with him nearly all her life. Her feelings had started out as gratitude and idolisation of the teenager that looked after her when her world had been thrown into chaos. They'd developed into so much more when she'd surrendered her virginity to him. Ellis hadn't been pleased when he'd found out and Nick was shifted out of the Bunker and into Omerri's employ permanently.

Theirs was no romantic love story. Nick's intense demeanour and his roguish good looks gained him a great deal of attention and he slept with scores of women. Occasionally even with Synjan. She didn't have a problem with the way Nick was. He'd never tried to keep his promiscuity a secret and she'd always known she was only special to him when it was convenient. What she *did* have an issue with was his relationship with Omerri, because she strongly suspected he'd given his heart to the woman he worked for. Omerri was at least ten years his senior, yet Nick would choose her over everyone else, just like Ellis would, if it came down to it.

That she was a constant second for both men stung Synjan more than she'd admit.

"Thank you," she acknowledged, returning his inspection coolly, watching as he began eating again. "You look good yourself although... shouldn't you be wearing something *prettier*?" she teased, gesturing at his silky black shirt with a swirling finger. Accompanied by black slacks and shoes, he was a monotone in a staff decked out like peacocks. Perhaps Nick was feeling rebellious tonight...or he hadn't dressed within Omerri's sight for once.

Nick laughed through his nose, grinning around his mouthful of food despite the fact that it wasn't amusement flaring in his dark eyes. His shirtsleeves were rolled up to his elbows and she saw sinews jump in his tanned forearms as he stabbed a little too enthusiastically at his dinner. She'd scored a point. It was a game no-one would ever win.

She tucked her hands into the pockets of her coat. "I have some news," she informed him, tilting her head towards the kitchen-hand who would be able to hear their conversation easily. It was her way of asking if he was trustworthy and subtly inviting Nick to move them into a more private place.

Nick glanced over her shoulder then back to her, his fork frozen over his food. "About him?" he demanded.

Synjan realised her gesture had been misconstrued and she was confused about why Nick was suddenly so tense. "What? No."

"About what, then?"

"About Kate," she said, thinking it might change the situation.

Nick visibly relaxed. Another forkful of food went into his mouth and chewed, watching her. "What about her?" A few wisps of glossy black hair fell onto his forehead, making him look dashing.

"I... well, you know she hasn't been coping at the Bunker," she began, feeling awkward because they both knew it was an understatement.

"She's a useless junkie," Nick agreed scathingly.

Synjan bristled. "Well, she's *dead*."

"And?"

Her mouth fell open. She'd wanted more from him than callousness. Surely Kate had meant something to him too? He'd known her longer and had also been her friend when they were children and living in the Bunker together. She'd expected it to mean more.

"Fuck you," Synjan breathed, betrayal controlling her expression.

Nick dropped his fork onto his empty plate with a loud clang and tossed it with a clatter onto the bench beside him.

"What do you want me to say?" he demanded, leaning intently towards her, appealing for her input.

Synjan shook her head, fighting back the tears she could feel pricking her eyes, her mouth screwed down tightly because she didn't trust herself to speak.

Nick looked disappointed by her reaction. "Shit, it can't have come as a surprise to you? She's been on the kit for more years than most ride it."

She shrugged and swallowed, wanting to rail at him and explain how it *had* been a surprise, actually, because *she'd* done it, it had been *her* fault. She wasn't sure it would matter. He didn't appear impacted by the news and he was the only one she'd thought would care. It was an extra blow of cruelty. No-one in this gods-forsaken city could show sympathy for one of their own dying, because it took too much energy away from surviving their own miserable life.

"It's for the best," Nick shrugged, straightening up. He took a step towards the exit but deigned to give her a little more attention before he returned to his work. "Who you gonna' put in as housemother at the Bunker now?"

So that was all he had an interest in. Not Kate, whose life was over but who would take her place. He probably had someone he wanted to offer up for the position, someone he owed a favour to that he could squeeze more out of by getting them a sweet position in Ellis' operation.

Synjan inhaled and glared up at him, feeling her love for him burn dark. "No-one you know," she ground out, effectively telling him it was none of his business.

Nick rolled his eyes. "Don't get pissy at *me*. I was just asking."

"Yeah. I understand," she agreed waspishly.

They stood there staring at each other for a few moments and then he gave the ceiling an exasperated look before he moved over, pressed his hand against the small of her back to hold her close and kissed the top of her head. "I gotta' go," he sighed. "You coming downstairs?" He was already three steps away from her, his arm stretching until the contact between them broke and the fact that he was willing to walk away when she was so obviously upset was the worst thing of all.

"Soon. I just need a drink of water," she said thickly.

"Fine, hurry up," he urged, gesturing towards the sink.

She glowered at him, no longer desiring his company. "You don't need to wait for me. I know the way."

"But it would be my pleasure," he responded with false cheer.

She frowned and looked away from him, staring unseeingly at the plate he'd abandoned on the bench. Perhaps it was the alcohol making her so emotional. Maybe it was just another symptom of grief.

A glass of water appeared in her line of sight and she looked up in surprise. The tall kitchen-hand stood before her, proving that he'd listened more effectively than the man she loved. He was strikingly handsome. He also seemed to care more because his lovely blue eyes were filled with sympathy and he wore a supportive expression.

"Thanks," she breathed. She realised at one point she'd folded her arms because she had to pull her hand out to reach for the water. She drank it all in a few swallows and smiled her gratitude when she handed the empty vessel back to him.

"Hey! Come on," Nick barked impatiently, appearing between them suddenly. His back was towards Synjan. He spoke to the kitchen-hand in a stern voice. "Why don't you get back to work?"

"What is your *problem*?" Synjan demanded, smacking Nick on the shoulder.

He turned to face her, a determined expression on his face. "You. Distracting my staff."

"He just gave me some water!" she tried to defend, gesturing at the brunette. He'd already turned away and was back at the stove.

"So I saw," Nick asserted grimly, grabbing her by the arm and marching her out of the kitchen.

"You're acting like it was a crime," Synjan spat, forced to take hurried steps to keep up with her taller companion.

"No, I'm acting like you're wasting everyone's time."

"That's ridiculous," she argued, wrenching out of his grasp as soon as they got to the hall. She glared at him, refusing to budge once he let her go. "You didn't even let me thank him!"

"He's got work to do."

"Who is he, anyway?"

"Nobody special."

"He's worked here a long time for 'nobody special'."

"So?"

"How is it that tonight is the first time I've even spoken to him?"

Nick laughed bitterly. "Are you serious?"

"Yes! Why are you stopping me from talking to him?"

"You're fucking paranoid, you know that?"

"Then why did you just drag me out of there like a child?"

"Because he's got fucking work to do and you're *acting* like a fucking child!" Nick screamed.

Synjan felt rather than saw the heads poking out of doorways along the hall, everyone no doubt wondering what the general manager was yelling about. She blushed, maintaining eye contact with Nick. "I'm not trying to argue with you. Settle down."

"I'm fine."

"Sure you are. What did I do wrong?"

"I thought you wanted to go downstairs?"

It was apparent he didn't want to discuss why he

was acting so oddly and she didn't want to draw any more attention to herself. The whole idea of coming up to talk to him about Kate was a mistake. Instead of replying, she pushed past him, intent on getting back to the club without him. His footsteps behind her were ominous until he walked into his office, leaving her alone without a farewell. She was infinitely relieved.

Once she was back in the basement Synjan went straight to the ladies' restroom. A woman was fixing her makeup at the expansive mirror and she pretended to do the same until the other left, then she simply stared at her reflection. There were no outward signs of the turmoil within her and she marvelled at her perfect veneer. The events of the day and her conversation with Nick were like tar within her, toxic and pervasive. Closing her eyes, she drew in a slow breath and resolved to shift her focus.

Kate's death would ruin her night if she didn't pull it together. She'd come here to avoid the abyss. If she didn't act, she'd wake up screaming tonight—she was prone to nightmares when she went to bed unsettled. Every time she killed, it was certain she'd awaken to find herself sweating, twisted in her sheets and staring wildly into the dark. The nightmares were either bloody and violent or repeated the day her family was killed.

The tonic to stifling those terrors was vigorous distraction. Sex. She'd come here to go home with an anonymous man, engage in hours of passionate exertion and drag herself back to the Office before dawn, exhausted. It was the only way to guarantee uninterrupted sleep. It was the only way she had control.

Synjan exhaled and opened her eyes. It no longer mattered how many women came to wash their hands while she stood there practising her smile. She lifted her breasts a little higher and played with her hair, readying herself for presentation. Her mask was impenetrable. She re-entered the dance area with determination.

The patronage in the club had tripled while she was upstairs. Wending her way through the press of bodies took some time. She left her coat with Misu and had another drink before she joined the dancers on the floor, enjoying the fast rhythm and pounding beat vibrating all the way through her.

While she danced, Synjan surveyed the clientele. Authorities were her target of choice. If they had a bit of rank, they were usually in Gredann for a specific task and were housed in some temporary, Authority-owned accommodation in Portside. She'd made the mistake of choosing a recruit before and wouldn't forget the hilarity of sneaking with him into a dorm room and finding it filled with eleven other sleeping soldiers. She'd backed out immediately and knew the right questions to ask now.

After narrowing her options, she settled on a pair of men seated at a table not far from the edge of the dance floor. One was blonde, one brunette, both nursing beers and talking to one another in between eyeing off the talent in the club. They were in their thirties and though they were looking, neither gave the impression that he was here to do more than find an appreciative view and an upbeat vibe to relax in.

If their posture hadn't given away the fact that they were soldiers, the way their gazes zeroed in on her the instant she decided to approach them would have. She respected men with good instincts and smiled as she sauntered up to them, drawn to the blonde. Unfortunately, when she was close enough to fold her arms on their table she noticed he was wearing a wedding ring.

"I gather you gentlemen are visiting the base, seeing as I haven't seen you here before?"

They shared a look before the blonde responded.

"Yeah."

When it became apparent she wasn't going to get any further details out of them, her respect for them rose.

"This your last night in Gredann?" She directed her question to the unmarried man. When he nodded, her smile broadened and she leaned in slightly, ignoring his companion. "Where are you staying?"

He shifted to face her. "They gave me a nice little contained unit up near Oceangate. It's called Port...something," he responded and Synjan allowed the warm timbre of his voice to sway her further.

"Portside."

"That's the one."

"I like the way you talk," she complimented.

"What are you talking about? *You're* the one with the accent," he teased and she laughed obligingly.

"So. Do you share your accommodation?" she queried, glancing pointedly at the blonde. His gaze lifted hastily from the curve of her waist and she liked the rakish grin he gave – unperturbed about being caught looking.

"Oh no. He's in a single. Lucky wick," the blonde answered for his companion.

Synjan turned to look at the brunette again and there was a lovely electric moment where he held her eye contact, silently agreeing to her unspoken proposition.

"What time are you portalling out tomorrow?" she asked, shifting her weight so that her hip was pressed against his leg, her breast to his arm.

"Eight hundred," he told her and lowered his arm to brush against her intimately.

"I'd be out at five." She was pleasantly surprised when his fingers slid beneath the hem of her dress and squeezed a thigh. She drew in breath and noticed his gaze focussed on her mouth.

"Sounds good to me," he confirmed.

"I'll get my coat," she told him. She made sure there was an extra swing to her hips so that he'd have something to watch as she went.

Overall, she was pleased with her selection. He hadn't needed a name and he was so keen to attend to her that he was already exploring. Of all the things she'd done that she regretted today, this was not one of them. Her dues were paid. Tonight was hers.

CHAPTER SIX

The Wailing Mothers

REAKFAST was a couple of rabbits and some berries. It would've been a fantastic meal for two people and a good meal for three, but there were six of them and Hawke was the lowest on the food chain. He was given one fire-roasted drumstick and four berries. He ate them too quickly, for he didn't taste them and it felt like he'd eaten nothing.

He rode in front of Carmen because he insisted and Carmen was agreeable. Hawke had chosen to ride with her not just because she was kind to him, though it had a lot to do with it, but because she'd left him to go toileting by himself. If anyone would give him a chance to escape, it would be her. Possibly even with her blessing.

Eddie wouldn't ride any horse other than Silverprint and Hawke hated him for that. Hatred boiled in him until the sun was high and it became a rancid, physical thing in his chest and throat. Carmen hushed him.

"Feeling that way will eat you up inside until you're hollow," she warned him. She had an ability as well, he discovered, which allowed her to know what others felt. He didn't question it.

"Then let me go."

"He won't give you a horse to get back," she told him.

"I don't care," he said, though he wanted Silverprint and he suspected that she knew.

Hawke's breath plumed in the crisp air. He tucked his hands into his vest and relied on Carmen to keep the rest of his body warm. She wrapped her fur-lined cloak around him. It didn't quite close up but their shared body heat helped. She was following Eddie and Jerrom, pulling up third at a hilltop, looking down on a village nestled in a snowy valley. The track they were on looked to be the only one in or out.

"I don't see it," Eddie said. There was no wind to snatch his words away and Hawke heard the conversation clearly even though it made no sense.

"Still too far. Will be beyond them."

Hawke looked where Jerrom was pointing and snorted. Beyond the village were mountains that looked inhospitable. They weren't going to get past them.

"Do we go around?" Carmen asked. A figure that was more clothing than person pulled up in the middle of conversation, blocking Hawke's view. Lyssa obviously didn't like the cold.

"There's no way around," Eddie replied. Hawke didn't need to see him to know he was talking. He recognised the bastard's voice.

"We're going mountain climbing?" Lyssa asked, her voice muffled by the scarf over her mouth.

"We are," Eddie confirmed. "Supplies first."

Hawke was planning how he would escape as they approached the village. He would throw himself off the horse and run into one of the buildings, and scream that he was their hostage if it looked like he couldn't get away. There was bound to be an Enforcer in a village so isolated. They were unlikely to have county patrolmen so far north. He tried to remember his lessons for the names of the villages a couple of days' ride north but came up blank—too many small communities peppered the base of this mountain range. He remembered that the mountains were called the Wailing Mothers and also knew the Narrow Pass would take a traveller through them safely, but only if they'd chanced upon the right town. He didn't share his information with the horse thieves, hoping they would be distracted and deterred long enough for him to see through his escape.

"How is he?" Eddie asked, riding Silverprint directly

into Hawke's view and causing Lyssa's horse—Wattlebrush—to snort discontent and back up. It was more proof to Hawke that Eddie was an unsubtle bastard who didn't even respect the others in his group.

"Thinking about escape."

The betrayal smacked Hawke so hard that panic swam into his chest and heightened his heartbeat and breathing. He'd felt safe in Carmen's hold. It was stupid, to think that she was on his side instead of with them. Of course she would favour them over him; she chose to *travel* with them. He hated her as much as he hated Eddie because even though she hadn't pushed him down or fought him, what she'd done was almost worse.

"Poor little guy," Lyssa said before her scarf dampened the sound of laughter.

He hated them all.

When they arrived in town, Hawke was side-saddle riding Silverprint in front of Eddie. He was trapped in the bedding cocoon, unable to move. Eddie's threats silenced him and they remained behind some of the outer buildings of the village while the sisters continued on. From the conversation around him, Hawke could discern that the women would be purchasing their supplies because of their mind-reading ability. It would make haggling easier.

"You could ransom me," Hawke suggested, earning himself a curious stare from Eddie.

"Your money will be useless soon," the leader of the horse thieves told him. "And you're worth more if you stay with us."

"I won't stay with you," Hawke argued, hearing the sullen tone in his voice and knowing that he was unable to hide his feelings from the group anyway, so why try? "I'll escape the second you look away. You can't watch me forever."

"No, Hawke Aron, I can't watch you forever. But

soon enough you'll have nowhere to run."

Hawke said nothing in return, unsure what the statement meant but not liking the sound of it. There was something he was missing. Since the horse thieves were travelling with a single-minded purpose, he knew whatever it was didn't herald good things for him.

"Where are you going?" he asked.

"North."

"But where north? You don't even know the name of the mountain ranges."

There was so long a pause that he thought Eddie wasn't going to answer.

"No, I don't know the names of them, but I'll be glad to see the back of them," his captor said. His comments were taking the form of a riddle, in Hawke's mind. Eddie's answer hadn't specified his intended location and Hawke thought that meant he didn't know.

"Where are you from?"

"You're full of questions today, Hawke Aron."

"Of Donovan Court," Hawke reminded him. His family weren't so wealthy that their influence extended this far north, but their estate was grand enough and their position established enough that he was proud of his origins.

"Hawke Aron of Donovan Court," Eddie amended.

Hawke felt his jaw tighten at the offensive way Eddie had stated his title. Like it was a joke. He struggled in the bedding and Eddie obliged him by unfastening it halfway down his chest. The cold air groped its way in as Hawke worked his fingers to the metal stitching and forced it down farther.

"Don't do anything stupid," Eddie warned.

"Like what?"

"Like yelling for help, saying we kidnapped you."

Hawke hadn't abandoned his plan and Eddie possibly saw it in his expression.

"If you do it, I'll cut you and we'll take off from here

on your horses. We'll be unprepared for the trip and it'll likely slow us down and maybe even kill us if the weather turns foul...but I will still make sure the last thing I do is take your life before I do my best to save my own. Do you believe that, Hawke Aron of Donovan Court? Do you believe I will end you if you sabotage me?"

Hawke looked from Eddie to the other two nearby. The one called Roderick—who would often be referred to as 'Rick'—was looking at the pair of them with detachment and the other one was staring at his horse's mane. No help from either of them.

"I believe you don't care whether I live or die," Hawke said. He was trying to be snide but Eddie corrected him.

"Oh, I care, because you're worth something to me. I'd hate to cut my losses."

Hawke did his best to slide the metal teeth fastenings upward again, because he felt cold.

They stayed in the village for the night. When Hawke learned from the sisters on their return that the small community was called Orrensville, his heart sank. The large strip of land that belonged to the Orren family followed the Wailing Mothers all the way to Narrow Pass. The Orren estate wasn't a rich one but could've been, if they'd decided to extort every hunter with tolls. The only way to find an ice-serpent was beyond the Narrow Pass, and it was free to travel through. Due to the Orren family's lack of business acumen, they'd been dismissed from Hawke's lessons, mentioned only in passing. They also failed to marry into other estates, so Hawke knew nothing of their daughters.

Their accommodation was warm, dry and spacious. There were four raised cots and six bedding mats.

Hawke assumed that he would be on one of the latter but Eddie directed him to one of the cots against the centre of a wall. There was a cot either side of him and another by the window. The mats were arranged closer to the door and Hawke supposed Eddie might think he'd try to escape in the night. Hawke thought he might try it anyway, except as soon as he sat upon the cot, the springs squeaked loudly.

Dinner was mutton stew; hot and comforting. Hawke ate without his usual aplomb and sped through the meal, eating his bread even after he ran out of stew to dip it in. His bowl was so clean that the table-maid picking it up commented on it and suggested they get another serving for him. Eddie growled that he could have another serving if it was free and the table-maid left them without comment. Hawke was angry, thinking Eddie had kept him from a second meal, until the table-maid returned with another bowl—not as full as the first one and given without bread, but Hawke was grateful and he thanked her earnestly. She gave him a warm smile and threw Eddie a filthy look. Hawke loved her for that.

He didn't want to sleep in his two day old clothes when they went to bed but he didn't take them off; he wanted them for sneaking out. He climbed into bed and Carmen laid the thin blankets supplied by the inn over him. The room wasn't too cold because the kitchen and stovepipe downstairs heated the inner wall, but it wasn't warm either. He refused the cocoon that he'd been using so far because it was difficult for him to wriggle out of. He'd thought she would insist but didn't and rolled it into an impossibly small bundle before shoving it deep into her backpack.

Hawke shivered beneath the blanket and curled himself tightly into a ball to preserve his heat, waiting for Eddie, Lyssa and Jerrom to finish playing their card game by lantern-light. The cold helped him to stay awake but he soon found his trials were for nothing; they spoke about drawing watch and Jerrom continued playing cards on his own while the other two went to their beds. Despair washed over Hawke as he suspected that this was not something they were doing just for his benefit but a common routine. Out of the five, one would keep watch over the others. They could effectively stop him from escaping just by continuing to do as they always did.

He would have to try a different method than sneaking away at night.

The next morning found him downstairs eating a hearty breakfast with the group. There would be no second serves but he soon found he didn't need extra. With a generous helping of eggs, ham and fire-toasted bread on his plate, and watered down grapefruit juice in a cup, his stomach was full and he was feeling good about his chances of escape.

"I need to fill the pipe," Eddie said, speaking of the lavatory. He got up and went outside and Hawke felt more relaxed when he was gone. Carmen was reading a book so perhaps she wasn't reading his thoughts. They'd told him he was a Shielder, so he actively tried to control it by thinking about an invisible tent around himself. He looked at Jerrom who was still eating and didn't seem to notice anything, but Carmen's expression was one he interpreted as annoyed.

"I'm cold," Hawke said, and hugged himself to sell the idea. He wasn't cold but he wanted an excuse to leave them.

"You're not cold," Carmen challenged, and Hawke's heart pounded as he had to explain his deception.

"You can't feel what I'm feeling. I'm cold!" he insisted, and reached out to touch the back of her hand with his fingers. The cup of juice had been chilly to the touch and he hoped his fingertips were translating that temperature to her. The warmth of the fireplace made for a stark contrast and she looked surprised.

"There's a small coat upstairs in my bag. It shouldn't be too big but I don't think any of my gloves will fit you," she said.

Jerrom spoke without looking up. "He'll try and escape."

"From upstairs?" Carmen scoffed.

Hawke took that as his cue to leave as fast as possible without looking too hasty. He went upstairs and into the shared room, not bothering to check for the coat though he planned on taking that with him, along with the cocoon bedding. It was going to be a long trip south.

The window, not too small for Hawke to wriggle out of, was stuck closed. Perhaps Carmen already knew it was frozen shut and that was why she wasn't concerned about letting him up here alone. Eddie's warning rang in his ears, but so far Hawke's attempt at escape hadn't compromised the horse thieves. Hawke took the coat from out of Carmen's pack and turned deeper into the corridor rather than towards the stairs that would lead him back to the dining area. He checked all the rooms but they were locked. There was one door that opened into a large storage room with piles of clean bedding. If he stayed in this room and hid while shielded, Jerrom (who could apparently 'see' where people were without using his eyes, Hawke had figured out) wouldn't be able to find him. The group would be forced to continue without Hawke, for fear of an alarm being raised. Once they were gone, Hawke could send word back to his estate. His father and Umber would travel here to take him home. This wasn't the escape he'd hoped for; his preference was to take Silverprint back with him but he was willing to sacrifice his horse if it meant he could escape the thieves without confrontation.

There was only one obvious hiding place; a wardrobe in one corner of the room. It had slatted doors and when Hawke opened it up, he was relieved to find it only had shelves on one side, while the other had some table-maid uniforms hanging within. He pushed them aside and stood in that section of the wardrobe, his head brushing the very top shelf where some cushions were stored. He poked his fingers through the slats to properly close the wardrobe behind himself.

He wasn't there long before he heard Eddie's familiar voice speaking to someone. The leader of the group didn't sound alarmed but rather happy. They didn't know Hawke was missing yet. He expected the voices to fade or possibly to raise upon discovery that Hawke was gone. Instead the voices came closer and he could hear the familiar rattle of hands trying doorknobs, just like he had.

Maybe they *had* realised he was missing? Why did they sound so happy about it? Perhaps they thought it was a game or that his attempt at escape was so pathetic that it amused them. Perhaps Carmen had read his mind all along and they knew he was hiding up here.

His stomach lurched and his chest tightened when the door to the storage room opened and Eddie and Roderick entered. Hawke quietly huddled back into the wardrobe as much as he was able and held his breath. They were sure to find him.

"Why are we in here, Ed?" Roderick asked. He sounded strange.

"The kid's in our room feeling sorry for himself," Eddie grinned. The explanation settled Hawke's heart when he realised that they weren't looking for him. "I'd prefer to do it here than on those creaky springs anyway."

Do what? Hawke was confused but didn't dare move for fear of discovery. He wanted them to leave. He wanted someone to go into the room and yell out that Hawke was gone, and for them to all go away to look for him before giving up. Or better still, leaving for fear that he would tell on them and have them arrested. He didn't care about justice anymore. He just wanted to be away from them.

He could hear odd noises. Hawke peered out from between the slats. He was shocked to see them cuddling and kissing. He'd seen kisses before when his father kissed his mother's cheek or even a peck on the lips, but nothing like this; they looked like they were trying to eat one another's mouths.

There were whispers and soft laughter and grunts as they rubbed against one another. Hawke looked away, embarrassed and mortified that he was intruding on their private moment. Why couldn't they have gone somewhere else? He wondered if the rest of the group knew about their relationship. The girls had to, if they were mind readers.

Eventually the soft groans and sighs of pleasure had Hawke peering out through the slats again to see what they were doing now. He was both fascinated and horrified to see Roderick bent over a tower of sheets while Eddie prepared to impale him.

Hawke gasped and sucked in breath and spit. His throat constricted as he spluttered and choked. Horrified, he covered his mouth with his hands to stop the noise but couldn't. His eyes watered with the effort of stifling his coughs. He hoped that the sounds he was making weren't as loud as the two men in the room.

A shadow was cast over the slats as someone approached the wardrobe door. Hawke was acutely aware of what he was about to be caught doing and what Eddie could be capable of doing to him.

When the wardrobe door began to open, Hawke shoved against it and had the element of surprise, knocking back Eddie whose pants fell around his knees because they hadn't been done up properly. His tormentor was caught between the wardrobe door and the wall when Hawke leapt out, barely seeing Roderick beyond the shocked look on his face.

He felt like his heart was in his ears, making it hard to hear, hard to think. He looked wildly from closed door to closed door and lunged forward down the corridor, which seemed impossibly long. He could almost feel fingers clawing for his back, to grab him by his clothing and yank him back inside. He was halfway along when Carmen appeared at the top of the stairs. Relief brought tears to his eyes as he flew against her and hugged her tight, begging her not to let Eddie punish him.

"What's going on?" she asked. Unbelievably, there was laughter. Hawke cringed against Carmen and risked a look behind, not seeing anyone chasing after him. Roderick was in the storage room holding his pants up at the waist and Eddie peered around the door, using it as cover. They were both laughing and Hawke felt a mixture of confusion, vulnerability and anger. "Why did you have him in there with you?" Carmen asked, sounding offended.

"We didn't *know* he was in here. Little shit was hiding and we didn't think to check first," Eddie said, then disappeared from view behind the door.

Carmen took Hawke with her into their room and sat with an arm around his shoulders on the bed until he stopped shaking. She asked him why he was so afraid but he couldn't give her an answer...because he *wasn't* afraid. He was furious. He wanted to punch something, to kick and scream and let the rage out. He couldn't do that, otherwise Carmen might think differently about him and decide he didn't need protecting. He needed her to continue feeling sorry for him, so that she might decide to let him go.

If only Hawke had ignored the two men. If only he'd had more control and not gasped. If only he'd curled up in the wardrobe instead of looking, he would've been free once they were finished.

If only he had someone else to blame for losing his first real opportunity to escape.

They left the next morning, with Hawke sitting in front of Carmen. She'd spent the last of their money getting him gloves, a scarf and a hat to go with the food rations they'd bought. As they rode, he ignored Eddie's jokes and barbs about being in the wardrobe. Eddie's comments stopped when they entered the Narrow Pass.

A respectful silence fell upon the group due to the size of the fissure they travelled through. The walls were very smooth but showed different colours of rocks layered on its surface. The ground was icy but the horses didn't falter.

Other people walked through with them; hunters, mostly, though there was a trio on horseback that looked like they were going beyond the hunting grounds as well. He wondered if they would end up going in the same direction.

The Wailing Mothers demonstrated their namesake as the wind howled mournfully along the Narrow Pass. It took on an eerie note, sounding more like a keening woman than the whistle Hawke was expecting.

"What's *that*?" Lyssa said, pointing. They followed the path of her finger to see figures carved into the side of the mountain wall; statues of children young and old but never adult, most of them smaller and younger than Hawke's eight years.

Winters in Orrensville were bitterly cold and summers were brief; only the hardiest survived. The townsfolk had taken their cue from the crying wind and immortalised their children who succumbed to the cold, making the walls of the Narrow Pass a monument to their memory. They served as a reminder that this was no place for the weak.

Hawke looked at the long line of boys and girls carved in stone. Their blank staring eyes lacked the detail of the rest of their faces and bodies and this gave them an appearance of being unrested. He leaned further into Carmen as they rode in silence and she wrapped her blanket more tightly around him.

Everyone that exited the Pass moved quickly through the light snow towards a scattering of trees marking the edge of a forest. They could've been after ice serpents or possibly chasing rabbits and deer. Jerrom and Eddie discussed something Hawke couldn't hear because the wind tore their words away from him.

They followed the others until there was a clear fork in the pathway. Everyone else travelled to the right with the hunters. Eddie led them to the left.

Travelling through snow-covered forest in a big group on horseback was slow. They didn't stop for lunch, instead pushing the horses onward and eating while riding.

Hawke worried about how the horses were faring. He was also unsettled by the lack of smells and sounds. Other than the horses and what they'd brought with them, only his eyes informed him he was in a forest. The trees looked brittle and imposing, their branches extending skyward at an impossible height for a trunk so small in girth.

The forest thinned out just after midday and they were in thicker snow by late afternoon. There was a discussion and agreement between all of them that they would need to stop and rest and feed the horses, and possibly make camp.

On their left was a massive snow drift, halving their chances of finding a good spot to rest. It had been unchanging enough that nobody noticed the tunnel entrance within the drift until they were almost atop it.

"Look!" Lyssa pointed out the tunnel, sounding excited. She'd bundled herself up in layers again so that she appeared more like a stack of clothes riding a horse than a person. Hawke wondered how she could ride like that.

The tunnel entrance had a light blue glittery sheen around the mouth, with glistening stalactites hanging from the top. There was something very pretty and magical-looking about it. Hawke didn't think the tunnel led anywhere, but it was an interesting looking cave. He watched Lyssa angling Wattlebrush to get closer.

Eddie and Jerrom were ahead of her, uncaring about the tunnel entrance enough to have passed it without a second look. Roderick was pulling up the rear. Hawke and Carmen were riding behind Lyssa, and had the best view of what happened.

Wattlebrush was uneasy about going closer to the tunnel mouth. The horse whinnied and tossed his head but Lyssa dug in her heels, forcing the horse to approach. One moment she was peering in and the next she'd reeled backward so quickly that she fell off the saddle, her foot momentarily caught in the stirrup before she landed with a puff in the snow. Hawke laughed until the round head of a large lizard-worm creature snaked out of the hole and captured Wattlebrush in its toothless mouth. The horse screamed as it was dragged into the hole with little effort. Lyssa flopped around on the snow, looking like a landed fish before crawling speedily away from the tunnel, sobbing as she went. Carmen repeatedly screamed her sister's name while spurring the horse to where Lyssa had found her feet after getting some distance from the glistening mouth of the tunnel.

Hawke covered his ears with gloved hands, unsuccessfully blocking out the screams of the horse that he could still hear, deep into the tunnel—and then they stopped. Carmen dismounted and threw her arms around her sister, the two of them hugging each other tightly. Hawke stared at the sisters until Eddie rode over and picked up the reins of Hawke's horse. It was then that Hawke realised sickly he'd missed a fantastic opportunity for escape. The group gathered a good distance away from the glistening tunnel.

"What was that?" Eddie demanded of Hawke, both of them still on horseback.

"Ice-serpent," Hawke said. He couldn't know that this was what the creature looked like, but at the same time he knew in his heart that this was the only thing that could have killed an entire pack of seven hunters, including his grandfather. He could imagine them investigating the strange glittering inner surface of the tunnel and then all being taken with one huge bite.

"They're not real!" Roderick protested, reminding Hawke painfully of Denis. He missed his brother so much that it hurt. He missed his home. He wanted to go back. He could feel a hot ball of emotion clogging his throat and he turned his face away to get himself under control.

"It looked real enough to me!" Lyssa yelled back. Then she turned on Jerrom. "I thought you would warn us about big animals!"

"The only thing I could see was the horse," Jerrom explained with a shrug.

"You telling me the ice-serpent's a Shielder, too?"

"You girls ride together, I'll take the kid," Jerrom offered.

"No, we have to make camp," Eddie said.

"Not here!" Lyssa argued. For someone who didn't talk much, Hawke thought she could make herself heard well enough when she wanted to be.

They skirted the ice-serpent's cavern and made their way farther north. Hawke reflected that it was unusual for an ice-serpent to be only a day's travel from the Narrow Pass; they were supposed to be difficult to be sighted. Perhaps those who saw them didn't survive to tell anyone about it.

The tents went up when the woods thickened. There were supposed to be ice-bears here. They should be hibernating by now but it was possible to get a rogue hunting late in the season. Hungry, tired bears were especially dangerous and Hawke relayed this information, not wanting to end up as dinner for one.

Jerrom went out hunting by himself regardless and brought back two rabbits and a couple of wild birds. He hunted especially well. The group was in strangely good spirits, considering they'd lost one of the horses today. It had something to do with a *Portal* being less than a day's ride ahead. They were all celebrating this news.

Eddie passed around a canteen and they each took a sip. Lyssa passed it to Hawke who accepted it and took a sniff. It was minty smelling burnwater. He pulled a face.

"Loosen up and have some, Hawke Aron, it'll warm your insides."

Her suggestion made sense. He was cold enough to try it and took a big gulp. Intense heat burned his mouth and throat before it forged a fiery path to his belly. He spluttered and coughed, the cold air that he gasped in making it worse. Laughter prompted him to try again, to show them that he wasn't useless...and it was true enough that the burnwater warmed him up. He knew burnwater was something people drank to forget their worries. He had a lot of worries he wanted to forget about.

After a few more passes around the circle, the canteen was empty and Hawke felt pleasantly warm and tingly. He watched Lyssa and Jerrom perform a stomping dance around the fire and there was a pause as chatter flowed around and over him. He wondered if he could bathe in voices, if they could clean him. Eddie's voice made him feel dirty, but Carmen's voice was like soap.

He listened as Roderick played a strange pipe

instrument that had a wheezy sound. Questions pierced the music; What was life like in Boronia? Was there any part of his life he didn't like? Hawke took the opportunity to vent; the constrictions of duty, the endless days of lesson after lesson, the social obligation for him to marry into a good estate because Umber had the most choice being first born, and Hawke being last born had so little choice that a marriage was likely to be arranged. He complained about his domineering father who had nothing to say unless it was a criticism and that he was an after-thought in the family, good for nothing except to be moulded into good marrying stock.

They told him they were Wanderers. They told him he was a Wanderer. Around the circle they explained what their powers were but Hawke couldn't make sense of them beyond the burnwater's effects. Navigator, Intuit, Catalyst – they were nonsensical words that he forgot the explanations of almost as quickly as he heard them.

Roderick had no ability, only able to travel from world to world with Eddie's help. They'd done so together for almost ten years. The sisters had only been travelling together for six. Jerrom hadn't Wandered until he met Eddie, who'd talked him into it. They'd paired up with the girls shortly after and had been travelling as a group for three years now. Eddie wanted to make a Fold, which required at least one Wanderer of each ability. Making a Fold meant the Portal would take them to the World of Worlds, from which every world could be visited. Hawke said that sounded nice. When they asked his opinion, he let loose a terrifying burp and then laughed.

He was vaguely aware of being led into the tent by Carmen and helped into his sleeping bag, smiling as Carmen fastened it with the whirring noise.

"What do you call that thing you pull?" he asked.

"It's a zipper."

Zipper. The word sounded deliciously entertaining in Hawke's addled mind and he giggled over it until he fell asleep.

He awoke with a thumping headache and the light reflecting off the snow was so bright it hurt his eyes. His mouth felt furry and there was an awful taste he couldn't get rid of, no matter how much water he drank. Riding in the saddle with Jerrom was much worse than riding with Carmen, because his horse's gait seemed more exaggerated than hers. He couldn't remember who was riding what horse, except he knew Eddie was on Silverprint.

Hawke pitched sideways in the saddle to empty the contents of his belly into the snow. Jerrom laughed the first time Hawke did this, but didn't the next few.

They didn't stop for lunch, instead eating their rations on horseback like last time. The thieves—*Wanderers?*—were keen to move on and arrive at the place where they were going. Last night's memory was murky and he was unable to recall anything beyond some music and dancing. There was conversation, he knew, but he remembered none of the details. The more he tried to think about it, the slipperier it got.

An hour later their driven tension turned into excitement and Eddie was whooping pleasure. Hawke was feeling better but even as he looked ahead into the blinding white of the snow covered ground and the clear blue sky over mountain tops, he didn't know what was different. Everyone got off their horses and Hawke was lifted down as well.

"What are we stopping for?" he asked loudly, to be heard over the excited shouts. Lyssa replied for she was closest.

"That!" she yelled, pointing ahead of them. Hawke

looked. Well beyond the powdery, flat snow was the beginning of a thick forest and a vast collection of mountains a great distance away. The sun was shining, the sky was blue and he had no idea what he was looking at. He looked back at a frowning Lyssa.

"Don't you see it?"

"The forest?" he hazarded, choosing the closest thing to them.

She grabbed his arm and marched him the few steps over to Eddie, who was hugging Roderick and had Jerrom in a kind of embracing headlock while Carmen laughed beside them.

"He doesn't see it!" she yelled at them.

The mood shifted and they all stared at Lyssa and Hawke. Hawke tore his arm from her grasp, disliking the way she'd handled him.

"He still has the blood," Eddie said.

"But he's no good to your plan." Carmen said. "Give him back a—"

"How do you know?!" Eddie thundered, whirling on her. "How would you know if he's good enough or not? He's enough of a Wanderer to shield himself from you and Jerrom! And with my help, he can do more!"

Hawke was lost by the conversation but he sensed it had to do with letting him go.

"Vote, then," Carmen said.

"I want to go home," Hawke said, trying to sway the vote in his favour. He watched every hand raise except for Carmen's.

"Grab the reins," Eddie instructed and took Roderick's hand. Once they were all holding onto each other or the reins of their horses, they all huddled together. Hawke was pulled into the middle and Carmen put her hand on his shoulder.

After everything that happened, he hated her the most for doing that.

CHAPTER SEVEN

The Hunter And The Car

THE Hunter was nestled in the crook of a large oak, the barrel of his rifle resting on a thick branch a couple of metres off the ground. It had taken him an hour of exploration, looking for the right place to set up. Most of his division preferred to hunt in an urban environment because it was easier to track and eliminate their targets there. The downside came in the mistakes—a few tourists had paid the price for looking unkempt in other-worldly clothing. He'd regarded his colleagues' miscalculations with contempt until he'd been fooled himself. He kept away from the cities now, even though the trails were warmest there.

He believed his targets were setting themselves up to Wander. They'd made large purchases of camping supplies and mixed weather clothing. He predicted they'd leave the city they'd bought their equipment in and head east to the small valley township nearby. There was only one road that would get them there—through the mountains—and it was what his sight was trained on.

There was no foundation for his guess other than his gut. He'd read somewhere that gut instincts were the result of finely-tuned minor perceptions. It sounded logical, except in his case his instincts were the result of finely-*trained* perceptions.

He watched as shadows shifted from one side of the tree to the other. He listened to birdsong and blinked away the sweat on his brow. He breathed his way through sore limbs and cramped muscles. Doubts rose but he'd learned to suppress them. Through his scope, he watched cars and trucks and the odd bus rumble around the curving road. He could identify drivers and passengers by their hair colouring and clothing. He watched intently for his targets.

Waiting was a bitch. He hated this part of the job. He got his adrenaline rush from tracking and making connections. There was a reason the phrase 'the thrill of the chase' was so popular. The climax wasn't as satisfying as the work he put into the hunt. In his opinion, the kill was anti-climactic...except results were what brought in the money.

A light blue sedan came into view and he trained the rifle onto it. He had to wait until it rounded the inside bend before he could see driver and passenger through the windshield. A brunette male was behind the wheel. There was a companion beside him but glare on the windshield made identification impossible.

The Hunter anticipated a blonde woman with short hair. His eagerness insisted it was them but reason countered that their car was supposed to be silver. They might've ditched it somewhere to make their trail harder to follow—this couple *had* been canny, which was why it had taken him nineteen fucking worlds to catch up with them.

As his mind sifted through the variables, he targeted the driver and applied light pressure to the trigger. He had seconds to decide, his entire world shrunk down to the interior of that vehicle, its two passengers, his one finger. He was unable to confirm both identities and he was weighing the consequences when movement in the back seat caught his eye. He abandoned the shot, moving his finger off and away. He struggled to make sense of what he'd seen because...it had looked like a small giraffe?

He continued to watch the car through the sight and as the road turned, the glare moved. This time he saw a woman with her hair pulled back into a ponytail. She was blonde but her hair was much longer than his target. It wasn't them. The most compelling evidence was the young child in the back seat, throwing the toy giraffe around. Their child's tossing game had saved their lives.

He huffed, annoyed at almost making a mistake. He was getting impatient and didn't have a spotter to double check him. Though the rest of his division were paired up, he'd refused a partner. He worked faster and more efficiently on his own and the results he'd garnered earned him that right. Partners only worked well when they trusted one another and none of them trusted him. It was a mutual sentiment. Some facets of his malignant reputation were organic, the rest he'd nurtured himself.

Twenty minutes later, the Wanderers appeared. This time he recognised the car. They hadn't dumped it, feeling safe because they were on the move. It was another advantage the wilderness had over an urban environment; the complacency and relief in his targets. It made them more like sheep and the trigger easier to squeeze.

He recognised the short, shaggy haircut on the woman. She was in the driver's seat while the man beside her was looking for something inside a bag on his lap. They were chatting animatedly as they drove.

They looked happy.

Steeling himself, he checked the wind, inhaled and aimed at her chest. He squeezed the trigger as he released his breath in a long, steady stream. This time there was no need for hesitation. The punch of the rifle was absorbed by his shoulder and his ears cringed with the bang, even with earplugs in place. Through the scope, he watched as the windshield exploded in an array of spidery cracks so intensely white that he couldn't see in. The driver couldn't see out, either. He didn't know if she'd been instantly killed but the car moved erratically, shifting to the oncoming lane before over-adjusting, rubbing the side of the car along the mountain. There was a railing that ran parallel to the road, designed to keep vehicles from driving over the cliff. The car hit it front on with such force that its bonnet crumpled and it vaulted over, hitting treetops in its speedy descent down the mountain side.

He swore, knowing that it was possible one or both of them survived. Unlikely, but possible. People had gone through worse and walked away.

He landed hard coming down the tree because he was stiff and cradling his rifle but was lucky enough not to turn his ankle. The impact caused a shooting pain to travel up his leg. He packed up quickly, dismantling his rifle and putting it into its case before slinging it over his shoulder. He grit his teeth as he moved between the trees, determined not to let the ache in his leg slow him down, estimating it would take him thirty minutes to travel through the forest to them.

As he drew nearer, he could smell the rank odour of petrol. The fuel tank must've ruptured on the way down. He was quietly working his way upwind so he wouldn't be affected by the fumes when he heard a giant rasping intake of breath and then a bout of violent coughing. Somebody *was* alive.

He could hear faint voices above as concerned witnesses discussed the situation with one another. They weren't calling out, perhaps guessing that nobody survived or maybe they'd exhausted their shouts. They would have called an emergency service by now. He wondered what the response time was for rescue operations like this one; would a helicopter come, a team of abseiling paramedics or something else? He was on a shorter deadline because of observant and well-meaning citizens.

He moved quietly in a quarter arc and now he could see the car resting on its roof, covered in branches and splattered with mud and leaves. Through the side window he identified the driver was still buckled into her seat, arms hanging limp and with a large dollop of red on her white shirt.

Somebody moaned from the other side of the car and then: "She's dead. She's dead, you bastard."

The announcement was slurred and filled with pain but it took him by surprise—not because he couldn't see the male yet, but because he thought the Wanderer had heard or seen him. *Impossible*, he reasoned, but he didn't know all of the Wanderer abilities. The Authorities had many powers accounted for but there were hundreds of others theorised. Regardless of what specific power they had, he was certain they all required focus in some form, whether being mentally aware or physically centred. This Wanderer was high on fumes. He was beside the car, seriously wounded and breathing in bad air. It was doubtful the man had any presence of mind to be able to control his powers.

The Hunter left his rifle case propped against a tree and pulled his pistol out of its holster. After checking it, he made his approach, keeping the weapon trained along his line of vision as he peered around the car. He wanted to know how badly wounded the guy was. It didn't sound like he would last too long before the fumes hindered his oxygen intake and he was fatally poisoned. It wasn't reason enough to avoid shooting his target; he'd prefer to be finished with this business.

He was tired and impatient and it made him reckless. He rounded the car on the assumption that the Wanderer wouldn't have a weapon handy. He found himself staring at a drawn revolver, the aim wavering but mostly pointed in his direction. He flinched back and a sharp crack filled the air, sending birds twittering out of the trees. The bullet didn't find its mark but it was close enough that he heard the breathy, high pitched whirr of it zipping past.

"Fuck," he said, prompting momentary ecstatic laughter from the shooter.

"I didn't getcha," the Wanderer slurred, sounding

bitter.

"No," he replied, thinking about what he'd seen in the brief moment before he'd retreated.

The Wanderer had been sitting peculiarly—there was something very wrong with one of his legs because it was bent at a weird angle. He was also sitting in a pool of petrol. There was the option of burning him alive, though starting forest fires in nature reserves would likely upset the local government.

"You're wrong, by the way," he reasoned, recalling that the Wanderer had a large brown saddle bag beside him filled with weapons and ammunition. The zipper had been pulled wide open and the Hunter had seen what was inside before he'd been forced to duck away. His mind connected the dots for him and he knew that this was the bag the man had been looking through when his travelling companion had been shot.

There was long, thoughtful silence.

"'Bout what?"

"I didn't kill her."

"You shot her! I watched her heart bloom!"

Her heart bloom? Apparently petrol fumes could make a person poetic. He made a mental note of the phrasing and continued to taunt the Wanderer, feeling the beginning of a headache at his temples. He better hurry this up before the rescue crew found two blathering fools at the bottom of the cliff.

"She committed suicide."

"She *what*?"

He could hear the strain in the Wanderer's voice.

"The instant she moved illegally between worlds."

"Fucking shoot me now and save me your sanctimonious crap." There was a thump that could've been the Wanderer slumping against the car. It was worth a peek around the front again.

He went in low the second time so he couldn't be easily targeted. He made eye-contact with the man he was trying to kill. There was a brief, frozen moment of assessment before they were both shooting and he was forced to retreat.

For a wounded guy, the Wanderer was taking care of himself quite well. The Hunter had a grudging respect for a man who wouldn't die easily. Pain made cowards out of most adults and this fellow was handling it well. Was it the fumes or grim determination? Wanderers were incredibly good survivors.

So were cockroaches.

He could hear sirens above them. He would have to work on the assumption the gunshots exchanged between them had been identified as such. The police or local military would get involved.

He could wait him out or go in shooting. Even though the latter didn't appeal, he didn't think he had the luxury of waiting. He didn't want the guy to get hoisted out by a rescue team who would then ship him off to some lab. He wasn't going to surrender the Wanderer now, not after losing over eight months to these assholes. He didn't want to waste a minute more.

The Hunter checked his magazine and then climbed up onto the car, squatting near the rear axle while he got his balance. He was heard, but there was very little the injured man could do about it. The shooting angle would be difficult for him and his broken leg would prevent him from rapidly turning for a better shot.

Carefully, he crept forward, trying to see better. The Wanderer fired wildly into the air, trying to get lucky. He watched as the wounded man twisted around, firing backwards, his arm straightening on the recoil because his gun was too big for that kind of trickery...and then came sounds of vomiting. The petrol fumes were affecting them both but the Wanderer had been sitting in it for forty minutes now.

He was in the middle of purging when the Hunter

shot him in the back of the head. The vomiting stopped and he remained as he was, slightly slumped over by the car.

Anti-climactic.

The Hunter jumped down and searched through the bag of ammunition, picking up a few choice items but leaving most of it behind. He pulled out his clip camera and took photos of the scene, including close-ups of the dead Wanderers, their gear and the licence plate of the car. It would help with the paperwork later...though he mostly kept it up to date with vocal reports transcribed by a secretarial assistant.

He returned to his rifle case and was gone by the time the first medics arrived on the scene. It didn't matter if forensic evidence led to the Authorities or to him personally—there was nothing they could do about it.

CHAPTER EIGHT

Shopping At The Fish Markets

A gust of wind rushed to meet her as she turned the corner and Synjan was forced to take a half step back before she could counteract it. The paved road stretched away from her at a steep downward angle. The long dock at the end of it helped funnel the wind straight off the Tutley River and up the breezeway with enough force to make the unprepared stumble. Smiling ruefully, she held the hood of her parka down with one hand and pressed onward.

The tall facades of warehouses rose above her on either side, their details lost in the murky dawn light but their presence reassuring to a woman who'd walked this street at least once every week of her life. It was the path to unique treasure. The brine clung to her face, causing her to breathe deeply and savour the cold air numbing her nasal passages. The taste of salt on the back of her tongue meant home.

She wasn't the only one heading to the fish markets as the day's first light began to creep from the wooden dock to the dew-slicked cobbles up the hill. A couple walked ahead of her—likely elderly because of the way they were carefully supporting each other down the uneven road—and another person followed ten paces behind. They were clearly not the first, either. A few others were heading back up the street, bags of paper-wrapped bundles swinging against invigorated legs and satisfied looks on their shadowed faces. There was nothing like an early fry-up to start the day. It was the Dockside way.

At the bottom of the hill there was another road running parallel with the Tutley. It stretched for many kilometres in both directions and there were numerous docks running perpendicular to it but Synjan had come to the widest, longest and busiest one. Here, the delta was only a kilometre or so away and the river at her broadest. The trawlers that had been out all night plundering the Western Sea would roll in here before dawn and find a place in the vast web of the marina to tie on and purge their haul. There were not as many trawlers now as there had been before the Authorities came, the old timers would tell you, but enough to keep everyone fed with the fresh seafood they loved.

It didn't matter how many times she saw it happen, Synjan was always amazed at the way they sailed in, avoided running into each other and found a berth with no fuss. They were like bees in a garden, focussed on their own task and unconcerned about what their brethren were doing.

It was a completely different story once the plunder had been wheeled over to the big dock for sale. In makeshift market booths stood boxes of ice piled high with every sea creature imaginable, the salesmen spruiking at the tops of their lungs to gain attention. Their words rose and fell in waves much like the water the market was built over, blending and spiking at her eardrums as she walked the length of the old jetty.

"Octopus! Get yer octopus here!"

"Fresh ocean shark, you won't find any fresher!"

"Blue-eyed wormfish! Bigscale clingerfish! Upright seaswimmers!"

"Western black pickerels, so fresh they're still swimming!"

"Spiny knifefish – miss, can I interest you—?"

Synjan shook her head, smiling as she walked on. All the stalls had lights over them and they were still on, even though the sun was making its presence felt now. The fishmongers took rejection in stride as long as it was delivered with a smile and it was the least she could offer.

At the third last stall she stopped and pushed her

fur-trimmed hood back, watching the old man working behind a low wall of iced crates. Affection for him welled in her chest. He didn't see her at first because he was busy serving someone but when it was her turn, his wrinkled old face lit up in recognition as soon as he spied her.

"Synjan! G'dawning," he exclaimed, the words filtered by a thick white moustache that matched the fly-away strands clinging to the sides of his head.

"Good dawning Baltham, how fare you?" she smiled.

"Oh, fine, fine," he enthused, hobbling over to stand behind the crate of scallops she stood in front of. "And you?"

"Can't complain."

"No-one'd bloody listen if you did," he told her conspiratorially and they both laughed at the familiar joke.

"I see you've had a good catch today," she announced, making sure to raise her voice as she looked pointedly at the produce in front of her. Baltham's hearing was best if he was faced while he was spoken to, the noises around them interfered otherwise.

"Yes," he agreed, his dark eyes twinkling with pride as she pointed out his success. "My grandson found a new bed and brought up a basket of huge beauties just yesterday." As he spoke, he indicated the crate next to Synjan, which held some white, circular mussels almost as large as the palm of her hand.

"He's done very well," she said loudly, nodding as she considered the discs. Normally she bought twelve – four each for herself, Ellis and Urvasi – but these were so large she was pondering whether to halve or even quarter her usual order.

"He's single, you know," Baltham told her slyly, lifting a knobbled finger and poking it towards the marina at her back.

Dutifully, Synjan turned in time to see a man wearing black clothes and a black knitted hat approaching, hefting two huge white crates he could barely see around. He glanced up to properly judge where his grandfather's stall was and caught them both looking at him at that moment. Colour flared in his cheeks as he made eye contact with Synjan. He hastily looked away to negotiate the small opening between display boxes that would allow him access to the serving side of the stall.

"And very strong," Baltham added gleefully, squeezing the newcomer's bicep as he dropped his heavy load on the floor at the back of the shop.

"So I see," Synjan grinned, making a show of looking Baltham's grandson over. It took little to keep the old man happy and this wasn't the first time he'd tried to set her up with one of his grandchildren. This one was new. She had no idea where he kept producing them from.

"What're you rambling on about, Pa?" he asked as he straightened, pulling his hat off and fiddling with it. He glanced at Synjan and then looked quickly back at his grandfather.

"Come and meet Synjan!" Baltham declared, hustling the muscular young man towards the front of store. "She's single too. Synjan, this is Paddy."

"Hello, Paddy," she laughed, withdrawing her hand from the glove it was in and holding it out across the seafood.

"Hi, Synjan," Paddy mumbled, blushing again as he reached out to shake her hand. He hesitated before he made contact, probably thinking that his hands were rough and not particularly clean after a night readying seafood for sale. Her lack of height usually made people assume she was delicate.

"It's good to make your acquaintance," she insisted and pushed her hand into his, unconcerned by the condition it was in. He would find that her skin was just as rough and twice as scarred as his. "I hear you found a new bed of scallops. Did you dive for these?" she enquired politely, indicating the seafood Baltham had told her about as she released him.

"Yeah," Paddy demurred.

"Have you been diving long?"

"Since I was small," he nodded, looking slightly more comfortable since she was carrying the conversation. His hands still fretted nervously at his hat.

"In the ocean?"

"And the river, yep."

"I think you're brave to do it, to go so far down without extra air, in all that cold water," she told him, her brown eyes widening to add to the effect of how impressed she was.

"Aw, it's nothing," Paddy laughed awkwardly. There was a pause during which he might have elaborated on his diving skills or even forged ahead with talking to her in the way his grandfather clearly wanted him to. Instead it hung between them, empty and obvious until he expelled a loud breath. "Well, I need to get back to washing down the boat. You have a good day, Synjan."

"You too, Paddy," she replied as he sidled past his grandfather and out of the stall. She turned back to see Baltham shaking his head in disapproval and laughed. "He's sweet," she complimented.

"And blind, obviously," Baltham muttered, flicking a hand towards Synjan that spoke volumes.

"Well, my dad always warned me against dating fishermen anyway," she said with a reassuring wink. Baltham would know she was lying and that made it okay. They were both aware her father hadn't been around long enough to advise her on whom to date. He'd been the one to introduce her to Baltham and his special sea bounty many years ago. "They don't smell all that good and they leave you in bed alone every night."

"Only a mad man would leave *you* alone every night," Baltham piped up cheekily and now it was Synjan's turn to blush.

"Okay! How about you give me a dozen of those big ones and I get out of here before this gets really embarrassing?" She was greatly relieved when he picked up a sheet of paper and started filling her order.

After she paid and they said their goodbyes, Synjan turned and headed back along the dock. She pushed her hands into the pockets of her jacket, the sea treats tucked safely in the string bag swinging on her wrist. She looked out towards the sea as she went, admiring the way the rising sun was lighting it up and how the shadows from the markets danced across the marina. She very much loved this time of day. The fresh smells, the growing light, the promise of new beginnings. Everything looked better in the morning.

CHAPTER NINE

May Portos Be Your Guide

AFTER three days and nights Daeson had enough. His enthusiasm from the first day dwindled as the road continued and he passed fields and forest followed by more fields and forest. It was all the same; same fields on one side, same forest on the other. He wanted to go on an adventure, not walk down an endless, unchanging road. He wanted to get to Stonehearth quickly but night crowded him and forced him to stop earlier than he felt the need to. The first night he'd kept walking, using the moonlight to see the road. He'd thought himself clever until he'd grown tired and then had to set up his tent in darkness. Hurling insults at his equipment hadn't made the task easier though it had helped with the stress. The experience had him finding a campsite and setting up before nightfall.

In the middle of the fourth day, Daeson left the road and went into the forest.

He'd been planning a short rest; there were fruits in his backpack he wanted to eat before using his ration of dried meat. The apples were showing signs of bruising and the peaches were soft and over-ripe but he didn't want to waste anything. The sign at Cloverlea had tallied ten days walk to Stonehearth—but some people walked faster than others, and summer meant more time in the day to walk. He hadn't thought about his pace until now.

Practical thoughts left him when he looked into the trees.

Between tall, thick trunks, he could make out nothing but darkness. Autumnal leaves blocked the sunlight, rustling in the icy breeze. The air was cold enough to numb the tip of his nose and chill his breath as he stood, panting lightly. Bumps rose on his skin and shivers rippled down his back, making him shift beneath their unpleasantness.

Something was there. Daeson almost expected to see eyes looking back at him. He saw no eyes and heard no sounds. No, there were sounds; birds in the trees, animals moving or snorting or digging...but they were muted. Panic crept into his thoughts and he tensed, ready to run. Before he took a step, the sensation ebbed away. Other than confusion, he felt better. The absence of panic left room for curiosity and he wanted to know who or what might be looking at him. There was a part of him—a rational part—that protested this peculiar calm; it wasn't natural, he should fight it and continue down the road, faster, faster. His doubts were easily dismissed for most of him wanted to investigate.

Daeson looked up the road and was overwhelmed by how it stretched away from him, curving out of sight around a hill. He'd never fully appreciated the size of the world beyond his town until this moment. There was a difference between being told about how vast it was and seeing it for himself.

There was nothing ominous about the moment he stepped off the road. The birds continued to chirp, animals scurried away and the sun filtered soft light through the first of the trees, creating shadow-play across his face as he walked. The temperature dropped but he'd expected that, as well as the grass being wet— the sun's rays had no chance to dry it.

He glanced over his shoulder; the road was still prominent and over-bright, making it seem unrealistic. The forest's depth was reassuring by comparison. His pants legs grew wetter as they were whipped by tall grass and small scrub with each step. He thought he could see a light up ahead.

His immediate thought was of spirit-lights; things from children's tales, along with houses made of cake that lured greedy children, scary beasts that lay beneath bridges and witches that fed on dreams. None of these stories had impacted Daeson's fears; he'd known they weren't truths as a child. He'd challenged his father, who'd laughed and praised him for having good sense—neither of them understanding yet that it was Daeson's gift and not his intellect that prompted his disbelief.

The light wasn't so much a light as a glow. It was hard to define the source of it, for the trees were a little clearer when he looked south and a little darker when he looked north. Twigs and dry leaves crunched beneath his boots with each step. He was surrounded by forest now, and the light was easier to follow. It would be easier to become lost, also.

The thought stopped him. Another glance over his shoulder revealed a small patch of road but he was farther away than he'd realised. A few more steps and it would be out of sight. Daeson understood the perils of trekking into the forest. He wasn't a tracker or hunter, he couldn't identify trails or clues about dangerous animals nearby, he had no weapons to protect himself with.

Logically, he knew he shouldn't go forward, yet he didn't feel compelled to go back. His heartbeat wasn't racing, his mouth wasn't dry, he wasn't trembling. He should be—he was facing real danger—but his instincts weren't in agreement with his ability to reason.

After a short deliberation, he decided he would be a fool to ignore common sense. Still, even as he headed towards the security of the road, he felt like he was turning his back on something good.

After three hours of walking, Daeson came upon a well-used campsite by the side of the road. The vacant space was marked with a white flag, indicating a well or spring nearby. The small clearing had been flattened by many visitors over time and the ready-built fire pit looked promising. When he got near it, the smell of fires-past welcomed him.

His tent went up easily; he wasn't rushing and he'd learned the tricks to it after putting it up and taking it down over the past few days. He collected firewood before looking for water, taking one of his flasks with him. Another white flag signalled the source of the water—there was a large pipe coming a short way up out of the ground, with a heavy metal cover atop it. A long rope attached a wooden pail to the cover.

With some effort, Daeson scraped the lid aside and tossed the bucket in the hole, already tasting the sediment at the back of his throat. Grit always came when drinking drilled water. He was encouraged by the sound of trickling echoing up the pipe—if there was an underground creek, the water had a good chance of tasting clean and fresh. He hauled it up with the rope, finding the pail had a leak at the bottom, but small enough that he could easily fill his flask. A quick taste energised him and made him feel good about his decision to stop at the campsite.

He was slow to leave the well, taking time to stare at the forest again. The inexplicable sensation to travel deeper into it remained. The call was stronger here. It felt like something invisible tugging on his thoughts, encouraging him to seek out an unknown prize. The forest was darker around the well, but he could still see the white flag that signalled the way to camp. The direction he wanted to go was opposite.

A frog began croaking, its loud bellow startling Daeson. It sounded like a roar because it was echoing up the pipe. Guiltily, he pushed the cover back over the well and hoped the frog had been there all along. He took another drink and noticed a strange light as he lowered his flask.

It was like the sun had set in the middle of the forest. The trees were stark in detail, bathed in pale luminescence. There was no heat. Daeson thought of moonlight next and looked up at the sky. He found the moon, fat and full among the swirls of stars. He also saw a pillar of light reaching into the sky that hadn't been there before. It rose out from the tree-tops ahead of him, extending farther than he could see. Daeson imagined it might be something made by the Gods themselves.

Was this the thing calling him? The idea felt both ridiculous and profound. He knew it to be true but didn't understand how such a thing could be. He had to know more. What was at the base? What could be projecting a pillar of light into the sky like that?

With his water flask still in hand, Daeson moved towards the light source. Back amongst the trees he couldn't see the pillar but the light from it guided him. He thought it strange that the light didn't hurt his eyes or make him squint, yet it was immeasurably bright and bathed him in a kind of...

well-being

...emotional purity. On his earlier trek into the forest, he'd experienced the same wash of calm. Had the pillar been there then? Had the sunlight hidden it? He thought it possible, even likely. Perhaps the beacon had been there all along? No! Someone else would've seen it! It would have brought others here, those curious enough to investigate the source. Some people shied away from unnatural things, that was a certainty, but many burned with a desire to know.

He thought he was getting closer. Daeson climbed a hill and found his answer at the crest, though it wasn't much of an answer at all. Even though he didn't understand what he was looking at, he was filled with wonder. The pillar's majesty couldn't be denied. It was twice as wide as him and the strength of its beam was constant. It didn't flicker like fire, nor did it have a wider or narrower base. It started at the ground and continued into the night sky.

It wanted him to touch it.

There was no strike of inspiration or understanding. He thought questions at the light, speaking to it in his mind as though it could hear him,. He shared his soul in case that would prompt it to tell him more. He only sensed the same thing.

It wanted him to touch it.

But it was just a light. How could it *want* anything?

There were dangerous plants in the world; the kind that displayed beautiful, vivacious colours and released exotic scents to entice bugs and other small animals to it. The plant would then trap or poison them in some way, feeding off the decaying creature for sustenance. This light could be like that. It promised him safety and comfort and well-being. It promised him enlightenment. None of these promises had any substance but he believed them anyway.

He swapped his flask to his left hand, so that he could reach out with his right. His fingers stopped just before the pillar began, his nerve endings straining to sense any warmth or clues about the light. It seemed not to have a physical presence.

"What are you?" he whispered to it. He got no answer.

He reached farther, so that his fingers were bathed in white light, marvelling that his hand seemed to be glowing almost blue inside of it. Before he could snatch it back, before he felt *anything*, he was gone.

CHAPTER TEN

Sacrificed

HAWKE was warm and safe. He floated and sank while his mind struggled to make sense of it. He couldn't, so he marvelled at the sensation instead and allowed it to fill his senses because it was nice.

Hollow murmurs interrupted the silence. Someone was speaking to him from the far end of an impossibly long stone corridor. He felt the heat of the sun on his face and his corridor disappeared.

The words grew louder and Hawke frowned as he awoke, not wanting to untether himself from the pleasant sensation. A raised voice sobered him and his eyelids opened before he squinted them shut; someone was shining light directly into his face.

"He's awake," Carmen said.

He felt the sneer on his face before he rolled onto his side, shielding his eyes from the light. The ground was a smooth furnace that burned his face. He cried out and sat up. He expected fire but he saw no flickers, heard no crackles and smelled no smoke. Above him was a cloudless and vibrant blue sky—the only ball of flame in sight was up there, though its piercing light left glowing trails behind closed eyelids. He heard the others talking.

"How are the horses?"

"They've all woken up except your one."

Your one. Hawke's anger flared because he knew the reference was to Silverprint. Hawke stumbled to his feet, trying not to touch bare skin against the ground. Why did the ground feel like it was on fire? What happened to the snow?

He saw his coat on the ground—he'd been lying on it. One of the horse thieves must have taken it off him and laid him atop it as he slept. But why had he slept? He didn't remember setting up the tent or climbing into the cocoon bedding. The last thing he remembered was standing in a huddled group.

"What did you do?" Hawke shouted, blindly searching for Eddie. He pushed past someone who was reaching for him. There was a strong scent in the air that reminded him of oiled saddlery and weaponry, yet it was different. Thicker, somehow.

"Gave you nowhere to run."

The reply was hauntingly familiar to the promise Eddie had made him. Hawke straightened and got his bearings, gradually opening his eyes but the quality of light was still too harsh for him to look about normally. Sweat traced a line down the small of his back from his tunic to his pants. His clothes felt damp and stuck to him.

"You're in a different world now, Hawke Aron. You've left your home behind," Carmen said gently from somewhere behind him. He whirled around.

"I didn't leave it behind! You took me from it!"

He felt spittle fly from his lips.

"You didn't sound much pleased with your lot when we asked you," Eddie challenged. "Complained about your place as last-born son, I recall."

"Rick's on his way back," Jerrom informed them, interrupting the argument before it could properly begin. Hawke felt a knot of anguish forming in his belly and the rise of bile in his throat before he unloaded it into a steaming mess at his feet. He earned himself some disgusted sounds from the others. Carmen's hand found his shoulder and he shrugged her off.

The sound of a familiar whinny nearby made him look that way. *Silverprint.*

The horse thieves—Wanderers, whatever they wanted to call themselves—were looking away from him except for Carmen. She looked at the ground, her posture making Hawke think she was ashamed.

He hoped she hated herself. She deserved it.

"Rick's running...but I can't see anything chasing him," Jerrom said, looking in the distance where there was nothing. Carmen joined the group.

Perhaps she'd dismissed him as too sick to be concerned about because nobody was checking where he was and what he was doing. His vision had almost adjusted to the harsh light of this world and he could see everything in stark detail, though he couldn't understand it. There were piles of what he had originally thought was rubbish but he could see now was scrapped iron and steel. They were gathered into huge mounds on each side of him, and someone had turned the ground into a giant slab of stone, with odd lines that reminded him of tiling. Why would someone pave the ground? It didn't look like a road, but like a floor.

Ignoring his instinct to gawp, Hawke approached Silverprint as the horse found his feet. His horse gave a soft whinny of greeting. Hawke could see the other horses nearby; not hobbled this time but with their reins tied around a large cylinder to keep them from leaving. Hawke risked a glance at the Wanderers who were moving away from him. He hurriedly untethered the horses before scrambling up onto Silverprint's back, using the cylinder as a stool. Amazingly, the other horses didn't run off like he expected.

"No, Hawke, wait!"

Lyssa had seen him and her cry drew their attention to him. With triumph, he yelled, flicking Silverprint's reins so that he would be urged forward into the group of horses. Hawke wanted to scatter them, but Silverprint surprised him by rearing up instead. Hawke fell sideways off the saddle but held grimly onto the pommel as Silverprint turned in a half circle. Hawke got his wish as the other horses scattered, their hooves clopping loudly on the flat-stoned ground. None of them could be stopped and Hawke was peripherally aware of someone getting knocked over when they tried to capture the galloping horse. He hoped it was Eddie even though it looked like it had been one of the sisters.

Silverprint was unhappy enough with Hawke hanging off him to buck. Sweaty hands had already made the grasp difficult and so Hawke fell against the unyielding stone, scraping off skin as he watched with disbelief as Silverprint galloped away, tossing his head like he'd been possessed.

"You dumb shit! You dumb fucking *shit*!"

Hawke heard the words clearly even though he didn't understand them. There was something harsh and guttural about the new language Eddie was speaking and Hawke understood that the pain he was feeling now would be nothing like the pain Eddie would bestow on him. Carmen was close so he ran to her and she knelt down to hug him close.

The hatred he felt for her was gone in an instant as he hid his face inside of her hold and felt her muscles tense.

"We couldn't use the horses here," she said, her tone fierce. "They were useless anyway."

Eddie's continued speaking the strange language while Carmen used Boronian. He could only understand her side of the conversation.

"Not for long, and he needs to hear that he's safe...No, but he's a child...We took him so now he belongs to us."

Hawke's instinct was to push her away but he squashed it down. She might be his protector at the moment but she was wrong. He didn't belong to them. He didn't even belong to this world. He would have to find a way to leave them and get back home.

There had to be a way and if there was, he would find it.

Carmen and Lyssa were the only ones to continue speaking his language. Carmen explained that the language the others were speaking was called Authoritan. They were now in a world with many Authorities. At first Hawke had thought of his world's Enforcers and Patrolmen but Carmen shook her head. She told him that Authorities didn't protect the citizens of a world, they only cared about their own interests. The Authorities had resources and destructive weapons beyond his understanding. Carmen told him about *guns* and described them as sticks that shot out lightning, sounded like thunder and could kill someone with a single bolt. She told him about steel carriages called *cars.* She told him that the Authorities had so many people working for them that they called themselves an *army*. Hawke said very little, wanting to scoff at her stories but not daring to. He was surrounded by mountainous piles of scrap in an overly-bright world with signposts in a language he didn't understand.

Every now and then he could hear thunder rolling in the distance but Carmen explained that those were machines in the sky called *planes*. At one point Carmen had pointed up into the sky and Hawke had seen a bird soaring high overhead. She said that it was one of the planes and Hawke had watched it for as long as he could before his eyes watered. He'd been dubious but believed her by the end, for the bird had not flapped its wings once and not deviated from its course.

They came to a large fence made of thin wire that looped back and forth in a pretty diamond pattern. It looked like it could be easily scaled until Hawke looked up and saw that there were large coils of evil-looking wire at the top. There was some discussion between Eddie, Lyssa and Rick which Carmen didn't translate for him. Jerrom didn't say anything but he pointed out past the wire fence and shrugged, then unshouldered his pack and set it down. After some rifling, he pulled out a tool that could cut through the wire fence. Eddie peeled the fence back, like it was a tent flap. Hawke moved through the flap with Carmen directly behind him, and stayed close to her side as Eddie pushed the fence back into position. Hawke didn't think it would fool anybody.

"If the Authorities see the horses, they'll know we were here but there's no point advertising our position further," Carmen told Hawke. After a calculated look, she explained more than Hawke wanted to hear. "Of course if this location is manned, then they'll find us quickly no matter what we do."

"You'll be thrown in a cell," Hawke said. The idea of the Wanderers being caught and imprisoned made him feel a malicious glee.

"We'll be shot and killed," Carmen corrected. "And you will too, for being with us. Sorry."

It was the apology at the end that sank his heart into his belly and made him feel like throwing up again. He'd not thought that the Authorities might assume he was one of them. He forced his feet to move and did his best to squash his nausea as Carmen offered him water from her canteen.

The paving ended at a ditch that they worked their way down and scrambled back up the other side. The ground was dry and loose and Hawke was having a hard time walking over it. A hand extended and he looked up at Jerrom. He accepted the help and was pulled to the top with a strength he hadn't expected from the quiet man. He sensed that Jerrom didn't feel hostility towards him like Eddie did, but Hawke also doubted that he would care for him or speak up for him like Carmen had.

Jerrom and Hawke fell into step with Eddie and after a short comment by Jerrom, the group veered purposefully towards a flat topped mountain range which they called a *mesa*. Hawke thought it didn't look real, as though the pointed part of a mountain had been lopped off by a sword.

They reached the base of the mesa before nightfall. Instead of using their rationed water, Eddie and Roderick dug a deep hole into the arid earth and found water below. Hawke was stunned. Carmen explained if a desert could support plant life, like the scraggly looking shrubs that surrounded them, it meant there was water to be found below the ground. Sometimes it took them digging a few holes to find it. The water tasted surprisingly fresh. Hawke drank to the last drop, which left his mouth feeling gritty because of the last impure mouthful.

They made camp, slept and moved on. There were less planes now and Carmen explained to Hawke that the planes were following a set *flight path*. Hawke didn't understand how there could be paths in the sky but didn't question her information.

Hawke disliked nightfall, as the temperature dropped to a brittle cold. The fluctuation between hot and cold was so extreme that he couldn't decide if this world was in summer or winter. At first he'd thought summer but the cold was so biting that he could feel it in his bones. It was a different cold to snow-cold. Snow-cold could be held at bay with layers, but this cold was so intense that it sank icy fangs through all of Hawke's clothes. Only the cocoon bedding was warm enough but he'd noted the group had decided to use two tents instead of pitching three, to share body heat even though they all had their own cocoons. It only occurred to Hawke while he lay among his sleeping kidnappers to wonder why they had a cocoon sized sleeping bag that fit him. It certainly wasn't an adult sized one. Lyssa was small but not that small...could it be her outgrown one? How long had this group of Wanderers been travelling? Was that supposed to be his fate too?

He'd always wanted a life full of adventure and to be allowed to travel but this wasn't the wish he'd made. He'd wanted to go with his brother Denis, to venture out into his own world, to hear about distant places and then visit them; not to explore entirely different worlds without any way of getting home.

He was in a place of mixed emotions; resentment at being taken in the first place, yet resigned to his fate.

Another four days passed in this same manner; walking from the base of one tabletop mesa to another, moving quickly whilst in the open, hunting for food and water whilst in the shade. Water was surprisingly plentiful, and the Wanderers knew which plants were safe to eat. Many of them were prickly and brought tears to Hawke's eyes. They stung hard and deeply, causing his hands or arms to throb for hours afterward. He'd learned to be more cautious when picking the flowers from the plants or cutting the limbs from them. *Cactus*, Carmen named them.

There were other plants they didn't recognise, which were left alone. They were strange, twisted tree-shrubs filled with delicious looking purple berries. Hawke observed a kind of lizard animal eating the fallen berries so he'd bent to collect some. Jerrom grabbed him and stated a firm 'No', as though Hawke was a small child incapable of understanding further detail. Carmen later explained that cold-blooded lizards were different to warm-blooded people, and just because a lizard ate them didn't mean he could.

There was always a lookout, and even at night Hawke would hear the distant rumble of planes that left a trail of thunder in their wake. It seemed the Authorities never slept; they were always busy doing something and going somewhere in their giant machines.

On the sixth day, they came across a smattering of

small, unfinished buildings. It looked like someone had started building a town and then given up. There were no stairs leading up to the porches—just a space where they were supposed to go. The porches themselves had no overhang and there was no glass in any of the windows. Hawke swallowed the impulse to ask questions that he knew would go unanswered. He'd fallen into the rhythm of the group.

Jerrom said something in Authoritan and grabbed Eddie's wrist so the dark-skinned man would look at him, forcing acknowledgement. Eddie asked a question back and got a positive answer. From their posture and how rapidly they were speaking, Hawke deducted that something urgent was happening. He was frustrated that he didn't know what was going on.

They split into three pairs and Carmen gestured for Hawke to join her and Lyssa.

"What are we doing?" he asked.

"Exploring. Looking for supplies."

He had no idea what kind of supplies they expected to find in a half-built town but he didn't question them. They'd surprised him with their resourcefulness already.

Roderick called out to them in a hiss. Hawke looked but couldn't see him. Lyssa must have because she ran to one of the false buildings and disappeared behind it. Carmen and Hawke followed.

There were three strange looking vehicles with large black patterned wheels parked in a row. They were slightly different from one another. Two of them had a saddle that could sit one person and the third one was a bit bigger, so it could sit two. The big one had a trailer hitched to the back of it, as did one of the smaller ones.

Carmen chose the one without a wagon. Hawke was about to squash himself onto the saddle behind her when Eddie stopped him.

"No, you ride in a wagon. There's space."

Lyssa and Jerrom both took the driver positions and Roderick climbed into the other wagon. Roderick was holding two sticks that he called *rifles* and handed one over to Eddie. Hawke was infuriated that he would have to sit in the wagon behind Eddie. Worse, Eddie sat on the saddle backwards, so that they were looking at each other. He wondered why the Wanderers had been so hurried, their search speedy and silent. On the breeze he heard many voices, shouting out in rhythm together.

"Go."

All three of the vehicles roared to life and pulled away from the town at speed. Hawke had been unprepared for the fast take-off and scrabbled for a hold before he rolled over. He found purchase and held on grimly, glad that he had four sides to keep him contained, otherwise it was possible he'd be bounced right out.

Shouts sounded behind him. Hawke chanced a look and saw a group of uniformed men and women rounding the corner of the building that they were now speeding away from. Hawke was astounded to see them sprinting.

Did they think they were going to *outrun* them?

The soldiers must've known what Eddie and Lyssa hadn't when they'd hopped onto the biggest vehicle.

It was the slowest.

Carmen was fastest, being on her own, and she passed her sister and Eddie without trouble. Jerrom and Roderick were making slower progress but still had no trouble pulling away. Hawke could see that Roderick was being jostled around in the back like him. Hawke clenched his teeth so he wouldn't bite his tongue.

He could hear bangs and cracks behind them.

Eddie screamed something at Lyssa over his shoulder and she answered him in Hawke's language.

"I'm going as fast as I can!"

It was easy to figure out what Eddie had requested of her by the answer she gave.

Eddie lifted the rifle up to his shoulder and looked down along it. He was almost bounced out of the saddle when Lyssa took them over a particularly harsh bump. Hawke looked over his shoulder and saw that the soldiers were gaining on them. On foot! He was both encouraged by the soldiers and frightened of them because they were the only people that could rescue him. But Carmen had told him they would kill him too; for being with this group, for being on this world, and for having Wanderer blood.

When he looked back, he saw Eddie had abandoned the gun idea and was now reaching for something just in front of the trailer. Hawke looked down and saw the large metal pin that attached his trailer to the vehicle Lyssa was driving. He understood what Eddie was about to do.

"NO!" Hawke reached out to grab Eddie's arm, to stop him from yanking the pin up and out, but he was too late. With a sinking sensation in the pit of his belly, Hawke slowed down in the unhitched trailer as Eddie and Lyssa picked up speed. They would get away now because they had sacrificed him.

He cowered as the first of the running Authorities reached him. The soldier looked puffed but was still able to pick Hawke up by his collar and force him out of the trailer. It was all too much. Thinking that he was about to be executed, Hawke started to cry, and was confused when two of the soldiers crouched so they could look at him with compassion.

CHAPTER ELEVEN

Trading With The Enemy

HE weather wasn't working in Synjan's favour. As so often happened to coastal cities situated between an ocean and a mountain range, it was a rainy afternoon in Gredann. The temperature had dropped, causing Synjan to pull on an extra jumper before she left the Office. She'd briefly considered driving Ellis' car but the vehicle always felt so ungainly to her and the route so convoluted when she had to stick to the larger streets that could accommodate the sedan. Then there was the problem of hiding it when she got to her destination.

It was easier to take one of the bicycles and wear wet weather gear. The whole point of her making this payment to Lieutenant Bennett at the Authority base was discretion. That couldn't be maintained if she drove up to the gates, even if she was heading for one that was out of the way. The bike could be left in an alley and would be there when she came back.

Discontented birds called overhead as they flew towards cover. She made the turn out of Dockside and pressed on to the smoother roads of Portside. The rubber wheels made a buzzing noise as she pedalled uphill, squinting beneath the plastic hood of her wetcloak. The rain had slowed for the time being, turning from the drumming tumult it had been into a soft, pattering mist upon her head. It was easy to see where she was going now. The streets were sparsely populated, the citizens not yet trusting the rain's latest tempo change. It allowed her a relaxing respite in a clean-smelling, muted world, where she didn't have to worry about what the evening would hold. She wasn't going to think about that until she had to.

It was only ten minutes of riding before she reached

her destination and dismounted, leaning her bike against a hot water system. She adjusted her clothing as she walked to the end of the alley and onto a wide thoroughfare named Hibiscus Court. The name was far prettier than the road. The alley she'd come from merged with it about fifty metres from the Port Cleary fence line. She leaned against a brick wall beside the road, a nondescript person giving the impression she was looking at nothing in particular.

This road was accessed mostly by food delivery trucks and the Authorities' industrial dump trucks that collected the base's garbage. She was staring at the huge entry point that they drove through. Gate Four was always locked. It was made from heavy metal and reinforced chain link, with rolls of barbed wire along the top. The trucks that came and went on this road were fewer and less important than others, so there was no guard post or full time security checkpoint here. All drivers had been vetted and they had their own key to unlock the large padlock and thick chain that was wound through the centre of the two gates.

Synjan had a key too. She'd been given it years ago by Lt. Bennett—the head of base culinary arts—when he'd signed on to Ellis' payroll.

A pair of soldiers moved parallel to the fence doing a perimeter check and a large group beyond them spilled out of the recreation hall beside the kitchen block. One of them was bouncing a ball as they laughed and headed in to the dining hall. Despite its lack of full time security, the area around Gate Four was well populated and patrolled regularly.

The reason this was Synjan's preferred entry was because of her Wanderer talent. It allowed her to sneak onto the base undetected. She'd always liked the rebellious quality of that notion, considering how dichotomous the Authorities and Wanderers were.

Synjan was a Navigator. The Authorities had

catalogued her particular talent but because the Portal occasionally moved, any information they had became obsolete. The thing was, Navigators could do more than find a Portal. Their power gave an alternate view of life.

Synjan perked up as the roadway beyond the gate cleared. She closed her eyes to get a better look, taking a breath and focussing her thoughts. As she did, she opened her mind and the world around her was revealed differently.

No solid, inanimate structures interfered with her internal vision. Without effort, she could clearly 'see' the people in her immediate vicinity. They didn't show up as bodies at first but as small spheres of light moving around atop a blue grid. The grid spaces were uniform and denoted the gradient of the land, becoming the reference point upon which people moved.

With each increase in concentration, Synjan was able to see a greater distance or more details in the people around her. Primarily she used her talent for looking at people. It was how she'd stayed safe moving around at all hours of the night in a city crawling with Authorities. If she wanted to locate the Portal, her energy was spent covering the distances required. Though she didn't need to choose between the two aspects, the more demand placed on her talent, the more intense her focus needed to be. She was well-practised at Navigating but the harder she worked, the more tired and thirsty she became afterwards.

She'd learned her limits the hard way, growing up without a Wanderer to advise her. One time, she'd pushed herself so hard she'd blacked out, waking up in a heap on the floor of an abandoned warehouse with her target hunting *her* nearby. She'd barely escaped with her life and learned to listen to her body's demands after that.

She called this process *mapping*. That was partly because it was what her father had called it but also because she used her mind to navigate the features around her like a traveller would consult a map.

Nick had asked her to explain her talent to him when they were young. Synjan had described the way her mind opened when she closed her eyes and felt the unique undulations of the land as an immediate visceral connection. He hadn't understood how she could know the depths of an ocean she couldn't swim or the height of a mountain she couldn't scale. Synjan related it to the way a blind Docksider they both knew used his hands to 'see' people's faces. Her mind was like that blind man, moving over the topography of the land. When her eyes closed, she 'touched' the land with her mind. If she wanted to see the Portal or someone more closely, she simply moved towards it, stretching out her mental hands.

He hadn't understood and she'd grown frustrated. Something he perceived as a mental ability was more than that to her, it was an extension of herself. She did it actively, much as she would smell a flower or savour the taste of a sugar cookie. The only thing he'd really understood by the time he'd walked away shaking his head was that she could find anyone she wanted and tell them apart. It was all he'd cared to know, in the end.

When Synjan actively mapped people, they shifted from the basic globe of light into a multi-hued pattern in the shape of their body. Each person was different so, like fingerprints, their patterns were also different. Some patterns she knew as intimately as she knew faces. After so many years spying on those around her, she could ascertain what someone was doing simply from their movements.

Most people had one dominant colour with other hues – single and multiple – woven through them in a pattern, which was why Synjan named them as such. When people were active, their pattern moved at a faster pace. When they were resting, it slowed down.

Bodies were colours infused with shapes or with contrasting shades or both, colours that dulled in sickness, strobed in anger, pulsed in pain, faded in death.

Pure; that's what patterns were. No pretence, no ability to rely on outward appearance. She could tell when their physical body was impeded or affected in any way. Colours ebbed, thickened around problem areas, bled into dominant shades like ink in water. Pleasure and pain showed up the same.

When people had sex, the flow of hues fascinated her. She'd learned about such things far younger than most, due to her talent and natural curiosity. Once she'd matured, she'd understood that it was at the moment of climax where the patterns merged at their place of joining and created a momentary glow—sometimes even a new colour. Then it would fade and the patterns would hasten less, drift more and resume their own cadence again.

Her Navigator's mind was much like a lover. She saw into the beings around her, knew them intimately and understood a tempo that even they were ignorant to. She saw colours she didn't have names for, that had never found their way to appreciation by human eyes. It was an absorbing inner world.

Ellis was different and she'd seen few others like him in her life. He had what she called a solid pattern, one singular colour. Only if she examined him *really* closely could she see undulations that could be a pattern. Like black ink written on black paper. Ellis had a solid khaki pattern and she'd often thought that appropriate, since it was a colour associated with camouflage and he was intent on not being noticed by the Authorities.

She had no idea why aberrations such as solid patterns existed amongst the kaleidoscope of the masses but she often wished for more of them. They were easier to remember. She also wished she could recall the patterns of her parents and sister but they were lost in the mists of a child's traumatised beginnings. It was something she tried not to think about too often.

Avoiding Authorities or sneaking into places illegally was not what her Navigating talent was meant for, of course. They were incidental perks. Her talent was truly designed for locating the Wanderer Portal. Every time she closed her eyes to map around her, it was there, at the periphery of her awareness.

It called to her sometimes in her dreams, taunting her with its beautiful swirl of shades and colours, enchanting her with its rhythm, hypnotising her with its promise. There were nights when she'd woken up gasping, already getting out of bed, her blood singing through her veins as the Portal lured her closer. Mostly it was far away but there'd been times in her life when it had been just outside Gredann and those times were torture. Big and bold, it dominated her if she allowed it, guided her when she needed it, comforted her when she craved it. It caused an unusual sensation in her body that was like two heartbeats, two body rhythms, like another entity just there, beyond normal sight but waiting to burst in on her senses whenever she used her talent.

She held the intimate secrets and the patterns of the people around her, while the Portal held *her*.

At the moment, it was closer than she'd have liked, probably a score of kilometres south of Poworth, which was five hundred or so kilometres south of Gredann. That was comforting in a way, too. To know she could travel to it in a day was almost like knowing the spirits of her family were watching over her.

For now, Synjan concentrated on all the patterns she could see between her and the gate, and then from the gate to the pattern she identified as Lt. Bennett's. He was a useful contact as he imported all sorts of unusual products for his chefs and his orders weren't closely scrutinised. He smuggled in small to medium-sized contraband at a reasonable price and was also a semi-reliable intelligence trader. Since he was only ten years off retirement, he was always keen to increase the contribution Ellis was making to his retirement fund. He was easily persuaded to go above and beyond.

She needed to enter the offices behind the kitchen to get to him. It was a mildly challenging location to access; there were plenty of staff members moving about and she wasn't wearing a uniform but there were no locked doors.

The perimeter patrol had moved north and the path to the kitchen was clear. Synjan jogged to the gate and withdrew her key. She slipped in and re-locked the padlock behind her—that was always the trickiest part from the inside and the rain slicking the metal didn't make it any easier. At the rear of the kitchen offices she used the plastic swipe-key Lt. Bennett had given her to enter. If she was caught in this building, she had no doubt she'd be put in a position where she'd have to decide what lengths she'd go to in order to protect the secret of her blood.

As she moved, she mapped continually. She couldn't close her eyes longer than a blink but that was all it took to ascertain who was close and on the move. In order to predict movements, she was looking at the complete patterns of those in the building, twenty-three in all. It was more strain mentally but it was a skill she'd been forced to perfect. Extended exercises such as these made her dehydration more extreme, but she was also experienced enough to know that she'd make it back to the Office before she drank the water required to replenish her.

Compared to some of the jobs she'd had, this was nothing.

After a short game of hide and go sneak, she let herself into Lieutenant Bennett's office, startling the older gentleman with her stealth.

"Girl, I swear you get quieter by the day," he breathed, pressing a pudgy hand to his chest and leaning back in his plush chair.

Synjan lowered the hood of her wetcloak. "Or you get more complacent every day, Lieutenant," she returned, unbuttoning her cloak enough so that she could reach inside and withdraw the envelope filled with cash.

He glared at her, obviously disliking her impertinence but taking the payment she offered. "What's this for, again?" he queried, lifting the paper flap to peer inside. After all the years she'd been delivering him packages like this, Synjan had no doubt he could count it with just a glance. He also knew exactly what it was for; he had a habit of opening up a line of conversation about it so he could complain if he felt it insufficient.

"It's your monthly stipend...with a small bonus. My boss appreciated the departmental newsletters you collected for us, to keep us up to date," she informed him, sickened by the greedy light that entered his eyes as he realised the whole wad of cash was his to keep. The Wanderer in her hated that they *paid* Authorities for anything. The realist swept the hate aside.

"Well, tell him thank you. Or her," he hinted, maintaining eye contact as he ran a fingertip across the edge of his earnings.

The lieutenant knew very little of the organisation he fed information to because Synjan was his only contact. Bennett didn't even know her name and just called her 'girl'. He obviously suspected she was part of Omerri's setup. Many of the things he'd smuggled in had been for her and the Queen of Hearts was well known at the base. Synjan disapproved of Ellis using his contacts to spoil Omerri, but now she had an inkling that her boss' pathetic devotion might actually be providing an unexpected misdirection.

Ellis would be tickled by this information when she told him.

"Here's our next order," she announced and dropped another note on his desk. It was typed and printed on Authority letterhead, just in case the information was ever compromised.

"Time frame?" Bennett queried, ignoring the demand list in favour of his money counting.

"A fortnight."

He looked up at her now, a disgruntled expression on his face. "You're kidding, right?" he snapped, shoving his money into the drawer of his desk and scanning the sheet.

"We believe you can do it, but a month is acceptable, if necessary. The sooner you do it, the larger your reward will be. We'll see how you go." She mapped to see who was around outside the office. It was a good time to leave so she turned without a farewell and left Lieutenant Bennett to his thoughts.

CHAPTER TWELVE

In The Hands Of The Authorities

THE armchair was so big that Hawke's feet couldn't touch the ground unless he scooted forward. He'd tried that once already, so that his tiptoes at least could touch the floor, but the giant across the desk from him had glared. Hawke sat up and didn't risk slouching again.

The man reminded him of his father, commanding the room from his grand chair. He barked out short, crisp sentences and did a lot of staring that made Hawke feel overwhelmed. He was flanked by two men that seemed eager to please him because they answered him quickly and bent eagerly to peer at any of the papers the big man shook at them.

All three were dressed in the same dark blue uniform, except the decorations on their jackets were different. The giant had the most decorations, with many lines and triangles on his sleeves and badges of colours on his chest. The man on his right had fewer lines and triangles and no badges. Hawke liked him best because he was the only one who smiled. The third man—without any decorations on his uniform—translated for Hawke without emotion.

"I want to go home," he said again. His demand had been ignored the first few times, then met with platitudes. This time, none of them acknowledged his words. The familiar anger and betrayal rose up in his throat and he held onto it because it was better than the greasy, nauseating sensation of fear.

It seemed his future was now out of his hands. They'd already processed him, pricked his finger to dot his blood onto a clear rectangle, and asked him a myriad of questions. He'd had to tell his story multiple times, in multiple ways and now they were talking around him. When would they start showing him the respect he deserved? They knew he was a lord and what estate he'd come from. Why couldn't they just put him back?

"I'm not the criminal. Those horse thieves were the criminals. I haven't done anything wrong, why are you keeping me here? It's time for me to go home."

The interpreter glanced at him. "Be quiet now." The bastard hadn't relayed his message. How was he supposed to communicate his needs when this buffoon was in the way? He wished the smiling man could understand him instead.

The giant began signing documents while speaking. Hawke felt like he was losing the opportunity to influence his outcome.

"What's he signing? I'm not signing anything. I don't care what—"

The giant looked at him and Hawke forgot what he was going to say. He'd seen that look before, on Eddie's face. It was the expression of a man who saw him as a means to an end.

Fear took over.

Hawke drew up his legs, hugging them. The friendly man looked down at the documents the giant was signing and interrupted the process. There was a lot of conversation that sounded like arguing except neither of them grew angry. He didn't know how anybody could have an argument without getting angry.

Eventually the friendly man was handed some documents that he looked very pleased with. He and the interpreter moved around the desk after performing a hand gesture for the giant's benefit and then Hawke was summoned off the armchair.

He was steered out of the room by his shoulder and into the corridor where the pair of men walked in step with him. He felt like a prisoner between two guards. Hawke listened to the footfalls and each step constricted his throat until it was difficult to draw breath. His heart pounded in his ears and he grew dizzy. He groped for the friendly man and his fingers clutched at a jacket. The man crouched down and peered at him, concerned.

"Am I being locked up?" Hawke asked. The interpreter translated for him.

"No."

"Are you taking me home?" Hawke asked hopefully.

"No."

It sounded so final. Hawke hitched in deep, shaking breaths that he couldn't control. He was held until the anxiety passed. He was embarrassed that he'd appeared weak in front of the soldiers.

"Why not?" He disliked the whine he could hear in his voice but he couldn't do anything about it.

"Because you know about other worlds."

"What does it matter?"

After the translator relayed his question, the friendly man sighed.

"Let's talk more outside."

Hawke didn't want to go outside. He didn't want to talk about it. He didn't want to stay here. He wanted to go home but nobody was going to do that for him. His hope was quickly fading.

They walked down a number of corridors until they reached the manicured lawns outside. The trio moved down a side path to a small parkland. The friendly man gestured with the document folder for Hawke to sit upon a slatted bench. Hawke's attention diverted to the small duck pond nearby. He stared at the ducks on it, marvelling that the animals on this world were the same as on his. He didn't think there were ice-serpents here though, the Authorities had been quite astonished by his recount of how he'd seen one take Lyssa's horse.

"Let's start over," said the man with a smile. "I'm Lieutenant Cayden and you are Hawke Aron Donovan."

The strange way that Cayden said his name captured Hawke's attention.

"No, I'm Hawke Aron *of Donovan Court*," he corrected.

"Not of Donovan Court. That's your *title*. We just use names here, so we shall use your family name. Donovan."

Hawke was sullen. The Wanderers had taken his world away and the Authorities wanted to take his identity away.

"That's not who I am," Hawke spat.

"It is now."

Hawke stared petulantly at Cayden.

"There's no point looking at me like that, it won't change anything. You're now a ward of the Authorities."

"What's a ward?"

"It means you're under our care. We will house you, clothe you and educate you until you're an adult."

Hawke's mouth dropped open and he turned away. Only the occasional quack from the ducks broke the silence as he struggled to process the direction his life had taken. Everything was different now. He was on his own.

"When will it end?" he asked, his question misinterpreted.

"You'll be an adult at sixteen if you're interested in civilian life, but your dependence can end at fourteen if you choose to enlist. There will be many more opportunities for you if you take this path."

Really? He was being pitched to now? Not only were they refusing to send him home, but they wanted him to sign up?

"Opportunities? I was told you kill Wanderers!"

Cayden blinked rapidly, a frown marring his features.

"Well—"

Hawke didn't give him a chance to continue.

"What do you want from me?" he demanded.

Cayden looked resigned. It took him a long time to reply this time but Hawke didn't interrupt again. He wanted to know the answer.

When Cayden spoke again, there was a long string of words that made the interpreter look increasingly uncomfortable. Hawke's interest was piqued but he also felt anxious.

"Since your blood test came back with the Wanderer gene and you've told us that you're a Shielder, it's an ability that the Authorities haven't fully explored. It would be a good decision for you if you help the alchemists figure out how you use your powers."

"How would that be a good decision?" Hawke scoffed. "Alchemists kill more people than they help."

Cayden looked confused and he and the interpreter had a discussion between themselves before Hawke received a better explanation.

"*Alchemists* is not the right word to describe these people but there's not a word in your language for what they do."

"But an alchemist is the closest thing?" Hawke guessed. That was bad enough.

"Yes."

Hawke looked dubious.

"It'll probably just be more blood tests," the interpreter said.

"So I give more of my blood on those little rectangles and that's it?"

"Sure."

"Lieutenant Cayden said I had to help them figure out how I *use* my powers," Hawke accused, feeling the interpreter was not the one who should be answering his questions. The superior officer obviously felt the same way because he spoke then, prompting another bout of talking over Hawke's head. He was pleased when Cayden's tone became chastising and the interpreter looked apologetic.

"He doesn't know details of the tests but you're unique," the interpreter finally said, his lips compressed stiffly. "They won't harm you."

Although he had no desire to comply, Hawke was pleased they recognised that he was special. "I want to be rewarded," he announced.

Cayden chuckled when the message was relayed to him and his eyes twinkled as he responded. "You will be. Especially if you commit to the Authorities. It will put you in a very powerful position."

Hawke liked the sound of that and he supposed that there might be a bright side to his deplorable situation after all. He was the only Shielder they had.

"Where will I live?"

"In a boarding school on the world of Varrell. It's an Authority-shaped world where they know about other worlds—we call them Charlie worlds."

"What do you call Boronia?"

"It is classified as Limbo. Authorities have discovered it but taken no action."

"Because they don't know about other worlds," Hawke finished, swallowing down the urgent, overwhelming sensation of despair that rose in him. He missed his world and his family with an ache so sharp it threatened to split his heart in two.

"Correct."

"Will I ever see it again?"

Cayden's expression was soft as he reached out and squeezed Hawke's shoulder. He had his answer.

He looked away again.

They stayed and watched ducks paddle around until Hawke said he was ready to leave. They returned to the building. Hawke walked silently alongside Cayden, giving his interpreter nothing to do or say. They walked through halls with rugs that met perfectly with the walls. It was like they'd been cut especially for the floor itself. The pattern of repeating diamonds—though pleasant—was boring. Hawke preferred the visions of battles or hunting or festivals on the rugs that decorated the floors of Donovan Court manor.

They trod on this until they reached a lush seating area. The armchairs were plush and could be manipulated with a switch that whirred a footrest up. Hawke delighted in pressing the button that lifted the platform for his feet and set them down again. He expected to be reprimanded for playing with it but nobody did. He kept doing it until they were approached by another uniformed man holding more papers. Cayden stood up to receive them and added them to his folder. He also received a rectangular card that he attached to a corded rope before turning to Hawke.

"Hawke, this is your lanyard. Put it over your head please."

The word *lanyard* wasn't one that had a Boronian match so Hawke heard it spoken again via the interpreter. He did as asked, then looked at the smooth card attached to it. There was an accurate portrait of himself on it, his fingerprint and some markings that he understood was the written language. He asked his interpreter what was on the card and was told it had his name, birth date, hair and eye colour and height, his home world and his assigned world, and that his sponsor was Lieutenant Cayden. Hawke didn't know what the word *sponsor* meant. Like lanyard, the interpreter had simply used the Authoritan word.

His interpreter shook hands with Cayden before they made a hand gesture to each other.

"Anything you would like me to tell the Lieutenant before I go?"

"You're not coming?"

"No."

He watched as the fellow turned and left them,

taking all ability to communicate with Lieutenant Cayden along with him.

Cayden took Hawke into the next room. It was huge and housed a large machine. Hawke was reminded of the scrapyard, though the thing in the middle of the room looked new and shiny. Soldiers were patrolling nearby, holding weapons. A diamond floor rug made a path to a door set into the machine's side. They walked along it to a female soldier standing guard. She instructed Hawke to press his hand onto a transparent booklet. When it glowed, Hawke flinched away. He was urged to try again and held his hand there a second time while the booklet glowed. When it chirped he was allowed to take his hand off. Hawke watched with interest as Cayden touched his own plastic card to the booklet so it would chirp, and then pressed his hand upon it.

They were allowed through the door.

Inside Hawke saw many rows of long, narrow chairs that were affixed on posts. There were buttons and switches on the armrests with a little hole at the end. They looked too tall for him to climb up on and he didn't like the idea of being lifted up onto them. He followed Cayden to the very back and watched as Cayden pressed a button, lowering the chair all the way down. It was low enough for Hawke to get on by himself. Cayden pointed out the button so Hawke could press it, lifting the chair up to its full height while Cayden selected the chair beside him. He was still far enough away that Hawke wouldn't be able to reach him.

Hawke played with the other switches, adjusting the chair in unusual ways. The only one he didn't like was when a lump pressed into his lower back. He played with them until he was approached by a smiling uniformed woman. She spoke the language everyone else was speaking but her tone was soft and comforting. She and Cayden exchanged a few words and then she crouched down and offered Hawke a blue and green marble. He took it and rolled it between his fingers before he noticed her point at her mouth.

"No."

Cayden made a gesture that attracted his attention and held his palm out. Hawke put the marble in it and watched as Cayden put it in his mouth and swallowed. The woman already had another one to offer Hawke and she picked up a bottle of water from out of a side pouch attached to Hawke's chair. He took it.

With both of them watching him encouragingly, Hawke put it in his mouth and washed it down with the water. He wished the interpreter had stayed long enough to explain what the marble was. He received a pat on his knee for doing as he was supposed to and then the woman went away.

His eyelids started to feel heavy and he struggled against the urge to sleep, even though he knew it had something to do with the marble he'd swallowed. He looked over at Cayden who was already dozing in his chair. Hawke relaxed and let sleep steal him away.

There was a queasy churning in his gut that Hawke didn't care for and his mouth filled with spit. He swallowed, disliking the slimy sensation that was left behind. He didn't think he would throw up but if the sensation didn't pass, it would become too difficult to suppress the urge. A chill ran down his spine, forcing his upper body to spasm.

"Hawke?"

He opened his eyes and it was too bright. Everything was white and it hurt his eyes. He made a protest and his memory played tricks on him, transporting him back to the hot world with the ground made of stone.

"Hawke."

The voice was familiar but he couldn't recognise it. Hawke squinted and was surprised when the glare moved away. The room dimmed and he tried sitting up but the dizziness was so strong that he fell back.

Some words were said that he didn't understand and then a woman's voice could be heard.

"If you need to purge, there's a bucket on your right. You will feel better if you use it."

He thought of Carmen and dismissed her. This voice was different. Not his mother, nor his sister. His family were on another world and he had no way of reaching them.

He turned to the right and threw up. The woman was right; he did feel better.

He was given some juice to drink which took the unpleasantness away.

He was in a room coloured mint green. Paintings of squares and triangles hung on the walls. He stared at them uncomprehendingly before his gaze tracked movement. Cayden crouched beside him, looking concerned. A plump woman dressed in white had her back to Hawke and was doing something at a table on wheels. It looked like the sweets trolley that the servants wheeled in after dinner time. Hawke doubted there were any goodies on this woman's tray. He looked at the small, empty bottle of juice in his hand and had to re-assess.

"I understood you," he told the woman. She turned around and he saw a harsh expression on her lined face. She was much older than his mother but didn't appear frail in any way. He thought she looked like an old warrior.

"I should hope so."

"You sound like you're from the South."

She took the bottle from him and the corners of her mouth twitched up. It made her look less harsh.

"Are you allowed to go back there?" he asked.

"One rotation was enough."

Her answer was bewildering and he lapsed into silence. Cayden and the woman spoke next and Hawke waited for a lull in their conversation before he spoke again.

"Did we move through worlds?" he hazarded.

"Yes. Was that not told to you beforehand?" she snapped. Hawke was glad her ire seemed not to be directed at him but he felt protective of Cayden when she glared his way.

"I don't like their way of moving through worlds as much as the Wanderers' one," he said. The woman looked back at him, her eyes wide but her expression angry.

"Don't say that, don't ever say that," she chastised.

Cayden asked a question and the woman said something that Hawke didn't think Cayden accepted. He gave them a calculated look but let it go. There was little else he could do.

When Hawke felt good enough to sit up properly, a black armband was put on him, puffed up painfully tight and then released after some beeping. A cold, metal thing was inserted into his ear and he had to hold still until it was removed. He was handed a very simple jigsaw puzzle to put together. Once it was done, he was given two small white pills to drink with water. Finally he was told he was healthy and to go with Lieutenant Cayden.

There were numerous corridors that they walked down before they exited. This time there was no garden opposite the building, only stone ground, benches, flagpoles and a sculpture of a triangle inside a set of circles. Hawke stared at it long enough for Cayden to comment.

"Authority logo," he said.

The word made no sense to Hawke but he didn't

question it further. He got a touch on the shoulder and then Cayden steered him to their ride. They both climbed into the back of a low black vehicle. The driver in the front seat had a wheel to drive it, like steering a ship. Cayden reached across and strapped Hawke in before doing the same thing to himself.

At first they moved slowly and Hawke had another look at the 'logo' sculpture as they circled it. Once they left the driveway, the window showed the speed they were travelling at before it began to go much too fast. It was peculiar how posts and trees zipped by, indicating their great speed.

Hawke looked at the uniformed man beside him instead. He thought Cayden wasn't much older than Umber, who'd begun running the estate alongside their father upon his twentieth birthday. Umber knew a lot about how to manage the property and all of the political and financial dealings that came with it. Hawke wondered how much Cayden knew about the workings of the Authorities and decided it must be a lot.

Outside the window was a lush green landscape dotted with large houses. Their grandeur reminded him of Donovan Court, though their grounds seemed impossibly small. He could see other vehicles of different shapes, colours and sizes passing them. He watched them all with mounting interest, wondering about the people inside them, who they were and where they were going. Did they worry about the same things his family worried about? What kind of lives did these people lead?

"Here's your school, Hawke. Willets Academy."

He didn't understand what Cayden said other than his name but it made him look. There was a long driveway, similar to the kind that led to his manor. The fence was tall and imposing, with pointed spear-tips. The wheels crunched over gravel, sounding ominous. His focus shifted and he saw the face of a small, frightened boy. He frowned at his reflection.

His stomach churned, only this time it wasn't with nausea. The vehicle was travelling slowly towards a very wide building, which was dirty cream in colour, as though it had once been white but then washed with grey water. Hawke counted six windows atop one another. Five raised floors and possibly a rooftop that he could walk on, because the top of the structure looked flat.

There was little decoration or pomp about the school. It was extremely practical. He'd thought with the sculptures and gardens he'd seen on the bases, the Authorities would create a school with more character. It looked like somebody had thoughtlessly left a giant block of sandstone in the middle of a field.

Hawke wasn't impressed. It was devoid of that extra level of care. To live in this building felt like he would be living among other outcasts. He was being sidelined; dumped in a place to be forgotten about. His anger returned with so much force that his head pounded with it. He was humiliated. He was indignant.

This was going to be his life now. He screwed his eyes shut and palmed them. The darkness helped the pounding in his head but got him attention he didn't want.

"Hawke?"

The concern in Cayden's voice was no longer comforting, it was irritating and meaningless. He heard a click beside him and looked over to see that Cayden had unfastened himself and was scooting over.

"No!" Hawke said more forcefully than he intended. Cayden backed away and pressed his lips into a thin line, holding back a comment that Hawke didn't think he'd understand anyway. He felt bad for the Lieutenant because he was the only nice person in this whole mess, but Hawke wasn't interested in apologising or being accommodating. He struggled with the strap across his chest and lap, fingers clutching at the clip that held them all together but he couldn't work it out. When he stopped trying with a huff and glared out the window, he felt and heard Cayden reach out and unclip it for him.

He followed Cayden out of the vehicle and expected it to leave as soon as the door was closed but it remained where it was. Hawke kept his eye on it for a lingering moment before he joined Cayden who was standing slightly apart from him.

Hawke sighed and nodded to indicate he was ready. He wasn't ready, but together they entered Hawke's new home.

CHAPTER THIRTEEN

The Depths Of The City

DAESON awoke to the raucous chatter of hundreds of birds. He listened to the cacophony of twitters and whistles in wonder. In spite of the noise, he felt relaxed and unburdened. It had been many seasons since he'd woken up refreshed; multiple worries and anxieties had woven their way into his dreams at night and spawned irritable days.

Something sharp dug into his back. He sat up and reached around, contorting himself until he plucked a stick off his tunic. It came unwillingly, taking some threads hostage. There were peculiar round thistles on it that he didn't recognise. Daeson tossed it aside and brushed more twigs and leaves off himself before standing to do a better job of it. He saw a conical brown object on the ground and stared at it for a long moment. Was it plant or animal?

Daeson stepped forward cautiously and nudged it with his foot. It rolled away, making him think it was a kind of seed, but it was huge and like nothing he'd seen before. There was a surge of confusion as he turned in a circle, looking up at unfamiliar trees. They went beyond strange and into the unfathomable.

The trees were *wrong*. They smelled funny. They were too tall. Their leaves weren't normal but needle-like. They were clustered closely together, hiding the sun's position from him. What little sky he could see had a strange tinge to it that he didn't associate with sunrise.

Daeson looked around but couldn't see his tent or the white flag that marked the well. He did see his water flask a little way off. He went to it and picked it up, turning it uneasily in his hands.

He wanted to pack up and leave. He remembered

walking uphill so why was he at the bottom of a slope? Perhaps he'd slipped and knocked himself out, then rolled down the other side of the hill. Daeson worked his way up the slope, figuring he would be able to see his tent or the white flag of the well if he made higher ground. At the top of the rise he emerged from the protective circle of the trees and stood in a clearing. It was unusual how suddenly it had happened—normally trees thinned out.

His unobstructed view of the sky presented a new problem.

The sun was *setting*, not rising. Hadn't it already set? Had he slept a full day? Where was his tent? Where was the road? Where was *he*?

Lots of questions without answers. Everywhere he looked made him feel like he'd been ambushed by a foreign land.

The grass he stood on was neatly clipped. Flowers and bushes grew in clusters that looked planted, not natural. He saw a smooth and narrow path wending around some gardens where it forked in three directions; he could see from here that one of the paths led to a gazebo.

A *gazebo*? He stared fixedly at it. His thoughts couldn't move beyond why the latticed construction was there and where it had come from. If it hadn't been for the siren that started up, he might've been staring at it until night fell.

The wail gradually rose in both volume and pitch. Feeling vulnerable without the rest of his things but not knowing how to find them, Daeson headed towards the noise. There was nothing else for him to do, nowhere obvious for him to go. There were no other people here but it looked like the kind of place that would attract folk. Someone was responsible for clipping the grass, though how they managed to clip so much of it and so evenly was beyond his comprehension.

At the fork, he took the path opposite the gazebo and it led him to the thing producing the noise. It was a tall iron post with four flared boxes at the top. He didn't understand how it could be so loud when there were no moving parts. The sound began to wind down until it disappeared, leaving silence in its wake.

The quiet was so deafening that it took his hearing a moment to adjust. Eventually he heard other sounds; a clanging bell, a rumble that sounded similar to distant thunder, and voices. The words they spoke were delivered to him on the breeze, broken and muted. They were too far away for him to make out but the wind gave him their direction.

He continued down the path, where it ran parallel to a wall that he assumed was the boundary of the gardens. It was too tall and smooth to climb but he could see the rooftops of buildings beyond. Was this Stonehearth?

He checked that his pouch was still looped on his belt. It was there and fat with coins. Inside his shirt he could feel the stiff paper that was the deed to his farm. He'd lost his tent and equipment except for his flask, but at least he could rent a room and buy food while he figured out where he was and what had happened.

The path widened and merged with another before it delivered him to a gate. It was shut and a chain was draped around it, a padlock holding everything together. His heart sank until he noticed that the padlock was open. Why would someone chain a gate and not lock it?

Perhaps there was somebody in the gardens with him. Daeson looked around but couldn't see anyone. The gardens were expansive though, with multiple paths leading to unknown locations. He didn't want to wander around aimlessly, looking for someone who might arrive at the gate and end up locking him in.

Daeson removed the padlock and unwrapped the

chain. The gate was well maintained, it swung outward easily and silently. Once he was on the other side, he rewound the chain after himself but left it unlocked, as he'd found it.

He turned and looked at the buildings before him. All of them were made of wood. If this city was Stonehearth, then shouldn't all the buildings be made of stone?

He knew names didn't always work in such ways, but Stonehearth was in the same region as Cloverlea, where the locals named things as they saw them. Daeson supposed Cloverlea meant nothing anymore, since every clover filled meadow had been turned into farmland. Stonehearth was supposed to have a quarry nearby, the town might have been named after that.

Doubt nagged at him. He'd had many days' walk to go before reaching Stonehearth. He couldn't have managed to get here in a single night, even if he'd been sleepwalking.

He couldn't be in Stonehearth. He was somewhere else. Perhaps one of the towns on the way there. He would have to reserve judgment until he met someone to ask. With no more voices on the wind to follow, Daeson set forth into the city, choosing a path at random.

The streets were as strange as the trees. They were narrow and slightly angled into the centre. It must not rain much in this city, if their guttering was so impractical as to channel water away down the middle of the street. Buildings towered on either side of him, making him feel small and vulnerable. The sensation persisted as he turned the corner into a wider street.

The buildings here looked more like houses and were lit from within. Daeson could hear laughter or murmurs of speech as he passed windows and saw silhouettes through thin curtains. He should have felt better that there were people here but they seemed distant and inaccessible. He knew he could knock on one of the doors and ask for help if he couldn't find an inn but the idea of asking a stranger for help was unpalatable.

What if he couldn't understand them? What if their language was as strange to him as the trees, the birds and the season?

When he'd left Cloverlea for Stonehearth, he'd been racing against winter. It would be harder to salvage a farm during the harshest season and selling it off-season would attract a lower price. All of this knowledge seemed like irrelevant now because it was hot. *Summer* night hot. It was as though winter had come and gone and taken spring with it. It left another quandary. How old was he supposed to consider himself, since he was a winter baby? On the first day of winter, he was to count himself sixteen...was he sixteen yet? Was he supposed to call himself a summer baby now?

An interruption to his thoughts came in the form of a young woman dressed in dark clothing. She'd stepped into the street from a small opening between two buildings, too small for Daeson to realise a person could fit. She was within arm's reach of him. What had she been doing in there? Hiding?

She looked his way and flinched. Even though they were between wall lanterns and night was taking hold, he could see the shock on her face. She hadn't expected to see him. He doubted she'd expected to see anybody.

Daeson had figured out the folk in this city stayed indoors at night. He thought it had something to do with the wailing post, that it signalled nightfall. What was so terrifying that they all locked themselves up at night? What was he supposed to be scared of?

"Good eve," he said. She sprinted away. "Wait!" he called, frustrated that the first person he'd seen hadn't stayed to answer his questions.

He chased her.

He managed to keep her in sight after she ducked down a narrow lane but she was increasing the distance between them. She was *fast*. After he exited the street and turned down the next one, he realised that chasing her was a terrible idea. She was hardly going to help him.

He stopped and placed a hand on his waist, looking up at the night sky—surprisingly devoid of stars—and slowed his breathing. He had stamina from working the farm but running great distances was not something he was used to. The streets were absurdly long here and their unusual slope made them more difficult to run through.

The air smelled different now and it caused his nose to wrinkle in distaste. Instead of the scent of greenery or the dry smell of the city, there was a salty quality that he could taste. Accompanying it was the overpowering stink of fish. The stench of long-dead seafood was everywhere, seeming to come from the wooden walls around him, the stones at his feet, the air above. He took a drink from his flask but couldn't wash the odour away.

In an effort to escape the smell, he continued down the street. It was wider than most of the others. The inn at Cloverlea was on the main street so it could easily be found by travellers. He hoped the same practice was applied here.

He stopped and turned when he heard a noise approaching from behind. There was nothing to see. The sound was like stones being ground into powder in the throat of a giant beast and it was growing louder. The sound was bouncing off the walls, disorienting him. He hurried into a side street and peered out, not wanting to meet the thing that was gargling gravel.

Light washed over his face and pierced his eyes. He squinted and retreated, running blindly through the street he'd chosen to hide in. All he could see were shadows and blooms of light and ended up running into something solid. He bounced off it and winced as he landed hard on slippery stones and rustling sacks, his back stabbed by a pile of stiff paper boxes. His flask flew out of his hand and rolled away. He couldn't see where it went because none of the wall lanterns were working in this side street.

He struggled to his feet as the crunching, grinding sound found him, bathing him in lights again. This time he shadowed his eyes with a raised arm and could make out two bright lanterns hanging on the bottom of a horseless wagon.

"Stop!" a man shouted. Daeson couldn't understand the purpose of the order since he was already standing aside, looking at them. He wasn't going anywhere. He was relieved by the voice, now that he understood the strange noise wasn't coming out of a living thing...or maybe it was, because the wagon was growling menacingly in wait. Figures jumped down from it. Daeson took a step back as they approached and was yelled at again. He didn't understand—the words were different this time. By the tone he assumed they were giving him more orders.

"...his clothes."

Two men closed in on him, carrying bulky sticks and dressed in dark uniforms. The lanterns on the wagon were too bright to make out details but Daeson could see one of the men had a stripe on his shoulder while his companion had nothing. They were both wearing bowls strapped onto their heads and were pointing their bulky sticks at him, advancing in a strange squatting posture.

They spoke to one another and then demanded a question of him, one of them gesturing with their stick, almost prodding him with it. Daeson didn't know how to respond; the language was familiar enough that he thought they might be asking him if he was from here but he couldn't know for sure. He'd rather give no answer than the wrong one.

"Sorry," he said, hoping that it was a word they'd know.

"Barrington! Bring me the cuffs."

Daeson didn't think cuffs were the same thing here as in Cloverlea—he doubted they were trying to give him laced hems for a sleeved tunic. He apologised again, attempting another step back only to be stopped by the garbage on the street.

He heard the booted feet of another man landing on the ground beside the growling wagon.

"Don't move!" the first man said. Daeson shrank away from a reaching hand. Something clinked on the ground behind the strange men, distracting them. "Flash!" he screamed. Daeson was startled by the shout and started running.

The world exploded and turned white.

Daeson stumbled to his knees and fell forward, scraping his palms on the ground. It felt like he'd been driven down by the force of sound. There was a high pitched ringing in his head, similar to the wailing post but worse because of the throbbing pain that accompanied it.

He couldn't see. Blooms of light filled his vision once more. Everything was shadowy grey, only the slightest contrasts helping as he felt his way around. He blinked and crawled, his palms were hot and itchy but unimportant for now. He was relieved when he found the paper boxes and sacks from before. He found the wall next and used it to stand up. By the time he was on his feet, he realised he could see the brickwork.

There were loud popping sounds behind him. Daeson turned to see two people lying on the street, washed in lantern light. One of them was dressed in a uniform while the other had a rope tied around his torso. They looked like they were hurt. Maybe they were dead.

There was nothing he could do to help them. Movement across the narrow street caught his attention and there were more popping sounds, though the noises were getting louder and sharper. There were other men with different looking sticks, pointing them at the horseless wagon. One of its lanterns went out, engulfing Daeson in shadows.

Confused by what was happening and thinking that this was his best chance to escape, Daeson ran. The popping stopped and muffled shouts could be heard at his back but he didn't want to know what had happened. He'd seen enough.

The street was very long and without any turns; the walls of buildings towered over him with no doors or windows that he could pry open. He wasn't even halfway when he heard the roar of the horseless wagon behind him. The sensation of being chased knotted his stomach and made his legs feel rubbery. He was unable to put on more speed and in his panic he couldn't even run straight, he kept rubbing his shoulder against the wall. The wagon caught up to him easily and kept pace beside him. Daeson looked at it but couldn't see anything. He stopped running to go in the opposite direction but the carriage squeaked to a halt and he was tackled. He landed roughly on his back, the air knocked out of him. It hurt to draw breath. The men bundled him into the wagon in spite of his weak protests and attempts to push them away.

"He's...him over...heavy," one of them panted, shoving Daeson onto the floor of the carriage. He pulled Daeson's arm back and bent it up between his shoulder blades, causing Daeson to cry out. The pain had the sobering effect of stopping him from fighting back—this was obviously what they'd intended with the hold.

"...he's wearing."

It was strange how some of their words were the same as his. What did such a thing mean? Was he in Stonehearth after all? Why didn't he remember travelling the rest of the way?

He couldn't see their speed, pressed as he was to the carriage floor, but he could feel it. They were moving so fast that it felt impossible and disorienting. Every so often the carriage would take a corner with a squeal and then it gave a shriek as it stopped. He slid forward along with his captor, before being hustled rudely out of the wagon. A coat that smelled of old, foul-smoke was thrown over his head before he could identify his surroundings. Before they'd covered him up, he'd only seen more anonymous buildings. He heard the carriage growl away.

"Leave me be!" Daeson ordered, the ferocity of his words muffled. He reached up to remove the coat from his head but stronger arms pinned them to his sides.

He heard metal scrape against something near his feet. He was strongly reminded of the cover he'd removed from the pipe-well. Were they going to throw him down one? Daeson's panic returned and he reacted instinctively, kicking out his feet, satisfied when he made a connection intense enough to hear a pained grunt. His reward was a hit in the head so hard that he lost consciousness.

He was moving again. Opening his eyes didn't reveal anything, the foul-smelling coat was still wrapped around his head—a little tighter now. He could tell that someone was carrying his legs by the ankles and another was holding him up under the arms. It wasn't a comfortable hold for him and he sensed it was a tenuous one for them. Before he could fight them off, he was dropped. For the second time that night, Daeson was winded. His back and tailbone ached from when he'd connected harshly with the ground. He moaned.

He heard jangling keys and the sound of someone unlocking and then opening a door. He was pulled up onto his feet and guided roughly through the doorway and onto a chair.

The coat was finally removed from his head and he squinted through the harsh light at the scowling man who'd taken it.

"What's going on? Is this Stonehearth? Who are you? Am I in trouble?"

The scowling man's expression shifted dramatically. He looked confused by Daeson's questions and when an answer didn't immediately come, Daeson looked around to see where he was.

They were in a small room. Daeson was sitting at a heavy table with a spindly wooden chair opposite him. They weren't from a matching dining set. He dismissed the observation and continued looking. All of the walls were painted a light grey, like polished steel. The wall across from him had a long, black rectangular window in it—no, the window wasn't black, he could make out the vague outline of shapes on the other side, as though the window was looking into a darkened room. But why would there be windows between rooms? Weren't windows supposed to be for looking outside?

The other man spoke, capturing Daeson's attention. He had a menacing look to him; heavy black brows over dark eyes. His voice was soft as he said something Daeson didn't understand. The man set the foul-smelling coat down on the table and sat in the chair opposite, looking at Daeson with an encouraging expression. Daeson assumed it was his turn to speak now.

"My name is Daeson," he said slowly, hoping that the word 'name' would be one of the crossover words.

"My name is Nick," he replied, matching the cadence

of the words though not the accent. Nick was an unusual name, Daeson thought. It was short and had no rhythm. It sounded like some of his name had gone missing, but it also suited him.

"Where...from?" Nick continued, using a few words Daeson didn't recognise but he thought the sentence was simple enough to answer.

"Cloverlea."

"...far...?"

Daeson shrugged, though he was certain he must've come a great distance. The seasons were turned around, as though he'd travelled to the very tip of the lands, where summers came in place of winter. Such an amount of travel was impossible...unless something had happened to him to make him lose his memory. Except how could he have gone so long with his flask still in hand, his coin pouch still full and his deed tucked inside his tunic?

Something happened when he'd touched the pillar.

Yes, something *had* happened. But what?

"Is this Stonehearth? Am I in Stonehearth?" Daeson asked, hoping that it was a name of a city Nick recognised, even if they weren't in it. Stonehearth was one of the bigger cities, though not as famous as one of the Great Citadels of Kharltae. People crossed entire oceans to visit those.

"Stonehearth? No." Nick followed his statement with a question that Daeson didn't understand. He stood up and rounded the table, reaching for Daeson's pouch. Daeson flinched and slapped Nick's hand away. Nick's expression settled somewhere between amusement and disbelief.

"My coin! Mine." Daeson's heart pounded, hoping that Nick wouldn't forcibly take the pouch from him. He realised it could've easily been taken from him when he was unconscious, so what was Nick after? No longer concerned that his coin would be taken, he continued guessing his location. He needed to anchor himself in some way. "Am I in the Quarterlands? King's Reach? The Great Citadel of Gorven? Across the Ocean of Perils?"

Nick's blank stare frightened him. There was no recognition in his eyes.

"Stay," Nick said and left the room.

Daeson stayed, looking at the black window. He could feel his breathing had quickened as well as his heartbeat. He didn't want to be overwhelmed by panic again. Panic wasn't helpful. He needed to be at his most sensible. He gripped the edge of the table hard enough that his fingertips became white and recited counting exercises until he no longer felt overwhelmed. So far he hadn't been hurt...though he'd been knocked out. Daeson reached up to feel for a cut on his head but there was none. He should have a headache but was lucky enough not to be suffering one.

Nick didn't strike him as a man of finesse. The shouting, popping battle between the bowl-hatted folk and Nick's people proved that they were violent and ruthless. Just because he hadn't been hurt yet didn't mean he wouldn't be.

The shadows beyond the window in the next room moved. He waited for the light to glow in the other room but it never did. The hairs on his nape prickled and he turned on the chair, showing the window his back.

Nick returned shortly after, asking questions slowly with words Daeson still didn't understand. Communication was difficult and Nick had little patience, his voice rising in pitch with each question. A rapping on the black window attracted both of their attention and Nick suddenly calmed.

"Okay," Nick said, a phrase that Daeson was getting used to hearing even though he didn't know its purpose. He looked back at Daeson. "Bed."

"Bed?" Daeson repeated, understanding that word and feeling hopeful that he would get some rest.

Nick threw his hands in the air and spoke to the ceiling. Daeson looked up but couldn't see anything. When he looked back at Nick, he was chuckling. This was when he realised that Nick must have been addressing the Gods.

"Let's go."

Daeson was led out of the room into a hallway that was undecorated and narrow. He followed Nick up a set of stairs and passed a few other men on the way. All of them acknowledged Nick and didn't give Daeson much of a look. All of them were dressed in black with bright turquoise shirts, a minor variation of the all-black clothing that Nick wore. They went up another set of stairs, this time entering a wide corridor with many doors.

Nick showed Daeson into a large bedroom. Everything was decorated in white; from the canopy bed that looked large enough to sleep four, to the dressing table, cupboard, and desk with matching ornate chair. The floor was carpeted in gold with white stencilled flowers. Daeson gawked at it all before Nick captured his attention by tapping his arm and leading him to an adjoining room. It was smaller but everything inside had a handle that did something with water. *Shower* and *basin* he understood. Toilet, not so much. Nick demonstrated its use by relieving himself into it and then flushing his urine away.

"Questions?" he asked. Daeson had none. He didn't want any more demonstrations.

Daeson followed him back through the room but stopped short when Nick opened the door to leave.

"You stay. Sleep," Nick said. "...get you...morning."

"Good night," Daeson bade.

Nick first frowned then smiled. "Good night," he repeated, and shut the door behind him. Daeson heard a scraping sound of metal against metal before Nick's footsteps carried him away.

He was certain he was locked in but Daeson tested the doorknob anyway. He'd guessed right. He went to the window next, where white painted iron bars were hidden behind lacy curtains. He could slide the glass upward for fresh air but when he tested the bars, he found them unyielding. They were so narrow that his torso and head wouldn't fit between them. If he called for help, would anybody come? Would they even understand what 'help' meant? From his vantage point, he could see he was a level higher than the street. He felt detached from it, like it was a picture of a strange place to which he didn't belong.

It smelled bad here.

It took him a moment to realise the smell was coming from him. He'd been walking for days without a chance to bathe and the grime was thick upon his clothes and skin. Daeson returned to the bathroom and pulled off his shoes. His clothes went next and soon the spray of warm water was relaxing him. He didn't question the magic that made it work; this was something he was happy merely to accept. After using the fragrant bar soap he found hanging on the end of a cord, he washed his clothes as best he could and hung them up on the shower bar to dry. There was a fluffy towel hanging nearby that he used to dry himself.

He had nothing to wear to bed. The wardrobe and dresser drawers were bare. He wished he'd searched them before choosing to wash his clothes, he could've at least worn his undershorts. Even though he'd only been up for a few hours, the madness of the night caught up with him and he climbed into the inviting softness of the bed.

He thought he wouldn't be able to sleep in such a strange place but he was quickly proven wrong.

CHAPTER FOURTEEN

Training With Freddie

"ANGLES, angles, angles!"

Synjan adjusted the trajectory of her punches accordingly.

"Keep your elbows in."

She did as instructed, though it was increasingly difficult to focus on the finer points after three hours of punishing training. She blinked, gritting her teeth as sweat rolled into her right eye. Her vision was hazy, tunnelled, everything focussed on his voice and the bag in front of her.

"Lower your chin. That's good. Square off. Come on, thirty more seconds, you can do it. Harder. Like you mean it! Ten... six more like that... five... two more... one. Alright, that's it, time."

Synjan staggered backwards; clothing saturated with sweat, chest heaving, wrapped hands swaying drunkenly around. She bent forward and rested them on her knees in an effort to get stable. Her shoulders felt like they were on fire, her arms were vibrating even though they were being held still and she was desperately fighting back a feeling of nausea. She'd be damned if she'd give him the satisfaction of throwing up, especially when every jangling fibre of her body was certain it was exactly what he wanted.

"Good work," he laughed jovially and pounded her on the back twice.

She groaned and succumbed to the force of his hits, collapsing in a sprawled mess on the padded mat. Mid-morning sun chose that moment to break through the cloud cover that had oppressed Gredann for the last week and slice through the slotted windows high up in the warehouse's walls. It managed to shine directly into her eyes. She squinted and turned her head instinctively, barely able to see Freddie as he left the mat. He headed for his gear to get a drink of water because yelling instructions at her was thirsty work. She closed her eyes again and went back to concentrating on keeping the minimal contents of her stomach where they belonged.

It was difficult to describe her relationship with Division Lieutenant Frederickson. She started out as just a job to him but after the time they'd spent together, their relationship was stronger than that of just trainer/trainee. He was in the Authorities but he was also a very close friend of Ellis'.

Freddie and Ellis had grown up together in the nearby town of Relmont but their friendship had fractured when Freddie joined the Authorities. Ellis moved to Gredann, creating a lucrative criminal enterprise.

Freddie was also aware that she was a Wanderer.

Synjan had never understood why Ellis had told Freddie her greatest secret, when he'd been exactly like her parents in cautioning her discretion. When she'd told Kate and Nick, Ellis spanked her so hard he'd left bruises and she'd found it difficult to sleep for a couple of nights. The rules apparently changed when it came to his old friend. When she'd nervously asked Ellis if he was sure Freddie wouldn't turn her in, he'd given her an intimidating smile and said, "Karaka herself could cast Freddie in flames and he *still* wouldn't betray you, Little One."

Against her better judgement, she'd learned to trust this Authority officer.

Freddie had come to train her in Gredann with surprising regularity, even while he worked on climbing the Authority rank ladder. When she was older, she'd learned that Freddie had a girlfriend named Tiln who lived in Hill End somewhere, which explained why he was there almost every weekend.

When she got older still, she was stunned to find out that the relationship had been an elaborate ruse orchestrated by Ellis. Freddie had merely complied, spending time with Tiln in order not to raise the suspicion of his colleagues about why he was taking almost weekly portal trips to an insignificant city like Gredann. After eighteen years, they were still a couple and he usually spent more time with Tiln than he did with Synjan these days. She often wondered if Freddie had grown to love her. What would it be like, to be part of a fake relationship that spanned eighteen years? Could it become real?

She was perpetually astounded at the lengths good men would go to when proving their loyalty to a man like Ellis.

"Are you going to lay there all day?" Freddie called out.

Synjan groaned as she rolled onto her side and squinted across at him, resenting the casual way he drank from his blue water flask and still managed to chuckle at her debilitated condition. "Will you carry me?" she whimpered.

Freddie tipped his head back and laughed uproariously. The happy sound echoed around the huge warehouse, bouncing off the extensive variety of dummies, punching bags, exercise mats, shooting targets and gymnastics equipment housed within. Freddie had an uncharacteristically happy demeanour.

He was also handsome and tall, broad and well muscled. The way he carried himself with an innate sense of purpose and confidence never failed to turn heads. His hair was blonde, hiding any grey strands that might have been popping up in his fifty-seventh year of life. The regulation cut certainly worked on him. He had extraordinarily white teeth and greenish-grey eyes with an ever-present sparkle. The only time she'd witnessed that glint go out was after he talked with Ellis. His square jaw and high cheekbones looked particularly gaunt after some of those conversations and she'd been afraid that she wouldn't get to see her friend again after seeing him looking like that.

He always came back, though. Training with Freddie had brought a unique amount of sanity into her young, turbulent life. At first, she'd been a weak six year old whose only form of consistent exercise had been on a dance stage and Freddie had despaired about what he would do with her. For a good month, the things he'd had her doing hadn't made sense until he'd incorporated some of his customised Authority moves and based the fighting manoeuvres he wanted her to learn on dance moves. Training her to move like water, allowing her to use flips, round-offs and cartwheels as forms of evasion had made sense to her. She'd found rhythm in fighting just as she had in dance and when the two combined, she'd found clarity.

Of course, there'd been an indescribable amount of pain, too. Freddie's theory was that experiencing pain in controlled conditions would help eliminate surprise in situations where she wouldn't have the advantage. He'd drummed into her that she was small and female and would come out second best in every fight unless she used better techniques, implemented faster strategies and manipulated the intangible elements of every encounter to her favour.

She'd kicked trees in parks until her shins bled. She'd punched the same spot on a wooden dummy until her knuckles grew calloused and the wood became indented. She'd run to develop extended stamina. She'd lifted weights to increase muscle mass and strength and she'd been knocked on her ass every single time they trained together.

Freddie had never let her win a bout between them. They always warmed up with a spar before her full training began, as Freddie claimed he needed the exercise to shake off the effects of the Authority portal. If his focus was compromised, she never saw it. She could very rarely claim victory and didn't, until she was nineteen. He praised her for any decent manoeuvres she made and pointed out his own weaknesses in an effort to focus her on overcoming him, but they both knew that unless she got access to weapons and the fight was real, she'd never best him. He was far too experienced.

With a sigh, Synjan got up. She was already hurting and her muscles were still warm. She knew what she'd feel like tomorrow and though she wasn't looking forward to it, she also was. She came to the warehouse—nestled in the heart of Dockside, a couple of blocks away from the Office—at least every second day on her own. She came to work out but it wasn't the same as it was with Freddie. He assessed her, challenged her, sparred with her and continued to shape her.

Even with her talent, if she hadn't been trained by Freddie from such a tender age, she knew she wouldn't have lived as long as she had. The situations she got into were difficult to get out of and it was only with the instincts he'd honed in her that she was as successful as she was. Ellis had a name that carried weight in Gredann and she knew she did too because of how she enforced herself. Freddie had taught her how to do that calmly, yet aggressively.

He'd also been her only counsel when her encounters had seen her limp away, leaving her opponent dead. Even though he hadn't understood what it was like to watch a pattern fade away in death and feel the impact of that life lost viscerally as well as physically, he'd killed enough people that he could console her. He'd given her a poem that summed it up – she still read it sometimes, when things went badly, because it was in his handwriting and it made her feel closer to him and to rationality. She knew it off by heart and recited it to herself when she was struggling.

Do not rejoice in your power
Nor wallow in despair
Be thankful of your victory
For you could just as soon be there.

Acknowledge; so their mortal sacrifice
Has not been giv'n in vain.
Were they a worthy adversary,
Be grateful for your pain.

Shed a tear of sorrow...or not
That choice is always yours.
Keep perspective in the moment
And an eye upon the cause.

Let this instant never rule you,
Though its mark fall on your soul,
For your journey now continues
And you must travel whole.

Killing wasn't rational. It was the least rational thing she did. She understood perfectly the ideal that if she didn't fight, she'd be the one bleeding out in some cold, dark place. Freddie helped her keep perspective. He hadn't written the poem, he said, he'd got it from someone, somewhere, he couldn't really remember, but it didn't matter. It perfectly summed up his attitude towards life and death and had become her mantra also.

"How long are you here for?" she asked as she walked up beside him, chancing a sip of water from her own bottle. She wanted to gulp but knew that if she took too much it would only end up on the cement floor.

"Staying tonight, heading out tomorrow," he informed her, sifting through his gear bag for a new shirt.

His uniform was on top and it caught her eye. He always changed before he came to her, arriving in generic shorts and a T-shirt if it was warm, longer clothes if it was cold. The few times she'd seen him in uniform had been jarring.

Still, his uniform was different to the rest and it was intriguing. Instead of the usual triangles and lines, he had a stylised hourglass with a vertical line running through the centre. The four quadrants were a different colour each: black, yellow, red and blue. They signified that he was the Division Lieutenant from Interworld Tactical Response, commonly called I.T.R. There were five gold bars on the top of his breast pockets too – medals of excellence and distinction awarded for his bravery and success in this role.

Even if she didn't love him in it, Synjan was proud of the features of his dress uniform, proud of what he'd achieved. Maybe he'd changed a friendship forever with the choices he'd made, but she could see that Freddie was as loyal to his blue family as he was to anyone else and she respected that.

"On a mission?" she asked brightly.

He observed her as he pulled on a light jacket. "Yes."

"What sort?"

"You know the answer to that."

She sighed and pouted playfully at him. "Confidential."

He chuckled and pinched her chin between his thumb and forefinger, peering thoughtfully down at her. There were many times when Freddie had described his missions in detail to her, after the fact. She'd been impressed and excited by the tales, swept up in the descriptions of adventures on distant worlds, saving people who were in danger.

One time, when she was twelve, her enthusiasm had culminated in him asking her if she'd consider joining the Authorities. It had been a very awkward moment. The way he'd shaped her, she knew she was a better soldier than most of the ones he encountered at work but that didn't mean she'd fit in with the system. Frankly, if she ever attempted to enter it, they both knew what would happen.

"You looking after yourself?" he asked her with genuine concern.

"Of course," she answered automatically, wondering what had caused such an unusual question.

"Ellis... he knows what he's got, how lucky he is with you, right?" Freddie murmured, his gaze roving over her face as his thumb stroked her chin softly.

"Yes... why?" she breathed, wondering what he was getting at.

Freddie released her with a shake of his head and attempted a smile. "No reason. I just worry about you. I want you to be happy."

She looked closely at him, trying to understand the subtext of his message. If she had to guess about what he was getting at, she'd have said he wanted to be sure she was happy with *Ellis*. He'd always been able to tell when she was having a harder time than usual and she supposed Kate's death must've been showing somehow.

"I'm fine," she said sternly. "Don't worry about me."

Freddie looked at her and it seemed like he wanted to say something else but as her expression relaxed, he simply nodded and looked more like his usual self. "If you say so."

"I do," she said and breathed a laugh as she punched him in the upper arm. "Now let's get out of here. Tiln's waiting for you and I think I hear a hot bath calling for me."

CHAPTER FIFTEEN

The Hunter And The Flare

HEADS turned as he made his way through the administration building and whispered conversations sprouted in his wake. The word 'Hunter' floated to him and he smirked at the way none of them could maintain eye contact. Paper soldiers in their crisp blue uniforms. He supposed they did somebody good somewhere, but it wasn't him. They were one step away from civilian as far as the Hunter was concerned—and it was a shallow step at that.

He swiped his I.D. card to enter a more secure section. The gazes that greeted him in here were bolder and lingered on his casual attire. He noticed the highest ranking officer staring at the bulge of his sidearm beneath his jacket and he headed for her. She prowled behind the curve of workstations set up facing a large screen on the wall, looking concerned about the scene of devastation displayed. Something important had been bombed and the tension in the room was palpable.

"Captain," he greeted, identifying the rank of her uniform.

"Hunter," she acknowledged in return, frowning.

"Where can I access the database?"

She pointed out an office. It was walled in bullet-proof glass and the blinds within were drawn, hiding the contents from prying eyes. He gave her a nod and strode over.

To get into this room, he needed to swipe his card, enter his staff number and submit to a retinal scan. Within was an Elite Divisions access point—the Hunters were just one group that had the security clearance to enter it and utilise the inter-world database access it provided. When an approving beep sounded and the door mechanism released, he turned the handle and entered, locking it behind him. Eco-friendly lighting sprang to life, flooding the room.

One strip buzzed overhead, competing with the grinding and clunking noises coming from the computer housed beneath the solid desk. The database was always on, constantly being fed information from other worlds and he could hear it working hard as he rounded the desk and sat. Moving the mouse made the whirring noises go quiet as the system readied the log on screen for him.

He swivelled in his seat, opening drawers to check out the supplies and ensuring that the industrial printer on the cabinet behind him had paper. He thought idly that if he ever needed to print out a star system map, this was definitely the base he would come to. All of these access points were similar in design across the worlds but the only thing guaranteed to be exactly the same was the database workstation and phone. This base's facilities were generous compared to most. He turned back to the huge monitor, logged in and got to work.

Truthfully, he was looking for the easiest score he could find. After hunting the last pair of Wanderers through nineteen worlds, he needed a break but Division regulations dictated that he needed to complete three consecutive missions before he got any personal time. Bureaucrats knew nothing of base hopping to get tech updates, slogging through inhospitable worlds and the frustration of trails going cold after weeks of recon. Time was irrelevant to them, it was all about results. Three was the magic number.

The database was clogged with flare reports. The Authority sensors recorded every time a Wanderer left a world because it gave off a unique energy signature that they had specifically-calibrated equipment to read. They'd never figured out how to read the energy signature of where the Wanderers arrived in the next world, as it seemed to be a different wavelength or spectrum or...whatever.

That was where a Hunter's skill-set came into play. Being able to find a pattern within the multitude of recorded departure flares was akin to penning an opera. It was vital to understand every factor at play – the worlds, the Wanderer descriptions, the timing between flares on the same and consecutive worlds and the likelihood of which Wanderer group had set them off. Hunters also scanned crime patterns because Wanderers were typically unable to make their way through any world in a civilised manner. Every element was important when it came to the data; it was his orchestra and it was his job to shape it into a symphony, rather than random, discordant notes.

After half an hour of scrutiny, he had what he wanted and he flagged it with a request for investigation and pursuit. A succession of two flares had occurred in the last week and, though others might dismiss them as disconnected, his gut told him differently. He knew the worlds reasonably well and had travelled through them a few times.

World ninety-five was Tahanan, a Charlie world aware of its position in the line of two hundred and fifty-three known worlds. He liked hunting in Charlie worlds best because they were easiest to get around in. They were shaped by the Authority hand and so carried recognisable brands that made it convenient for Wanderers to replenish their supplies. This convenience often relaxed them and made them sloppier. The best thing was public co-operation. Citizens of a Charlie world knew who the Authorities were and didn't get in the way.

World ninety-six was an Echo world, not just shaped by Authorities but structured around a single purpose. The world of Finalis was designed to host championship challenges in every imaginable form of competition. Each continent boasted a vast range of sophisticated facilities. Such an obnoxious world had high tech, high security and a high media presence, which made identification easy. After reviewing available closed circuit systems footage and some low-level crime reports, he had visual confirmation of a Wanderer group as described by local authorities on Tahanan – two men and one woman. They had stolen a vehicle and were suspected of stealing food and other supplies in both worlds, leaving a clear path of where they'd been. These Wanderers seemed intent on movement rather than savouring the experience, so although he had no idea where their Portal was, he could predict their path through Finalis.

The trio were not pausing to appreciate new cultures, took no time to contribute to the worlds they were passing through and had no desire to invest in or nurture new relationships. No, these ignorant Wanderers were going to continue running through the worlds as fast as possible, uncaring of who they took advantage of or what crimes they committed in pursuit of their own interests.

The Hunter Division was created specifically to stop this kind of exploitation. By their choices and travel thus far, this trio of Wanderers had proclaimed their intentions and the danger they represented was clear. They would pay for their disregard of law and common sense with their lives—quickly, if his calculations were correct.

The phone rang and he lifted the handset, running through the required process of identification and confirmation of his request. The repetition of the script was automatic after all these years but his reward came in the final sentence.

"Your request is approved, effective immediately."

A thrill of excitement ran through him as he acknowledged and hung up. This mission was very convenient. Each world held numerous continents and oceans of possibilities as far as hunting went but he'd been at the game long enough to know how this job would play out. The Wanderer criminals would be on Finalis for some time, so he had the luxury of choosing whether he'd catch up with them there or on the next world, Baxter. The potential to resolve a long-term issue made the decision for him.

After taking the time to book his portal trip to Baxter and submit a request for immediate notification of the next departure flare on Finalis, the Hunter logged out and left the office. With every step, the exhaustion of the last mission left him and he was filled with a renewed sense of purpose.

CHAPTER SIXTEEN

Omerri Backhouse

CLOUDS wrapped soft arms around him, keeping him warm and cosy. Daeson shifted in their hold. He didn't need to open his eyes to know daylight filled the room. The sun was already up and it felt wrong not to be up with it, but at the same time everything in him was rebelling. He didn't want to leave this safe and comfortable place.

Somebody sat on the bed. He opened his eyes to see who'd invaded his space. She was a goddess dressed in white.

Daeson propped himself up on his elbow. The lady sitting upon his bed was not a goddess after all. He could see why he had mistaken her for one; she was radiant and beautiful, with shiny black hair that fell halfway down her back. Her eyes were a vivid blue, a much lighter shade than his own. Her skin was pale and he took this to mean she must be one of the very rich, with no need to work outside. As he stared at her in awe-struck wonder, the corners of her red lips pulled upward into a gentle smile and he was encouraged by it to offer her a smile in return.

"Good morning, Daeson," she said. "My name is Omerri."

He was surprised she knew his name before he realised Nick must have told her.

"Good morning, Omerri," he replied. He'd wanted his words to sound assured but he could hear the uncertainty in his own voice.

"Did you sleep well?" she asked. She shifted on the bed so she could face him more directly and her hand settled atop his blanketed hip. It was a natural enough movement for her, perhaps even an innocent place for her hand to be, but to him the touch was intimate and he twitched.

"Very well, thank you."

She was breathtaking and intimidating, yet comforting and familiar. How could she achieve such a thing? It was the idea of familiarity that helped him make a connection; she could speak his language! "I can understand you."

"Yes," she said, offering nothing except a smile.

They stared at one another as he waited for her to give him an explanation. When he realised that she wasn't going to tell him anything, he opened his mouth to ask. She spoke the moment he drew in breath.

"There are clothes for you behind the screen. They may not fit you perfectly but should be no less comfortable than what you normally wear. I would like you to dress yourself and join me for breakfast." Omerri's hand moved off Daeson's hip so she could gesture at a tri-folded wooden screen in the far corner. Last night Daeson had dismissed it as decorative because of the many heart-shaped holes in it. There had been nothing behind it but now Daeson could make out the dark shape of a stool or small table. Omerri stood and waited for him to get out of bed.

The mention of breakfast had Daeson's stomach rumbling encouragement but he hesitated. He made a nonsensical sound, feeling trapped.

"Is there something wrong?"

"I'm not wearing anything." His admission brought heat to his cheeks and he wondered if she would think he was a barbarian for not even having undergarments. "All of my clothes were dirty," he justified.

Omerri moved across the room, her long white dress clinging to her figure as she walked. Though her body was covered, he'd never seen anything so revealing and wasn't sure he should be watching her. She pulled down a robe hanging on the back of the door. Like the stool, it hadn't been there last night. It was unsettling to think she'd moved things around the room as he'd slept.

Omerri brought the robe to him and held it up, politely looking away. Daeson was grateful and shuffled to the edge of the bed before throwing the covers back and standing. He slid his arms through the sleeves and shrugged the robe on when he sensed Omerri letting go of it. Once it was knotted safely closed, he turned to face her while caressing the sleeve, marvelling at how soft and fine the wool was.

Towering over her, Daeson felt ungainly. Omerri was a tall woman in comparison to those in Cloverlea but they had fuller figures and athletic bodies. Omerri was a delicate wisp.

She looked up at him with an expression he couldn't decipher and smoothed the creases of his robe upon his chest with her palms. He didn't understand her actions but he was enjoying them.

Omerri's hands dropped and she led him towards the screen, indicating for Daeson to move behind it. From the small table, he picked up a strange pair of stretchy shorts which he guessed were undergarments. Before disrobing, he peeked through the screen to find her looking his way. She would likely see a great deal as he undressed. Feeling self-conscious, Daeson turned his back and stepped into the shorts, pulling them up beneath the robe. Once they were on he felt safe enough to untie the robe and let it puddle on the floor.

"You have a lovely body," Omerri said. He was startled by her compliment. His assumption was correct; she could see plenty through the screen. With a mixture of embarrassment and pleasure, Daeson pulled on his outer pants and shirt.

The clothes were a lot more colourful than he was used to. Varying shades of brown were the most he wore at home, but here the only brown thing he wore were the shoes. His pants were blue and his shirt was a green and white check.

"Am I wearing too much colour?" he asked, stepping out from behind the screen. He wanted her approval and was fairly sure he would get it, since she'd selected his clothes for him.

"You're wearing just the right amount."

"These pants feel strange," he said, rubbing his hands against them.

"They're called jeans. They're made of denim," she told him.

Jeans. Denim. The words sounded as strange as the material itself. He said them out loud to concrete them into his vocabulary.

"Come along, let's do some breakfasting."

Daeson followed her out of the bedroom. When she opened the door, it reminded him about last night.

"Why was I locked in?" he asked.

"We didn't know what kind of man you were. It was safer for us to lock you in."

Her words weren't truthful which made him uneasy. The reasoning was sound but the lie made it suspicious. He pondered it with a frown as she spoke again.

"I hope the room made you feel like a guest rather than a hostage."

"I liked the room but it was scary that you were keeping me in it."

"Scary?" Omerri repeated as though tasting the word for the first time. He thought she might not recognise it even though she was fluent in his language.

"I was frightened."

Omerri gave his arm a squeeze. They passed an open door and Daeson glanced in to see a man tucking his shirt into his pants beside an empty bed. The bedroom was decorated entirely in blue. Were all the bedrooms decorated in different colours? How many bedrooms were there?

"Do a lot of people live here?"

"Nobody lives here, though many do sleep over."

"So this is an inn?"

"It's more than that."

It was a very busy inn—or whatever this business was—for there were many doors down this corridor. Most were open, revealing their colourful bedrooms, but it was the closed doors that Omerri commented on.

"Never knock or interrupt anyone in a room with a closed door," Omerri instructed. Daeson nodded his agreement. "If you need to talk to someone, come downstairs."

They stood on the landing of carpeted stairs that angled steeply downward. Daeson reached for the bannister as they began their descent. The stairs turned halfway and at the bottom Daeson saw a woman with her back to them shouldering the wall. Her hair was the same vivid red as her boots and she wore a silver dress that looked like a short towel wrapped tightly around herself. The strangest thing about her was the tendril of smoke that curled and dissipated in the air just above her head. The woman must've heard Daeson's feet thudding down each step because she looked over her shoulder. Upon seeing them, her eyes widened before she reached down to crush the little white stick she was holding into the soil of a nearby pot plant. When they reached the bottom of the stairs, Daeson became aware of an acrid, unpleasant smell and screwed up his nose.

"Ruby, darling," Omerri began before she spoke in the twisty language. By Omerri's tone, he could tell the red and silver woman named Ruby was being reprimanded. Ruby didn't look his way, keeping her eyes on the floor as she repeated a few phrases over again: "Yes, Omerri. Sorry, Omerri."

She hurried upstairs once she was allowed to go and then Omerri and Daeson were alone.

"It's a disgusting habit," she told him.

"What is?"

"Smoking."

He looked down at the little white stick that Ruby had squashed into the soil. In Cloverlea, he'd heard about smoke-houses, where special burning grasses were set alight inside enclosed rooms and people sat within until they passed out from the fumes. He wondered what the appeal of smoking and smoke-houses was, if this was the kind of smell they had.

Omerri took him into a large dining room with dark wood-panelled walls, no windows and a candle on every white-clothed table. There was a large tanned man seated nearby, hunched over his breakfast. He looked up when they entered. His fork paused on the way to his mouth before he finished the bite, picked up his plate and disappeared through a swinging door on the adjacent wall. The retreat struck Daeson as peculiar. Omerri seemed not to notice as she selected a table with two chairs for them to sit at.

A different man entered the room through the swinging door, carrying two glasses and a jug of water. He placed them on the table and pulled out Omerri's chair for her to sit down. Daeson sat opposite, mentally reprimanding himself.

"The usual, Miss Backhouse?"

"Yes, please," Omerri replied, then put in a further request. Daeson poured water for the both of them, to display his good manners. Once the man was gone, she thanked Daeson for her glass and explained that she'd ordered a few different meals for him to try, so he could see what kind of food he liked. He took large swallows of his water while considering which of his questions to ask first. He blurted out the simplest one, needing to fill the silence.

"Are you the owner here?"

"Yes, I am."

They stared at one another some more. He liked

that she was giving him time to think but he wished she was more forthcoming.

"What about Nick, is he an owner too?"

"Nick works for me," she said proudly. There was a gleam in her eyes that looked unkind. It prompted Daeson to think about all Nick had done; attacking the bowl-hatted men, grabbing Daeson and knocking him out, locking him up in a little room and asking him difficult questions.

"What kind of work does Nick do for you?"

"Would you like to breakfast with Nick instead?" she asked. Her tone was pleasant but he knew he'd displeased her. He wanted to take back his question. How had things soured so quickly? He struggled for a solution and found none. Staring at the tablecloth between them didn't help as what was said couldn't be *un*said. "I'm still making bad decisions," he mumbled.

"Why do you say that?" she asked. He looked up at her, surprised that she'd been able to understand him since he'd spoken his words softly. Her hearing was impeccable.

"I ran my farm into the ground, making it worthless before..."

deciding to move on. He couldn't phrase it in such a way because he hadn't decided at all.

"...I left."

She nodded, accepting his explanation. They were interrupted by the man who'd taken their food order. He returned with a tray that held small plates, glasses and cutlery on it. Daeson watched the man arrange the tableware into neat rows, with a small plate to the side and nothing in front of Omerri, then repeating the layout for Daeson. When he left, Daeson picked up the new glass and admired it, amazed by its quality.

"You have glass where you're from," Omerri told him, though her tone was questioning. Daeson set it down and nodded.

"Yes, but not so thin."

"Let me show you a trick," she said before licking the tip of her finger. She set her fingertip upon the rim of her glass and circled it, enticing a lovely ringing sound. Daeson puffed laughter and grinned at her. The tension was gone between them.

"What is the name of your home town?" she asked.

"Cloverlea. Have you been there?" he asked hopefully.

"No. Didn't you have anyone to help you on your farm?"

"When my father died, I took over...but I didn't do a very good job."

Omerri reached across the table and covered his hand with hers. He felt obliged to mimic the gesture, and ended up sandwiching her hand between his. Her skin felt cool and soft. "I was going to find a buyer for it at Stonehearth."

"Stonehearth is a bigger city?"

He nodded.

"How were you travelling?"

"Walking."

"It wasn't too far away?" she guessed.

"It would've taken a quarter moon."

"Moons are called months here."

Daeson was silenced by this information. The word was unusual but made sense. The twisty language overlapped his own at times, and he felt like that was significant but couldn't grasp how. Perhaps if he was cleverer he would be able to solve the riddle. When the swinging door opened between the dining room and the kitchen, Omerri extracted her hand. Daeson sat up as a delicious smelling meal was brought over to them. The server held three plates in his hands like a juggler. The first plate was for Omerri, who had half a grapefruit and a peculiar white lumpy substance with green flecks throughout. Daeson had a plate piled with eggs and bacon set before him, and a second plate of short stacked pancakes to one side. The server left and Daeson watched with dismay as Omerri poked her fork into the white mess.

"What is *that*?"

"Scrambled egg white with herbs."

"Does it taste better than it looks?"

Omerri tinkled laughter and shook her head. "Not really."

He was enchanted by the sound of her laughter. He wanted to make her laugh again but didn't know how so he shovelled food into his mouth instead. The meal was delicious and he was ravenous. In spite of their breakfasts varying so greatly, Daeson and Omerri finished at the same time. As he licked his fingers she took her napkin and dabbed at the corners of her mouth. Her elegant gesture humbled him and he shyly reached for his own napkin.

"Would you like more to eat?" Omerri asked.

"I've had enough, thank you," Daeson said, wiping his fingers.

"Did you ever reach Stonehearth?" she asked.

"No. I had seven days walk to go when I camped on the side of the road for the night and I saw—" he hesitated, unsure how to share his experience.

"What did you see?" she asked in a hushed voice, leaning closer.

"At first, nothing. It was what I felt, in here." Daeson touched his chest. He told her about the way he'd been drawn into the forest during the day but hadn't succumbed to it until nightfall. With difficulty, he described the brilliance of the pillar of white light, believing he couldn't properly communicate the spectacle of it.

The swinging door opened and Omerri made a quick gesture to shush Daeson. He held his tongue while the server cleared their plates. She made a request—Daeson thought something needed to be collected—and once their server was gone, she smiled warmly.

"Well done." Omerri reached for her water and took a sip. Daeson did the same, pleased to receive her praise and curious that she didn't want them to be overheard.

When she stood, Daeson followed suit, tucking his chair under the table before he started collecting plates. Omerri stopped him.

"Leave those for Kite to collect." Daeson wondered if Kite was the man who'd served them throughout their breakfast. Omerri took his arm and led him out of the dining room and down a corridor to a door where a man was waiting. He was Daeson's size but closer to his father's age.

"Good morning, Miss Backhouse," the man said with a nod.

"Good morning, Hammond."

Hammond didn't look at or acknowledge Daeson. He opened the back door and stepped outside first, his head turning left and right as though looking for something. When Daeson was outside he looked as well but there wasn't much to see beyond a narrow alleyway sandwiched between tall buildings. When he checked back with Hammond, he met a narrowed stare. Daeson lowered his gaze, studying the cobbled street and dismayed by the hostility of the people in this city.

They stood in the shadows of four storey buildings while they waited. It was chilly and every so often a strong gust howled up the street. Omerri was only wearing a light dress and Daeson didn't miss the way she held her elbows to keep warm. He puffed his frustration and Omerri looked his way.

"Is something the matter?" she asked.

"I wish I had an overcoat to give you," he explained.

Omerri smiled at him before shuffling closer and tucking herself against him. He held his arm up and out but if felt awkward leaving it hanging there. Slowly he lowered it, his hand holding her shoulder in a half-embrace. It was a more intimate hold than he was comfortable with but he didn't know what else to do with himself. He stood rigid, not moving lest he disturb her.

A black horseless carriage entered the street at the far end and Daeson flinched. Omerri whispered some comforting words to him, including Nick's favourite letters, 'O' and 'K'. He liked the soothing quality of her voice and was relieved when the carriage approached them with a soft purr.

"This is my car, Daeson," Omerri told him as she pulled out of his hold. She tugged on his hand to draw him over to the carriage with her. He didn't remember much about last night's ride other than being thrown around the inside of the car, but he did recall there had been no roof. This car was fully enclosed and sounded quieter.

"Car," he repeated. It was a short version of the word carriage, which should help him remember what to call it. Since it moved without a horse, it made sense that it earned itself half a name.

Hammond opened the car door for Omerri to enter. She sat and then scooted along to allow Daeson to climb in after her.

The space within was large and the seats were soft and comfortable. Omerri named a few different places she would be taking Daeson but it was the last destination that excited him.

"I've always wanted to see the ocean."

"Then we can look at the ocean as long as you like," she promised. She pressed a button on a panel set into the door beside her and a dark screen lifted up with a whirr, separating them from the driver.

The car turned down a few streets where the buildings weren't quite as high. There were few people dressed in colourful clothing, walking along. When the car turned down the next street, Daeson was amazed.

People were everywhere; sitting down at tables that were set out on the footpath forcing other people had to walk around them. There were shops with large windows that people stopped in front of to have a look inside. There were people riding things on two wheels that Omerri called *bicycles*—so many bicycles; a lot of them with baskets or little trailers behind them. There were also bicycles without pedals that Omerri called scooters.

"What do the wailing posts do?" Daeson asked when they passed one of the flared iron trees that he'd seen last night. He pointed it out to Omerri.

"They tell us when the curfew begins."

"Curfew?" Daeson repeated the unusual word, finding he had some trouble wrapping his tongue around it.

"When nobody is allowed outside anymore."

"Why not?" Daeson asked.

"The Authorities control our world. They want everyone here to know it."

He'd heard the term 'Authorities' from Nick, who'd spat on the ground after mentioning them. Omerri's tone matched Nick's sentiment.

"I haven't heard of them," he admitted. "Are they like the Flag Guards?"

"I don't believe so. You didn't have Authorities on your world."

"'On my world'?" he repeated. He regretted his question when he saw her expression. She looked like she hadn't intended to tell him.

He knew. She didn't need to explain further because he knew. He'd considered it when he'd woken up in a strange garden in the middle of summer. He'd suspected it when he'd found the wailing post. He'd known it when he'd been accused of wearing strange clothes and speaking a slightly different language. Still, the similarities had given him hope that he'd merely travelled very far...but Nick hadn't known any of the places he'd mentioned. He'd discarded all the evidence because it made no sense, but he had to acknowledge the differences that were now surrounding him.

"You shifted worlds, Daeson," Omerri said, her voice gentle. "The pillar of light you told me about is the Portal. You're a Wanderer, Daeson. You're special."

Special. So special that he'd been dumped on a farmer's doorstep as a babe. During winter, no less. How long could he have survived in the cold? So special that everything he touched had either been ruined, unwanted or trickery. He hadn't been able to *give* his farm away. Now it would become one of those abandoned places that people would call cursed. Maybe it *was* cursed. The Portal had whispered promises to him to entice him to touch it, but the joke was on him because all it had done was deliver him into a world he didn't understand.

Omerri was still talking and he reined in his focus.

She told him about Wanderers. They were people who travelled between worlds using the Portal. Only Wanderers could use the natural one. Only Wanderers could even *see* it. They could bring others through with them but the Portal was reserved for their touch only. Omerri spoke wistfully as though it was a spiritual experience.

"Are you a Wanderer?" he asked her.

Omerri gave him an edgy look. "We're not discussing me."

"But you know a lot."

She huffed. "I'm trying to help you," she explained. "You don't yet know the dangers you're facing, and this world will be kinder to you than others."

Her words were convincing, yet horrifying. She interpreted his expression correctly and sidled closer, leaning into him and placing her hand upon his arm. He smelled the faint aroma of grapefruit on her breath when she spoke again, softly.

"No, I am not a Wanderer...so I envy you. I envy the opportunities you have and the talent you were born with, whatever it is. You have a weapon to protect yourself with, or a way to flee your enemies, while I am forced to face them or ask permission to leave. You have freedom, in its purest form. Even the world itself can't cage you."

Daeson was moved by her words. He sensed it was a very personal thing that she was sharing with him—that she measured herself against an ability she would never have because it was something inherited through blood. He felt unworthy. He felt ashamed. He felt ungrateful for hating something she considered wonderful. He wanted to make it up to her by sharing his knowledge in return with her, but he only had one thing.

"Truth," he whispered.

"Truth?" Omerri repeated softly, returning him to the here and now. She was pressed against him, the side of her breast brushing against his arm. His heart raced and he quickly judged that she was trustworthy. She was helping him and showed reverence for his world-travelling ability. He turned to see red lips slightly parted as she awaited his response. There was something exciting about her painted mouth. He didn't question its appeal but he did confess to it.

"I know when people are lying." He thought this would amaze her further but she retreated instead. He was disappointed when she moved away to assess him. "Have I made you angry?" he asked.

"No," she said. He was relieved when her words felt like truth. "You know everything I think and feel, don't you," she said. It was phrased like a question but it sounded like an accusation.

"I would only know them if you lied about them," he explained. She was quiet for long enough that he felt the need to prompt her. "Do you know something about my gift?"

"You must be an Intuit, but I don't think you're a full blood. That kind can see more than they should." She sounded cold, the information she relayed might as well have been a yield report for all the emotion he could detect from her voice.

"I don't go looking for lies," Daeson offered. "I don't seek out what's not my business."

"At least I haven't lied," she said, which was true and yet not. She didn't remember.

"You have, but I didn't think it was my place to question you."

She looked shocked.

"When did I lie?" she asked. She sounded upset.

"When I asked why I was locked in the room and you told me you didn't know what kind of man I was."

Omerri breathed a short laugh of relief and explained herself.

"By then, I already knew you were a Wanderer by your clothes and your speech."

Daeson nodded. He forgave her for the lie because it made sense that she would want to ease him into the truth. She'd told him everything as soon as she was able.

"What did you call my gift?" he asked. One corner of her lips pulled up as she looked at him with an expression he couldn't decipher.

"Intuit. I assume it comes from intuition. The Authorities are not known for their creativity when it comes to naming things."

"Why would the Authorities name my gift?"

She shook her head and raised a hand briefly to dismiss the question. Perhaps she was going to explain the Authorities later. So far she'd only mentioned them briefly but the Authorities were something he wanted to know more about. They sounded important.

"Do you have to switch it on?"

"Switch?" Daeson asked, confused about the way she used the word. A switch was a stick for hitting.

"Do you need to look inside yourself to know when someone is lying?"

"No. I just know it."

"Is there anything else your gift does?"

He looked at her beautiful face, at the intensity of her gaze and the way she was slightly leaning towards him, interested in what he had to say.

"I can't lie."

It was strange to admit this out loud after hiding it for so long. His father had warned him that it could be used quite potently against him. Not even Cleric Faelin knew he was unable to speak lies; he'd managed to avoid others finding out his whole life. Until now.

Omerri looked intrigued. Now that the secret was out, it was easy to keep talking.

"I used to try to when I was little. My tongue glue to the roof of my mouth and my throat would seize. It didn't take long to make the connection."

"Aw," Omerri pooched out her lip. "Did you get into a lot of trouble?"

He wondered why she would think such a thing.

"No."

She shuffled closer to him and reached up to stroke fingers through his hair. The sensation caught him off guard but gave him delightful shivers down his spine.

"Were you a good boy, Daeson?" she asked quietly.

"Yes," he said.

"And now you're a good man?"

"Uh, I do my best," Daeson said. The way she was caressing his head was both mesmerising and distracting.

"What do you think of me?" Omerri asked, her

fingers massaging the base of Daeson's neck in a way that was very relaxing.

The question struck him as unusual but it was easy enough to answer well. He knew she was testing him, using the knowledge of his truth-telling against him, but he forgave her. She *was* helping him.

"I think you're a nice lady. I think you're generous and kind, to help me. You're...really pretty."

He didn't think he would have admitted this last but her touch boosted his confidence.

"Thank you," she said warmly. Her fingers left his hair but she remained near him, their arms brushing against each other. He mourned the loss of her touch because it was nice but he felt that he didn't know her well enough to be familiar in return.

They were driven past a place with a very high fence. Behind it were uniformed men and women wearing bowl hats and carrying long black, bulky sticks. Omerri identified them as Authorities and described the sticks as *guns*.

Finally, she spoke about the Authorities. She explained that they had manufactured their own portal using giant machines and charged people a lot of money to travel between worlds. Using words that Daeson didn't quite understand, she told him about their strict portalling regime; they demanded a blood sample from every traveller to identify the correct inoculations, touting that they were preventing the potential wiping out of entire civilisations over a mild strain of the flu. They were also using the samples to identify Wanderers, who would forever remain on their files. She told him about their philosophy; that travelling between worlds was a responsibility not to be taken lightly and therefore the use of all portals other than theirs were illegal.

"So I've travelled illegally?" Daeson asked, understanding enough of her explanation that the

Authorities were a grand organisation spanning many worlds and that he was unlikely to escape their notice forever.

"Yes, but you're lucky to have come to a place where it's normal not to have papers. Many births and deaths are undocumented here. Once you learn the language, the Authorities won't know any differently."

"Where am I, anyway?"

"In the city of Gredann, on the world of Trent."

It was a relief to finally know the name of where he was. Without it, he had no chance to settle, but he still needed to know what would happen if the Authorities found out about him.

"What will the Authorities do if they catch me?"

He braced himself for bad news, but he was still shocked by her answer.

"They arrest you, they experiment on you and if you run away from them, they have people to hunt you down."

His face felt numb and his hands became fists in his lap. The cabin of the car was suddenly claustrophobic and too hot. He felt Omerri draw closer and she lifted his arm and placed it around her shoulder. Daeson allowed himself to be manipulated into position and stared at her once she was settled.

"Oh Daeson, darling, I'm so sorry to be the one to tell you."

Her words surprised him out of his thoughts, for they weren't expected. In his shock, he challenged her.

"But you're not."

Her shoulders tensed beneath his hold.

"No, you're right. I'm glad to tell you. I'm glad I can protect you from them and I'm glad that you weren't discovered by someone else."

Daeson was humbled by her answer. To survive in this world, he would have to trust someone. It would be in his best interest to stop questioning her every comment, lest she tire of his suspicion.

They rode together in silence. The car took them on a winding road that angled steeply upward. Looking out the window, Daeson saw a cluster of orange rooftops above tan buildings, the sunlight stripping away the mask of bleak greys that had made up his first impression of the city. This view made it look beautiful and he thought he might be able to live here after all.

The car delivered them to a plateau and idled as Daeson got out, holding the car door open for Omerri. The wind whipped his hair and clothes, pulling at his body with enough force that he had to consciously resist it. Omerri took his arm and walked with him to the edge of a cliff, her hair like a wild bird flapping about her face.

He was careful not to go too close to the cliff's edge, but he didn't need to. Daeson looked out at the ocean where it met the horizon and was speechless. There was a vastness about it that helped him grasp the size of the world. Of this world, at least. To imagine many oceans like this one, on many other worlds and accessible to him through a beam of light; he didn't understand what or how or why it worked. It made no sense to him. It was like speaking of magical things found in children's tales, or of the greatness of the gods.

He could see many dark dots upon the water in the distant horizon that Omerri said were merchant ships, heading out to or coming back from foreign lands. There were also many boats, both small and large, close enough that he could make out the details of. They peppered the ocean as they sailed, or were driven like cars using engines—Omerri briefly described how Cloverlea's hand-cranked machines cranked themselves in Gredann.

Omerri said something that he missed because the wind stole her words away. He turned to see what she wanted but she was already on her way back to the car, hugging herself. He watched the wind play with her dress, pulling it taut against her form or lifting it up high enough to reveal a great deal of her shapely legs. Before she reached the car, Daeson turned back to the ocean for a final look and then trotted after her.

CHAPTER SEVENTEEN

The DOME

IT took less than a week for Hawke to learn that his school was similar to his home life. Like at Donovan Court, he had regular classes, teachers and rules. Unlike Donovan Court, he had no servants to take care of his menial tasks. He had to make his own bed, launder his own clothes and was even rostered on to serve meals and clean toilets.

He had no friends because nobody spoke his language. He dedicated his free time to learning theirs. There was a television room in the library where he watched a puppet show at the same time every day. The puppets and their juvenile antics taught him how to say the alphabet and identify numbers. Hawke would never admit how much he enjoyed the show—he thought himself too old for puppets.

He'd learned that some of his classes were different to the ones the other boys in his dormitory went to. With the exception of art, music and athletics, he would be segregated from the main population. Learning the Authoritan language was a priority for all those who didn't speak it. He was surprised to find that there were many boys in the school who'd come from other worlds and didn't know the language. One of their exercises was to introduce themselves, so he quickly learned most of the class had parents who'd newly signed up to the Authorities. The rest had tales of being arrested, like him.

Art was his favourite class. It was interesting and relaxing and kept him independent from the other boys. It was a class that on Boronia he'd been kept from, for male painters were an absurd idea. He was pleased that the Authorities had no such ideas about gender—he'd learned that on Authority worlds both women and men could learn any skill they wished. He also liked that nothing in art was incorrect. He quickly learned to love abstracts.

Music was more difficult, though the teacher was impressed with Hawke's guitar skills. The guitar was similar to the yinnarow. When flipping through a book of stringed instruments, he'd come across a picture of a yinnarow and the teacher called it a *ukulele*, a difficult word for Hawke to pronounce. In one week, he'd only had a chance to try out a few instruments but he was fond of the percussive range.

He'd expected athletics to be skill building as well, like hand to hand combat or fencing, but it had mostly been about running and performing repetitive exercises. He didn't know why they were jumping up and down instead of learning how to fight, but he didn't know how to ask. He did as he was told.

Cayden arrived to collect him on the seventh day, which was supposed to be a relaxation day except there was an assembly held early in the morning in a huge pointy building behind the block-shaped school. The pointy building had beautiful paintings inside as well as leadlights on the windows that reminded Hawke of the tapestries at home. These ones seemed to follow the story of a man, and Hawke's gaze moved from window to window to see different scenes of things the man had done, like talk to a crowd from upon a hill, or fight with some other people inside a building, or having a meal with some friends at a long table. Before Hawke could sit with the others on some uncomfortable looking benches, he was tapped on the shoulder by a teacher and taken out of the pointy building. Hawke wondered why he couldn't be in the assembly too.

He saw the Lieutenant standing and talking with another uniformed man, who was older and had a strange haircut; he was bald all around his head except for on the top, where he had a lot of hair twisted into a mess of small braids that stuck straight upward. He also had a beard at the very tip of his chin and styled in the same braided fashion. The man was broad-shouldered and imposing in spite of his peculiar appearance.

The teacher left after a few words exchanged with Cayden. The strange man addressed him in Boronian.

"Lord Hawke Aron of Donovan Court, Region of Galantyne, World of Boronia." Hawke was excited and hopeful to find out who this man was, for he was observing the accepted culture of greeting. "You meet Filip Don Effertrey, Region of The Tortured Isles."

A pirate? Cayden had brought him a pirate? Hawke's smile faded as he understood that this man wasn't going to take Hawke back home. He was here for something else. Hawke looked at Cayden, disappointed.

"No."

"Don't judge so quickly, Lord Hawke. I cannot control where I am born as much as you cannot control where you are now."

Hawke looked at the pirate dubiously. Apart from his strange hair and beard, the uniform he wore made him part of the Authorities.

"What are you here for?" Hawke demanded.

Filip Don Effertrey crouched near him and Hawke stepped back instinctively. Even though he was mistrustful, Hawke was curious about the pirate for he'd never met one before. He'd only heard the stories about what happened to ships that dared enter the region of the Tortured Isles, or even those that neared the perimeter.

"I owe some people favours."

Hawke looked at Cayden but Filip shook his head and chuckled.

"Not to him, but to those who must owe him."

Hawke looked at Cayden again, who seemed anxious. Of course he didn't know what the conversation was about, and he'd put his trust in a pirate, which Hawke thought was insensible. He wondered if Cayden even knew Filip was a pirate. The Lieutenant extended a hand for Hawke to take and he accepted, walking alongside him as he chatted. The pirate walked behind, translating everything to Hawke on Cayden's behalf as they approached a waiting car.

"How are you getting along?" Cayden handed Hawke his lanyard.

"I have everything I need," Hawke replied, putting it on.

"What does that mean?"

Hawke considered how much to tell Cayden and thought there was no point telling him about how overwhelmed he was by homesickness.

"It means I'll be fine."

Cayden looked dubious but he didn't challenge the statement. Hawke didn't know if he felt relieved or disappointed about this.

The three of them sat in the back seat with him in the middle. It was snug but not squashed, though Hawke wished that the pirate had sat up front beside the driver.

"We're going to a place called the DOME. We'll be staying there for three days. Filip will be translating for you."

Hawke was irritated by the news.

"What about my music and art classes?" he asked.

Filip didn't translate for him but spoke to him directly. "I guess you'll have a few less songs and paintings to show off," he laughed. Hawke was livid but helpless to interject as Cayden and the pirate spoke back and forth. Obviously Cayden realised something had been said but was unlikely to have been told the truth.

"What's this DOME?" Hawke asked after an uneasy silence.

"It stands for Domiciliary Observation and Medical

Examination. It means they're going to do tests on you, Lord Hawke."

"I can do without the extra translations."

"All part of the service," Filip grinned.

"Feel free to take that part away."

The portal trip made him sick again as the trio travelled to a world called Austra. The recovery room here had murals of a hilly green landscape on all four walls. Hawke preferred it to the mint green walls of Varrell.

Smiling people in Authority medical uniform fussed over him, concerned about his well-being. Hawke acted a little sicker than he felt for the pretty brunette. She sat by him and wiped his brow while Cayden and Filip smirked nearby. He wondered if they would spoil his fun but neither of them said anything. Hawke was dismayed by the attention his medic gave the pirate when she finished tending to Hawke and suddenly it wasn't fun anymore. He muttered something and Cayden asked for clarification.

"I said the woman has no taste."

Filip laughed.

The portal stop was on the base that held the DOME. Because of the name, Hawke thought the building would be spherical but it was an ordinary looking rectangle.

"Why are all their buildings so boring?" Hawke asked as they walked across the grounds towards it.

"The Authorities are nothing if not practical," Filip replied. "Practical buildings, practical names, practical solutions."

Hawke didn't think it was practical to make everything the same but he didn't know how to argue about the dangers of mediocrity so he held his tongue.

The DOME looked like the foyer of a grand house when they stepped inside, which wasn't what he'd been expecting. Armed guards stood at the entranceway but looked relaxed rather than alert. Their IDs were checked and their hands scanned before they were let into an elevator. Like the ones at Willets, it was spacious and plain. An Authority soldier went in with them and stood at the back, his weapon pointed sedately at the floor.

Cayden swiped his card and pressed a button. There was a sensation in Hawke's belly that he despised because he hadn't expected the elevator to plunge downwards. He could tell when it was coming to a stop because he could feel the pressure in his legs.

The doors opened. The floor they stopped at was very busy. There was a mix of people wearing yellow pyjamas and caps as well as more uniformed people. Filip and Hawke were scanned first, but after Cayden was scanned he was handed a special pass which he clipped to his lapel. Hawke kept close to him as they moved through the crowded halls.

"The prisoner trusts his keeper," Filip said. Hawke didn't reply, though the comment resonated in him.

They arrived at a door that required Cayden's pass before it swished open. The corridor beyond held fewer Authorities in uniforms. There were more pyjama people, only some were in pink as well as yellow. A man in pink approached them with a booklet that he wrote on with his finger, and scanned Cayden's pass and identification card with it. Hawke was interested to note that he was in a very special location.

The three of them were led to a room. Hawke stood near the door and looked at what appeared to be a child's playroom. He wasn't fooled by the bright pictures on the metal walls or the jigsaw rug that covered most of the laminated floor; this place was a holding cell. A large rectangular mirror was set into one wall.

"You can investigate the room," Cayden said. Hawke took that to mean he should, so he walked around, touching a few things that he found interesting.

He found and switched on a radio after fiddling with the different buttons and switches, and left it quietly playing instrumental music. There was a large chest that he investigated. Inside was a wooden train set that he took out. Underneath all of the pieces was a blue pennant. He left it there and assembled some of the track. He pulled it apart before getting too far and tossed all the pieces back into the chest, his motivation for play lacking in this strange location.

Hawke stood and faced Cayden. "Am I here to answer questions?"

"Yes."

Hawke didn't need translation by Filip but the pirate repeated it anyway in Boronian.

"I know what yes and no means," Hawke said indignantly. Filip remained impassive and he wondered if the pirate was going to continue to translate the simple words or not. Hawke looked at the mirror again. There was no need for a mirror that size in a room like this, unless it was like a television or window.

"They're not going to ask questions about the Wanderers anymore, are they?" he guessed.

"Do you want me to translate that?" Filip asked.

Hawke shook his head and approached the table that was close to the mirror. Two chairs faced each other on each side and he wondered who would be sitting on them. He gripped the back of one of the chairs and pushed down on it.

"Is it going to hurt?" he asked, looking at Cayden. When Filip translated for him, Cayden's expression was a mixture of compassion and guilt.

"No, Hawke. No more than visiting a doctor."

Filip chuckled when he translated this, using the word *apothecary* instead of doctor because it was the closest word, and he knew that they delivered princely sums of pain on a regular basis. Having been through a similar conversation when he'd first met Cayden, Hawke knew that it wasn't the same thing. He was annoyed by the pirate's sadistic humour. Hawke was determined to let him know that his joke didn't have the desired effect.

"I know that an apothecary is different," he said snidely.

"Not that different," Filip smirked.

Hawke glared and Cayden intervened. He sat upon the chair so they could speak at eye level.

"I have a son about your age. A little younger. He doesn't like going to the doctor either but he knows it's not always bad. I think he's more worried when he doesn't know which way it's going to go, if it's going to hurt or not. When he knows he's getting a needle, he deals with that quite well. He's a brave boy, but I don't think he's as brave as you."

Filip translated.

"What's his name?" Hawke asked cynically, curious about the Lieutenant who he hadn't pictured as a father. He suspected the story might be made up for his benefit.

"Octavian, but we call him Tavi mostly."

"Does he go to my school?" Hawke asked

"No, he goes to school on his own world. On my home world, Ulsa Maya. Would you like to meet him?"

"You'd take me to your home world?" Hawke asked, surprised.

"Yes, for the holidays. You'll also have learned how to speak the language by then. I'm sure you and Tavi will have a lot to talk about," Cayden said.

'Holidays' was a word that Filip used directly because there was no Boronian word for it. Filip described what it meant, and Hawke thought it sounded nice. He supposed he'd been on 'holidays' with his family on Boronia when they'd gone on picnics or visiting with others at their estates, but those had been day trips or overnight trips, and the 'holiday' idea seemed to last a great deal longer.

A man entered the room with a young woman, both dressed in pink pyjamas and wearing long white coats over the top. The woman carried one of the booklets that were written on with fingertips and the man held the lapels of his coat. Lieutenant Cayden shook both of their hands and introduced Filip to them. Both of them sat at the table and Cayden arranged for Hawke and Filip to sit across from them. He positioned himself on a low stool not too far away and listened in. Hawke was glad for his presence.

"I am Doctor Norovian Glauka and this is Doctor Kelly Turner. We are going to ask you some questions that we would like you to answer truthfully."

The questions revolved around moral issues, such as if he found something stolen, would he return it or keep it. Hawke answered them instinctively. He was given some logic puzzles that displayed on the booklet; he could move the pictures around with his finger—it was like the disc shows but he could touch it. After he solved the puzzles, he began pressing different buttons on the device. It was quickly rescued from his inquisitive fingers.

"We shall perform a flag test now. If you show me a green flag, you will be rewarded. If you show me a red flag, you will be punished. A blue flag will randomly give you one of those options. Did you find a flag while you were waiting?"

Hawke thought of the blue pennant underneath the train toys.

"No."

The woman made some notations on the booklet. When she gave a nod, the next question came.

"We will perform a new flag test now. If you show me a blue flag, you will be rewarded. If you show me a green flag, you will be punished. A red flag will randomly give you one of those options. Did you find a flag while you were waiting?"

"You just changed the colours around," Hawke stated. "You can't do that."

Filip translated for him and the woman smiled while the man shrugged.

"These are the new rules. Blue is reward, green is punishment, red can be either. Did you find a flag?"

"What kind of reward?"

The woman made more gestures on the booklet and Hawke supposed she was writing down his answer.

"You cannot know. Please answer the question."

"No. I didn't find a flag."

Glauka's eyebrows lifted.

"You know I found a flag!" Hawke accused.

"I do not know," the man replied.

"You must've seen."

"I was not in the room with you while you were playing. I do not know if you found a flag or what colour flag you found."

"You probably saw through the window."

"There is no window here, we are underground."

Hawke pointed at the mirror.

"That is a mirror, not a window."

"And I thought that was a booklet, not...a magic thing," Hawke said, pointing. Cayden barked laughter and was summarily told off for it.

"It's called a tablet," she said offhandedly. "You can have a chocolate bar if you show me a blue flag."

"I don't want a chocolate bar."

"Cake, then."

Hawke shook his head.

"You may name your reward."

Hawke blinked. "I can say what I want?"

"Yes."

Hawke went to the train box and tipped it over. Train tracks and carriages tumbled out with a crash. He knelt down and dug through them before he got the pennant out and held it up. The woman doctor made many notes on her tablet.

"Well done. What would you like?"

"I want to go home to Boronia."

"Oh, Hawke," Cayden said from his seated position nearby, and Hawke looked at him, knowing that his reward wouldn't have come but needing to make the point anyway.

"It was supposed to be a food reward," Glauka insisted.

Hawke threw the flag down and glared at the doctors who were both watching him closely. He didn't like the way they were looking at him, studying everything he did and said before writing it down.

Cayden spoke, causing Glauka to huff.

"I'll take you home. One day, I'll take you back home. I swear it."

Filip translated for him and Hawke wasn't sure if Filip was playing a trick on him or not, but he threw his arms around Cayden anyway and pressed his face against his uniform. The promise should've made him feel emotional but other than gratitude, there wasn't much hope inside him.

Lunch was brought to him in the playroom. After he ate, he was taken to a white room with lots of different equipment in it. He changed into a light green gown and sat on a chair that was very much like the ones inside the Authority portals, only he didn't have switches and buttons. Cayden and Filip were both in the room with him, explaining everything. He did his best to appear stoic but he was scared. There were screens that showed light patterns and machines that made bleeping sounds. A team of doctors had a discussion over his head in a language he didn't understand—neither Filip nor Cayden translated what they said. Nearby was a tray of nasty looking tools that Hawke didn't like the look of.

He was given a large bottle of water to drink and urged to drink it all. He only got halfway through it before they took a blood sample from him. A peculiar helmet hooked up with wires was strapped onto his head. He watched as photos appeared on a television, all of them landscapes or from different parts of the world (worlds?) in various seasons. After the photos finished, the helmet was taken off him. He hoped all of the tests would be as easy.

They weren't. Every other test was either physical or hurtful. Machines both large and small were hooked up to him, clipped to his skin, giving him small voltages or large doses of pain. His skin was red and sore in some places, bruised in others. Cayden was there to hold his hand, but by the end, Hawke no longer wanted to hold it.

Hawke was returned to the playroom where there was more food and water on the table for him but he ignored it and whirled on Cayden instead.

"Why did you bring me here?"

"I know it seems like a lot, but I thought you would prefer three days every few months rather than—"

"I don't care about the arrangement, I want to know why you're bringing me here at all!"

Cayden looked confused as Filip interpreted. "We talked about this. I explained it all to you."

"All you explained was that I didn't have a choice."

"You have a choice," Cayden said. "You can deal with it, you can cry about it or you can fight it. It might not change what happens here but it will change how you feel about it, and also the outcome you get from it."

"The outcome? Am I risking vague rewards and empty promises?" Hawke snapped. "The Wanderers treated me better. At least they didn't lie."

Filip didn't translate for him. Cayden looked at him expectantly but the pirate stared at Hawke.

"You don't want me to repeat that, Lord Hawke," Filip said to him.

"They'll figure it out anyway. They have their tablets and television discs. Everything I say in here is written down."

Filip's lips quirked a smile, though his eyes were cold.

"You're smart, Lord Hawke. Smarter than most but dumb, too. He's getting impatient. Give me something I can say to him."

Hawke's gaze flicked to Cayden whose lips were pressed so tightly he had a slash for a mouth. With his hands on his hips and his feet slightly apart, Cayden looked imposing.

"Tell him I'll do his stupid tests. But I want a favour from him for later."

Filip laughed and translated. Hawke watched as Cayden received the news. He and the pirate spoke back and forth for a short while until Filip saluted and Cayden let him out of the room with a swipe of the card.

After a short time, a bed was rolled into the room and unfolded. He watched as two yellow pyjama people dressed it before leaving him and Cayden alone.

"Tired?"

Hawke didn't recognise the word but when Cayden mimicked yawning, Hawke nodded. He wanted the day to be over and sleeping would be the fastest way to end it.

His dreams were filled with campsites and ice serpents.

When he awoke, he was alone but not for long. A new set of green pyjamas in his size had been provided for him and as soon as he was clothed in them, a man dressed in yellow carried in a tray with breakfast and took away the uneaten meal.

Hawke supposed it was morning but he had no idea. Time was irrelevant in an underground room. He was hungry enough to eat all of his porridge.

He went to the mirror and tidied his hair with his hands and thought about how nothing made sense anymore. The Wanderers had not only taken him out of his world, they'd taken everything he knew from him before throwing him away. Now he was with people who could put him back but wouldn't because he might betray their secret.

He looked around at the things in the room; interesting things, colourful things that he couldn't have even imagined on Boronia. It was all fake. It would've been better if he'd stayed in a room that looked like a dungeon cell...at least that wouldn't have been hypocritical.

He stood and grabbed the chair he'd been sitting on. He could lift it but it was heavy because it was sturdy—he'd felt that much while leaning on it yesterday. He imagined what the medics behind the mirror might be writing down before he swung the chair and smashed it against the glass. It hit hard and he expected to come away with spidery cracks but there was only a small circle where the chair leg had impacted. He tried again but the second hit left no damage. Abandoning the chair, he searched for something else to use. He grabbed the radio because it was the heaviest thing in the room but easier to use as a weapon, and bashed it against the glass. On the fifth slam, plastic yielded and exploded under his hands, shards cutting through his left hand. He swiped his blood across the mirror, leaving streaks like warpaint.

The door opened and pink and yellow clad people streamed into his room to restrain him. He was surprised that his actions had provoked this response. Apparently they thought he needed five grown men to restrain him. He didn't fight them, though the one that grabbed him had thick fingers that bit painfully into his upper arms. Two of the pink clad men had been carrying cases with them, and they opened them up to reveal not syringes like he expected, but bandages.

He was silent when they washed his hand and inspected it, armed with tweezers. His silence meant nothing, for his attack had been silent, though he had no intention of fighting these men.

Neither Filip nor Cayden said anything to him about his bandaged hand when they came to collect him. Hawke figured they'd been told but he was upset that Cayden wouldn't at least ask how he felt.

He only had puzzle tests to solve—perhaps they thought he needed a break. If that was the result of his outburst and wound, then it was worth it. After he solved them all, Dr Kelly Turner had a long talk with him She started out reading questions from her tablet but then set it down and chatted with him about school. Hawke would've felt more at ease if Filip hadn't been sitting beside him translating everything. Hawke complained that there wasn't an invention that could translate everything for him. He didn't think Filip would translate this but he must've because Turner chuckled and told him that she'd pass on his request.

Before the session ended he was asked his reasons for trying to break the mirror. He shrugged. He thought she'd press him but Dr Turner only told him that he wouldn't be needed for a few months while they investigated his results. Hawke continued to sit, unsure of what to do until Cayden stood and held out a hand. Hawke took it and left the room with Cayden, Filip following behind.

He was taken back to his room and changed into his clothes. He was unsure why because all of the tests had been performed on him while he'd been wearing pyjamas. Once dressed, he was led to the elevator. It went up as fast as it had gone down, and when the three of them left it, Hawke realised they were leaving.

"I thought I was here for three days, not for two."

"Your psychological tests were cut short."

"So all I had to do was try and break a mirror?"

Cayden didn't answer right away. They moved out of the DOME and set down the path that led to the building that housed the portal. Hawke was between the two men.

Cayden volunteered advice.

"I wouldn't do that again. Glauka wanted to keep you longer because of that. Turner and I argued against it, but I don't carry much weight with these people."

When Filip translated, he had a peculiar look.

"What? What are you thinking?"

Filip frowned at him.

"Tell me all of it."

"That's all he said."

"There's something else though, isn't there?" Hawke challenged.

"Not at all."

"You're a bad liar."

Filip chuckled. "It appears so."

"So tell me."

He expected the pirate to stall but he answered.

"The people I owe favours to are very high ranking. They've helped me on the Isles a great deal. If I'm here helping *him* out, it means he has more influence than he says."

"More influence?" Hawke repeated.

"Be careful, Lord Hawke. You're sailing bigger seas now."

"What does that mean?"

"Choose your battles."

"So...I should do what the scientists want?"

Cayden cleared his throat. Hawke looked up in time to see a pointed look directed at Filip, who translated then nodded at Hawke.

"Because it works so well for you. Taking orders."

Filip gave him an admonishing look. "I beg pardon,

Lord Hawke. You must know best."

The front doors of the portal building slid open to let them in and Hawke knew Filip wasn't going to be with them much longer.

"Pirates have no masters. Why would you give that up?"

"What makes you think I gave it up?"

Hawke stared at Filip's smug expression and realised he'd made the wrong assumption.

"You go back?"

"All the time, little Lord."

Rage threatened to choke Hawke. Why were the Authorities allowing criminals like pirates to go back to Boronia while keeping him away? The excuse of having other-worldly knowledge was no longer valid. A pirate was less trust-worthy than a nobleman's son. How dare they afford Filip this benefit?

The worst part was that Cayden had fed him the lie and Hawke, like a fool, had believed it. All he was asking for was to go home. Why was that so hard?

Cayden must have sensed a shift in tension and made a querying remark that Hawke didn't understand. It wasn't translated for him. He doubted he would've been able to answer past the constriction in his throat anyway.

The portal trip was uneventful. Filip didn't come back with them and Hawke was glad. The car ride would've been silent except Cayden tried making broken conversation. Hawke ignored his attempts. Once they were on the Academy grounds, Hawke unfastened his restraint and flung himself out of the car so fast that he fell. Without noticing the cuts on his palms, he picked himself up and ran away.

Cayden called out his name but he didn't turn back. He couldn't spend another moment with a man who was betraying him.

CHAPTER EIGHTEEN

Meeting The Queen

THROUGH the barred window, the sky was tinged with dawn's soft light. In spite of the early hour, Daeson could hear the thudding of heavy footsteps along the corridor and the low murmur of muffled conversation through the walls.

He reached for his bedside drawer and pulled it open. Only two things were inside; his property deed and coin pouch. He unstrung the pouch and took out one of the coins before laying back on the bed, turning it in his fingers. A picture of measuring scales was stamped on one side and the tallied weight marked on the other. He waited for the ache of homesickness to overwhelm him because it was expected, but he *didn't* miss the farm, he *didn't* miss Cloverlea. It didn't seem right but that was how he felt and he couldn't change it.

He tossed the coin back into the drawer, shut it and got out of bed. He found more clothing and a fresh pair of underwear when he checked behind the screen. He took them with him into the bathing room and set them atop the counter near the sink before toileting and showering. The convenience of an indoor washroom was something he'd fast grown used to.

Once dressed, he found the shirt a little loose around the shoulders but the pants—*jeans*—fit well. He didn't like them. They were clean and comfortable but they smelled like they'd come from another person. He felt like an impostor. Surviving here meant adjusting quickly, which included learning the twisty language. He thought he might be able to pick it up fast as he understood most of it already. He would learn even faster under Omerri's instruction, since she could translate for him.

He was looking forward to seeing her.

Daeson tentatively tried the door and was pleased when it opened. He moved down the corridor, going the same way he'd gone the day before. There were more closed doors this morning. Curiosity drew him close to one of them, where he could hear the sounds of grunts and rhythmic thumping through the door. He was filled with a mixture of amusement and embarrassment, knowing he shouldn't be eavesdropping. He didn't know how long he'd stood there listening but a door opening nearby motivated him to get moving.

He hurried downstairs and stopped to get his bearings in the corridor on the ground floor. Towards the front of the house, he could see a ginger-haired man dressed in black pants and a turquoise shirt. Daeson offered him a brief smile before heading towards the kitchen. He hoped to start the day with another hearty breakfast because he always had a clearer head once he had a full belly. Before he could get more than a few steps, someone cleared their throat behind him.

"Excuse me, sir. This way, please."

He turned to see the ginger-haired man approach with a helpful smile and a beckoning hand. Perhaps Omerri had arranged something for him and this fellow was supposed to take him there. Daeson went to the man with a smile but said nothing, not wanting to give away his loose grasp of the language.

"Do you have a coat?"

The question was simple enough for Daeson to decipher.

"No, I wasn't given one," Daeson replied. He wasn't feeling the cold but perhaps it was supposed to go along with his new outfit. The ginger-haired man laughed like Daeson had said something highly amusing, and clapped him on the back.

"Your girl must've treated you well, sir."

Daeson didn't fully understand the man's words but assumed he was asking about his time spent with

Omerri yesterday.

"Omerri was very nice," Daeson agreed, hoping his answer was satisfactory.

It wasn't.

The fellow's face changed from a smiling, friendly expression to an indignant one. He grabbed Daeson's arm with a growl.

"Don't talk about Miss Backhouse that way, scum. You couldn't afford her favour even if she was sellin', which she ain't."

Daeson only understood 'Miss Backhouse' but the tone translated the rest. Perhaps he wasn't allowed to call Omerri by her first name. He apologised while he was being marched towards the front door but didn't pull away until it was opened for him.

"No, I can't leave," he said, feeling panic welling up from his stomach to his chest. Where would he go? Omerri had told him to stay in the house, to keep himself safe. Daeson grabbed each side of the door frame but didn't have time to brace himself.

"Out!" Ginger insisted, pushing against Daeson's back. Daeson was now through the door but was still holding onto the frame. His shoulders screamed in protest as Ginger shoved forcefully against him. He didn't think he could hold on for much longer. In the background, Daeson could hear the shrill sound of a woman laughing.

"Leave off, Ladd," a man said.

The shoving stopped and Daeson leapt back inside the house. The woman was still laughing and he saw her looking at him through a little window in the wall, like a horse at its stall door. She was behaving more like a donkey though, braying laughter the way she was. The man who'd spoken was Nick, standing in the foyer and frowning at Ginger. *Ladd*, Daeson recalled.

"He insulted Miss Backhouse," Ladd replied waspishly.

Nick grunted and tipped his head for Daeson to join him. He hesitated before hurrying past Ladd. He didn't know why the man had wanted to throw him out, but he understood that Nick had come at the right time and that the staff here followed his orders.

"Getting into trouble already?" Nick asked.

"I wanted breakfast," Daeson said.

"I'll eat with you."

Breakfast with Nick wasn't like breakfast with Omerri. Nick said very little but he stared a lot, and his dark gaze was intense and moody. They didn't order a meal but they did get served one. It wasn't fancy but it was filling. Daeson and Nick ate like their food was about to escape their plates, and once they were done, Nick pounded his chest a couple of times to help him burp. Daeson didn't feel the need to join in.

"Why'd you get up so early?" Nick asked.

"I get up at sunrise," Daeson provided.

"Why?"

"I always have."

"That's not a fucking answer."

Daeson blinked his surprise at Nick's gruff reply. It was unexpected, though he let it slide, thinking that Nick must've misinterpreted.

"I grew up on a farm. I've always risen before the sun to do my chores."

Nick muttered something at his empty plate. Daeson didn't know if he was speaking to it, to him, or to it about him. He chose to say nothing and ignored the awkward silence that followed. Nick was the first to speak.

"Omerri doesn't get up until ten."

"Ten what?"

Nick stared at Daeson for a long moment and heaved a sigh. Daeson felt self-conscious about being thought a simpleton, but he couldn't explain his ignorance, not if he wanted to keep his Wandering a secret. Nick stood up and Daeson did the same.

"Jade can take care of you until Omerri wakes up."

Daeson nodded politely until he figured out Nick's words.

"I don't need—"

Nick barked an order at him and pointed to the chair. Daeson sat back down, feeling cowed and infuriated at the same time. He didn't want to be under Nick's influence but he felt like he had no other choice. Nick was a bully but until Daeson could understand more of what was going on around him, he thought it would be better to do as he was told. Nick left the room and Daeson waited.

A woman eventually appeared in the dining room's doorway and her gaze found him. Her hair was untethered, long, dark and straight, and her eyes a vibrant green. She was dressed in a short transparent black negligee over a green bra and underwear. The skimpy outfit didn't hide much. It took him a moment to realise he was staring and he pointedly looked away to be respectful.

"Hello. Daeson, is it?" she asked as she moved closer, her voice soothing. "Nick sent me to look after you. I'm Jade."

He peeked at her from the corner of his eyes. When she extended a hand towards him, he angled himself away. "What's the matter?" she asked, dropping her hand.

"Your name isn't Jade."

"It's not my real name but that's what I'm called here."

Her explanation was truthful, though Daeson couldn't decipher it. She spoke quickly and through a broad smile, which made her words more difficult to understand.

"Are you cold?" he asked.

"Not really. Do you want me to change?" she

gestured at her clothes.

"Yes, please."

"Alright, follow me."

"I can stay here."

Jade tilted her head and regarded him. "If you ditch me, I'll get into trouble."

Daeson looked at her blankly. She seemed not to need a response because she left. He waited again, this time having something to watch as Kite first cleared the table then wiped it down. Jade returned quickly, with her hair tied back and wearing a short green dress.

"Want me to show you around?" she offered.

"Could you speak slower?"

"Sure. Would...you...like...to look...around?" Jade shouted while using expressive hand gestures. Was she being serious? Daeson answered anyway.

"Yes." The idea of knowing his way around the building appealed greatly.

"Okay, we'll start with upstairs." Jade spoke loudly and pointed upward.

He followed her and she pointed out rooms, identifying them by their decorated colours, all of which matched Daeson's language. She referred to his room as 'the white room'.

"Do you live in the green room?" Daeson asked.

"I like the way you say 'room', pooching out your lips like that. It's cute," Jade said. He smiled at her and she returned it. She'd forgotten to speak slowly but it didn't matter. "I don't live here, if that's what you just asked me. I have my own place next door. Not far enough away I think, because I'm not going to be working here for years and years like some of the girls. I have a plan."

Daeson let her chatter wash over him. Jade liked to talk and he liked listening because she had a nice voice and everything she said was truthful. The best thing about her was that she made everything sounded happy. He was glad she was spending time with him, even though it was only because Nick had asked her to.

When they were touring the floor on the upper level, Jade mentioned Omerri.

"What did you say?" he interrupted.

"Omerri's rooms are upstairs, so we won't go there. She likes her privacy." Jade looked Daeson over and gave him a sly smile. "*You* might end up there."

He didn't know how to react to such an idea. It seemed an inappropriate suggestion. When he didn't say anything about Omerri, Jade led him back downstairs, saying 'club' a few times. Daeson didn't think she was going to show him a hefty stick to beat people with so went willingly, curious about what he would end up seeing. Her excitement was contagious.

The 'club' ended up being a large room in the basement. Daeson followed Jade through a carpeted area filled with tall tables and stools and stepped onto a raised wooden stage where Jade began to sway and move around in a dance Daeson had never seen before.

"Why is it so dark?" he asked. There were strange pink and blue glowing lines that he could see by and tiny spots of light in the ceiling, but it felt like night down here.

"Here, I'll put the mirror ball on for you," Jade said cryptically, gesturing upwards and moving towards a black desk in the corner of the dance floor. Daeson looked up to see a sphere hanging above him. It looked like a small, shiny moon. With a loud clacking, the ball slowly began to spin. Daeson was captivated as spots of light danced around the glowing room—it was like watching stars move rapidly across the sky. He was suddenly accosted by loud singing and thumping so great that he could feel it reverberating in his chest. The noise was so thunderous that he pressed his palms flat against his ears. He couldn't block it out so he yelled for it to stop. Even after the noise was gone, there was a ringing in his ears.

"You don't like music?" she asked, leaving the black desk where she'd been controlling everything.

"Why did you make it so loud?" Daeson asked.

"That's the volume it's always at. It's so you can feel the music in your body." She gave a little shimmy.

"Music is for listening," he told her.

Jade shook her head and tapped his shoulder playfully. "No, buddy, music is for feeling. It can shape your *mood*, your whole state of mind, you know?"

"I don't know," he replied, not realising her question was rhetorical.

Jade giggled. "Okay, buddy, very funny." She moved to a long counter that ran parallel to a wood-panelled wall and Daeson followed her.

"I've never heard that kind of music before," he explained. As soon as the statement was out of his mouth, he wondered if she would find such a thing suspicious.

"Not many people have," she said. She launched into a complicated description about how the music was recorded, which he didn't fully understand. He managed to catch that it came from another world. "The Authorities really like dancing to it." She gestured for him to sit on one of the counter stools.

"The Authorities?" Daeson repeated warily.

"This is their favourite hangout. Don't worry, buddy, they won't close this place down. They're the ones we bring the alcohol here for."

She moved around to the other side of the counter and slid open a wall panel, revealing long rows of bottles. He thought he knew what they were; different kinds of intoxicants.

"This is a *tavern*. An underground tavern...and instead of minstrels you have the, uh...magic music."

The way the music had filled the room everywhere at once had felt like magic, though it hadn't sounded very magical.

"Tavern, sure," Jade repeated with a grin. "Sit and survey while l make a drink."

Daeson watched as she mixed a drink and chatted. He did his best to join her conversation but when she spoke very quickly he had no chance. Every now and then she held up a bottle and named it for him. He recognised rum.

A triangular glass was placed in front of him that held a vibrant pink liquid.

"I can't," he said, shaking his head.

"Sure you can, it's free."

"I'm too young."

She giggled but it faded quickly. "What? You're not serious? How old are you? You look twenty-five."

"Sixteen," he said. Jade smiled like she was uncertain but she must have decided he was telling the truth for her eyes widened before she looked at him compassionately.

"You poor little lamb, you must be from the outer province, yeah? In Gredann, you're an adult when you're fourteen. You can thank the Authorities for that. So, here you're allowed to drink."

Daeson pulled the pink drink closer to himself and sniffed it. It smelled sweet and vaguely of apricot. Jade smiled at him expectantly. Because he didn't want to ask Omerri or Nick, he asked Jade about what this house really was.

"Is this...do men come here and...are the bedrooms for hire?"

He thought she would be insulted but Jade just laughed and nodded.

"Yes, buddy. This is a brothel known as the Queen of Hearts and I'm a favour-giver. Now drink up before you lose your nerve."

He took her advice.

Daeson finished his seventh drink and was watching Jade make another. He hadn't enjoyed the taste of some of her efforts but she'd figured out quickly he was a fan of the fruit liqueurs. He'd drunk a few drinks with strange names like Melon Ball and Appletini.

"Don't get him drunk," Nick complained, appearing from the shadows. Daeson wondered if this was the reason Nick wore black clothing all the time. He was the kind of man that liked to keep himself to himself— Daeson had met a few such men in his life and didn't understand their strong desire for reclusiveness. Kurgan had been one such man.

"He's not drunk," Jade replied, sounding excited. "Daeson here has never had a drink in his life, yet he's downing them all like water. Hasn't slurred once."

Nick was thoughtful. "How many has he had?"

"This is his eighth," Jade replied, setting a tiny glass in front of Daeson. He'd learned that the small ones were called shots and were supposed to be drunk in a single gulp. He reached for it but Nick grabbed the shot glass first and swigged it. Daeson felt vindicated when Nick pulled a ghastly face as he set it down.

"What the fuck is this shit?"

"It's a Jungle Run."

"Why the fuck are you giving him girl drinks?"

"They're not 'girl drinks' you macho wannabe. He likes them."

More arguing and gesturing between Jade and Nick towards Daeson had him shifting uneasily in his seat.

"Okay. It's okay," Daeson said, capturing their attention by patting the air. When Nick glared at him, he felt his insides wither but he made himself stare back, not wanting Jade to get into trouble. He was surprised when Nick's tone changed to something quieter.

"Jade, back to work. My turn now."

"Yes, boss," she replied, and left quickly.

Daeson found it interesting that Jade conceded since she'd been ready to shout at Nick on his behalf. He watched her go and looked back at Nick who was staring at him intently.

"Not for you."

"Pardon?"

"Jade. Not for you."

Daeson blushed and nodded his understanding, unable to speak. Nick moved away to switch off the mirror ball, grumbling about it as he did so. Daeson looked curiously at the line of glasses that he'd drunk from. He'd seen the after-effects of those who drank too much at the tavern; his father had warned him of the addled state it put one's mind in. Daeson was certain he should've been affected but he felt no different. Did that mean intoxicating drinks were weaker here than on his home world? Or perhaps the folk where Daeson was from were hardier. It was curious that Jade had considered him almost ten years older than his true age.

"No more drink," Nick ordered, but he took the stool beside Daeson.

"No more," Daeson agreed.

"Omerri..." Nick faltered after speaking her name and then looked Daeson over. He looked unhappy.

"Omerri is on her way?" Daeson prompted, feeling obliged to fill the growing silence.

Nick nodded. "Omerri tells me you have a special gift."

Daeson's stomach flopped and then knotted at the obvious betrayal. He wished he hadn't understood Nick's words but the meaning was clear. Omerri had shared information about his talent to Nick. The hollow sensation in the pit of his stomach persisted as he remembered her promise to keep it a secret. She hadn't lied to him...had she changed her mind? She'd made it clear that sharing such knowledge risked his life, yet she'd immediately told Nick?

"Don't look so gutted. It makes you useful. It's good to be useful on this world. She knows that."

Daeson stared at Nick unhappily. "Useful or used?" he asked.

Nick had the decency to look sympathetic to Daeson's plight. "Yep."

CHAPTER NINETEEN

In Defence

SYNJAN looked up from her desk in surprise as Ellis entered her workspace. She'd been updating an accounts ledger but her hand stilled. She sat upright and pushed her reading glasses to the top of her head.

"I've just received a disturbing telephone call. I need you to head out."

"Now?" Synjan complained, looking at her watch. It was half past five and she'd been intent on finishing her work before dinner. When her gaze returned to take in Ellis' expression, she regretted her query. His lips were thin and his hands were fisted by his sides.

"Apparently the delay in settling the Sandy Avenue property has worked against us," he said stiffly. "I was informed that the building's been breached and there are *squatters* inside."

He sounded repulsed by the notion.

He'd purchased a new office building in Portside a couple of months ago—she didn't know the specifics behind his impulse buy but suspected it was because he wanted to dabble in the less shadowy, more legal role of industrial landlord. Unfortunately, the transfer of ownership had taken an extra month to complete due to legal problems on the developer's end. They'd finally received the keys to the building two days beforehand but neither of them had gone to inspect it, believing it to have been locked up safely while the purchasing limbo persisted.

Any other businessman would have called the Authorities to inspect the property after being informed that it had been compromised but Ellis was far too cautious for that. This was what he had Synjan for; he'd prefer she go and ascertain how problematic the situation was before he asked for Authority intercession. Who knew what the trespassers might have been up to in a brand new, empty office building with two months' unfettered access? With his name on the deed, Ellis wasn't going to leave potentially incriminating discoveries up to the Authorities.

Synjan thought carefully before she said anything else likely to aggravate her boss.

"Do you have a description?"

"There are three men."

Synjan waited for more information to come but, as the silence stretched, she realised he had nothing else to give. She chose not to criticise or query the reliability of the informant. Instead, she dropped her pen, set her glasses down on the desk and stood up.

"Right. I'll find out what's going on. Has it got utilities connected?"

"As far as I know, yes. I believe you'll find live telephones, too. Some of the offices were outfitted for display purposes."

Ellis was uncharacteristically vague. Synjan didn't need to exacerbate an already tense situation so she left without further comment.

The smell of cooking dinner taunted her as she bounded up the stairs and hurried into her bedroom. She needed to change from her casual clothes to something more utilitarian. Tight black pants and a jacket that moulded to her figure allowed her freedom of movement. She pulled on steel-capped boots to protect her feet. A small calibre gun holstered in her bra provided backup security but she also put her favourite, larger gun in a backpack along with her hip holster and extra ammunition. The bag would make her look like she was heading home from work and rushing to get there before the curfew siren sounded. Finally, she braided her hair and tucked it under a snug black leather hat to keep it out of her eyes.

Rushing into the kitchen to retrieve a water bottle, Synjan almost ran into Urvasi as she turned from the stove, wiping her hands on the apron stretched around her.

"Synjan!" the older woman exclaimed, taking a step backwards and clutching melodramatically at her chest.

"I'm sorry!" Synjan cried, placing a comforting arm around the housekeeper's soft shoulders.

"I didn't hear you come up."

"I know, I'm sorry," Synjan repeated, rubbing Urvasi's upper arm a couple of times before she stepped away to open the refrigerator's door.

"Are you going out?" Urvasi asked rhetorically—she knew very well what Synjan shoving a water flask into her pack meant. "I was about to start serving!"

"I thought as much," Synjan sighed sympathetically, offering a smile of consolation. "It smells *delicious* but this—it can't be helped, I really have to go and check something out."

"Does Mr Ellis know?"

"Yes, he insisted it be done *before* dinner."

Urvasi muttered something against Ellis beneath her breath as she retraced her steps in order to emphatically turn the stove off.

"Please keep me a plate, I should only be an hour," Synjan vowed as she jostled her backpack to test that the items inside didn't rattle.

"It will be in the oven for you," Urvasi agreed resignedly.

"Thanks, you're a gem!" Synjan called as she hurried out of the kitchen and back to her office to collect her flashlight. Ellis was still in there.

"Don't go far. I may need to call you," she warned.

His expression was grim as he watched her check the light worked. "I won't," he promised.

"And don't lock up here, I'm not taking my keys. How am I getting into Sandy Avenue?"

He scowled and led her into his office.

"This is the master key." He held it out towards her.

"Ta," she grunted and zipped it carefully into the pocket of her jacket, aware of Ellis' intense gaze. The weight of his expectation was never more apparent than at moments such as these.

"Be careful."

"Of course."

Shoving her arms through her backpack, she ran downstairs and headed out onto streets that were already wearing the cloak of dusk. A few people were walking quickly towards their destination, so her haste didn't make her obvious. She mapped minimally as she settled into a steady jog, taking the most direct route out of Dockside. The sound of her booted feet on uneven thoroughfares was familiar and comforting. As she wound her way west, the departing sun coated the tops of built-up warehouses and crooked, weather-worn homes with its last rays. Down on the ground, the shadows were thickening like old timers gathering to resist the Authorities. They would soon head out on their curfew hunt.

Spurred on by the thought of concluding her business before the patrols hit the streets, Synjan sped up.

Despite her efforts, night had overcome the city by the time she reached Sandy Avenue. She circled the long building, reconnoitring by street light until she found a secluded entryway at the back to use. Ensuring the door was locked behind her, she re-secured the master key in a zippered pocket and crouched in the dark stairwell to unpack her bag. She closed her eyes, opening up her mind to get a true indication of what she was walking into while strapping her holster around her waist.

Contradictory to Ellis' tip off, there were four patterns at the north end of the building. She judged them to be on the top floor because of the height distance between them and her. Three moved around quite freely for the number of minutes she watched them, but there was a fourth person lying down in a corner that she suspected wasn't a willing part of their gang—especially when one of the trespassers began doing something brutal to that person...a woman. She chose not to look too hard at what was happening and focussed on her preparations instead.

Confident she wasn't about to be discovered, Synjan flicked on her torch and examined her surroundings before setting the light down. It was wise to assume that the squatters had set themselves up in a defensible position, with exits available. The three men didn't seem to be interacting with one another, all seemed occupied with different things. Anything could be happening up there.

Synjan took the time to rehydrate, re-check her equipment and pull her gun out of the pack. After a quick once-over, she holstered it and turned off her torch. While her eyes adjusted to the dark, she did a few stretches and thought about how best to approach the strangers on the top floor.

Ellis would want to know who they were and why they were there. He'd also want her to punish them soundly for having the audacity to trespass in his building, so she'd need to account for hurting them, though not necessarily killing them. A great deal of her success depended on what she found when she reached the men, but even a vague plan was better than guesswork. *Focus is your first advantage, preparedness your primary weapon.* It was Freddie's mantra and she'd absorbed it. Mentally primed, she re-shouldered her back pack and set off up the stairs.

She sincerely wished she'd paid more attention to the layout of the building when she and Ellis had inspected this place. Her talent couldn't tell her about internal doors, the structural integrity of walls or the exact dimensions of the clusters of offices she was running past. She usually had an accurate memory for details but this business was always going to be legitimate and wouldn't involve her. She hadn't given it another thought after that single visit.

Mistakes are only clear in hindsight, Ellis would tell her.

She did remember that each floor was divided in half by a folding wall that could be opened if a single company chose to purchase the whole floor. The real estate agent had opened it up for them. The collection of differently-sized offices with permanent walls was in the southern half. The squatters were in the long, open, loft-type space in the northern end. If they were going to come directly at her, they'd have to get through the dividing wall, giving Synjan a little extra time to choose a good hiding spot.

Reaching the topmost landing, she eased the stairwell's door open, hoping its newness meant it would make no sound...and all her plans of a surprise advance ended.

They had it rigged with some poor-but-effective booby trap. What sounded like fifty metal pans crashed to the tiled floor on the other side with an unsubtle clamour. She shoved the door all the way open, hurdled the debris and ran as far down the hall as she could get while the settling pots masked her steps.

She mentally watched them scatter. She slipped inside an office off the central corridor and crouched behind the semi-open door. The meagre light coming through the windows showed the large room was bereft of furniture. She slid her backpack off and pulled a large plastic cable tie out of it, placing it on top after propping the bag against the wall. Her concentration returned to mapping the squatters.

One of the men had gone down some stairs at the other end of the building – he wouldn't be a problem for some time – while the other two came her way. They walked together, pausing to open the dividing wall as she'd expected, before they moved into the southern half, exploring every office. They moved cautiously, not knowing what to expect.

The systematic approach of the two squatters disappointed her. They didn't rush straight at the noise she'd created like the mindless fools she'd expected them to be; they secured their immediate perimeter first, working their way consistently towards the perceived threat. They would meet it in their own time.

She watched them walk, the way they looked through the rooms, each man's size, what hand he favoured; getting as much information from their patterns as she could. Their impatience got the better of them by the time they closed in on where she was. They'd split up and were exploring each room individually. Mentally she could see that they were wielding guns or flashlights; she assumed both.

The smaller of the two came towards her office first. Synjan used his cautious entry through the doorway against him. He was holding a torch and gun before him, so she sprang at him. She swept his weapon upward with her right arm before following through with her left, jabbing him in the throat with rigid knuckles. Her plan skewed as he released his gun and torch to clutch at his throat.

The torch flew wildly into the room where it clattered against the wall. The gun was tossed with as much gusto and it clipped her sharply on the eyebrow as she squared up to her opponent. The skin split and blood spilled down her face. The gun fell to the floor with a thud.

Closing her stinging eye, she delivered three quick punches to the intruder's face and a knee to his groin. He was having too much trouble trying to breathe to defend himself. When he dropped, he landed face first on the carpet. She was quick to lean down and get a grip on his clothes.

He was a dead weight but the imminent arrival of his colleague fed the adrenaline coursing through her. She dragged him farther into the room then snatched the plastic cable off her bag, zipping his wrists together behind his back. He was choking and gargling senselessly while fighting her restraint but her knee on the back of his neck ensured he made no progress.

She was bathed in light as his partner appeared in the doorway. Synjan rolled behind the door as the newcomer opened fire. She arrived unscathed and pressed herself flat against the wall. The door was a flimsy barrier between them.

Confident he had her pinned down, the shooter concentrated on the door. The shots were purposeful yet spread randomly, as though his intent was to drag this out. He called out a taunt—"Gotch'asshole! Yer fuckin' *dead*!"—and cackled laughter, revealing that he was enjoying his dominance. His desire to bask would work in her favour.

Synjan wanted the opposite; she wanted to end this quickly. Her best chance was to change position from behind the door. Rapid action should give her some advantage. Swiping blood out of her eye, she rolled back to her original position, coming up smoothly behind her only other shield in this room and drawing her weapon. Her eyes were closed, her mind map active and she took a calming breath.

Both men reacted to her new position at the same time. As the light swung her way, the tethered man tried to lift himself up, giving her more cover than she'd expected. The second re-aligned his aim but it was too late.

One of her bullets sank into his chest, the other hit him between the eyes. His gun spat out one last shot before his pattern faded from the head down and he dropped into a heap.

She aimed at the man in front of her only to note that his pattern was paling as well. Confused, she opened her eyes and saw by the light of two abandoned torches that the bullet from his associate's gun had caught him in the neck. The wound sprayed feebly then settled into a lurching stream, feeding the spreading blood pool on the carpet.

At least *she* hadn't been hit.

She holstered her gun, scooped up her backpack and torch and jogged out of the room. Years of training kept her footsteps even, despite the fact her ears were still ringing from the echo of unmuffled gunfire. It would be a while before her hearing settled entirely.

The final squatter hadn't missed the cacophony and his pattern was heading upward at a run. She matched his pace and reached the opening in the central dividing wall just as he stepped out of the northern stairwell. She didn't hear the door close—he was likely trying to mask his whereabouts—but she saw his pattern enter cautiously.

Remaining where the shadows were thickest, Synjan looked into the open space ahead of her, the back of her sleeve pressed to her eyebrow to staunch the flow of blood. She needed her eyes to ascertain what she was walking into.

There were windows set nearly the whole way along both sides of the northern half of the building. The far end was dark, the moon not having enough strength in its quarterly phase to encroach. Peering from left to right, she realised that many of the windows were covered with what looked to be paper, while others had more substantial things like blankets over them. Square support columns stretched in two orderly lines from end to end, wreaking further havoc on the milky light leaking into the room but creating some useful pockets of shadow.

There was enough residual glow to see that nearly the entire floor of the office space was filled with rows of plants. Calloshene plants. Hoses had been rigged up to the overhead sprinkler system, snaking down inside the long plastic tents covering the huge batch. *This* was what the squatters were here for; to harvest a lucrative crop of drugs that would, ironically, hurt Ellis' business in more ways than one. Creative scum.

Muffled footsteps caught her attention and she mapped to see where the third man was. He was coming towards her from the right, sticking to the shadows and the protection of the pylons. He didn't know what trouble he was facing but he was wily, deciding not to use his torch so as not to give himself away. Had she not been a Navigator, it would have been an admirable challenge to locate him in the eclectic light. He moved like he knew what he was doing.

He stopped suddenly, listening. "Sam? Mutt?" he hissed into the heavy silence.

It was good of him to identify the others for her.

He crept forward again when there was no response. As he did, she also moved, leaving her backpack behind and dropping onto one knee at the opening of the dividing wall. She held her position out of view, both hands wrapped around her gun, her eyes closed and waiting. When he reached the last pylon and was staring at open space, he sensibly paused again, no doubt listening for some indication of whether he was alone or not.

Faced with no other choice, he eventually streaked towards the moveable wall. When he crossed into open space, Synjan leaned around and shot him. She aimed for his knees and his gut but got his thigh and his shoulder. He also didn't drop his gun as she'd hoped. He fell down screaming and firing, issuing rage-filled expletives into the office space, most of which she couldn't make out amongst the noise of his bullets being let loose.

Synjan slipped farther back into the corridor, waiting until the shooting stopped. It took a while, as the squatter was tough and he dragged himself the rest of the way to the wall while offering covering fire, but then the blood loss and his wound must've got to him. Or he'd run out of bullets. There'd been no point counting them, she had no idea what model of gun he had.

When there was only the sound of his laboured breathing and she could see him sitting up against the dividing wall, Synjan flicked on her torch. She stepped in and then back out into the corridor, hoping to draw any fire he had left. He looked in her direction but didn't shoot, so she edged in again. She took careful aim with her light and gun in case it was a ruse. She doubted it was because his pattern was so sluggish.

"What's your name?" she asked as she approached cautiously. She kept her torch beam just out of his eyes.

He sneered in her direction. "Suck me, bitch."

"Who do you work for?"

"None of your fucking business."

"What's your name?"

"Fuck you."

"Who do you work for?"

"You're a dumb cunt, aren't ya'?"

She was close enough to secure his gun but she was wary about him grabbing her. He was lean and tall and he'd no doubt best her even with two bullets in him, if he got hold of her.

"Toss your gun. That way," she ordered, flicking her light towards his right arm, away from her.

He followed her instruction, the movement difficult because he used his left hand to do it. "It's empty, anyway."

"Mine's not. Answer my questions so I don't put a bullet in your other leg."

He glared at her, his face screwed up with hatred and pain as he considered his options. She waited him out, her gun trained on his left knee.

"Harry," he eventually spat.

"And who do you work for?"

He pursed his lips, hesitant about answering this question.

"How about this. Judging from the brashness displayed in breaking in here to *my* boss' place and the amount of product you've got growing, I'd guess you work for one of two people. Devin Muscat or Lisa O'Grady. O'Grady... or Muscat," she repeated, watching his face for a reaction, as Freddie had trained her to do. "Muscat? O'Grady?" The lighting wasn't perfect but she was fairly sure she had the right read. "Muscat, then."

"I told you fuckin' *nothin'*, bitch!" he frothed.

"Yeah. I'm sure he'll believe you when you tell him that," she smirked, circling around him and kicking his gun even farther away before she bent down and picked it up. "You just wait there for me," she instructed and gave him a wide berth again as she backed into the corridor to her backpack. She tucked her torch under her arm, had a quick drink of water then retrieved another plastic tie. She retraced her steps, approaching the squatter with her gun and torch raised cautiously.

"I'm gonna' fuckin' bleed to death anyway, if you don't hurry up and call it in," he complained.

"Shut up and show me your hands. Behind your back," she instructed, doing him the courtesy of moving past him so that he could lean his unwounded side on the wall.

With great difficulty, he shuffled around, bawling when his arms were pulled together. She ignored his cursing and tied his wrists together anyway, needing to do one last thing before she decided what to do about this situation. She needed to check the woman.

Once the squatter was secured, she holstered her

gun and jogged through the criss-crossing shadows, noting that the pattern she was heading for was not moving rapidly at all. The woman's heart was beating very slowly now and though Synjan hoped to reassure her with the human thumping of her feet on the new carpet, she doubted she noticed. She approached the ebbing life form with caution.

A filthy mattress had been placed in the corner. Since there were no windows close by, Synjan could see nothing beyond the bottom end of the mattress. Two bare feet, easily as dirty as the bedding, with ropes wrapped around the ankles was all she could make out at first. The ropes were long, secured to something on the wall for the left leg and to the nearest pylon for the right leg. They were caked with grime she suspected was blood, but the moon wasn't able to give her a lot of help there.

With trepidation, Synjan moved her torch's light upward and was glad she hadn't come to this job with a full stomach. She switched the light off, breathing rapidly and swallowing the saliva flooding into her mouth. She would *not* vomit.

When she was ready, she turned her flashlight on again and took a better look, having to reassure herself by mapping that this girl was actually still alive. And she was a girl, not a woman. Her breasts and hips indicated that she was perhaps fifteen.

She was tied down, spread-eagled, completely naked. Her body was a mass of cuts and bruises, her face puffy and swollen from innumerable punches. Her hair was knotted and bloodied on the grimy pillow she'd been given, some of the dark brown tresses glued to her face by blood. The hair tips moved slightly as shallow breath wafted in and out of the girl's slack mouth.

A huge bloodstain marked the mattress between the girl's open legs, her pubis bruised and swollen, inner thighs cut. A glass bottle, having once held a fizzy drink, lay abandoned against her right knee, the blood coating it attesting to its use as the most recent instrument of torture. At the base of the mattress were a few other blood-smeared phallic implements, as well as a sizeable collection of used condoms.

Movement caught her eye as she looked in this area and she focussed the beam of her torch on the girl's left ankle. It seemed the flies buzzing around had made use of the open wounds inflicted by the girl struggling against her bonds. If not the flies, then some other insect—there were definitely maggots of some sort wriggling in there. The unhealthy blackish green colour of her foot was probably not due to just dirt or bruising, either.

Looking closer in her mind, Synjan saw now what she hadn't had the inclination to see before; the girl's pattern didn't include a left foot or right hand. The movement of blood stopped around her wrist and calf. Synjan didn't lift her torch to inspect the hand. The sight of the undulating ankle was bad enough. The girl had to have been tied up for weeks. Of course, the stench had already alerted her to that fact.

She switched off her light and took a few steps away, turning her back on the scene. The adrenaline that had carried her through the previous encounters was abating and she was trembling in its absence. For all her previous strength, seeing this girl left her weak and she sank to her knees, folding herself up, closing her eyes and pressing her forehead to the carpet in an effort to think clearly.

Unfortunately, it wasn't the first time she'd faced a situation like this, though the previous times had involved vengeful adults, neglected animals or small children locked in cages by their own parents. The children were the worst. She'd been only thirteen when she'd found the toddlers in the basement of their home and she'd telephoned Ellis in hysterics, begging for Authority intervention to help those two little babies.

He'd responded to her weakness but not to her plea, sending the clean-up crew plus Ren to kill them for her. It had traumatised her for days, watching the light of those tiny patterns fade. Although the desperate thirteen year old that wanted to help still existed in her, she'd seen and done too much in the decade since. This situation wouldn't have a different outcome.

Synjan's mind whirled, tracking the pitiable pattern behind her and imagining what her time here must have been like. She'd been normal, before all this, just a young woman going about her life when she'd been targeted by sick individuals that sought to rape the youth out of her, to destroy everything that made her an individual. They'd branded her with their inhumanity. Her life was all but gone and even if she survived this horror, she'd never be the same. No-one who'd lived this much ugliness would see life in quite the same way again. Synjan knew from personal experience that beauty was hard to find and impossible to appreciate, once ugliness had cauterised the senses.

Synjan straightened up off the carpet, staring unseeingly at the plants around her. A hole had opened up inside her and she felt dizzy, despite the fact she wasn't moving. She was teetering. A waterfall of hatred washed over her. Those men had done this, had broached Ellis' property and brought with them a hapless victim to amuse themselves with... while the *plants* grew? Was that how fucking evil they were? This poor girl was just some sort of trivial amusement to them?

The hate consumed her as she stood and walked back to the girl, carefully stepping over the rope to crouch near her head. She closed her eyes and hummed a note that filled her ears, breathing heavily. The noise, the breathing, the hatred vibrated around her like a protective barrier so she didn't see when the bullet went through the girl's brain. The void where her pattern had been was welcome, though.

Synjan strode back to the squatter she'd left tied up at the back of the room. She could see his mouth moving as she walked up to him, deliberately shining her light in his eyes this time, but she didn't hear his words. Whatever they were, the hate curtain absorbed them and they stopped when she aimed her gun at his face and pulled the trigger. He died more pleasantly than he'd lived, she decided, but the hole inside her wasn't fuelled by the need for justice. Just for peace. For them and for herself.

She was concerned that the gunfire coming from the building might have alerted the Authorities, even though it was in a commercial area. By the time she'd found a display office and placed a phone call to the Bunker's clean-up crew, she knew she was safe from discovery. She gave them instructions about the safest route to travel, sipping shallowly from her water flask as she talked, and then went downstairs to wait for them outside the door she'd entered by.

Time was moving while she stood there, she knew that, but she didn't allow herself to think as she waited for her colleagues. Her gun was still holstered at her hip, her backpack on and her thumbs hooked through the straps near her armpits. She stared at nothing, losing herself in the dark of the night, emptying her mind and listening to her breathing, the beat of her heart. It was another technique Freddie had taught her. He called it meditation, but she hadn't used it very often. She needed it now.

Some time later, movement beside her registered. She faced Jaycob, Lale and Praven when they appeared, preceded by torch light.

"By the Gods!" Jaycob exclaimed in his nasal twang, flinching back as he came upon Synjan standing silently near the shrubbery. Habitually, he pressed his dark-rimmed glasses higher on his nose with the hand not holding his torch. "Synjan."

"Hello, Jaycob."

He regained his composure quickly and leaned closer to peer at her. "You okay?" he wheezed.

"Fine."

He shone his torch in her face, causing her to turn her head. "You're covered in blood," he argued vehemently.

"It's nothing," she assured him, even though she couldn't, in that moment, remember how or why she had blood on her.

He looked unconvinced but got on with business instead of arguing. "How many 'em got here?" he asked.

"There are thr-*four* bodies," she corrected herself hastily. "All on the third floor. Two in an office in the southern end, two in the northern end."

A figure loomed out of the darkness behind him to whisper something in Jaycob's ear. Praven. The complete opposite of short, fat Jaycob, Praven had long, greasy-looking brown hair, drooping around his morose face as he bent forward into the circle of light thrown by Jaycob's torch. His eyes moved slowly from his best friend towards Synjan as he finished speaking, then he withdrew silently again.

"How big are they?" Jaycob queried speculatively.

"Uh," Synjan was at a loss. She saw that Praven and Lale had wheelbarrows filled with equipment. She had no idea what they did to dispose of bodies – she'd never *wanted* to know – but she supposed such information about size was relevant when there were four bodies, two wheelbarrows and it was their business to clean everything up. "Three men, one woman," she hazarded. "Two of the guys are biggish, the other was shorter?" She had no idea if her information was helpful or not, but it felt like a morbid discussion either way.

"Look, no mind. You move on, we got it," Jaycob told her kindly.

Her head wobbled in something she hoped was a grateful nod and she held the key out to him. When he took it with a promise to return it on the morrow, she sidled past their wheelbarrows and started her run for home. This time she mapped constantly, avoiding trouble and concentrating on the pockets of people she could see, drinking water as she ran.

CHAPTER TWENTY

The Hunter And The Librarian

HE tyres of his pickup truck crunched over gravel as the Hunter pulled into the space closest to the doors. The parking lot held more cars than he expected so early in the morning. He pushed the truck door closed but didn't lock it before moving briskly up the front path and through the double doors.

The smell of old books assaulted him. He was used to modern libraries where the buildings were new and the books were replaced as needed. This library was far from modern. The building itself was heritage-listed, with fifteen foot ceilings and exposed beams. The heating system was having a hard time competing against the cold outside. Nobody had taken off their sweaters or jackets.

Standing close to the doors and taking stock of the space within, he expected someone to offer their assistance but nobody addressed him. The counter was unattended on his right. He could hear soft talking and the chink of a spoon coming from a doorway beyond. With their morning duties done and early visitors only just arriving, the librarians were making themselves coffee.

The Hunter circumnavigated the main floor, observing the patrons. Other than a mother reading to her young child, everyone was over sixty. When he approached the counter from the opposite side, he could see one of the librarians through the doorway. She was dressed in a light blue striped shirt and black pants, a large white name tag clipped onto a breast pocket. She saw him coming and set down her cup so that she could come out and serve him.

As he drew closer, he could read her name was

Susanne. Her smile was warm and helpful. Why wouldn't it be? He was a library patron because he'd come to the counter from among book shelves, not from the entrance. It was a subtle psychology, the impact of which couldn't be measured, but he felt it would help when he had questions he wanted answers to. He was a strong believer that first impressions mattered.

"How can I help you?" Susanne asked, her gaze taking in the fact that he carried no books before she made eye contact again. Her smile didn't falter and he approved.

The Hunter handed his ID wallet over so she could have a good look and understand he was an Authority Hunter, though she might not understand the title. Not all of the librarians in this city had been friendly to him. Providing his ID gained him their grudging cooperation.

Susanne accepted it from him with an uncertain expression. While she studied it, he unfolded a piece of paper from his pocket and swapped it for his ID. As the librarian sighted the picture, he thought he saw a brief reaction; that she recognised the woman in the identikit. It was slight but it was enough. His instincts demanded he stick to his script, even though he wanted whatever knowledge she had immediately. His heart rate accelerated and he drew in a slow breath, internally counting the number of seconds she looked at the picture.

The librarian didn't speak so the Hunter had to.

"She's a person of interest in connection with multiple crimes," he stated. "She currently operates under a false identity. We're trying to find out what name she's going by."

Susanne was wide-eyed at his words. The woman that she was connecting to the picture obviously hadn't struck her as a criminal.

"Is she dangerous?" Suzanne asked, leaning forward slightly so that her voice wouldn't carry across the room.

He mirrored her pose and hushed his tone also. "You recognise her." He phrased it like a statement, trying to lead her into confessing her knowledge.

She hesitated and glanced over her shoulder for help. Her co-worker had already come out of the kitchenette and disappeared somewhere into the library, but the movement was telling. She didn't want to be an informant.

"I can't say for sure."

He stared at her, debating his course of action; threaten her for withholding information or cajole her into doing the right thing? Staring turned out to be enough.

"There's a lady who kind of looks like this, but it can't be her," Susanne said with an awkward giggle. She looked around again but there was still no-one in sight. The silence continued to stretch and even more information came out of it. "She's a mother."

He smiled. Susanne was the kind of person who didn't want a nice stranger to get into trouble. He knew how to get information out of her.

"It's possible she's not who we're after," he said, assuaging the librarian's fears. "I have to exhaust all leads though, otherwise I'm not doing my job. How about you get me her name and address and I'll clear things up with her directly?"

He hadn't won her over. He could tell by the dubious expression on her face. He was positive she was considering denying him the information, so he tapped his finger on the ID wallet on the counter, reminding her who was asking. She looked at it and then back at him, resignation in her eyes.

"Name and address?" she confirmed.

His smile widened.

CHAPTER TWENTY-ONE

Night Terrors

SYNJAN had no idea how long she'd been gone but it felt like hours. True to her instruction, Ellis hadn't locked her out but she had to let herself in via the side entrance because the garage was closed. The metal staircase led to a window on the second floor and after she locked it behind her, she went into her office to leave her torch there.

Distant aromas reminded her she'd told Urvasi to keep her food but she knew she wouldn't be able to stomach it. On her way upstairs, she detoured into Ellis' office and swiped a full bottle of dark amber alcohol and a heavy crystal tumbler, carrying them with her straight into her bathroom. Setting them beside the sink, she leaned into her large tub and turned the taps on. The hot went as far as it could go, but less cold was running into the mix. She poured herself a shot of alcohol and drank it, needing to take a breath in through her nose as it burned down her throat. It had a lovely dark, fruity aftertaste that she greatly enjoyed and she knew it was either very expensive or imported from another world. Or both.

When she opened her eyes, she was staring at her own reflection and grunted. The side of her face was coated in blood. The girl flashed into her mind and she leaned into the sink, scrubbing the blood off roughly and checking the mirror repeatedly to be sure it was gone. Her vigour re-opened the cut above her eye and she wondered whether it would need stitches. She staunched the flow with her sleeve and was relieved when it stopped soon after.

She went back into her bedroom and dumped her backpack, holster and guns on her desk before stripping and heading back into the bathroom. She tipped some strong-smelling bubble bath into the filling tub and then went to the toilet, losing track of time again as she unwound her braid and finger-combed her blonde hair out.

The mound of bubbles rising towards the rim of the deep bath caught her eye and she flushed the toilet before climbing into the tub. The silence when the water was shut off was like pressure on her skin, leaving an intangible itch across her arms and shoulders. She broke it by standing up and leaning over to regather the bottle and glass she'd brought in.

She was onto her sixth nip when Ellis walked into the steamy, fragrant room and she was feeling much better by then.

"I was in the lounge," he criticised.

She smiled up at him, taking a sip of alcohol. "I didn't notice," she responded pleasantly, enjoying the warmth all around her and the heat that circulated in her head, making it easy to talk to him for once.

Ellis looked thoughtful as he turned his back to the mirror and leant against her bathroom counter, folding his arms across his chest. Her gaze ran over him, appreciating the economy of his movements and the way he looked so damn neat in his slacks and knitted jumper.

"You're not wearing shoes," she marvelled, seeing that his socks matched his sweater.

"You're not wearing anything," he countered and she giggled appreciatively as she poured herself another drink. When she'd filled the glass more than half full (including a bit of spillage), she carefully placed the uncapped bottle back on the corner of the bath behind her left shoulder. "You took that from my office," he accused.

"Yep."

"Why?"

"I wanted to drink it." She gazed adoringly at the

pretty liquid, refracted so fascinatingly by the bumpy glass it was in, before she took another sip. It had filled her up now, better than any dinner, and though it was getting harder to swallow, the taste was only getting better.

Silence rose between them but only one of them was comfortable with that, it seemed.

"So," Ellis said tersely, drawing her gaze to his face.

He wasn't wearing his glasses but she chose not to point that out. "It was a mess. A big, ugly, motherfavouring mess," she decided.

"Was the information inaccurate?"

"Sort of." She got distracted by taking another swallow and forgot to elaborate.

"Synjan!" he barked.

Her eyes widened and an old fear seeped into her, cold and sharp, as she remembered the times she'd made him angry while growing up. He would punish her, but her brain was quite scrambled and it took her a few moments to remember why he was so angry anyway.

"I... uh," she blinked and then the panic cleared. "There was a girl!" she exclaimed, pointing at Ellis as if he was the winning candidate in a lottery game. "The information was right about three men but they had a girl there, too."

"So there were four?" he frowned.

"No, she wasn't with them. They just had her tied up and... and..." Words failed her and she frowned, fighting off that memory and looking at the reassuring prettiness of her glass again. She took a mouthful and had to hold it in her mouth for quite some time before it would go safely down her throat.

Ellis was quiet too, no doubt thinking about what she told him. She hoped he understood about the girl without the need for more questions.

"The men. What happened with them?"

"I killed them. Well, I shot two of 'em and the first guy got killed by his buddy and—OH!" she exclaimed excitedly, slapping the water and causing a splash that left her blinking momentarily. "They've got drugs there!"

"Drugs?"

"Calloshene, I think. Plants. They were using the water in the office to grow them, it was all rigged up."

Ellis' jaw set and she was glad that it wasn't her causing him to look like that this time. "Those impertinent... who were they?"

"Harry, Sam and Mutt," Synjan answered slowly, counting them off on her fingers before she pointed at Ellis again. "And! I'm fairly certain they worked for Devin Muscat, that fucker!" she spat sanctimoniously.

Ellis looked thoughtful so Synjan went back to her drink, surprised that when she lowered it next, she could almost see the bottom of the glass. One more mouthful and it'd be empty. Again. She glanced at the bottle over her shoulder, reassured when she saw it was still half full.

"I assume you called Jaycob?"

"Yep. An' he brought Praven and Lael, too. It was a big job, wiv' all those plants to clean up, plus th'bodies. He'll bring the key back tomorrow," she advised, not realising that her final words were slurred into incomprehensibility because she chose to finish off the last of her drink in the middle of it.

"Don't you think you've had enough of that?" Ellis frowned.

"Nope."

"You're drunk."

"You're an ass," she replied conversationally and reached behind her for the bottle.

"That's uncalled for," he growled as he stepped in and easily removed the bottle before she got hold of it.

Synjan mournfully watched it fly over her head.

"Hey! Give it back!"

"You don't need any more. You need food, water and sleep," Ellis announced as he twisted the cap onto the bottle.

She pouted and decided he wasn't serious. "What about... if I," she sang teasingly, shaking her shoulder towards him like she'd seen the private dancers at the Queen do, rolling it in a way she thought was delightfully alluring. "Show you a little o'this... and these," she purred, brushing the concealing bubbles off her breasts and cupping them as she struggled to stand up. It was awkward, because she'd forgotten about the glass in her left hand and it didn't lift her breast as she expected it to. Plus, getting vertical was a whole lot more dizzying than she'd anticipated.

"Synjan, put the glass down!" Ellis ordered, slamming the bottle onto the counter hastily and moving closer to the tub as Synjan gained her feet unsteadily.

"Or this, I know you want this, I've seen you lookin'," she murmured impishly, half turning away from him and waggling her bottom towards him. This was certainly not the first time he'd entered her bathing room while she was naked and he'd always looked at her like she was an unreachable delicacy he wanted to devour. She hated that look.

"Give me the glass," he commanded.

"Fill it for me'n you c'n have—" she tried to hold the glass out backwards while shaking her rear, bending forward so he could get a good look but it all fell apart when she lost her footing.

Ellis stepped in and secured her seamlessly, snatching the glass away and wrapping his other arm around her middle, squeezing her to hold her steady.

To Synjan, all the effort she'd put into forgetting about the girl was gone the moment he touched her. The moment a man touched her.

"Don't touch me!"

"Synjan—"

"Don't you fucking touch me, let me go!"

"Just wait a—Synjan, you're going to hurt yourself!"

"I don't fucking care, just let me go, get your hands off me—!"

She fought valiantly, trying to push his arm away, clawing at his hand, scrabbling at his fingers and attempting to peel them off her midriff. Something black and desperate was beating inside her chest, clogging her throat, filling her face with tears and snot. Her words echoed off the tile walls like the gunshots in that office and everything was twisting, rolling and deafening. She squirmed wildly in Ellis' grasp, kicking the bubbly water and recoiling when it splashed into her face.

It all became too much. The copious amount of alcohol she'd consumed decided, with the help of all her thrashing and Ellis' squeezing, that it was going to come straight back up.

She wasn't sure but she thought Ellis actually swore as her stomach purged itself and it sprayed all over the tiles, on his arm and dribbled down her naked body into the tub. Still, he didn't let go, he just stood there supporting her until nothing more was coming out. Her body was still heaving though, and everything was spinning.

"I can't...I don't...Ellis?" she whimpered. "Make it stop."

"Skin of the Gods," he muttered as he lifted her out of the tub and walked her to the shower stall. He turned the water on, checked the temperature—all while holding her against his hip—and then pressed her unceremoniously against the far wall. She slid slowly downwards, finding these tiles were an inviting kind of cool and the spray was bearable once she managed to get her hands up to block it from going up her nose.

Ellis moved off to do something with the bath and she decided that some water to drink was a good idea after all. The alcohol didn't taste nearly so good coming back up. She lapped at the shower spray, doing her best to catch enough in her mouth to rinse the aftertaste away.

"Have you washed with soap?" Ellis demanded.

She flinched as he appeared suddenly and his voice boomed around inside the shower.

"Fuck, not yet," she complained.

"Get up and do it, then. You have vomit in your hair."

"You're so judgemental," she mumbled, doing her best to stand. His hand on her elbow was a help.

"And you're a sloppy drunk and an ungrateful brat," he retaliated, grabbing her hand and squirting shampoo in it.

She washed her hair and rinsed it. When he pressed a cake of soap into her hand, she used that, too. She registered that he closed the shower door to let her do that herself, which she was grateful for. She was also glad that he didn't leave entirely.

When he ascertained that she was clean and fully rinsed, Ellis shut the shower off and held a towel up for her to step into. Silently, he began drying her.

"I can do it," she protested feebly, attempting to take the towel off him.

"You can barely stand on your own."

"I...it's wearing off."

"Stop that."

"Stop what?"

"Covering yourself. You were just offering it to me."

Her cheeks heated and her gaze lowered but she couldn't bring herself to move her hands. "Please," she whispered but she wasn't sure what she was asking for.

"Your hair is too long," he sighed impatiently. "It's wetting everything I'm drying."

"I usually wrap it up," she explained timidly.

"Do it, then."

He stood nearby while she reached for her other towel and flicked her hair forward so she could wrap it. She managed to get the towel around but straightening up again made her incredibly dizzy. Ellis was marching her across the room before she even realised what was happening and this time, she managed to get the next wave of vomit into the toilet and stay clean. After that, he wrapped her in her bathrobe and walked her to bed.

It seemed she was only just managing to burrow under the covers when he was standing above her, holding a bottle of water out. She sat up to take it. Her bedside lamp was on and she noticed he was only wearing a singlet tucked into his slacks now. Embarrassment flooded her as she realised she must've vomited on his sweater and she made sure she swallowed two good mouthfuls of water in contrition.

"I'm sorry," she told him, finding that the world dipped and swayed less when she rested her towel-wrapped head against the headboard of her large bed.

"Good. You'll be sorrier in the morning," he lectured, sitting on the bed beside her with something in his hands.

"What's that?" she frowned.

"A first aid kit. Your eye's bleeding."

She closed her eyes and felt him wipe her eyebrow before he pressed a band-aid there to keep the cut closed.

"His gun hit me when I punched him."

Ellis hummed a noise of acknowledgement and she sighed heavily, opening her eyes because her mind wasn't showing her the memory of that man at all; all she could see was the girl. When she lifted her eyelids, a waterfall of tears escaped.

Ellis' expression softened and he caught one with his thumb. "Don't, dearheart."

Synjan's heart was bleak and broken. The black hole

had spread throughout her and she was sure her soul was dead. Someone, somewhere, had to be wondering where that girl had gone. Someone had to mourn her. "I killed her," she admitted, her voice cracking.

He nodded.

"Why, Ellis?" she beseeched. He looked confused so she clarified. "How can people... do the things they do to each other in this city?"

He shrugged as he caught another of her tears, cupping her face in his hand.

She pulled away to swallow some more water. "You've been around longer, you should know," she chastised petulantly.

"The truth is... I think it's because they can," he told her and his deep voice was lovely and curled inside her chest but his words seeped into her mind and just made her cry harder.

"It shouldn't be that way," she sobbed. "It's not fair."

"No. It isn't. But it doesn't just happen in this city, it happens everywhere, on every world. Wherever there are predators and prey. People are animals too. Despite their intelligence, to the strong go the spoils. That's why I made sure you were strong," he told her reverently and pulled the towel off her hair. Gently, he began to dry the long strands that fell upon her chest, between his towel-swathed hands.

"Strong isn't better," she whispered, watching his green eyes. They were directed at what his hands were doing, rather than at her and she wondered at the mind behind them.

"Better is as better does. But strong will survive longer, and figure out the way life should be lived."

"Not if they're animals. Those men tonight... they were animals. It wouldn't've mattered how long they lived, they'd never have figured out the right way to treat people."

"No, but you were stronger than them."

"Just a better trained murderer."

Ellis looked at her sharply but whatever he saw in the way she was staring at him, he didn't have a response for. He lowered his gaze back to drying her hair. "You shouldn't drink. It's never worked out well for you," he reprimanded.

She barked a bitter laugh, knowing exactly what he was insinuating. He'd rescued her and sheltered her, given her a family (of sorts) to support her in her time of grief. Unfortunately, he'd also condemned her by training her to become everything she could be. Then he gave her guns. Inevitably, she'd killed someone.

Her entire being had cringed in horror at the sight of that first man's pattern fading. The life leaked out of him and he was simply gone. Just like that. A bloody corpse, a shell at her feet. No more life pumping through him, no more adrenaline firing in his veins as he attempted to hit her, to hurt her. Everything he'd been had been eliminated in just a few heartbeats because of her.

The utter simplicity but fundamental wrongness of it all had shaken her. It wasn't right that people were so fragile. She'd been eleven years old and she'd known her mistake was irreversible. It wasn't right that people could take other people away. It wasn't right and it wasn't fair. And she was wrong for doing it.

She'd stood there a very long time that day, staring at the body. Seeing someone lying down was not abnormal, but the blood...and he wasn't breathing. No pattern, no breath, no movement. It was supposed to be otherwise. People moved, even in their sleep. She'd been born wrapped in a cocoon of fluttering life, undulating where her eyes looked, warm where her body was hugged, pulsing where her inner sight ventured. Life in forms her young mind couldn't comprehend, shared in ways her parents promised she would understand when she was older, beating inside and around her in a primordial rhythm she couldn't explain but felt, as a Navigator.

Then she'd taken that from somebody. She'd personally stopped the movement and the dance for him. Every life she'd taken since then impacted her in the same way. They were another mark of her dead soul. Ellis said it was because she was stronger and that was why she was still standing but a lot of times she thought it was just dumb luck. One day, her luck would run out.

In the meantime, she had a support network, a cleanup crew to take the bodies and wash the blood away, sanitising the scene to remove all traces of them. Little by little, piece by piece, she was being cleaned away, too. Sometimes she felt like she was little more than a shell, following through on her training, surviving. It didn't feel like living, even if she could still move and breathe.

The nightmares proved she wasn't strong. After that first kill, she'd blocked them with the alcohol and the drugs that were always present in the Bunker. It had worked, too. But she hadn't done anything properly and she'd made a lot of mistakes. She was constantly scared of taking another life and the nightmares that followed, so she'd kept drinking. Eventually Ellis had punished her out of wanting that netherworld, he'd hurt her until she saw that there was no escape. She had to own the consequences of her actions.

He was referring to her past mistakes now.

Keep perspective in the moment

And an eye upon the cause.

He didn't like seeing her out of control. She got the feeling he strongly disapproved of how she was squandering the gifts he'd given her and part of her despaired over that, too. She owed him everything. For all that tormented her, he'd given her as many reasons to rejoice. To be thankful.

The problem was, she couldn't remember the good things on nights like these. Her perspective was not on any cause, just on getting through to the next dawn without losing her mind.

He leaned over and kissed her forehead, taking the towel and turning off her lamp as he stood. "Good night, Little One. Get some sleep."

"Good night, Ellis. I'm sorry," she sniffled, and wriggled back down under the covers again, closing her eyes and clutching her water bottle carefully. "I love you."

"I love you, too."

CHAPTER TWENTY-TWO

Half An Enemy

"PASS the salt, please."

Hawke reached for the small flask beside the pepper mill but another hand snatched it first and handed it over. Hawke was intimidated by Cayden's wife, who he felt only tolerated his presence and had grudgingly accommodated him during every major school holiday visit for the past three years. He'd been too grateful for the escape from the boarding school to decline the invitation, but he felt like Mrs Cayden considered him an inconvenience.

With the approaching Christmas celebrations, he'd thought she might be in a better mood. Cayden had been promoted from Division Lieutenant to Captain just before the break. When picking Hawke up from Willets, Cayden told him the news. He'd admitted that his promotion came because of the results Hawke had garnered at the DOME. Cayden had spoken of his gratitude at Hawke's compliance and praised him.

It had been a rewarding moment for Hawke. The tests at the DOME had eased up after the first few visits and had almost been reduced to a blood drive. Dr Turner had become his main contact and she was still full of questions about how he was getting along with others, what his life was like now and how he felt about it. He didn't see the point of it but he enjoyed talking with her because, unlike the school counsellor, she was completely separate. He also liked that she shared information with him—things that he didn't think he was supposed to have been told.

Through Dr Turner, he'd found out that his blood had led to some kind of important discovery. The DOME now had some special rooms that could shield the more dangerous Wanderer talents. He'd asked what kind they were and Turner had told him about Elementalists, who could make a tiny flame into an inferno, or a glass of water into a flood. He'd felt better about the tests after that.

Cayden had also reminded Hawke about his opportunities in three years' time. He was eleven now and fourteen was the earliest age that someone could sign up into the Authorities. It was the expected outcome for those who went to an Authority-run Academy like Willets. Hawke was still not sold.

Cayden thanked his wife for the salt, not noticing the subtle power play on the table. Hawke wasn't even in the running, though he felt like she was always trying to best him. It was unusual to think of an adult playing such games but he had no other explanation. Maybe she thought he was clumsy and would drop the salt shaker. The crystal piece did look expensive.

Drue sat across from him, glaring. She looked a lot like her mother already, with the same eye and hair colouring, the same facial features, the same expressions. She also styled her hair the same and wore the same kinds of clothes. His sister Giselle would be horrified if she wore anything similar to their mother and would certainly not fashion her hair the same way. He wondered why Drusilla would want to mimic her mother so closely. She was old enough to forge her own path at twelve. If she'd been in Boronia, she would be allowed her own sword by now.

The thought sent Hawke into a dark mood and he pushed the food on his plate around with his fork. Thinking of home did not make him happy.

Pain flared in his ankle. He grunted and looked over at the cause. Tavi stared back at him with wide eyes. Hawke knew it was Tavi's method for pulling him out of his reverie. Tavi was a friend and Hawke didn't have many. He smiled back and tried to kick Tavi's feet in return but couldn't reach him and so the pair of them ended up wriggling and snickering until they were told off by Mrs Cayden. Drue scoffed and rolled her eyes and Tavi did the same, exaggerating the movement. Hawke didn't laugh or get involved in that game, choosing to spike a roasted potato and place it in his mouth.

He didn't feel like eating but made sure to finish what was on his plate, to be polite. Mrs Cayden made a comment about clearing the plates and Hawke was the first to volunteer. He, Drue and Tavi silently took the empty plates away, stacking them on the kitchen bench. Hawke washed, Drue rinsed and Tavi put everything away. Once the chore was completed, Hawke made sure to return and thank Mrs Cayden for the meal before he and Tavi raced upstairs.

"Drue wants a tattoo," Tavi said as soon as they entered their shared bedroom. A rollaway cot had been set up in the corner for Hawke to sleep on.

"No way," Hawke said, wondering if Mrs Cayden had a tattoo.

"Why do you think she's been sucking up so hard?" Tavi asked, launching himself across his bed. Hawke flopped onto it beside him and Tavi took this to mean a wrestling match had to take place. After Hawke fought him and then had him pinned into a position that had Tavi laughing pain-tears, he climbed off and continued the conversation.

"I thought she was always like that."

Tavi laughed but shook his head.

"Nah, she's okay. She goes weird whenever you come over. Maybe she likes you," Tavi batted his eyelashes and made kissing noises into the air before waggling his tongue after it. Hawke knew Drue didn't like him that way—or any way—at all.

"She doesn't like me."

"She doesn't even want an interesting one," Tavi said. It took Hawke a moment to realise Tavi was speaking about the tattoo.

"What does she want?"

"Four bars of music on the back of her shoulder."

Hawke was familiar enough with sheet music, thanks to his classes at Willets and his tutoring on his home world. Sheet music between the two worlds had been eerily similar.

Learning that Drue wanted to tattoo music onto her shoulder won Hawke's respect, even though Tavi thought it sounded boring.

"What instrument does she play?"

"Flute and cello."

They listened as the subject of their conversation came upstairs. Hawke had never heard anyone so heavy footed as Drue. She stomped everywhere, all of the time, proving that girls weren't naturally delicate.

Hawke and Tavi spoke quietly, changing the subject to what gifts they hoped to get for Christmas. Hawke wanted a telescope but he doubted he would get one. Tavi spoke of paints, guitars and kayaks. Hawke had the impression he might get all those things, but certainly the last one, for it slotted in with his father's love of all things watercraft.

Cayden yelled up the stairs for everyone to get ready for bed because they were going to have a big day tomorrow. Hawke was excited about what was planned; a full day's cruise out on the Caydens' yacht. Hawke had gone for a few jaunts on it, but they'd only lasted a couple of hours. This time there were plans to spend the whole day on board, and to visit a small island that was supposed to be a great picnic spot. Hawke didn't care about the picnic, he would've preferred to stay on the boat, but Tavi was excited about exploring 'new lands'.

His interest in world travel had been the thing that had bonded them. Unlike the boys at Willets Academy, Tavi had been fascinated by Hawke's stories of travelling from world to world. Hawke hadn't had much to talk about in that respect, and Tavi had seen more worlds than he had through the Authority portals—but Tavi had been fascinated with the idea of adventure.

Tavi was the only person Hawke had properly described his home to, and how he'd lived before he'd been taken. When describing his manor and title, he realised that he'd been born on a harsh, rustic world, but he'd been on the privileged side of it, for his family had money and land. Even so, he would never be grateful to Eddie and his crew for taking him from it.

"Want to get some dessert?" Tavi asked, his brown eyes big and round and filled with promise.

"There wasn't any tonight," Hawke pointed out. The routine for desserts was one night off and one night on, and tonight was a night without.

"Drue told me she helped make macaroon pie today, and there were extra macaroons."

Macaroon pie was Hawke's favourite dessert, a preference he shared with Drue. The idea of spare macaroons in the kitchen waiting for hungry hands to steal them away was too alluring to ignore, so Tavi and Hawke snuck downstairs.

It was a risky venture, as both Tavi's parents were watching a movie on the downstairs television. The lounge and the dining room were connected by an open doorway, but the armchairs and sofa were around the corner and the visibility to the kitchen entrance was blocked. He and Tavi had successfully performed a midnight snack mission once, only later discovering that Tavi's parents had both been awake and in the lounge when they'd feasted in their room.

Hawke and Tavi wore woollen socks to hide the sound of their steps, and neither were as heavy footed as Drue. They tiptoed downstairs with Hawke in the lead and he was about to reach the landing where it turned and led the last three stairs down when low-spoken voices stopped him. Tavi stopped directly behind him, Hawke could hear his friend breathing over his shoulder. The voices sounded like they were in the dining room, so he didn't want to risk peering around the corner. It was easy to tell who was speaking, for Cayden's low pitched voice couldn't be mistaken for Mary's.

"You spent too much on him."

Hawke thought she meant Tavi, until he heard the response.

"Darling, the boy has nothing."

"That's not our fault. That's their fault. Why are we the ones paying?"

"It wasn't *his* fault," said Cayden.

"He's one of them!" Mary hissed, and Hawke felt his stomach drop. He couldn't feel Tavi's breath but did feel a tug on his sleeve. He ignored it and continued to listen. He didn't think he'd be able to unfreeze anyway.

"That's not his fault either," Cayden said, repeating his earlier sentiment but sounding less like he was trying to be reasonable and more like he was getting angry. Hawke liked that Cayden was vouching for him but he hated that he had to.

"No? Then why did they take him? Why would they, unless he wanted to go with them?"

Hawke was caught between wanting to yell out a protest, to rail at her for assuming that he'd somehow asked to be abducted, or shrinking a hasty retreat, to curl up into a ball and pretend that the worlds weren't aligned against him.

He wasn't orphaned from his family, he was orphaned from his place in a world. None of them fit him, none of them felt right. He was a stranger in all of them and incapable of returning to Boronia—the only world he understood but would still not fit in because of the secrets he would have to keep.

"Mary, he didn't want to."

"Did he tell you that? Because Wanderers are liars.

You already know that, considering the Division you're involved with."

As she spoke she walked; Hawke could hear her steps and her voice carrying through to the living room and Cayden following. His words to her weren't clear, just a rumble as he moved away from the doorway and kept his voice low. Another tug on the sleeve from Tavi pulled Hawke into motion and he turned and moved upstairs, trying to keep quiet, even as he began to tremble.

Back in their room, he moved around to the far side of his bed, away from Tavi who looked at him with concern, away from all eyes. He sat with his back against the cot and hugged his knees, hiding his face in the pocket of dark space his arms created.

Tavi sat beside him and put an arm around his shoulders and they sat like that while Hawke choked on the sobs that shook his whole body. Eventually, they gave way to sniffles. Tavi moved away and returned with a box of tissues that Hawke used wadded handfuls of to wipe his eyes and snotty nose. Tavi disappeared again and returned with a glossy magazine that Hawke didn't recognise.

"Looking through this always cheers me up," Tavi whispered. Hawke was momentarily confused by the cover. The title read 'Authority Brats' and it had a photograph of a girl in her late teens with her shirt unbuttoned but not quite showing the full cup of her young, pert breasts. He blinked at it; the appearance of the magazine was surprising.

Tavi flicked through it, explaining how he'd got it from one of his friends who had two older brothers and they'd nicked it from one of them. Hawke didn't ask how Tavi had managed to get it home, he was just interested in what the magazine had to offer. He'd never seen anything like it.

There were pictures of more naked girls in

suggestive poses, but the most he got from them was purely educational, until he arrived at the archery girl. There was a photograph of her from front on, looking just off to the camera at whatever her target happened to be; perhaps a pheasant or something, considering the light quality of the bow and arrows she was using. Her upper body was completely naked and Hawke questioned the credibility of shooting arrows in the nude, but whoever this girl was, she held the bow and arrow correctly. She knew how to properly nock and draw. He spent a long time looking at her face, which was serious, like a huntswoman should be. Tavi began to turn the page but Hawke stopped him, so he could follow through his inspection of her body. The photograph ended at her navel and he wondered if she was wearing anything at all.

There was a twitch inside his pyjama pants that wasn't unpleasant but certainly not anything he wanted to call attention to. He gave Tavi the go ahead to flip to the next page, while shifting position, trying to hide an erection that grew without his permission.

Tavi grinned at him but he didn't look directly at his friend. The two of them investigated more pictures, the heat escalating until there was a completely nude girl holding a beer bottle.

Hawke was fully hard by the time they reached the end of the magazine and he'd given up trying to hide the tent in his pants. He was glad that Tavi had one too, and seeing those pictures with Tavi had felt deliciously naughty. He adjusted his pyjama bottoms so that they weren't uncomfortable and watched as Tavi flipped back to Hawke's favourite page—the one with the archer. His hand was down his pants and he was stroking himself. Hawke looked away and focussed on the girl.

"Has anyone touched it?" Tavi whispered.

The question brought Hawke's attention back to his

friend.

"What?"

"You're stuck in a boarding school. I've heard stories about what happens in places like that."

Hawke thought of the hooliganism that happened but there was nothing sexual going on; at least nothing that he knew about.

"It's not like that."

Tavi looked disappointed and Hawke stared at him, bewildered. What had he been wanting to hear?

"There aren't any girls at my school," Hawke explained.

"So? Everybody has hands. It's really nice when someone else touches it. It's different to your own hand."

Hawke had no doubt that it was nice but he hadn't had any opportunities to try anything with anyone. The idea of being touched there was exciting though.

"Girls wouldn't know the best way to touch it anyway," Tavi said, then reached over and shoved his free hand down Hawke's pants.

Hawke watched it happen, surprised that Tavi would even want to stroke him. Even though Tavi was a year younger, Hawke considered him much more knowledgeable. He'd already kissed a girl.

As Tavi's expert hand slid up and down, Hawke let his eyes drop to the magazine. He looked at the archer's breasts and then stared at the place where the photograph ended, at her navel. Now that he'd seen pictures of fully naked women, he knew how to imagine her there. He pretended that she was sitting beside him, her bow and arrows to the side, and touching him. He closed his eyes and found himself short of breath.

Tavi shifted his wrist so the elastic of the pyjama's waist band would drop down, unrestricting his movements. Unlike Hawke, he seemed not to be getting carried away. Hawke climaxed and was shushed by Tavi for groaning. They used handfuls of wadded tissues to clean up and flushed the evidence away. Once they were lying in their beds in the dark, Hawke summoned his courage to whisper a question.

"Why did you do that?"

"Because I knew you'd like it."

"Did you...want me to do it back?"

"Only if you want to."

Hawke felt guilty for not wanting to. It was only afterward, when he was almost asleep, that he remembered Eddie and Roderick and that moment in the cupboard.

CHAPTER TWENTY-THREE

A Dark Path In A Dark World

FOR the seventh time in as many weeks, Daeson stood in the dark room looking through the window into the interrogation room. He remembered how frightened he'd felt while sitting there facing Nick and not understanding what was happening—but the memory was disconnected and intellectual. The room looked different somehow, perhaps because he was familiar with it but he still felt uncomfortable. This time, instead of a vinegary suggestion of fear, his tongue tasted a sour note of disapproval.

Daeson studied the man seated in the chair opposite Nick. He wore a fisherman's woollen cap pulled down as far as it would go. It covered his brows and most of his ears. His posture of crossed arms and hunched shoulders amplified his defiance. The fisherman wasn't talking and Daeson couldn't help Nick if there were no truths or lies to report on.

This questioning was unlike the others Daeson had observed. In the past few weeks, Nick had organised all of his contacts to come by—the ones that didn't serve at the Queen but were part of his after-curfew unit. The conversations had been pleasant, the questions seemingly innocuous until Nick asked about some stolen money or Authority contacts. The answers had all been truthful except for one man, who Daeson exposed. Nick expressed his thanks and Daeson had felt important and pleased with himself. When Daeson asked what was going to happen to the man, Nick shrugged and said he would not be hired again. It wasn't until later that Daeson wondered if there was a greater punishment that he wasn't being told about.

The fisherman had attracted Nick's hostility from

the start. Nick progressed from sneering to yelling, spittle flying from his lips with the force of his words. The twisty language was called Authoritan and Daeson now understood it. He still thought it harsh and it encouraged spit. The fisherman would either blink or wipe it away when it landed on his face.

Daeson watched with a churning gut as Nick questioned, bullied and threatened. None of Nick's promises of violence were lies. Daeson was at a loss because he didn't like what Nick was saying but the aggression was justified. Before coming into the room, he'd been told that the fisherman had put one of Nick's contacts in danger—a woman called Olivia. Nick explained that Olivia had been sent to give the fisherman some money and to return with a package. She never came back. Nick wanted to know if the fisherman's explanation of her disappearance was truthful. It had seemed a simple task but neither of them had expected the fisherman to remain silent.

It felt like a very long time before Nick gave up on his questioning and spoke to Daeson through the window, not quite making eye contact because he couldn't see him in the room.

"Get Xenik and don't come back."

Xenik was one of the security guards; a man so tall that he had to duck under every doorway. Daeson hesitated and continued to listen as Nick spoke quiet threats to the man in the chair. The details were horrific. With a queasy sensation gnawing at his belly, Daeson knocked on the glass to draw Nick from the room and then stepped out to meet him in the corridor.

"I said get Xenik!" Nick barked, opening the door just enough to yell this. He was closing it when Daeson protested.

"No."

The door clicked shut before it opened again. Nick's eyes were wide and his expression furious. Daeson clenched his fists and braced himself.

"I'm not going to let you...do those things to him."

"He's not talking because he's responsible."

"You can't be sure."

"His silence tells me he's involved in some way. Does it matter if he killed her himself or set her up for someone else?"

"You don't know if she's dead."

Nick's fury settled into disdain. "Grow up, Daeson. She's either dead or she took off with the money. Why the fuck would he say nothing if she just took off?"

Daeson could see he was losing the argument but he didn't want to know that a person was being tortured down here while he went about his business upstairs.

"Maybe he fell in love with her and they were going to run away together."

Nick blinked then laughed. His mirth didn't last long.

"He either murdered her, or he sent her to her death. Why do you want to protect him?"

If Nick had been the one to send her out, hadn't *he* been the one that sent her to her death? He couldn't say that. Not because it wasn't truth but because he didn't want to risk enraging Nick further. He was unpredictable, ruthless and violent.

"The Authorities—"

"—don't care," Nick finished.

Truth.

The chair scraped in the room because the man inside had moved and Nick turned to order him to sit down again. After a long pause, he turned back to Daeson, his expression soft.

"Get Xenik for me. That's all I'm asking you to do."

Daeson's stomach lurched but he gave a slight nod. He thought Nick might not see it but he disappeared back into the room and closed the door. Collecting Xenik and instructing him to go into that room was granting Nick permission to carry out his threats, but Daeson didn't have the fight in him to stop it. They were criminals hurting criminals and he had no influence.

If it wasn't for Omerri, he wouldn't stay.

He made his way upstairs and after some inquiry, discovered Xenik was having a cigarette break in the back alley. He went outside, feeling cold in spite of the warm night. Beneath the buzzing glow of a streetlight, Daeson found Xenik standing in a group of three men, one of which was in uniform. An Authority.

Daeson didn't understand how such a thing worked; why the Authorities didn't just permit the existence of a club that defied their own laws, but even *visited* it. They drank alcohol that was purchased without a liquor licence. They danced to music illegally imported from other worlds. They arrived in their uniforms to avoid paying the entry fee and enjoy discounted drinks, all while ignoring the hypocrisy of their own making.

Xenik was the first to notice Daeson's approach, looking over the heads of his companions. They stopped talking when they became aware of another presence. Daeson managed to say 'um' but no more words would come out. Xenik guessed anyway. "Nick want me?"

"Yes."

He felt like he was going to be sick. Daeson hastily returned to the building and went into the closest bathroom to splash cold water upon his face. He thought of the man downstairs, wondering why he hadn't spoken. Even telling lies had to be more reasonable than staying quiet. Why hadn't he at least tried to protect himself? It didn't make sense.

He thought of Omerri, who explained things to him in ways that helped him understand. He knew that Nick did everything under her instruction—that she probably wouldn't stop what was happening, either; but she could give him a reason. She could tell him something that would help quiet the horror.

He knew she'd already retired to her rooms. He'd never visited the penthouse before but he needed to speak with her now. Walking rapidly, Daeson made his way to the topmost floor, where he faced a polished golden birch door. It was difficult to summon his courage until he thought about the man downstairs.

He knocked on the door.

Omerri took her time answering it. Daeson endured the wait with a pounding heart and a dry mouth. There was a tightness in his shoulders and jaw as he stared blindly ahead. When the door opened, Omerri stood before him, dark brown hair falling in lustrous waves over her shoulders. She was dressed in a wispy robe over a silken nightgown that stole his breath. She'd had a winning smile in greeting but upon seeing him it faded.

"Daeson, darling, what's wrong?" Omerri reached out and took his hand, pulling gently. "Come in."

As she led him to a sofa, he got an impression of a room dressed in rich burgundy, white and gold. He was sorry that he couldn't properly appreciate this special moment.

On the sofa, she cuddled up to him and he wrapped his arm around her. After living here for two months, he was used to her cosying up to him...but it was increasingly difficult to suppress the effect she had. He felt flush, dizzy and his whole body thrummed with awareness. Some nights after being near her, he would take his shirt to bed with him because it smelled of her. Those were the nights his dreams were sweetest.

He was grateful he did his own laundry.

Entertaining such thoughts made it difficult to speak.

"Tell me," she whispered. He'd forgotten why he'd come here. It was with horror he remembered and he tensed.

"Nick," he said.

The tension mirrored in her shoulders.

"What about him?"

"I don't like what he's doing. I don't want to help him hurt people anymore."

She melted against him. "Aw honey, he's not supposed to make you hurt people," she said, her hand caressing his thigh.

He sucked in breath and struggled to recollect his scattered thoughts. "No, he's..." With a great deal of concentration, he forced out his concern. "*I'm* not hurting people. *He* is. Doesn't that bother you?"

She leaned away from him. There was a cold spot on his leg where her hand had been.

"This world is harsher than your world. Justice is served accordingly."

"Justice?" he scoffed. "You're feeding into a cycle of revenge."

"And on Kharltae you burn your criminals before banishing them," she pointed out.

Daeson shook his head, thinking it a different situation altogether. "Their crimes are counted on their skin, it's not about torturing or killing. It's a warning."

"But they can never escape their pasts," Omerri replied. "A mark tells you nothing. They could've killed someone or stolen an apple."

"Nobody gets *marked* for a stolen apple," Daeson argued.

"It depends who you steal it from," Omerri said.

He couldn't deny that truth. There was injustice on Kharltae, but that didn't make this situation right.

"I'm not here because of crime on Kharltae," he argued.

"That's right, you're not. You're here because of crime on Trent, and you don't like how Nick is dealing with it."

Her tone and the way she was looking at him reminded him of Anna, and the advice she'd given him.

Stop looking for the bad. Was he doing that now? It wasn't like Nick was doing good, but there was no justice in either world; people did what they thought best. There were no guards here to police the community, just Authorities. They'd already proven their double-standards and irregular convictions.

"What Nick is doing isn't right," Daeson protested feebly. He wished he could go back to the part where she was touching him, her softness moulded against him and her voice breathing through him. He didn't have the words to express his opinion and it was hard to recapture the despair he'd felt when watching Nick work.

"Right and wrong isn't something you can take at face value."

Daeson was astonished; his father had said exactly the opposite. Right and wrong were things not to be quarrelled over or up for negotiation.

"How can that be?" he asked.

"If the man below had put me in danger instead of...the girl—"

"Olivia," Daeson supplied. Omerri nodded. He could tell what she was going to say before she finished saying it, but he still didn't have an answer ready.

"If it were me instead of Olivia, would you allow him to go unpunished?" She waited out his silence and rested her head in the crook of his shoulder. "It's not so easy to answer now."

For the first time, her proximity brought him clarity. Replacing Nick with himself and substituting the unknown Olivia with Omerri, he understood why she argued that right and wrong were a matter of perspective.

On Kharltae, there'd been Lessons preaching revenge as the coward's tool, but imagining Omerri being torn out of his arms and hurt made him burn with vengeance hotter than a blacksmith's forge. Women especially were vulnerable—it didn't matter the world, it was the way of *all* of them—and they needed protecting. When their fragility was compromised, he knew that justice must be meted out.

Realisation washed through him. Omerri surrounded herself with strong men—*dangerous* men. Daeson had come to her because he disapproved of their brutality, he now saw their purpose. If Omerri was ever hurt, Nick would not stop until he avenged the mistreatment of the flower that bloomed amongst the thorns of this garden.

He experienced a momentary wash of unreality as he recognised a gratitude for the way Nick was. Sometimes, violence was necessary if justice was to be rightly upheld and though he mightn't like the appearance of it, he shouldn't be so quick to judge.

"I..." he began, but he didn't know how to finish. He wanted to ask her forgiveness, to tell her that he understood now, but the magnitude of it was overwhelming.

Stirred by his prompt, she tilted her head just as he shifted on the couch. His movements caused her to undulate against him, her beautiful face filling his vision as they settled even closer together. His pulse leaped and his mouth watered, her perfume fogging his mind. He was intently aware of the gentle rise and fall of her breasts and the scarlet urging of her mouth.

Omerri began to say something and he swooped, thinking she wanted him to kiss her. He saw his mistake immediately. With wide eyes, she swerved away from his seeking lips, narrowly avoiding contact and uttering a small exclamation of protest.

Daeson froze, mortification balling in his throat. They stared at one another, shocked into silence. He shot to his feet but there was no escaping the haze of embarrassment because Omerri simply watched him stand, still saying nothing. He gestured between them, his hands limply sawing the air while he tried to find the words that would express his regret.

None came to him. He had to leave before he made it worse. With a few unintelligible, apologetic utterances, he turned and fled the penthouse.

Breakfasts were awkward, the conversation forced. Daeson expected Omerri to stop coming but it didn't happen. A week passed before he realised that Nick wasn't asking him to identify liars when he brought people into the interrogation room. He assumed Nick would ask for his involvement again but for now Daeson enjoyed the break.

He spent his time helping the girls tidy their rooms; even Ruby—whose sharp tongue often lashed out at him or others—was nicer when she had help getting her room in order before beginning her shift. He and Ruby were tucking in the corners of freshly laid red sheets when Onyx entered the room and flopped onto them.

"Get off my bed, scummy," Ruby ordered, grabbing one of Onyx's legs by the ankle and pulling. The satin sheets made sliding around easier but Onyx made her escape by kicking out at Ruby and laughing gleefully.

Daeson didn't mind Ruby; he wasn't fond of her but she was alright when she was out of Onyx's influence. The same could be said for the dark skinned woman, as the pair of them brought out the worst in one another. Daeson didn't understand why they spent so much time together when they seemed to always be arguing or making one another miserable. If they weren't insulting each other, they were insulting other people together.

He left the room but not before Onyx made a detailed comment about what he was permitted to do with her. He ignored it as best he could, not wanting her to think he would accept such an offer. Onyx might be beautiful, but so were snakes. He thought about what she did with the men who paid to be with her and misjudged Jade's doorway enough to bump against it as he came through.

"Ouch, buddy. What's up?"

"Here to help," Daeson said, rubbing his upper arm, even though it didn't hurt. He tried not to look guilty about thinking of Onyx giving favours.

"Just the bows need doing," Jade instructed, gesturing at where she'd tied lengths of green ribbon to different articles of furniture. Daeson went to a chair and made careful bows.

"Why are Onyx and Ruby friends?" he asked.

"Because they're the same," Jade said, her tone betraying how little she thought of them.

"Ruby is nicer than Onyx, when she's on her own."

"Only because Onyx has been here longer."

Daeson finished making the second bow and had to kneel down to get to the ones tied the chair legs. He didn't know what Jade did with the ribbons or why they needed tying every shift, but he wasn't going to ask. He anticipated that Jade would fill the growing silence with more chatter. He'd learned that comfortable silences weren't her thing.

"They've both given up on their dreams. They've decided that this is the best they can do and they're upset about it so they want to get a win wherever they can. They probably think real friendship is baking cakes."

Daeson burst out laughing at the idea of baking cakes for his friends and Jade laughed along with him.

"I don't understand," he said when the laughter died down.

"Yeah, I thought you didn't. It's a saying...put in certain ingredients, get a predictable outcome. As though real friendship is boring?" Jade chuckled at

Daeson's thoughtful expression. 'Baking cakes' was a metaphor that hadn't given him the nausea of a lie. They were interrupted by Pearl who knocked on the open door and waited for them to look at her.

"Gregory's asked for a double. Want in?"

Daeson returned his focus on the chair bows but couldn't seem to get them quite right.

"Which Gregory? Soldier or dockworker?"

"Dockworker."

"How does *he* have that kind of cash?" Jade said, but she was walking to the door, which made Daeson think she was going to accept Pearl's offer.

"Got promoted."

"Alright. Daeson could you finish up in here for me?"

"Okay," he replied, keeping his gaze fixed on the ribbon that refused to turn neatly around his thumb. He completed the ribbons in Jade's room as quickly as he could, even though they didn't look very neat because of his hurrying. He wondered if there was *any* job at the Queen that he could be comfortable working.

A month passed. Omerri ate her scrambled egg-whites and accompanying fruit quietly. Daeson had learned the names of many fruits as Omerri's breakfast cycled though them. Today she had a sweet green fruit called Honeydew; a name he thought strange as the fruit didn't look or taste like honey and there was nothing dewy about it.

He wasn't sure what he was doing wrong; many of his comments led to long silences. Perhaps she'd woken up unhappy. There were days he'd had like that; the misery of his heart had felt like it gathered tangible weight in his chest, his sadness a heavy chain. He'd learned the best way to cheer her up was with compliments but today the best reaction he received was a tight smile.

"Am I not good company this morning?" he asked finally. He suspected that her interest in him would never match his interest in her. She was a sophisticated woman with complex thoughts and he worried that his simplicity would never be enough to capture her attention. It was possible she was too polite to tell him there was nothing left for them to talk about.

"Daeson, darling, I'm afraid *I'm* not good company this morning," she declared. Her smile was sad and in seeing it, he felt guilty for being focussed on himself. "I don't feel...myself."

He knew what she meant. He'd felt that way for two years, trying to be the farmer he knew he wasn't. He'd wanted to meet his father's expectations and failed, which left him with nothing. No legacy. No identity. His sense of self had been invested in that farm and he'd turned his back on it.

"I've felt that. I've pretended to be more than what I am, trying to keep up with everything and feeling like it's going to fall around me. Wearing a mask while inside I feel hollow."

Omerri gaped at him and he wondered if he'd offended her again, but then she stabbed her fork in his direction and nodded briskly.

"*Yes*. Hollow. That's the word. You've said it so perfectly."

Her excitement at hearing how well he'd described how terrible she felt was both amusing and horrifying.

"That's awful. I'm so sorry."

"It can't be helped." She picked up her wine-glass filled with water and took a lingering sip, watching him over the rim. "I didn't expect you to have such thoughts."

"Why not?"

"You seem a positive man."

He found her words encouraging and he wanted to accept her flattery, but it wouldn't be right to mislead her.

"I try my best, but my thoughts and my feelings don't always agree. I know what I'm supposed to feel and when it's not the same, I..." he shrugged, unsure how to describe it.

"You feel guilty?" she guessed.

"Yes, but I also feel...ungrateful, somehow."

"Because you resent having to keep up appearances," she said with a firm nod. It wasn't what Daeson meant but Omerri looked satisfied with the answer she'd given so he didn't argue.

"Is that what you're doing?" he asked.

"Keeping up appearances? Of course. This whole world wears a mask, darling. Everybody makes nice with everybody else, but it's always about getting everything you can out of them. If you're not using, you're being used. Maybe both," she admitted.

Her words sounded bitter but he had a question for her.

"Nick told me that the first day I was here," Daeson said, for the conversation had impacted on him. "I'm being used for my truth, aren't I?"

"Not anymore," Omerri said softly, breaking eye contact and looking down at her plate. He felt bad for provoking her when she was already vulnerable.

"I understand why you would," he conceded. "In a world where everybody lies, it must be refreshing to know that you can find the truth."

Her gaze lifted and she gave him a smile that thrilled him.

"I want to be the reason for all your smiles," he gushed.

"Oh Daeson, you're a sweetheart." He flushed embarrassment but was also pleased that she'd used his name instead of 'darling', though he liked when she called him that too.

"Your mood will lift," he encouraged. "Especially since you have a birthday to celebrate."

She was setting her water down and the glass clanged harshly against her plate. The stem snapped and glass shattered in her hand. She flinched as water spread over her plate and the tablecloth. They both looked at her bleeding palm as she held it aloft.

Daeson leaped from his chair and crouched beside her, reaching for her wounded hand and wrapping both of his around it, to contain the flow of blood. He wished he knew what to do beyond that. He didn't even know how deep the cut was, or how to tell how bad it was. All he could do was hold her hand and wish it better. He could feel heat radiating from it, as though he was holding the bell of a lantern. He didn't know why her hand was so hot—it wasn't normal. He associated burning skin with fever.

The sound of the kitchen door alerted them of Kite's approach. "Miss Backhouse?"

"Leave us!" she ordered, her tone hurrying him back into the kitchen. Omerri pulled her hand out of Daeson's grip. Blood was smeared over her palm. Daeson pressed his lips together, his heart pounding in his chest, wondering if she would shout at him like she had at Kite.

Omerri grabbed a napkin then flipped the edge of the tablecloth up and over her plate to contain the water spill. Daeson watched as she cleaned blood off her palm. He hissed in breath, imagining the pain she felt. She made no such sound, instead holding out her hand for him to inspect. She'd cleaned it well and both blood and cut were gone. He stared in confusion; how had she manage to wipe the cut away?

"Is there something you'd like to tell me?" Omerri asked. She sounded upset but she looked excited.

"I don't know. Your hand got hot."

"Did you do this?" Omerri whispered, her eyes wide. He couldn't decipher her expression. He shrugged.

"I don't know what happened."

"You healed me."

Daeson shook his head. "*Your* hand got hot."

She was quiet for a long moment and they held their positions; him crouched before her and Omerri staring down at him. The hand that was no longer wounded reached out to brush his hair, fingers playing with a strand behind his ear. The action caused shivers to burst along his spine and he couldn't help but shift at the force of them. Omerri smiled and it reminded him of the smile she'd had when he'd woken and met her for the first time; when she'd looked like a goddess.

"Darling, you're a Healer. I don't know how, because you're an Intuit, but you're also a Healer. You're more special than I realised."

He felt a mix of emotions at her flattery: pleased that she had answers for him. Thrilled at her touch and adoring expression. Uncomfortable with her testimony that he was special.

"I don't feel special."

She smiled and ran her thumb across his lips. "I can fix that," she promised.

CHAPTER TWENTY-FOUR

The Hunter And The House

THE piece of paper the librarian gave him led the Hunter to a two-storey house in the suburbs. The lawn was manicured, the path bordered by flowers and there was a wind chime hanging beside the front door. He hadn't expected anything so tidy, so normal.

He left the pickup near the kerb rather than pulling into the driveway. Even though his vehicle wasn't marked as Authority-owned, he didn't want to give the residents any cause for concern. He wore no uniform and his pistol was concealed beneath his bulky jacket.

Her case had gone cold almost a decade ago but he hadn't forgotten her. She'd been protected by the people around her, selfishly allowing them to sacrifice their lives on her behalf.

Shrubs and trees shielded most of the front lawn from neighbours but he could be seen from across the street. It was best to walk with purpose and entitlement. There were four stairs leading to the front verandah and the door beyond, which he took in a couple of long strides. His hand remained loose at his side, close to his weapon, as he knocked on the door.

There was no movement inside. After remaining where he was for a reasonable period of time, he followed the wraparound verandah to the back door. The back yard's primary feature was a kennel but it looked old and dilapidated, as though a dog hadn't had the displeasure of living in it for some years now.

The back door was locked when he tried the knob. Forcing it would be easy but he didn't want to advertise his presence. He ran his fingers along the lintel but there was no key. Looking down, he saw a trio of differently sized pots with flowering shrubs in them.

The smallest one looked like it had been moved a few times so he looked underneath it.

There was a key.

He picked it up and slotted it into the lock, where it easily turned and opened the door. It led into a laundry. A half-filled basket of dirty clothing was set on top of the washer, detergents and other cleaning products lined up neatly on the shelves above. He moved past and through an open doorway, into the living room.

It was tastefully decorated. The walls held paintings that mirrored the furnishings in the room, the rug matched the curtains and a wide-screen television filled a short wall. Beyond, the dining room was simple but elegant, with high backed chairs and a floral centrepiece on the large table. The kitchen lay behind it, with a few modern appliances on the counter tops and figurines artfully arranged on a display shelf.

A photograph nearby caught his attention, delaying him from investigating the other rooms. As he took a step closer, his phone's ring punctured the silence. Flustered, he pulled out his phone and turned his back to the photograph so that he could concentrate on the call.

"What?" he barked.

He was told about a flare on Finalis. His Wandering trio had arrived on Baxter, which meant he had to report to Fort Winston. The Hunter acknowledged his expected time of arrival and hung up. The phone was carefully stowed in his pocket.

He was slow to turn back around. He'd been wanting to catch this woman for decades and the chase might be over now. Confirmation was there, behind him, yet he'd seen something in the first glance that he hadn't expected and he wasn't sure he wanted to know after all.

Ridiculous. He turned and approached the photograph. It was in a sleek silver frame; a young couple holding a baby smiled at him through the glass. He recognised the woman. She was definitely his target. The librarian had informed him she went by the name Narelle Lawson now. How many times had she changed her identity?

But it wasn't just her that had him tightly gripping the frame. It was the man beside her; a kill he'd made a dozen years ago. He hadn't realised they'd been a family.

Not that it mattered.

Even as he thought it, he knew he didn't feel it. For some reason, it did matter, and he didn't want to think about why. Not now. He had a mission to complete.

He left the house as he found it, intending to return.

CHAPTER TWENTY-FIVE

The Morning After

SYNJAN awoke to the taste of stale memories and twisted dreams. It was dark and the air was cold but her attention to this was sharply surrendered the first time she moved her head. Pain bloomed, bursting against her skull like a firebarrel before pulsing down her spine and crawling across her face.

Recollections of the bloodshed followed by her heavy drinking the night before slunk across her consciousness and she realised why every part of her ached. She could feel the layer of despair still smothering her; her skin was a pressurised cocoon. She knew she had to push her way out before it became toxic. It didn't take her long to know how she would do it.

She was still cuddling the water bottle Ellis had given her, but it was empty. Carefully, she pushed back the covers, flinching as the pre-dawn cold bit at her exposed flesh and groaning as every movement made her head throb. Like an aged woman, she dragged herself into the bathroom. She used the toilet and washed her face, swallowing two tablets that would lessen the pain, gulping water directly from the tap. She didn't look into the mirror.

She dried her face and went into her bedroom, closing her eyes and turning on her bedside lamp. It still managed to penetrate with an initial flash of brilliance but she moved away and sought some underwear and warm clothes through shuttered eyelids. The clock beside her bed told her it was almost four, so she didn't have a lot of time.

She left the household curled in their beds, skulking along oil-dark streets towards her seaside destination.

The curfew wasn't lifted yet and she was too hungover to map, so she took a route she knew would be friendly; past the Queen of Clubs and through Portside.

With every step, her head hurt less and her mind cleared a little more. By the time she reached Whale Lookout, her shoulders had relaxed and she could turn her head freely. One thing the Authorities did do right was pain medication.

She walked cautiously to the edge of the highest cliff in Gredann, wary of stepping into space and tumbling to her death in the impenetrable darkness. Listening to the scrape of her running shoes diminish as she found the edge, she squatted and then sat on the rocky clifftop, dangling her denim-clad legs into the abyss before her. She took a deep breath of salted air and squinted at the vast horizon of water, though it didn't help her see any better.

The moon was gone and the sun wasn't ready to get up. She could make out the occasional flickers of white in the turbulent sea below. The wind was gusting too, nudging her in different directions as she rested her hands by her thighs, fingers thoughtfully exploring the texture of the stone she was perched on. She'd worn a couple of layers of warm clothing on her top half and all of it was zippered and tied down but still the restless wind tried to snap the hood off her head, to whip in beneath her jaw and attack the warm skin of her neck and ears.

She loved this place. It always cleared her head and soothed her heart. Her father, Cronson, used to bring her up here; from the time he had to carry her until just a few days before he died. They'd navigate the hushed streets of Portside and climb through the strip of forest bravely defending the businesses from the ocean's wrath, to this perch on the cliff. From here, they could see to a faraway watery horizon but also look down to the left, where the Tutley River met the Western Ocean.

Just beyond the generous delta sprawled the Shipman's Docks, though she couldn't see all of them from here, even when the sun was up.

There was a serenity and comfort she felt in knowing that the trawlers would be headed back now. Baltham would be setting up his scallop shop and his grandson—she'd forgotten his name—would be finishing up another long run from wherever he'd found his latest treasures. Perhaps she'd go down there and buy something for breakfast, even though she'd only visited a few days ago. It felt like longer in some ways, but that was just because of her life and her job. Time was capricious and always Synjan's master.

It was why Dockside meant so much to her. Despite the fact that it was filled with as many nightmares and monsters as it was friends, it was also a reliable beast. Its rhythms were ancient, dictated by the tides and turning with a predictable, reassuring regularity. Though the faces changed, the dance remained the same; the ocean was full of life that the trawlers caught a small percentage of. What they brought back was always enough and the docks played their part by being the beating heart of a people who valued the old ways over the new.

Of course, they weren't anywhere near as efficient as Port Cleary, the docks around which Oceangate was centred. It lay beyond her sight, around the curve of the cliff to the right. Port Cleary was built by the Authorities to change and upgrade Gredann in a way they'd convinced people was good for them. The only thing that had changed was the Docksiders' trust. When the Authorities built their warren of a dock and sent out their super-powered ocean boat that disrespectfully fished fifty times what the trawlers could in a single day, the generations of Docksiders finally turned against them. Profit was all that beat in the dead, technological heart of Port Cleary. Nobody in Dockside respected people with such a high disregard for tradition.

Synjan straddled the two worlds out of necessity. It suited her because she got a taste of each. She could appreciate the benefits and shy away from whichever burned her when the detriments struck her down. Like last night's unwelcome reminder of what horrors people could do to each other.

She drew in a deep, deliberate breath through her nose as unwanted images flooded her thoughts. The alcohol hadn't committed them entirely to the vault of nightmare fodder within her mind so she was forced to push them aside consciously. The taste of fear and the bitter sting of regret weren't so easily dismissed.

"So what now, fool?" she asked on her outgoing breath, the quiet words snatched by the wind and dispersed into the ether. It was a habit to chide herself in times of difficulty, to force clarity when emotions clouded her view. It helped her think.

Ellis was right, of course. As much as she was tempted by the notion that she could simply run to the Portal and Wander away from here, she knew he hadn't been lying the night before when he'd told her the cause of her dilemma. People. People were on every world, and every world had the same scope for kindness and barbarism that hers did. If she travelled, the only change would be that she'd have no security and the landscape would be different.

Once, she'd believed everything would be fixed by leaving. She hadn't been able to work past her own emotions then. She'd been fourteen and had experienced some particularly bad things – a deal gone wrong where she'd killed her way out, an Authority interrogation where she'd been terrified they were going to take her blood and Ellis punishing her for all of it. She could find no clarity, nothing good in Gredann and she was aware that she'd reached the age her mother was the first time she'd Wandered. It had all added up to Synjan packing her bags and plotting to get to the Portal. Then the McGaw incident happened.

She didn't want to think about him but she had to. The girl in the warehouse wouldn't rest until she did.

McGaw had worked as Ellis' second in command. He was around long before Synjan came on the scene; he'd been with Ellis the night he'd found her at the hospital. McGaw towered over everyone and was almost as wide as he was tall. He was roped with muscle and always wore a suit that looked like it would tear right down the middle if he flexed too hard. He'd had a habit of silently staring at everyone with dark, suspicious eyes.

Synjan couldn't even pretend toughness with McGaw, which was exactly the way Ellis wanted it. McGaw had always been the man who'd beaten her whenever she'd made a mistake. Despite her training with Freddie, she'd learned to fear him and, more importantly, to never act against him. She also learned to hate him because of that incapacitating terror.

She'd killed him when she was fourteen. She'd been despairing over her life in Gredann and decided to flee with as much money as she could carry. She'd accessed Ellis' vault of Authority dollars and stolen a hefty wad, sneaking back up to her room to pack it. McGaw must have been hanging around because he'd followed her upstairs.

When he walked into her bedroom, she froze in the middle of shoving the money into a bag. It was very obvious what she was doing so he didn't bother to ask before he backhanded her. She stumbled into the wall and he was upon her instantly, deflecting her attacks and delivering some devastating ones of his own.

By the time she landed on top of her packing on the bed, both her eyes were swelling shut and her nose was broken (not for the first time). Her body had screamed in pain and she'd begged and sobbed, pleading with him to stop but her anguish washed over him like waves on a beach. He was more like a machine that night than he'd ever been, yet when he dropped his pants and advanced on her, terror such as she'd never known had taken over.

Despite her injuries, she tried to turn and crawl away from him, to escape what she knew would come next. He dragged her back and in her clawing desperation, her hand fell upon her bag. Inside was her gun. As he wrenched her jeans over her prostrate rear and the cool air signalled her doom, she spun around and shot him. She kept shooting until her magazine was empty, even though he'd jiggled and snapped backwards until he hit a wall and then slid down it, brains and blood pouring into his dead hands like he was trying to catch it.

Ellis found her standing over him in that condition, clicking an impotent trigger and crying. He'd gently taken the gun from her hand, righted her clothes and taken her to the hospital. She'd dislocated her shoulder, fractured her left forearm and broken a rib. They'd given her some strong pain killers that had helped her sleep for almost two days. By the time she was lucid again, the entire mess was 'taken care of'. That's what Ellis had told her as he'd kissed her forehead and insisted she rest.

After that, she hadn't been in any condition to Wander and though he hadn't ever come out and said it, Ellis expected her to step into the gaping hole McGaw's death had left in his organisation. It had been her fault he'd died and even if the circumstances vindicated her, the outcome was the same. Ellis had lost his most trusted employee. Job by job, she'd assumed that responsibility, silently apologising for her actions, deeply regretting the situation. Ellis had been genuinely upset and, even though he mourned McGaw for a long time, he never criticised Synjan; he'd supported her and even admitted how sorry he was that he hadn't seen sooner that it might happen.

He'd apologised to her.

A decade later, sitting on a cliff top watching the sun bleed colours into the sky as dawn conquered night, she could see clearly how that event had shaped her life. Yet her question remained.

What now, fool?

"Be grateful for your pain," she answered herself, tilting her head forward once more. "And keep perspective." Yes. Last night had been hard but she'd been through hard before. She'd destroyed McGaw and he'd seemed insurmountable at one point in her life. He was dead and she was still here, still whole. As much as there were times she couldn't bear to even open her eyes to look upon one more horror, there was always this—a new dawn that lit up the darkest corners of her soul and managed to remind her of what she did have.

She had Ellis; his love, support and trust. Trust was not a commodity available for purchase. She had Freddie; his support, faith and empowerment. It had taken many years to become as strong as Freddie had always assured her she would be and with it had come immeasurable confidence. She had Nick; his respect, friendship and affection. She knew she was stupid to have given her heart to a man that had a different woman in his bed every other night, but his influence on her life couldn't be denied.

There was something else in Gredann that she couldn't walk away from. Her family was buried here.

She would never understand why she'd been the only one of the Walker family to survive Gredann's greatest tragedy; a train line collapse on one of the highest peaks in the Rin Sayriss mountain range. They'd been travelling to Bardon City, accompanying her mother on a working weekend away. Cronson, Sorrell and eight year old Chandler had been counted amongst scores of fatalities. Synjan had been one of few survivors.

Though she didn't visit their graves as often as she once had, being close to them was still important to her – as evidenced by the well-loved wooden kitten she carried most places with her. Sometimes she lost which pocket she'd left it in and panic overcame her, but she'd always find it.

Her father had been a hobby carver. His work for the city's waste management department hadn't been glamorous or mentally challenging, especially once the hydraulic trucks were brought in by the Authorities. He would express his creativity with wood and a carving knife. There were a few beautiful pieces she'd managed to recover from her family home when she was young – she had keepsakes from her mother and sister as well – but none was more important than the kitten, because it had been a name he'd called her. He'd also made it and given it to her a few days before his death.

She pulled it out of her pocket and looked down at it, seeing it mostly from memory in the muted light. It sat across two of her fingers, curled up with its tail resting across its nose, eyes closed and a blissful expression on its face. Her father could make wood come alive because the kitten was detailed and expressive. From every angle, it looked authentic. It was well-loved, the curve of its spine worn smooth with the brush of her thumb in countless pockets through the years. It was a symbol of her family and a comfort in times of fear, a representation both of what she'd lost and could never lose.

Synjan tucked the kitten back within the warmth of her pocket. Returning to places that were significant to both of them kept her father alive in a small way. Her sister and mother had never cared for this sport. The Navigators alone had shared time atop this cliff, making out the shapes of the various boats rising and falling on the waves, racing towards the rising sun from wherever they'd fared in their search for seafood.

She and her father used to make a competition of their return and barter rewards for who saw the first boat, laughing when they turned out to be wrong and whooping when they were right (mapping was against the rules).

She smiled vaguely to herself as pinkish orange light speared the sky above her, highlighting a shadow speeding towards the dock. A new day was beginning and she'd sighted the first trawler; she turned to where her father would've been but saw only empty space.

A shiver ran down her spine then rippled through her body. Bringing her knees up to her chest, she hugged them and turned back to watch the way the little boat was tossed from one wave to the next. Its yardarms and the nets swinging on them looked like the kicking legs of dancers.

Nothing and nowhere was perfect. Despite what she'd lost, she'd made gains in her life too. The nightmares weren't easy but they kept her honest. They reminded her of the cosmic balance she dangled within and also rooted her more firmly in reality. What she had now, she didn't want to lose in the future so it was in her best interests to protect it.

Her thinking clear and her soul reaffirmed, Synjan stood and left the cliff when the entire vista before her was washed with soft pastels. Her walk back to the Office was brisk and invigorated, her intention to appease Ellis with an act of repentance firm but formless. She'd said some deeply embarrassing and offensive things in the grip of the alcohol and her cheeks coloured as she watched her feet walking. Would he punish her for what she'd said? It wouldn't be out of character and it certainly wouldn't be undeserved, yet she dreaded it all the same. Ellis wouldn't accept excuses.

Excuses hand the devil your soul, he always said with a sneer, and she knew this was exactly the reason he believed it to be true. There were many reasons for her behaviour but, ultimately, they were all excuses for a failure she shouldn't have entertained, let alone embraced. She had a lot to apologise for.

When she stepped into the dining area, Synjan saw she wasn't the only early riser. Ellis was seated at the head of the table, chair pulled back and one leg crossed over the other. He was reading the paper intently while Urvasi cooked breakfast. Two places were set at the table and Synjan approached dutifully, sitting at Ellis' right hand.

"You have impeccable timing," he told her dryly, looking at his paper as he folded it closed.

Synjan shrugged, unsure about how to lead in to what she needed to say.

"How's your head?" Ellis asked, reaching over to press his fingertips to the area near her eyebrow.

"It's alright," she answered quietly. "I took some pain blockers this morning." She looked at him as penitently as she was able, searching his green eyes for any sign of recrimination or forgiveness.

Urvasi arrived at the table with their plates, smiling as she laid them down. As Synjan gazed at the bacon, eggs and toast, the delicious smells reminded her how long it had been since she'd eaten. Her liquid dinner the night before hadn't been nutritious, even before her body had rejected it.

"Thank you, Urvasi," she said, picking up her knife and fork.

"There's more in the kitchen if you want it," the maid offered pleasantly, pouring orange juice into two glasses before being dismissed by Ellis.

For a while, only the sound of eating filled the room and the silence was companionable. Synjan was aware that Ellis was watching her, and she ignored him just as studiously, until she was ready.

She took a drink and cleared her throat as she replaced the glass on the table, looking hopefully at him. "I know I don't have any right to ask your forgiveness for what I did last night but I want you to know; I'm very sorry."

Ellis chewed and swallowed before he responded, his words as economical as his gaze was steady. "You said that last night. Repeatedly."

His words had a deflating effect on her and she exhaled as she stared at him, feeling every bit the child she'd always be in his eyes. "It... doesn't make it any less true," she offered humbly.

"Perhaps," he shrugged lightly, turning his attention to cutting a piece of bacon to stack with his egg on a matching portion of toast. His every move was measured and Synjan couldn't help but be insulted by his perfection. It had to be purposeful, to highlight her flaws. "But this is one of those times where your words are irrelevant in the face of your actions."

She stiffened. "My actions at that building were faultless."

He paused to look at her from beneath his lashes. "We wouldn't even be having this conversation if they weren't," he chastised silkily.

The hairs at her nape prickled. She watched him chew his fastidiously crafted bite, afraid to say anything lest he move beyond veiled threats.

After he swallowed, he drank some juice and steepled his hands over his plate as he considered her. "Where were you this morning?"

"Whale Lookout."

"How long were you there?"

"A little over an hour, I guess."

"And?"

She was momentarily at a loss. He knew she went to the lookout when she was troubled, when she needed some time to piece her thoughts together... and then she realised what he was asking. Relief flooded her.

"And my mind is back to where it should be. I got lost and I'm sorry I took that out on you. You didn't deserve it," she told him sincerely, reaching over to touch his forearm. She was reassured when his other hand dropped on top of hers, holding her in place. "I have nothing but gratitude for everything you are and everything you've done for me. I shouldn't have lost faith in you, not when you were trying to help. I'll do better next time," she promised.

Ellis smiled at her and his approval was clear to see. "That's my girl," he said softly, patting her hand.

"I love you."

"I know you do," he told her warmly, releasing her hand in order to pick up his cutlery once more. "Yet old men crave the whispers of fealty, for fortitude, heart and hope."

"Old men," she scoffed, returning to the remnants of her own breakfast.

His smile widened briefly before he looked up at her as if he'd just remembered something. "Speaking of men, Nick telephoned here for you last night. When I told him you were out, he requested you contact him this day."

"He didn't say what he wanted?"

Ellis shook his head. Synjan's positive mood dissipated as she was forced to think about her schedule and what Nick could possibly want with her. It would be foolish to think it was personal rather than work-oriented. She would telephone him after she finished her breakfast. Work could wait until her mind, spirit and body were in order.

CHAPTER TWENTY-SIX

The Criminal Portal

AESON'S dream of selling apples at a fair was interrupted. He opened his eyes to peer blearily at the person shaking him. He grumbled a protest at a woman's silhouette. The dream lingered enough for him to consider this woman might be unhappy with her apple before Jade identified herself.

"Get dressed and meet me outside."

Before Daeson could reply, she was out of his bedroom and had closed the door. Time was abstract—he had no idea if he'd slept for a few minutes or well into morning. The room was dark and he fought to escape from his cocoon of sheets. He wasn't sure where 'outside' was going to be; if she meant his room or the building itself.

He fumbled around in the dark and selected the first pieces of clothing his hand landed on and stepped into his joggers. When he entered the dimly lit corridor, he could see Jade standing a short way ahead, dressed in a nightgown.

"Am I—?"

Jade shushed him before leading him downstairs and to the back door. When she and Daeson stepped into the alley, they found Marcus waiting outside. He was the night shift guard for the back door and out of all of the security guards, Daeson got along with him best.

"Here you are!" Marcus said, as though Daeson had been hiding instead of sleeping in his own bed.

"Have a good time," Jade bid before she retreated into the Queen and closed the door. Daeson turned his confused look to Marcus who gestured down the alley. Daeson turned and saw Omerri's black limousine parked a short way ahead, its engine silent. The car door at the back was open and Daeson headed for it.

When he rounded the door, he saw Omerri's slender legs crossed over one another. His pulse quickened at the sight of them before he joined her.

She wore a short, flared dress that ended mid-thigh—a choice unlike her elegant gowns. The neckline of her dress dropped impressively. He'd seen a great deal more of the womanly form due to the other girls wearing skimpy outfits; certainly he'd seen Jade wearing less than what Omerri was now...but looking at Omerri was different.

Once Daeson settled beside her on the seat, she rested her head upon his shoulder and placed her hand on his leg just above his knee. Daeson considered putting his arm around her but shifting would disturb her position and he didn't want to ruin yet another moment.

The car purred to life and the driver pulled out of the alleyway without needing instruction. They drove into city streets that were fully deserted, through Hill End and then out of the city. They passed a few Authority patrol vehicles but weren't stopped even though they were out after curfew.

"Do they recognise your car?" Daeson asked.

"They don't stop limousines," Omerri replied.

He wondered who else was allowed to break curfew. Obviously anybody with enough money could bypass the laws. He was sour at the thought of this injustice. Omerri's influence extended beyond the money she made to the people she knew, as most of the Queen's clientele were Authorities or successful merchants.

Questions about Omerri's business danced at the tip of his tongue but he suppressed them, not wanting to spoil their time together by risking upsetting her. He was quiet until they started passing farmlands.

"Where are we going?"

"Somewhere nice. Trust me."

He trusted her. He enjoyed the feel of her beside him; the soft touch of her skin, the delicate aroma of her perfume—something floral with a spicy undertone that made him think of winter flowers and harvest time. Her hair tickled his ear and he moved his head as slightly as possible. She shifted when he moved a second time and snuggled against him in a way that encouraged his arm around her. He couldn't resist the view she offered him of her cleavage.

The street lighting disappeared. The full moon revealed they were passing fields with runnels of freshly sown wheat or corn. They made him guilty enough for him to frown.

Omerri looked up at him and he held his breath, his shame forgotten beneath the tingling quality of their connecting stares. He hoped that she would smile at him but she didn't; instead she leant in closer and tipped her head upward so that their lips were almost touching. He could smell her breath, minty and cool, and he was aware this moment would pass him by if he thought about it too much.

He tilted his head to meet her, brushing his lips against hers and partially opening his mouth when she did the same. He echoed her movements, soft and subtle, his eyes closed to focus on the sensation of the kiss.

Their first.

It went on for a long time like that, soft and pliant. When her tongue stroked across his lips, he was startled enough by it to pull back before trying to kiss again. Her hand rose between them and the feel of it resting upon his chest was enough to stop him. He was worried but her eyes were smiling through her thick, dark lashes. He grinned back, relieved that she wasn't upset with him, and then she snuggled against him again.

Happiness radiated across his chest.

The limousine turned down a driveway with a single lamppost near the entrance and bounced down an ill-tended dirt road. Daeson expected them to stop at the farmhouse and was surprised when they were driven past it, heading for the large barn beyond. Night-time shadows couldn't hide its run-down appearance but he could see the problems were mostly cosmetic. He thought the barn might've been yellow once, but now there were flakes of paint and patches of dark wood showing through.

The driver got out and opened the door for Omerri. As she shuffled across, the hem of her dress rode up higher so that Daeson could see the full length of her leg. He stared until he realised the driver was waiting for him to get out on the same side. Hastily he shuffled along to exit the car and took Omerri's hand when she held it out for him. She ended up leaning on him a great deal as her shoes weren't appropriate for walking on grass and dirt. He wondered why she would dress up when she was visiting a barn in the middle of the night.

Daeson looked over his shoulder in surprise when he heard the limousine start up. Omerri watched alongside him as the car performed a large turn and drove back the way it had come. Daeson looked at Omerri who was smiling mischievously up at him. He sensed that she was waiting for a question from him, but she'd already told him to trust her so he would prove himself by not questioning her now...though he did wonder how they were going to get back.

When Daeson entered the barn he didn't know what he was looking at. Many floor lamps blazed light and heat across the area, revealing the scene before him in stark detail. There were no stalls or animals—just a large grey semi-circular pod in the middle of the barn that looked like it had been squashed at both ends. It was the width and length of a small car. Multiple large cables fed out of it and connected to a lineup of small rectangular boxes. Above some of the boxes were flat panels, most of them showing moving images.

A grey-haired man sat in the chair at the centre of them all, facing them. He'd been startled when Daeson and Omerri entered but after seeing them, turned back to the pictures. A woman approached them who looked about his age, though her hair was still a youthful blonde. She smiled warmly and Omerri dropped Daeson's arm so the women could hold each other's elbows and kiss the air near each other's cheeks.

"Karen, darling," Omerri said, "promise me all will be well."

"I promise all will be well," Karen repeated. "Let's get started."

Omerri looked at Daeson enquiringly and he nodded, perplexed that Omerri wanted him to check this woman's statement for the truth. What was going on?

Omerri and Daeson both stood on a weigh scale where their weight was measured and written down. Omerri refused to let Daeson anywhere near her while this was being done. They were examined briefly while Karen explained to Daeson what they were checking for; the stethoscope for his heartbeat, the black cuff for his blood pressure and the thermometer for his temperature.

After everything was recorded and looked over, Daeson was directed to sit inside the grey pod. The space inside was smaller than he'd anticipated and he had to hunch over while getting in. There were two bulky chairs inside. Both had thick black strips of material stitched into the arms.

Omerri joined him once she was finished with her check-up and Karen stepped in after her to attach the black straps around Daeson's wrists and ankles, and also loosely around his neck. He was told that they were made from *Velcro*. She then tied down Omerri the same way and left the pod. Daeson listened to the man recite a bunch of numbers and measurements before announcing the countdown had begun. Daeson couldn't hear anyone counting down.

Karen returned with a tray that held two syringes. She explained that they would be put to sleep to keep them safe. Daeson was comforted by the truth of her words and flinched when she jabbed the needle into his arm. He'd expected her to be gentle. He watched her prepare the second needle for Omerri as sleep stole him away.

He awoke to the sound of two people arguing. Omerri slept in the chair beside him. He was still in the pod in the barn and through the side opening he could see the woman, Karen. When she looked over at him, her expression changed from confusion to panic. Daeson's heart jumped because she looked terrified. Something was wrong.

"Oh my God!" she screamed, and ran over. Before she got to him, the pod door slid shut with a clonk, shutting out all light. He tried to sit up but the straps held him in place, choking him. He could still hear her shouting outside and scratching for a hold on the automatic door.

"Stop it, stop it, stop it! He's awake! He's awake!"

"I can't!"

"You have to stop it! He woke up!"

"I *can't*!"

Daeson fought his restraints and felt one of them rip. The man shouted at Karen that she shouldn't open the door or they would all die, so Daeson stopped resisting.

The shock of this news ran his body cold. He could hear his heavy, shaking breaths. His eyes felt like they were open very wide, but he could still see nothing so he closed them. He whimpered and then cleared his throat. He had to calm down. He couldn't jeopardise the lives of three other people to save himself. His fingers were clenched tightly on the chair arms when the vibrations began. There was a low hum that accompanied it and then a rumble. Somewhere outside of the pod he could hear a growing whirring pitch.

He had to make himself relax. Maybe that was why being put to sleep was safe, because people were relaxed. He sank into the chair as best he could but he still felt tense. The Velcro at his throat made it hard to breathe.

The pod shook and he could hear things rattling around him. He remembered the cables and wondered if any would fall off. He was overwhelmed by a strange sensation of compression and force upon his body and he opened his eyes. He could see only blackness but his mind insisted that he was being lifted up and spun around inside the pod.

Abruptly, there was no sound. After a moment he thought he could hear the whoosh of wind, except he couldn't feel anything. He thought he'd stopped spinning but there was still a sensation of movement, as though he was being propelled somewhere at great speed. Finally, he could see something other than black; streams of colour around him, heading towards a small dot of white. It was like being in a tunnel, except the colours were racing him to the end. One of them passed very close to him and he felt a burst of acceleration, as though he'd been pushed. When the dot enlarged, he saw it was a picture of some kind of room. He couldn't make out details until it got bigger—or until he got closer, it was difficult to understand what was happening.

Perhaps this was what portal travel was like when awake and he was watching his entry into the next world. Was this the room he was going to arrive in with Omerri? He knew he was being too hopeful. The feeling in the pit of his stomach wasn't like his truth talent; it was a mixture of suspicion and defeat, a sensation he didn't care for.

The room rushed at him, causing him to throw his arms up to shield his face, anticipating impact. None came. He opened his eyes to a grand golden atrium.

There was a balcony that curved around the room held up by curtained columns. The roof depicted a mural of birds and butterflies. Each wall panel showed varying landscapes of hills and valleys. Sky blue and light pink cushions were clustered at the foot of each panel, creating a welcoming atmosphere. The room was exceptionally bright, as though somebody had harnessed the sunlight and imprisoned it. The problem was, everything that he looked at directly was rippled and watery, solidifying only after he took his gaze from it and stared at something else.

He wasn't alone. He couldn't *see* anyone but he was certain he wasn't alone. He didn't know how he could know such a thing.

He must be dreaming. He'd started with a nightmare of his worst fears and then the dream had transformed into something calmer. He was asleep after all.

"You are not asleep, Daeson."

Truth from a voice that echoed around him. But did his talent work in dreams? This was not like his regular dreams, which were filled with nonsense and half-imagined scenarios. This was both vivid, yet not. He looked from one rippling column to the next and rubbed his eyes before opening them again.

"You cannot see clearly because we are not properly connected."

This time the voice came from his right and Daeson turned to see a woman wearing a sapphire blue gown. The material rippled and melted into the floor. He couldn't see her properly but he got an impression of brown hair piled high on her head and vivid blue eyes.

She was a striking figure. She looked like a water goddess, because of the way her dress behaved while she walked closer. It looked like she was wearing a river. This *had* to be a dream.

"Dreaming is another place. Not here."

Where was *here?* This room wasn't anything like he'd seen before, not even on a tapestry or in a storybook. He focussed on the statuesque woman.

"You shouldn't use the artificial portals, Daeson. It is not safe."

"But the one I touched was safe?" he asked. He hadn't visited this watery room when using the Portal made of light.

"It is natural. It is safe."

"I didn't want to leave my home," Daeson said.

She said nothing.

"Who are you?" he demanded.

"I am your mother."

Shock chased away the rest of his questions. This woman, with her strange declaration and ability to gather him into a dream-room so she could talk to him, *this* woman was the one who'd given birth to him and then left him on Kharltae. She was able to contact him through powers that he'd inherited. It made an awful yet exhilarating kind of sense.

"Why now? Why are you speaking to me now?" he challenged.

"I was unable to before. Do not use the artificial portals, Daeson," she repeated. He was aware that her form was becoming more shimmery and unreal before he realised what it meant.

"No! Wait!" he cried, but the room transformed into an aquarium, except all of the fish were on the outside and he was on the inside. He stared at them uncomprehendingly, wondering if this was another dream-room. A tall, skinny man rushed to stand in front of him. He gave an almost comical sigh of relief before he moved away. Daeson watched as he went to a large black box and picked up a spoon-shaped object from it. The man spoke into the spoon.

"He's okay. They're both okay. She's still sleeping it off but her vitals are fine."

She? *Omerri*! Daeson found her on his other side, lying on a slender reclining chair. A bald man held a stethoscope to her chest and when he caught Daeson's eye, he gave a thumbs-up. Daeson knew this gesture was positive and felt some of the tension escape him. He could still hear the one-sided conversation the first man was having on the phone.

"No, you must've imagined it…he *can't* have been awake, he's come through alive. Maybe you saw him twitch or something." A longer pause. "I've seen someone have a fit before being sent through and *they* made it through to the other end…No, of course not, but in this business…"

Daeson shuffled forward to get out of his recliner and was ordered to wait by the man tending to Omerri, but Daeson ignored him. Once his feet landed on the floor his knees gave way. He managed to save himself by grabbing onto the arm of the chair.

"Fuck, I'll talk later, this guy's keen to get going. There's obviously nothing wrong with him if he's already trying to walk around." A brief chuckle and then: "Yeah, stay out of trouble. Bye."

Daeson could stand on his own by the time the man returned to him.

"You feeling okay? You need a bag or anything?"

"A bag?" Daeson asked, bewildered.

"Yeah, never mind. I've never seen someone get up so fast before."

"Okay," Daeson agreed. The skinny man's statement was confusing but wasn't important enough to pursue. There was a metallic taste in the back of his throat that he wanted to be rid of though. "Can I have some water please?"

He expected to have it pointed out to him but a glass of water was brought to him. The skinny man helped him hold the glass until it was obvious that Daeson could manage it on his own. He gulped it down quickly, wanting to get to Omerri's side before she woke up.

He sat beside her and held her free hand while the bald fellow checked her periodically. When he made noises about being happy about a readout, the doctor picked up a thing that looked like a perfume bottle with a breathing mask attached and held it over her, squeezing the pump twice. Omerri opened her eyes with a gasp and her face lit up when she saw Daeson. Joy bubbled up inside of him at her reaction.

Omerri remained in her chair for a long time and spoke with the two men as she recovered. Daeson kept quiet and listened as they discussed people he hadn't met and didn't know. When one of them mentioned someone called Ellis, Omerri gave him a menacing look before slyly checking on Daeson. She didn't seem pleased that he'd noticed the exchange.

She struggled to her feet soon after, relying heavily on Daeson to hold her up. He didn't think she should be walking around yet but the doctor wasn't concerned so Daeson didn't say anything. Before they left the room, the bald man handed Omerri a large yellow envelope.

CHAPTER TWENTY-SEVEN

On The Lookout

AFTER the Christmas break with the Cayden family, Hawke returned to Willets. He knew the routine of the Academy well enough now to take advantage of the staff's festive mood. Their holiday spirit had allowed him to scam two huge lemon-frosties for himself after dinner. The icy drinks were his favourite treat. There were two women that worked in the kitchen who thought he was charming; he'd used that charm on each of them separately and then stolen away to consume his ill-won rewards in isolation.

Now he wished he hadn't because he had a strong urge to pee. He hated getting up in the middle of the night. Moving around a mostly-silent dormitory in darkness didn't bother him but the rules put in place after lights-out were ridiculous.

Going to the toilet was allowable but only with the presence of a hall monitor at your side, to make sure the toilet was the only location visited. Hall monitors were normally older kids who'd earned the responsibility of patrolling the corridors and ensuring everyone was in bed, but sometimes they could be teachers. Hawke didn't need an usher to take him to the toilet and back; the whole idea was humiliating.

He wriggled to the edge of his bed and rolled back the covers. He dropped his feet out first, toes landing on freezing laminate over concrete. He should've worn socks. As soon as he was out of bed, he could feel the chill in the air. It was summer; outside it was warm but Willets was always cold indoors. At least in winter there was a chance the heating might be turned on.

He snuck across to the door, passing Salty on the way. Salty's real name was Saul Nolte, even though there was nothing about his character that suited the nickname. Apparently having a real name close in sound was enough. Hawke hadn't attracted a nickname yet and he was pleased about that.

He'd received a few derogatory remarks though, mostly about his bloodline. At first the questions about where he went and what he was doing were general and driven by curiosity. He'd answered them cautiously until he'd perceived genuine interest, then Hawke had supplied tales of his abduction and won some wide-eyed respect. He hadn't even needed to exaggerate...much.

The secret about his having a strain of the Wanderer bloodline had been mistakenly outed the moment he'd spoken of the DOME. He'd known that Wanderers were tested there but hadn't considered it was reserved solely for that purpose. Since most of the Willets kids were Authority brats, they knew of the DOME's reputation and word had spread.

Still, in spite of the odd snark from students, Hawke had come to appreciate his Authority-provided home. He was learning about things that his world didn't even know about and his future had broadened incredibly. He would never thank the Wanderers for taking him away from Boronia, just like he resented the Authorities for keeping him from it...but that didn't mean he couldn't be grateful that he was here now.

As Hawke peeked around the corner to check for hall monitors, his heart sank.

Farther up the corridor, standing in an open doorway—for there were no doors that led into the bedrooms, privacy was not something afforded students at Willets—was a boy that ran in Polsen's circle of friends. Circle of hooligans was a more apt description for this particular grouping of boys—the kind that liked to exercise power over other, weaker members. Bullying was frowned upon at the Academy and there were always phrases of 'serious allegations' being made and 'behaviour that wouldn't be tolerated'. Hawke thought the teachers meant well but they couldn't help because they had no proof, and everyone was too scared to speak up. Even if a group of bullies were expelled, others waited on the sidelines to take control and it would be easy to find out who told. Surviving in the goldfish bowl that was Willets, meant keeping out of the way of the biggest power-groups.

He hopped from one foot to the other, doing the dance that all people did when needing the toilet badly. He froze when the lookout glanced up the corridor in his direction, but then the lookout turned away again. Most of his attention was on the north end of the corridor, as this was the direction that would bring a hall monitor.

While they both waited for one to come, Hawke thought about why there was a lookout on that dormitory in the first place. He'd heard rumours of homework auctions held at night and he suspected this might be a room that was hosting one. There was an intelligent kid called Naveen who slept in that room. He was a perfect target for Polsen to puppeteer, though he wasn't terribly wise to have attracted their attention. Hawke would prefer to be world-smart over being book-smart any day. Kids like Polsen would be all smiles while getting what they wanted but he'd turn on Naveen as soon as the supply stopped.

Polsen wasn't any kind of smart. He would only ever do well as long as he had someone do things for him. Hawke knew the benefits of taking advantage of others but his methods separated him from thugs like Polsen. Hawke played on his charm, so that people wanted to do things for him—like giving him a lemon-frosty. Polsen exploited the fear he put into others, which meant that as soon as someone bigger and nastier came along, his kingdom would fall. He had no finesse.

Hawke couldn't wait for the hall monitor any

longer—he would have to take the risk of being seen by the lookout. The toilets were in the other direction so his back would be turned. He doubted they would even know who he was, for Hawke kept a low profile, circulating amongst select boys—the kind who blended in, like him. Hawke waited until there was one more brief glance in his direction and then he made his move.

With bare feet making barely a sound on the ice-cold floor, Hawke ran lightly on the pads of his feet to the door that led to the toilets. He hurled himself inside without a look back. Hastening into a stall, he experienced the bliss of pent-up release as the horrid knot that had formed in his bladder loosened. He washed his hands carefully, procrastinating because he wasn't looking forward to making the dash back to his room. He was probably going to be seen. If he waited a little longer, a hall monitor might appear and escort him back safely.

He thought he could hear footsteps.

Hawke moved to the bathroom door and slowly pulled on the handle, so he could peek through a crack and see who was outside. The person on the other side of the door shoved into it with force, smacking the door into Hawke's forehead. Pain exploded like fireworks behind his eyes and he stumbled backwards, catching himself against a urinal. His forehead blared, interfering with his thinking as he struggled to stand.

"It is him, you were right," a voice sneered. Hawke squinted at three boys past the throbbing in his head. His stomach dropped when he saw Polsen glaring at him, flanked by two other boys. One of them Hawke recognised as the lookout. "Hello, Lab Rat."

The sarcastic greeting helped Hawke realise that he had a nickname after all, just not one that had been repeated to his face.

They were in the same school grade but Polsen was a year older than everyone and Hawke was a year younger, putting two years' age difference between them. There was a significant difference in bulk, too. Even with the advantage of age, there was something clumsy about Polsen, like he'd stopped bothering to try and be anything better. It only served to lower Hawke's respect. Why should anyone fear a brute who would never be important beyond the Academy?

"I won't tell," Hawke said, thinking they might've been worried he'd reveal their nightly escapade.

"No, you won't," Polsen said agreeably. Hawke felt like they had more on their mind than just covering their tracks. They intended to beat him up. The way they'd addressed him was a clue as to why though Hawke knew that 'why' didn't matter to a boy that thought power and influence were won through fear. They were Authority spawn and they knew he had Wanderer blood.

Perhaps Hawke shouldn't have shared so much about his abduction experience.

Polsen's swing came at him so slowly that he managed to avoid it by stepping back and hitting the arm aside. Even with his throbbing head Hawke considered himself smarter and faster. Polsen's face reddened and he signalled the other two boys to advance along with him. The lookout was the quickest and closed in on Hawke before he could reach a stall. Hawke thought it would be easier to contain his space so each boy would have to attack him individually, maybe even hold them off long enough until someone came to help. There was no time or room for that now.

He managed to elbow the lookout in the throat. It was more luck than skill. Polsen and the other guy rushed him and there was little Hawke could do. The first punch hit him in the cheek and pain flared so hot that the smack from the door seemed minor. He didn't know which way the ground was but gravity got him there. He landed roughly and became the target of a kicking contest. He curled up to protect himself as much as he could. Blows landed on his back, legs and arms as he covered his head. Hawke kept expecting a bone to break—perhaps some of his fingers that were wrapped around his skull—but nothing did. He was lucky he'd fallen partially underneath the sink counter, where they couldn't get at him properly.

They left him as quickly as they'd begun to beat on him. Something had interrupted them. He could hear a weird, keening noise echoing around the bathroom tiles and wondered what it was before he identified it as himself. As soon as he realised he was the one making it, it stopped. Tears and snot streaked down his face and pooled on the floor. He opened his eyes and was surprised not to see blood – he was sure he would've started coughing it up. His back ached, his neck ached and he didn't know if he'd be able to stand up.

The reason for the other boys' exit was made apparent when a hall monitor entered the bathroom. He was one of the assistant teachers, which commanded him more authority. Hawke recognised him but didn't know his name because he helped with the year levels well under Hawke's age.

"Can you stand up?"

Hawke was already trying to get to his feet but was struggling. He wasn't being helped by the hall monitor but was grateful for his presence anyway. He'd scared off Polsen and that was enough.

"Think so." Hawke used the counter as a support.

"Need first aid?"

"No."

"Wash up, then. I'll wait outside."

The hall monitor left him to deal with his wounds and Hawke was both surprised and indignant. He hadn't been asked to name the culprits, although he wouldn't have. He hadn't been treated with care or even assisted. There was no concern for what had happened to him, from a teacher. The betrayal from this man far surpassed anything Polsen and his mindless friends had done.

Hawke washed his face, taking his time because he was having trouble moving his arms. They hadn't been kicked much but his back and shoulders protested when he lifted them. Once he was finished, he ignored the sorry state of his reflection and shuffled across to the door, using the counter to help him. He felt nauseous the instant he thought about reaching across and pulling on the handle. He must've taken too long because the door opened and he flinched back from it, causing a shooting pain to spike up his neck.

"Need a hand?"

It was still that same, impersonal offer. Hawke wanted to tell him to shove off but at the same time he knew that this man was his saviour—even if he didn't care to be—and Hawke needed his help, like it or not.

"Yeah."

He hobbled back down the corridor to his room and the hall monitor covered him up once he was in bed. It was the most considerate action the man had taken. The hall monitor checked the other boys were still asleep in their beds with a perfunctory look, then left the room.

It took Hawke a long time to get to sleep.

The next morning had him facing a panel of three; the principal, the student counsellor and the head teacher in charge of his school year, Mr Blatch—the only one out of the trio that Hawke liked. Mr Blatch hadn't treated him differently to the rest of the boys under his charge. Hawke worked hardest in his class, even though mathematics didn't come as naturally to him as with the other subjects.

The student counsellor was a woman who insisted on being called by her first name, Naomi. She seemed at a loss when it came to counselling him. The first session he'd had with her, she'd prattled on about his grieving the loss of his family. He'd said nothing, thinking instead that she didn't know what she was talking about because his family wasn't dead. He'd ignored her offer of assistance after that, avoiding her request for appointments with excuses so thin he thought she would call him out. She never did.

The principal was an imposing man—a retired Authority soldier who'd held some ranking before becoming a teacher and then a principal. Rumours had him at various ranks before being honourably discharged or sometimes even dishonourably discharged, which Hawke knew was bogus because he wouldn't be in charge of an Academy if he'd been kicked out. He was the only person Hawke knew with a combined name. Principal Fielder-Wiley had grey hair and Hawke's young eye couldn't determine if he was thirty or sixty. With an aquiline nose hooked over thin lips, he looked more like Hawke's namesake.

"Your sponsor is on his way to meet with us," Fielder-Wiley said in a voice that was both rich and deep. Unlike the hall monitor teacher from the previous night, the principal spoke warmly, sympathetically. Hawke didn't mistake it for true affection—he'd sat through many school assemblies listening to the cadence of this man's voice. If a person could address hundreds of students at once and make them feel as though he was personally speaking to them, then it was a talent Hawke was wary of and mistrusted. "I understand you haven't identified your assailants?"

Hawke shook his head but the silence stretched for so long that as each second ticked by, he felt further compelled to speak.

"I don't know who they were," he said finally.

Fielder-Wiley grunted his discontent.

"They jumped him from behind," Naomi supplied, repeating the excuse Hawke had given her. Hawke deduced she must've spoken out of turn because the principal slowly turned his head to look at her. She wilted under his gaze.

"Hawke," the principal said. It made him feel uncomfortable to hear his name coming from this man's lips. "Do you understand the no-tolerance policy we have at Willets for fighting?"

Fighting meant expulsion for those parties involved. There were no warnings, no detentions, no suspensions. There was talk of how there were students in the past who'd organised boxing matches, even going so far as to have gambling attached to them. Apparently it had been difficult to stamp out, so a strict no-fighting rule had been imposed. One thrown punch at another student meant a new school for the aggressor.

"Am I being expelled?" he asked, shocked.

He hadn't considered this as a possibility. He didn't want to leave Willets. He liked being here. He enjoyed every class, even the difficult ones. He'd lived here for three years, this was his only home. Even though he went to Cayden's house for the holidays, it didn't feel like he belonged there. Thinking of the Authority officer who'd extended his heart and his home to him made a wad of panic lodge inside of his chest. It perched there, thick and heavy, as he imagined the disappointment in Cayden's face.

"No." Hawke felt relief surge through him. "But you should consider that your attackers will not go unpunished," Fielder-Wiley growled.

The idea of Polsen and his slack-jawed friends being thrown out of Willets was bitterly satisfying. He couldn't accept the promise and name them, though. Everyone would know that he was the cause of their expulsion and then his existence at Willets would be unbearable. His nickname would likely change from Lab Rat to just Rat. It was not a title he wished to earn for himself. Plus, revenge was sweeter if he could dole it out himself.

"I didn't see them," he repeated.

Hawke held eye-contact with the principal, ignoring the weighty silence and refusing to fill it.

"You will have daily detention for a period of six weeks."

"For being attacked?" he cried.

"For protecting the boys who attacked you. For allowing them to continue their behaviour. For putting other students at risk."

Hawke said nothing when the Principal fired these reasons at him. He was sullen; detention duty meant cleaning classrooms, being a server at mealtimes and disqualification from participating in any after class entertainment. That meant no movies on movie-night, no excursions and he would miss out on the travelling funfair that was supposed to camp on the Willets grounds four weeks from now.

There was a soft knock on the door and Fielder-Wiley's secretary announced Cayden's arrival. He was clearly surprised at Hawke's bruised appearance but said nothing as he was invited to sit. Hawke was instructed to wait outside. There was a wooden bench out there that matched the pews of the school church. He sat and listened, unable to hear anything. It didn't take long for there to be raised voices but he still couldn't hear the details of what was said—the voices were merely sounds. He recognised from the voices that the heated discussion was between Cayden and Fielder-Wiley.

A short time later, Cayden stepped out of the office looking determined and he spared a smile for Hawke. Naomi followed him and Cayden made a point to shake her hand and thank her. Hawke made a mental note to show her some respect, considering she was obviously an ally.

"I hope we can talk later," she said to Hawke when walking past.

"Okay," he promised before standing at Cayden's side. The two of them left the office and walked without speaking until they were in the central courtyard. Nobody else was here, for all students were in classes.

When Cayden and Hawke sat on a bench, the questions came.

"How many?"

"Three."

"You know them?"

"Yeah." Hawke hoped Cayden wouldn't ask who they were.

"Why not name them?"

"Because that's not how it works."

"Do you need help?"

"No, I can keep out of their way."

"Did you hold your own at all?"

Hawke looked out over the paved stones, not wanting to look at Cayden because he was embarrassed for being unable to properly defend himself.

"I got one in the throat."

"Good job." Hawke was surprised. It was strange to think that Cayden condoned fighting when Willets obviously didn't. "I've managed to reduce your detention by half. You'll still have three weeks of dogsbody duties, I imagine."

"Thank you," Hawke said, stunned and extremely grateful for Cayden's accomplishment.

"Nobody can help you until you let them."

Hawke wasn't sure what Cayden meant, especially when he'd reduced his punishment without Hawke asking. Wasn't that helping without being asked? Or was Cayden disappointed that Hawke was protecting his attackers with his silence? Surely an Authority would understand the unwritten rules of a boarding school for Authority brats?

"I can't stay. I have a lot of work to get back to."

"Thanks for coming." Hawke stood up when Cayden did and they faced each other.

"Not an option," Cayden said, holding out his hand. Hawke shook it, feeling oddly formal before they left the courtyard, heading in opposite directions.

CHAPTER TWENTY-EIGHT

The Hunter And The Tip-Off

THE Hunter was thinking about the photo when he was asked a question. He answered smoothly, his tone firm and decisive.

"Pursue."

The silence that followed was conspicuous and caused him to look up. The uncertain expression on the young soldier's face told him that his internal preoccupation had made the situation awkward. She glanced at the Team Leader, who was standing nearby, before she looked back at the Hunter.

"Uh...so does that mean you *do* want sugar in your coffee?" she hazarded.

Shit. He was sitting at the conference table at one end of the Elite Divisions Tactical Centre, nursing the file report he'd been given when he'd entered a short time before. He'd been pretending to read quite convincingly while a dozen Authority Officers tapped away at their computers and scanned countless local authority communication channels at the other end of the room. They were the army of blue ants gathering information to help him find the three Wanderers he'd started hunting from Finalis. His mind was not on the task at all.

"No sugar," he corrected and she looked relieved as she scurried off.

The Hunter looked at the Team Leader, who had the grace to ignore the interchange and stick to the mission.

"See anything you like?" he asked, nodding at the file lying open on the table before the Hunter.

Apart from cradling his own mug of coffee, the T.L. didn't look like he'd been up all night. His team of hardworking underlings weren't looking nearly as shiny. The older man obviously had a great deal of experience with all-night sojourns, sifting through the pile of information his home world had to offer.

"Not yet," the Hunter answered tersely and was pleased when the T.L. wandered away again.

As soon as the superior officer approached the work stations, he was accosted with codes and possibilities – every crime currently occurring across the twelve states of Calibria that fit the parameters the Hunter had provided.

"Sir, I've got a twenty-eight in progress in Western Calibria!"

"Pursue."

"Team Leader, what about a twenty-eight that's been resolved in South Calibria, three suspects in custody?"

"Disregard."

"Sir, a thirty and a sixty-one in Townsend?"

"On a beach?"

"Um…"

"Never mind, disregard."

It was the Team Leader's job to interpret the local authority codes and prioritise according to the likelihood that the crimes being committed were perpetrated by the Hunter's targets. Being so time-sensitive, fast decisions were necessary and the T.L. was efficient.

The Hunter received his coffee and took a cautious sip before he forced himself to peruse the offences report he'd been given. Though they'd occurred in the last twenty-four hours, they established a pattern that he could extrapolate from. The T.L. had ranked the list so he didn't have to flip past page one.

"Did you pursue this one?" the Hunter asked, tapping the first report.

"Dead end," the Team Leader nodded, pointing at a nearby whiteboard covered in words and numbers, a great deal of which had been crossed out or partially erased. The T.L. was very fond of updating it, so there was probably some value in examining whatever was on there, except the Hunter couldn't make sense of it.

Impatience spiked at his insides. He wasn't as close to finishing this mission as he'd expected. For all the data being offered up, it didn't feel like any of it had traction. He didn't want to be here at all. The photo was there, mocking him from the periphery of his focus. He wanted to be back at that house, it was where he needed to be. Not just looking at a silver-framed family but talking to the woman inside it.

He took a deep breath, fighting the preoccupation consuming him. He needed to concentrate on the mission. His breath released and another was drawn, slowly and purposefully, his mind clearing along with it. The noises in the room blended and faded into the background, the lights hazed in his unfocussed vision and everything became the rhythm and flow of his breathing. He relaxed, breathing steadily and reduced to base instincts. Soon after came a feeling of clarity.

"Disregard all incidents but those to the east," he ordered, the noise of the room rushing back at him.

"East?"

The Team Leader stared at him from a short distance away, half-turned towards an intern presenting him with a folder of information. His gaze was disconcerted and the Hunter was overwhelmed by the feeling of being a rat in a lab.

"What the fuck are you looking at? You heard me! Do your fucking job and focus on the east!"

The Team Leader blinked but turned to give the order to his workers anyway. There was a brief scramble of action while they assimilated the directive and adjusted their listening equipment accordingly but they soon settled back into their routine. After a brief pause, the codes began coming in again. This time, the Hunter listened, silently approving when the Team

Leader wanted to pursue everything.

"Sirs!" A male officer in the back corner was so motivated by his intel that he shot to his feet and looked from the Hunter to his superior before he continued. He had everyone's attention. "I've got a forty-two in progress in Yulanigh Bay, description matches targets. Local authorities are listing prior codes twenty kilometres west in Robin's Nest – eighty-six, twenty-four, twenty-five, nineteen. Sixteen, twenty...thirty-three with fifty-six! Fifty-six confirmed *now*!" the officer yelled excitedly.

The Hunter looked to the Team Leader, who was writing furiously on a notepad, even as he strode towards him.

"You've got a theft from a camping outlet, a holdup at a convenience store, stolen car, collision with pedestrians, a car chase travelling east and an abandoned vehicle in a populated area. Foot pursuit has been undertaken, two men and a woman matching your description are being followed. Gunfire has been confirmed."

"That's them. How far from here?" the Hunter asked as he ran for the door.

"An hour by aircraft."

"Get me one!"

"On it!" floated out to him as he ran down the hall.

He sprinted towards the base airport, feeling like the notes were aligning at last.

CHAPTER TWENTY-NINE

Mwavey

CHILDREN were everywhere; holding the hands of their parents or peeking out from behind their legs, playing games in the playroom close to the foyer or running around between holiday-goers, bumping past everyone and their luggage. Daeson had never seen so many families gathered together, wearing such colourful clothes. The noise of conversation echoed around the room and he almost missed Omerri's request for him to wait at one of the settees while she handled her affairs.

He was approached almost as soon as he sat down by a little girl.

"You're sitting on my friend."

"I beg pardon?" Daeson asked, getting up and checking that there was nothing under him other than a cushion. He'd expected a toy of some kind but the little girl made some strange gestures in the air as though helping someone off the chair.

"Her name is Kelly. She's imaginary."

"Oh. Is it safe to sit down again now?"

"Yes, I helped her off, but she's a bit flat."

Daeson sat down and grinned at the little girl who looked like she was fluffing up an invisible pillow.

"Do people sit on her a lot?"

"Sometimes. It's okay if they get up straight away though."

"I'm glad I didn't squash her too much," Daeson agreed.

The little girl's pretend game intrigued him; while growing up, he'd never been able to play such games with the other children on Cloverlea because he'd been unable to speak the lies required...but this girl's version skirted on the edge of truth enough that it didn't make him feel queasy and he could even participate. She was confident for someone so small—her youth accentuated by blonde pigtails and a bright green romper. Another girl that looked similar noticed them talking and came over.

"Sophie, you shouldn't talk to strangers," she ordered, and reached for the little girl's hand.

Sophie spun away. "Go away, Lila!"

"Sorry, I didn't mean to sit on Sophie's imaginary friend," Daeson apologised. The older girl looked uncertain and checked over her shoulder for her parents. Daeson followed her gaze to see a couple in deep conversation at the front desk. Omerri stood in line behind them.

"Do you have a daughter I can play a game with?" Sophie asked.

"No, sorry. Is Kelly not un-squashed yet?"

"Kelly's not real," Sophie's sister interjected.

"Kelly is real to me, but she can't move the pieces on the board," Sophie sulked, pointing at a game that was set up in the middle of the playroom.

"Can I play? You'll have to tell me the rules," Daeson offered.

Sophie's face lit up and her sister gave him a suspicious look but the two girls led him to the middle of the playroom where they quickly taught him a complex game with rules that changed at their will. Halfway through their game, as he was laughing along with Sophie, Lila thumped him on the shoulder and pointed.

"Your lady friend is watching us."

Daeson turned to see Omerri staring at him with a peculiar expression. He thought he might've done something wrong so got to his feet.

"Have a nice holiday," he bade the girls, but couldn't leave without Sophie throwing herself at his legs for a hug. He indulged her, her sister more reserved and hanging back. He went to Omerri with an apology on his lips but she shook her head.

"I think it's lovely that you like children," she said warmly, and took his arm.

The wind whipped Daeson's hair and salt spray stung his face. The sound of water slapping at the hull of the boat was distinctive and rhythmic, like drumming. He raised a hand to acknowledge the last of the small sailboats they passed, their thin triangular sails creating a rainbow of colour across the ocean's surface. Most of the sailors waved back, though some were too far away to see.

When the boat picked up its pace, Omerri retreated into the cabin beside the captain, protected from the elements. She sat upon a stool, looking out the windshield ahead instead of back at him. Daeson didn't mind, he was grateful to her for bringing him to Mwavey, a world where tourists spent exorbitant amounts of money to stay in underwater hotel rooms.

The yellow envelope that was given to Omerri upon their arrival contained items that she'd arranged for herself; a retail card with credits for a shopping trip (she'd used it in the hotel lobby shops to buy him clothes and a strange pair of rubbery sandals with a strap insert between his toes), a hire ticket for the services of the boat they were on and some keys for the house that they would be staying at. From her description, Daeson believed the house was a place she visited every year but there'd been no joy, no excitement in her voice when she mentioned it.

It took them twenty minutes to reach a hilly tree-covered island. A large house perched at the topmost point and Daeson marvelled at it. It looked huge. Were they going to stay in that large house all by themselves?

He glanced over at Omerri who was looking his way but he couldn't see her expression behind her dark, oversized glasses. He went to her, wondering if she wanted to talk to him. The boat slowed as he joined her.

"There'll be nobody on the island apart from us," she boasted. Daeson was surprised.

"Am I here to do the housekeeping?" he asked, disappointed. He'd thought she was bringing him here because he was special to her. That's what she'd said when he'd healed her.

Her laugh tinkled. "Of course not. There'll be staff, but we won't notice them."

He believed she wouldn't notice them, but he might.

The dock extended out over the ocean, its grey salt-weathered timber striking against the cerulean of the shallow waters. The boat gently butted up against it and the captain expertly tossed the rope over the pylon and pulled it taut, keeping the boat in place. Daeson admired his experienced manoeuvre while Omerri slid off the stool and positioned herself near the doorway.

The captain helped her across the step onto the dock as Daeson collected the shopping bags. He was also helped across and he thanked the captain who said nothing in response. The man hadn't said much to them since greeting them when they'd first hopped on. Daeson had the distinct impression that he was more comfortable with boats than with people.

Omerri strode purposefully down the dock without looking back. Daeson hurried after her and only caught up when she stopped at a strange little box on a post. It had a keyhole and a button. Omerri took out her keyring and inserted one of the keys into the slot before pressing the button. Daeson stood at her side, curious and expectant. Now that there was no longer the ocean breeze to cool them, the heat and humidity felt oppressing. He wished he'd had the chance to change into the new clothes Omerri had purchased for him. The long pants were making him sweat.

While they waited, he noticed a low green guard rail set into the ground, well camouflaged. There were two depressions either side of the rail, as though something had rolled over the grass and leaves many times. He could hear the growly rumble of an engine not too far away. A vehicle appeared, driverless, along the railed path. It turned slightly when the railing did and came to a stop in front of them. It was a strange kind of car, with a plastic roof and no doors or windows at the sides, but long enough to seat six people in three bench seats.

"Did pressing the button call it?" Daeson guessed.

"Yes, but the button doesn't work without the key," Omerri explained, getting in. Daeson placed the shopping on the seat behind her and then climbed in after her.

"How does it know where to take us?" Daeson asked when he saw that there were no controls—just a blank dashboard.

"It only goes to the house."

The car moved forward at a measured pace, following the guided rail path that cut through the jungle. Large colourful birds whistled and squawked in the trees, exotic plants displayed vivid flowers with overpowering scents, and a peculiar looking furry animal jumped onto a tree branch close by, causing Omerri to shriek and cling to Daeson.

"Is it dangerous?" he asked, leaning forward in his seat while tucking Omerri into his side.

"No, nothing on Mwavey is, I just...I think they're creepy."

Creepy was not a word he knew but he could guess the context. He hid his amusement by looking back behind them, as though keeping a wary eye on the little animal.

The car drove out of the foliage into a clearing that held a central fountain. Standing in the centre was a bearded king holding a trident, aiming it menacingly at the waters that spouted at his feet.

"Who's that?" Daeson asked as they drew nearer, wondering if it was a volcano god.

"Oh, he's from an Authority world. I can't remember his name."

Daeson no longer felt as comfortable as he had upon leaving the resort. Even though they were in this private sanctuary, the Authorities' influence extended to them still.

"Why not put up a statue from this world?"

"Because there are no statues from this world. There were no people here."

"None?" Daeson asked, wondering if this was another of Omerri's perceptions.

"That's what the brochure said."

When the car came to a stop, she hopped out and took off her sunglasses before smiling at him and headed for the house. He admired the way her skirt flicked as she walked. The car made a clunking noise as it settled and he climbed out before it could drive away again. He rescued the shopping and followed after her.

The house was even grander close-up. The windows and doors had white flourishes on the trimmings and countless balconies. Painted light blue and white, it blended in with the crisp sky above and not with the dark green jungle it was nestled in.

The front doors were much taller than Daeson and silent when they swung open. The house within was a cool oasis from the oppressing heat. Ceiling fans with broad paddles woven from straw slowly circulated overhead.

"They do a good job," Daeson said, surprised at how well they kept the house cool.

Omerri turned at his comment and then glanced up. "Darling, they're doing very little. The house is air-conditioned."

He didn't know what her words meant but didn't want to betray his ignorance. She left him standing in the foyer and made her way up the sweeping staircase that led to the first floor landing. He watched her climb the stairs to the top, until Omerri noticed that he wasn't with her.

"Daeson, come upstairs and I'll show you around."

He moved forward, slowly at first, speeding up until he was taking stairs two at a time. Omerri's smile was broad and welcoming, and Daeson took the hand that she offered him.

Daeson didn't see anyone in the house other than Omerri. He would hear soft footsteps or the sounds of doors as they snicked closed. Sometimes he saw movement out of the corner of his eye but would always be too late to see more. Cushions upon couches that he sat on were righted before his return and his shopping, which had been left in the doorway, had been taken away to a location he didn't know. He assumed Omerri had arranged for his new clothes to be placed in his bedroom—he just had to find out which one was his. If he hadn't known that the house had many staff within to serve them, he would find the unseen movements unnerving. Lunch had been lain out for them, but when it came to dinner, an intimate table had been set with a food trolley beside—their meals kept warm under anonymous cloches.

"Is there much to see and do here?" Daeson asked, laying down his cutlery. He'd finished the food on his plate. Omerri had moved onto her wine and nursed the glass close to her bosom. She hadn't touched what was left on her plate for a while.

"You could go swimming, there are lovely beaches here," she suggested.

"I don't know how to swim."

"I'm sure you'll learn how to paddle before we leave."

"Is there anything else?"

"There are a few hiking trails you could follow behind the house. The paths are marked blue or yellow, depending on how long you wish to be gone for."

"Which are shorter?"

"I don't recall. I haven't gone down the paths." She sipped her wine.

"Is that because you're afraid of the bears?"

"There are no bears," she said with a frown.

"Um, the monkeys that look like little bears. Poo…pee?"

She blinked at him. "Oh! The Puku monkeys." She screwed up her nose and shook her head. "They're one of the reasons. There are many bugs around as well that I would prefer to avoid. It's quite cloying, walking through the jungle. Most of this island is covered in jungle, except for the dock, the railcar and the house."

"You know a lot about this island," he pointed out.

"I come here every year," she said before taking another drink.

"I don't understand why, when it makes you sad."

Omerri's brow twitched and her gaze lowered to her glass. She and Daeson watched as the red liquid was gently swirled around. "It's not this world that makes me sad," she said quietly.

He thought he knew why. He was torn between guessing the reason for her sadness and keeping his silence so she could divulge it to him. It would be meaningful if she knew that he was in tune with her, but thought it might mean more to her if he could prove his patience. The longer he waited, the more he noticed she was avoiding eye contact with him. Perhaps she wanted to be pressed.

"Mwavey is a beautiful world, but that's not all it

has to offer," he told her. Omerri pressed the napkin to the corners of her lips and then looked at him expectantly. "There's culture and language and refinement. There's depth and surprises to be found."

"It's a manufactured world. Nothing is natural," she argued, but her expression was more vibrant.

"That makes it more complex. It's more difficult to make something refined," he said.

Omerri tinkled laughter and reached across the table to stroke Daeson's hand. His fingers twitched in response before he took her hand in his own, wondering if she would pull away. His heart hammered for fear of her rejection but she was gazing at him, smiling. He was struck by her beauty—she had a level of sophistication that far surpassed his own, an intelligence that he couldn't hope to match and he should've felt inadequate in her presence, except he didn't. He felt happy, buoyed by her attention and flattered that she was interested in him enough to bring him here with her. Obviously there was something in him that she valued.

"Am I here because I healed you?" he asked tentatively. He risked her pulling her hand away but he needed to know what it was she saw in him.

"Yes, but there's more to you than that," she said, squeezing his hand.

"My truth?"

"That, too," she admitted. "But even more."

He was relieved.

"You're hard on yourself, Daeson. You're a very intense young man. As attractive as that is, you should enjoy your youth while you have it."

Something in her tone became hard as she completed her sentence.

"Why don't you celebrate your day of birth?"

Her hand retreated and hid under the table.

"Because it's no longer a celebration of the past, but

a reminder of what lies ahead."

"There's no point looking at what lies ahead," Daeson disagreed. "It's never as you expect it."

"That may be true for you, darling."

"It's true for everyone," he said, holding Omerri's gaze. "When I went to sleep last night, I didn't know that I would be spending the day here. When I touched the pillar—the *Portal*—I didn't know it would bring me to you."

"Something divine brought you to me," Omerri agreed softly.

"Or I was brought to something divine," he replied. Perhaps his words were too forward, for she seemed taken aback and light colour rose on her cheeks. He thought she was pleased, for she smiled before she looked away.

After their dinner, Omerri led him upstairs.

She took him through her bedroom and out the double doors onto the wide balcony, where he could see an indigo sky and a sliver of red. It wasn't the right colour for the moon, and too big.

"What is that?"

"The moon."

"Why does it look like that?"

"On some worlds it is red and large."

The moon's strange appearance created a feeling of displacement in him. "Is it the same moon?" he asked.

"I think so."

"Don't you know?"

"I don't really care."

He was surprised by her dismissal.

"But don't you wonder why the Gods made more than one world?" he asked. Her expression let him know he'd made the wrong assumption. "Don't you believe in the Gods?" he asked, suspecting that she might not. There were no clerics on Trent, though there were places of worship. He thought it made the temples lonely places to visit.

"No. I never have. Do you think me uncivilised?" She looked at Daeson, her gaze questioning. She looked vulnerable.

"No, but where do you think you'll go when you die?"

"Let's not speak of death," she whispered. He thought he could see her shivering and he regretted asking.

Instead of speaking and ruining the moment further, he wrapped her in his arms and rested his forehead on hers. Her hair smelled clean and like flowers. He nuzzled against her and the movement had her looking up at him. Their faces were very close but he didn't dare try to kiss her again...until she licked her lips.

"Can I...?" he began to ask, feeling awkward and hopeful, the word 'kiss' difficult to say in case it led to another embarrassing moment.

"Please do."

With her permission, he kissed her. Her lips were soft and plump, warm and inviting, and sticky with the strawberry taste of her lip gloss. He'd expected their kiss to be delicate and it started that way, but quickly deepened into something that stirred a great desire in him.

It was after that kiss that she led him away from the balcony and to her bed, and taught him what it was like to love her.

CHAPTER THIRTY

Nick's Proposal

SYNJAN preceded Nick into his office and perched cautiously in the visitor's chair in front of his desk. She was trying not to frown but failed when he shut the door then sat opposite her. Nick never closed his office door. Someone or other demanded his attention from the moment he walked into the Queen to the moment he walked out. Whatever she was here for was obviously serious if they were keeping it between the two of them.

"Have you collected your mail lately?" Nick asked, his gaze intense.

"What?" Synjan asked, bewildered. Her gaze fell to take in the way he was resting his forearms on his desk, his body leaning slightly forward and his fingers rolling slowly against one another as he stared at her. His demeanour was grave and she'd known from the tone of his voice over the telephone that he wasn't fooling with her, but... the question didn't make sense.

"You heard me," he said impatiently.

"Yes, but—"

"Have you collected your mail?"

"Urvasi collects the mail and gives it to Ellis," Synjan snapped, finding she was bristling because she couldn't fathom where this conversation was leading. She shifted in her seat, straightening her pantsuit jacket.

Nick looked grim and she thought there was condescension lurking in his brown eyes. "So you haven't seen the announcements."

"Clearly," she responded perfunctorily, now wanting him to get to his point. "Enlighten me."

"Oh, it's nothing important," he said airily, creating a carefree arc in the air with a hand as he sat back to glower at her in an even more superior manner. "Just that the Authorities have sent out fliers and letters stating that they'll be registering every Trent citizen, officially entering them into their records. Cataloguing us. Now it's Gredann's turn to fall into line and get their 'Authority Citizen' I.D. cards."

"I.D. cards," Synjan repeated, and a rivulet of ice spilled down her spine.

"Yes!" Nick declared with a false joviality no doubt meant to further condemn her ignorance. "They'll be going street by street. Herding everyone through their little tents – like dumb fucking cattle, if you listen to the old timers tell it – taking photographs and sighting birth certificates to issue the cards. If you don't have a Trent birth certificate, they'll kindly take your blood to help identify you."

"They're looking for Wanderers," Synjan said hoarsely.

Nick's expression became a scowl and he sat forward again, his casual pretence gone. "You think?" he sneered.

"When's this happening?"

"It's already started. They're nearly finished in Hill End. It was all very civilised up there so they're setting up stations in Portside. Very soon after they'll migrate to Dockside – and you know how well that's going to go down."

Synjan could imagine quite clearly what such an intrusion into the most traditional area of the city would look like. Riot gear would be donned to tear down the barricades the staunchest opposers would make, there'd be scuffles in the streets, a myriad of arrests and forced blood takings at the end of it, regardless of how much the Docksiders wished to resist. Things were about to get complicated.

"It'll be a war zone," she murmured regretfully.

"To put it lightly. But you have a birth certificate, so you'll be fine," Nick said, and his tone caused her to look at him more closely.

"So do you?" she offered slowly.

"Yes, but there's someone close to me who doesn't that I need to protect—that I need your help to protect," he clarified. He waited for her to think through the implications.

"Someone without a Trent birth certificate? A Wanderer?" she asked sharply.

"I didn't say that."

"Why aren't you asking Ellis for his help? He could have one forged for you, or buy one. He has a lot of connections."

"I have connections," Nick spat, obviously affronted by her implication that he wasn't as resourceful as Ellis was. "But this can't involve Ellis," he asserted.

"Why not?" Synjan frowned, but even as she asked the question the answer came to her. Omerri. Synjan's expression shifted and Nick obviously realised she'd made the connection.

"Don't ask me why she doesn't want to share this with him," Nick beseeched, raising his hands and presenting his palms to her in a surrender gesture. "She just doesn't."

"And of course you'll do her bidding."

Nick tilted his head and gave her a look that made her feel like a jealous nine year old once more. She didn't enjoy the sensation and found it difficult to get her next words out. "Who is this person, then?"

"I can't tell you that, either."

"Because it's a Wanderer?"

"You're like a dog with a bone, aren't you?" he wondered.

"And you've avoided answering that question twice."

"The less you know, the better."

She couldn't argue with that logic but she burned to know who in Nick and Omerri's sphere of influence might be a Wanderer that needed protecting from the Authorities. She couldn't think of any other good reason to go to all the trouble of having a closed-door meeting with her about getting a birth certificate for a non-native...well, okay, she could, if she tried.

All this subterfuge would be necessary if it was a case of needing a new identity due to criminal activity. Sadly, that was a far more likely reason for all of this. Since Nick wasn't deterring her from suspecting a Wanderer, it was good reason to believe her imagination might be taking her down the wrong track. It was just like him to use a false assumption to avoid discussing the truth. It was a disappointing thought.

"Why me?" she demanded.

"Because I need someone who can get onto the base and move around without making too many ripples."

She raised her eyebrows but said nothing.

"I have a contact organised to issue the card, you just have to get some information to them first and it'll be done."

"Surely some of your other contractors could do it?"

"Are you saying you won't do it?"

"I'm saying that I don't like keeping secrets from Ellis and this whole thing sounds a little too... convoluted for something you're telling me will be a simple exchange."

"Well, it won't be easy to get to the contact," Nick admitted.

Synjan pursed her lips, thinking about Port Cleary. "The administration building?"

"Yeah."

Her heart sank, though she wasn't surprised. She could access many areas of the base without too much effort but they were the general areas only. She didn't go to restricted buildings that needed heavy identification to get into because she didn't have it. Sure, she had a uniform and could dodge or talk her way around most people, but she didn't have a badge, fake or not.

"I don't see—"

Nick opened the top drawer of his desk and pulled a card out. He tossed it in front of her. At a glance, she knew it was an Authority I.D. but she picked it up to examine the details. The picture showed someone that could have been her – even *she* had to look at it more closely.

"This is why it has to be me," she scoffed, giving Nick a wry look.

One side of his mouth lifted in a grin she knew wasn't nearly as sheepish as it appeared. It caused a flutter of awareness in her chest regardless. "Not at all. I swiped that card because she looked like you."

"Won't she miss it?"

"Who checks their I.D. on a weekend?"

Synjan's eyebrows lifted. "You want me to do this today?"

"Tomorrow is fine."

She couldn't believe the smirk on him, though there was something in his eyes she couldn't decipher, behind the bravado. It didn't seem as confident.

"How'd you get it?"

He snorted a laugh. She didn't need details.

"You've got a lot riding on me agreeing."

"There's no other choice. It has to be done or my associate will be in a situation you wouldn't wish on your worst enemy."

Synjan felt his pointed look was luring her into considering the person she was doing this for was a Wanderer, but that also had a familiar aura of manipulation. Nick wanted her to feel sympathy so she'd agree to do his job for him. There was a lot more to this than he'd told her but she didn't blame him for not leading with minor details. He was waiting for her to agree, even if it was a token gesture.

"How much will you pay me?"

Nick's expression lightened and his smile was broad and lovely. "Let me tell you everything you have to do and then we can negotiate," he said as he sat forward and got down to telling her all about what he was already calling her 'mission'. Synjan listened avidly. Once he was done, she sat back, chewing on her lip.

"You don't look convinced," Nick sighed.

"It's just... you want this done by *tomorrow*?"

"Has to be. My contact says it's the best time to do it and I'd like to get that I.D. back to its owner before it's missed, if possible."

"And what if Ellis finds out?"

"What if he does?" Nick scoffed, swinging back in his chair and folding his hands nonchalantly over his flat stomach.

Synjan despised his casual attitude. "I can't risk him being angry with me."

"You worry too much."

She couldn't tell him how her recent actions had made things delicate at home. "Hey, I already lost one family, I'm not going to do anything to jeopardise what I have now."

"Ellis is hardly family."

"Don't be such an ass, you know he practically is."

"And don't you whine at me about shit you know is far from the truth," Nick spat. He agitatedly yanked the lapels of his jacket. "Ellis doesn't look at you like his kid and he sure as fuck doesn't worry about the shit he gets you to do like a real parent would. He doesn't even care that most of the jobs he sends you on could get you killed!"

"Don't be ridiculous, of course he does. He worries about me—"

"Yeah, that was so evident in all the bruises he put on you while you were growing up."

Synjan blinked, feeling like she'd been slapped. Part

of her mind grew increasingly frantic as Nick's words bled into the silence, the rest of her didn't care. It was too busy being horrified by the fact that her dearest friend had just voiced something she'd wrongly felt was a secret. Reasonably, she knew he'd always known but she'd found his silence on the subject as comforting as his hugs or his verbal reassurances. That he'd spoken of it now, so offhandedly, was as much a violation of her trust as it was humiliating.

She stood abruptly, embracing the anger that flooded into her. Nick anticipated her move and was on his feet just as quickly, reaching across the desk and grabbing her wrist.

"Synjan, wait—"

"Fuck you," she spat, pulling against his hold, knowing that she could get away from him if she really tried. He was off balance.

"Look, I'm sorry, don't go. I just meant to say that you don't always have to worry about what Ellis thinks!" Nick gushed, looking into her eyes with a sincerity that touched her, even through her indignation. "You've been beholden to him your whole life but you *can* do things by yourself, you know. You're a capable woman."

"I owe him everything," Synjan hissed through gritted teeth.

"Nobody's arguing with that!" Nick cried, letting her go in order to straighten up and hold his hands palms out. "I'm just saying the man is your boss, not your father. If he finds out what you're doing for me, you can tell him it's your business, not his. Because it's not his business!"

"He mightn't be my father but he's the closest thing I've got."

Nick pulled an odd face and Synjan could tell that he wanted to say something he knew she wouldn't like. He seemed to be thinking of another way to phrase himself and the effect on his expression was disconcerting.

"Close has the same flavour as failure and leaves you with the same reward."

It was another saying of Ellis' and she supposed it was as diplomatic a way of issuing his message as he could get. The anger departed almost as suddenly as it had come, leaving Synjan feeling raw.

"Yeah, I understand that," she frowned. "But your opinion of my beliefs won't change them."

"Synjan. The Gods themselves couldn't change your beliefs," Nick scoffed, picking up the ID card and holding it out towards her.

Synjan looked him in the eye as she took it, not wanting to think about why she was suddenly feeling so helpless and sad. She wished that conversations about Ellis were less exhausting than spending time with him. She wished she could actually blame someone other than herself. "As long as you respect them...and stop trying to mess with my head," she accused. The card swivelled between two of her fingers and pointed at him.

Nick chuckled and stepped around his desk to embrace her. She allowed it, resisting the urge to wrap her arms around him but succumbing to the desire to rest her head on his chest as he spoke.

"I don't want to argue with you. If you weren't so damn stubborn, you'd see I'm trying to tell you I respect you. You're better than all of us. The day you figure that out is your last day in Gredann," he promised, leaning down to kiss the top of her head.

It was Synjan's turn to laugh, though it was a weary sound, released in a muffled cough against Nick's chest. They were words he'd said before but she'd always demurred, unable to see herself ever climbing out from under her obligations in such a manner. It was a nice dream, though, and hearing him say it was always reassuring.

"I'll go home and see what I can shuffle around tomorrow to get this done, okay?" she told Nick, pulling away reluctantly. "I think our best window is nine of the clock, the base is at its quietest then."

"I'll see you here at half eight, then."

She smirked at him over her shoulder as she pulled the door open. "If you're lucky."

His laughter warmed her as she headed down the hall and out the back.

CHAPTER THIRTY-ONE

Oceangate

HAWKE was the first to see the Unit Commander on arrival at Oceangate.

Fifteen students and two teachers had filled up the Authority portal save a single chair. The excursion was one Hawke had been looking forward to going on, even though he wasn't that interested in engineering. It was the idea of coming into a different world that excited him. He wouldn't have minded travelling to Austra, except he and Cayden would portal straight into the base that held the DOME and he saw nothing of the world. Cayden explained it was much like Varrell, with the same lifestyle and only a few quirks of different cultures.

Civilisation was being shaped by the Authoritan hand, and while Hawke was impressed by the idea of shaping entire worlds, he was also horrified by it. To think of Boronia being shaped to end up the same way as every other world made him sad.

The Unit Commander looked out of place; he wore a black fatigue jacket over his blue uniform but it wasn't the difference of his clothes that made him stand out...it was his cool, assessing stare. It reminded Hawke of the way Dr Kelly Turner looked at him when he was doing puzzles for her—or when he spoke to her about his brief time Wandering.

He found he'd started to enjoy his sessions with her. There weren't many secrets he kept from her, but the fact he liked talking to her was one of them. Tavi was another. He still heeded the advice of the woman who'd attended to him after his first portal trip and didn't talk about his preference for the natural Portal over the Authority one. After so many trips, he found he was developing a resistance to it; no longer getting sick and waking up sooner after every trip. Waking up early was how he'd spied the peculiar soldier first.

Instead of a weapon, he held an envelope, though there was a holster on his belt and the butt of a very big handgun in it. It had a silver grip and didn't match the other handguns that the Authorities had strapped to their belts. The soldier was taller than the other men in the room and broader across the shoulders. He looked like a wrestler.

Hawke had watched some of the wrestling matches on television during his recreational time in the common room at Willets. He loved the wrestlers' costumes, even though a lot of the other boys thought they were silly. They didn't get it—the costumes were part of a story. There were heroes and villains and, even though the fighting was staged and dramatic, Hawke believed it took a lot of skill, staged or not. The hits were hard and the falls made him wince, and he loved cheering on his favourite.

This soldier, who'd decided that Hawke was the boy he wanted to look at, could easily have been one of those wrestlers. He could be the embodiment of the Authorities, and he would wear blue tights and a black cape, because he would be a bad guy, even though he was fighting for justice. Hawke didn't know the phrase 'anti-hero' but the concept appealed to him just the same.

The soldier was staring at him a bit too long now. Even though Hawke had been staring back, his awareness of being sought out interfered with his daydream. He looked over at the other boys stirring. There was a lot of fussing of nurses in this room and he rarely saw people beyond the few guards at their positions.

As soon as Mr Blatch stirred, the soldier that could've been a wrestler watched him instead. He looked ready to pounce. Mr Blatch wasn't exceptionally skinny or small, but Hawke didn't think he had much of a chance. The soldier approached once Mr Blatch was on his feet and handed over the envelope while introducing himself quietly. Hawke saw groggy surprise on Mr Blatch's face.

The envelope was opened—it hadn't been sealed—and the page inside was read. There must not have been a lot written on it because he looked over at Hawke almost immediately.

His heart sank.

He'd been looking forward to the Oceangate tour and it appeared he was going to miss out. He knew it was just propaganda, designed by the Authorities to take groups of boys from boarding schools like Willets and show them how awesome signing up could be, but it was still interesting to come to a different world and be shown around it, instead of being injected and tested and asked a bunch of questions.

"Hawke, since you're the first one awake, you can go along for a look at the tactical centre. I'm sure you'll enjoy it."

Hawke stood and grinned, because it sounded like the letter didn't have his name on it. His heart was no longer in his stomach but felt like it would soar out of his chest. He wanted to jump around in excitement for getting something randomly special. The soldier had been looking at him and waiting for the teacher to wake up—he'd probably figured Hawke would be the boy who got to go! Nothing sinister in that. Thankfully nobody else had woken before Mr Blatch, dividing his chances.

"Hawke, ensure you follow uh…"Mr Blatch looked to the soldier, his eyes searching for an ID tag.

"Unit Commander." A rank was provided instead of a name. Mr Blatch seemed less alarmed by this soldier's anonymity than by the idea of Hawke not doing as he was told.

"Follow the Unit Commander's instructions," Mr Blatch said, distracted by the groan of another waking boy nearby.

"Yes, sir," Hawke said, and hurried after the long-legged stride of the nameless Unit Commander.

He was excited about seeing the missions room. As they moved through the base and he started seeing less soldiers and more civilians, Hawke got the impression that the story might be bogus. He could feel his shoulders slumping and his steps dragging. He felt as though he'd been punched in the gut, because the emotional hit felt just as compelling as a physical one.

Had the Unit Commander taken advantage of an opportunity to select Hawke? Did he know Hawke was going to be first to wake? If he'd been last, would this soldier have waited until they were all lined up and eager to visit the missions room and just happen to choose him?

"So where am I really going?" Hawke asked, not wanting to go anywhere with this soldier until he knew more. Right now he was mostly safe, surrounded by the Authorities and other people.

The soldier looked down at him and Hawke thought he detected surprise. It was hard to tell whether it was really there or if he was imagining it because he was looking for it—*hoping* for it.

"You're going on a mission."

It wasn't the answer he was expecting and he didn't know whether to be excited or not.

"Because of my blood?" he asked, already knowing the answer in his heart. Why else would he stand out for a mission if not because of his Wanderer blood?

"Yes," the soldier responded, sounding like he wasn't pleased about it.

"Is it a dangerous mission?" Hawke asked, slowing his pace. The Unit Commander slowed with him and gradually they came to a stop in the foyer. Hawke could hear the swish of automatic doors opening and closing, letting soldiers and civilians inside and outside.

"You just have to talk to someone."

"How is talking to someone a mission?" he asked dubiously. The soldier frowned and gestured for him to start walking. Hawke took a step backward instead. The soldier glanced around to see if they were attracting attention and Hawke did the same.

There was an ID checkpoint near the doors, which Hawke took to mean that this base ran on a higher security level than the one they'd left on Varrell—a portal-stop for tourists.

He guessed this wasn't an official mission. This was like his DOME visits, where he made promises not to talk about the specifics. He tended not to talk about anything at all, and Dr Kelly Turner had commended him for making the smart decision. He wondered why she would say such a thing, when he'd already divulged to her it was because he had nobody to confide in.

"The sooner we leave, the sooner we get back and you can join your buddies."

Buddies, Hawke thought resentfully. Screw his non-existent 'buddies'. Let them think he was having a wonderful time in the missions room. The idea of running back to people who didn't give a shit about him—maybe even hated him because of his differences—decided him. He would go on this mission and rub it in their faces.

The Unit Commander went through two checkpoints with Hawke, and both times he'd been treated respectfully, almost with awe, after his ID was checked. Hawke didn't have his ID lanyard on him because that was something Cayden kept for him, and the temporary ID papers were still with Mr Blatch, but he didn't need them. Whenever Hawke's presence was questioned, the Unit Commander declared that Hawke was under his charge, and nobody took it further.

Hawke wasn't concerned for his safety, even though they left the base and were travelling into a part of the city that was small, compact and dirty. He hadn't questioned the Unit Commander's authority once the other soldiers checked his ID. Now that Hawke was alone with him, he realised that just because someone had influence didn't necessarily make them a good person—and Hawke had been naïve enough to walk out of the base with him, without anybody knowing where they were going and what they were doing.

"Who will I be talking to?" Hawke asked.

"You'll see."

The lack of a detailed response had Hawke studying the Unit Commander's profile, which looked stern. He was concentrating on driving but there was something underneath that focus. Hawke could tell there was underlying anxiety, though he was too young to pinpoint details. Instead of identifying tension in the soldier's shoulders or the white knuckles of a too-tight grip on the steering wheel, he was forced to trust his instinct that something wasn't right.

Where was the Unit Commander taking him? He'd experienced first hand the bias against him for being what he was...what if there were extremists that wanted to eradicate all of his kind? Was that why the Unit Commander looked tense? Because the soldier was taking Hawke somewhere that would lead to his violent end?

"Is this a return trip?" Hawke asked through a dry mouth. His head felt stuffed with cotton wool and the noise of the engine was too loud in his ears.

"What?" The Unit Commander gave a few quick stares between him and the road ahead. "Yeah, kid. You'll be fine. Jeez."

It was the 'Jeez' at the end that made Hawke believe him. He knew it came from the preaching of the Authority church. Since arriving at Willets, Hawke had sat through services on Sunday mornings and listened to tales and questions of morality. Sometimes the dilemmas were interesting, most of the time they weren't. This man had sidestepped blasphemy and was shocked by Hawke's insinuation that he might be hurt. Hawke felt better—not safe, but safer.

They went deep into the heart of the city, where Hawke saw horses pulling carts and lots of bicycles rigged with trailers or baskets to carry things. He'd spied just two vehicles in this place and both of them had been trucks small enough to manoeuvre around tight corners or fit in tiny alleys.

The Unit Commander parked in a nook behind a large warehouse and then zipped his black jacket up, hiding his uniform as best as he was able before getting out and then meeting Hawke around the other side.

Wordlessly, Hawke watched the Unit Commander unlock the back door and followed him into the warehouse. It was completely empty except for a cluster of furniture in the middle. He couldn't see more than that because they were too far away.

The Unit Commander walked with him towards the cluster, their footfalls echoing in the expansive space of the warehouse. Hawke looked around—there were many steel racks ready to hold goods, but nothing was in them.

He wanted to ask the Unit Commander a question but he didn't want to speak into the empty space. For now, he would just walk to the furniture and see what was going on.

As they got closer, he could see that the cluster looked like a lounge room without walls. A large floor rug connected the furnishings; in the centre was a coffee table and two armchairs diagonally facing it, and at the back was a floor lamp. It was the kind of lamp that could direct a spot of light on something, or someone.

A man sat upon one of the armchairs and the floor lamp was aimed at him. He was well-dressed in a light grey suit, with a bright emerald tie. His eyebrows were dark and low over his eyes, though he was smiling, not frowning. When Hawke drew close, the man stood and stepped forward, extending his hand for shaking. Hawke shook it.

"A pleasure to meet you, Mr Donovan. If you would kindly take a seat?" The man's voice was rich and deep and reminded Hawke of Principal Fielder-Wiley, who could make anything sound warm and genuine.

The Unit Commander walked away and Hawke called out after him. "Hey! How am I supposed to get back?" He wondered if this mission wasn't a return trip after all. The Unit Commander hesitated but didn't turn around.

"He's not leaving, he's just giving us some privacy." The well-dressed man reclaimed his armchair and crossed his legs. Hawke thought it looked prudish. The man reached out and twisted the lamp around by its post, so that its spotlight was cast on the coffee table. Hawke looked at the long cable that came out of the lamp and attached to an extension cord that disappeared into the darkness of the building. He didn't know what this bizarre setup was supposed to mean.

"You're not much of a talker."

"The Academy warns us not to talk to strangers," Hawke replied.

"And yet here you are," the suited man said, smiling. His eyes crinkled at the sides but Hawke still felt like he was being studied. After so many years of being a subject in the DOME, he knew how to recognise that look.

"Who are you and what do you want?" Hawke asked after it was obvious the man was waiting for questions.

With a wide smile, the man settled into his armchair, getting himself comfortable. In spite of wanting to remain aloof, Hawke found him fascinating.

"My name is Howard Ellis, and you and I have a great deal to discuss."